MW01680921

When the Wind Met the Embers

The Ashford Saga: Book Two

Alaina Hope

When the Wind Met the Embers

The Ashford Saga: Book Two

Alpha reading by Hannah G. Scheffer-Wentz, English Proper Editing Services

Copy and line editing by Gabby D'Aloia, GCD Editorial

Cover art, map illustration, and internal illustrations by Kelci Parsell, Kelci2D, https://kelci2d.framer.website

For those whose heart has frozen over, because they knew no other way.

May you find a place safe enough to thaw.

N
W
E
S
Inphis
CYNTH
BAY
Gatlyn Castle
HOLLIS
Mineshaft
Hilfik
Salic
Mountains
Genisyn
Obysum
Delfisch
Forest
Fallaine
Ravine
Mines
OCREIN
ISLES
SISRYM
SEA

ANVALI OCEAN
Jackton
Glaytred Forest
Neokell
Acrynd
LEVAST ISLES
Kyrish
Wittuck Woods
The Haven
Cairnyl
Telawol
Yarpeck Woods
Breckshyre
Diorum
The Cabin
ECHEN BAY

Chapter One

It had been twenty-eight days since I murdered my own father.

Kin-slayer.

That was what I was. That was all I'd ever be known as.

I clenched my hands tight, trying to erase the feeling of my father's blood dripping off them. Though I knew it wasn't real, my mind seemed to enjoy playing these tricks on me as of late.

Cruel, wicked tricks.

Taking a deep breath, I focused on the feeling of the warm, mid-summer air filling my lungs. I counted down from ten, then peeled my eyes open.

I was in mine and Byn's bedroom, located in the private royal wing of The Haven, which was in Cairnyl, the capitol of the South of Inphis.

So far away from what I had once considered to be my home.

I was no longer on that battlefield, in that tent where I had fought my own flesh and blood.

It seemed my mind needed to be reminded of that sometimes.

I brought my hands to my face and took them in. They were clean, of course, with no blood in sight. The life blood on my hands that day had been surprisingly easy to wash away.

The markings left on my soul... well, that was another story.

I had to remind myself on days like these that I'd had no other choice than to put an end to Father. He would have stopped at nothing to continue to corrupt the continent—after wreaking havoc and chaos on it.

There'd been no other option, I told myself.

I vaguely remembered Byn, my loving husband, trying to coax me from bed earlier this morning. In response, I had tucked my head deeper into my silk pillow and drifted in and out of sleep once again. He, as well as the rest of our Valwain, had been doing their best to keep me active and my mind busy, but this week had been especially difficult. The memories had plagued my thoughts without end, etched into the depths of my heart.

A knock on the door drew me from the spiral of my mind.

"Go away," I said without lifting my head from the pillow.

Without a sliver of warning, the door to the chambers swung open, and Matea swaggered in as though these were her own chambers.

"What are you doing in here?" I asked her, pulling myself up into a sitting position and gently wrapping my wings around myself. My hands idly stroked one of my gray-tipped white feathers.

"Anything I can to get you out of this bed. Out of this room, actually," my half-sister replied, and though I wanted to be annoyed at her, I appreciated her honesty.

As she rounded my side of the bed, I noticed she was holding a large plate of different fruit slices. Their sweet aroma floated through the air towards me, and without warning, my empty stomach released a ferocious growl, reminding me that I couldn't recall the last time I had eaten anything. It must've been days.

"And *this* is why I brought the snacks," Matea said. "Robyn said he couldn't place the last meal you'd had. I figured some food would help."

She set the plate on the small, honey colored wooden table next to the bed, then sunk to the ground and rested her back against it.

"You know, you can sit up here," I offered.

Matea waved a hand dismissively. "I'm alright where I'm at. Now, either eat or start pouring your heart out to me." She phrased it as a joke, but I knew the underlying offer was legitimate.

Picking up a slice of a soft peach, I bit into it and nearly groaned as the sweet flavor and syrup coated my tongue.

After devouring that slice along with two more, I caught Matea peering up at me.

"Thank you," I said softly after a beat of silence.

We both knew this act of service was my sister showing she cared and that she was worried. Though I'd felt unworthy of that depth of love as of late, I still deeply appreciated it.

She nodded, not one for sentimentality, and asked, "What was it this time? Robyn said there's a few different memories of those moments that plague you."

I couldn't help but look down at my hands again at the thought. Noticing the syrup sticking to my fingers, my hands began to shake.

"His blood," I said quietly, holding them out farther from me, my heartbeat beginning to race. Gravity caused the syrup to roll down my skin, and I couldn't help the shudder that ran through me.

"Can... can you—" I stuttered.

"I've got you," Matea said, standing and reaching for a cloth she must have brought in with the dish of fruits.

Sitting on the very edge of the bed, I felt her lean closer and, with a gentleness so unlike her tough exterior, she wiped the syrup and juices from my fingers.

I watched meticulously, unable to look away, the same way I had when I washed my father's life blood away twenty-eight days ago. Her olive, sun-kissed skin was such a stark contrast next to my pale complexion, sometimes it was difficult to believe I was related to such a beautiful female.

With that thought, along with the absence of sticky residue on my skin, I looked up at my half-sister and studied her.

Her eyebrows were still scrunched together as they had been when she was concentrating on my hands. Her eyes were a striking combination—brown surrounded by a ring of green. Her wavy hair had grown out, sitting just below her shoulders now, and I realized I must've missed that detail in her life while I'd been stuck in this bed.

Her eyes shifted to meet mine, and her expression was guarded as always. Though, since we'd met, I'd noticed that her walls had cracks. The slight downturn in her lips displayed her worry, and suddenly I was grateful for all the times I had snuck out of Gatlyn Castle in the North as a child and teenager to study those around me.

"I don't know what's worse..." Matea said quietly. "Knowing them and then losing them, or losing them before you ever knew them."

Matea had been left with our maternal grandparents when our mother and her father went to war and never made it back home. Meanwhile, I'd been led to believe I had killed our mother in a freak accident as a child, and twenty-eight days ago, I truly did kill my father—for the sake of what was best for our continent.

Matea still believed our mother was out there somewhere, and after my last interaction with my twin, Dimitri, I wasn't so sure her theories were that farfetched.

"Part of me wishes I never knew them at all," I responded. "Then there would be less about them to miss."

Matea nodded slightly and looked as though she wanted to say more, but something seemed to shift her train of thought. "What's one thing that makes you feel alive?" she asked suddenly.

I tilted my head at her in a silent question, but she motioned for me to answer, so I took a moment to think.

Being with Byn always helped. Being surrounded by flowers and wild grasses and the nature of the South. Swimming in Echen Bay, watching the fish move all around me.

"Something we can do now," Matea clarified, pulling me from my thoughts.

I pondered for a moment, then answered, "Flying."

"I knew you were going to say that," she groaned, but lifted herself from the edge of the bed anyway. "Laurence should be here any moment with Eden."

"Pardon?" I sat up a little straighter.

"I want to do something with you that makes you feel alive, Aviva. If flying is what it takes to show you that you're missing out by staying cooped up in here all day—all *week*—then so be it. Though, I'd much prefer it if something here with both feet on the ground made you feel more alive instead."

"You really don't have to—"

"I'd suggest you get dressed in the next few moments, unless you want Laurence seeing you in whatever you have on under that blanket... Actually, I don't think Robyn would be too happy about that."

Faster than she could react, I grabbed the pillow from behind me and swung it towards her. Catching her off guard, it hit her in the side and she stumbled back a step.

"*That's* for doing this without telling me," I said, swinging my legs over the side of the bed for what felt like the first time in ages.

Matea, not wanting to show her surprise, crossed her arms and pointed towards the washroom and closet. "Go get ready," she ordered.

I couldn't help but laugh at the absurdity of it. "You do know who you're talking to, right?"

"Queen or not, you're still my sister—*apparently*. My sister, my duty. Now, *hurry up*," she said, huffing in annoyance that wasn't entirely one sided.

"Alright, alright, I'm going." I walked across the chambers to the washroom. Matea shifted to be closer to the balcony, likely looking for Eden and Laurence, before peering back at me. I resisted the urge to roll my eyes at her as I shut the door behind me.

It may have been twenty-eight days since I'd murdered my father, but it'd been twenty-one days since I had *officially* met my half-sister.

And I thought she might just be my new best friend.

***

Soon enough, I found myself freshly washed and donning a pair of plain brown leathers, consisting of flexible trousers and a form-fitting tunic. Lacing up a pair of matching brown boots, I headed out of the washroom while braiding my pale white hair away from my face into one thick plait. I fluffed my bangs, which I noticed as I caught a glimpse of myself in the mirror were framing my face perfectly today.

I tugged the balcony door open to find Matea, Laurence, and Eden waiting. Their conversation ceased as I stepped out into the near-blinding sunlight. I couldn't remember how long it'd been since I'd seen my own griffin.

I cleared my throat, looking towards the older male before me. Not only was he here right now, but if Eden's shiny feathers meant anything, he had been taking great care of her in my stead.

"Thank you." I shifted my gaze towards Matea. "Both of you."

They both smiled and exchanged a quick glance, subtle pride written across both of their features.

"It was nothing, Your Majesty," Laurence said kindly.

"Now, let's stop wasting daylight and get up there," Matea exclaimed, grabbing Eden's reins from Laurence with a confidence I knew she was faking.

She hated the simple *idea* of flying.

The fact that she was still willing to do this with me made my appreciation for her run even deeper.

"Matea, you really don't have to—"

"I want to," she reassured me. "Come on."

She settled into the custom-crafted saddle on Eden's back, affectionately scratching the top of her head after settling in. She hid her nerves well, but not well enough. She absent-mindedly picked at the skin around her nails before focusing her energy on gripping the reins. It seemed that nervous tick was another thing we had in common.

"Just don't drop me, alright?" Matea whispered to the griffin, who in response let out a sharp chirping sound.

Tilting my head skyward, I gazed upon the scattered clouds moving at a leisurely pace above. I tucked my wings closer into my body cautiously. I desperately missed it up there, but was I ready to fly again?

I couldn't help but think, *After everything I've done, do I deserve this privilege?*

Picking up on my hesitation, Laurence rested a hand on my shoulder. "Let yourself enjoy something again. Take this opportunity and *fly*, Aviva. Fly... for those of us who cannot."

Swallowing the lump in my throat, I nodded and took a step forward, towards the middle of the large stone balcony. Slowly, I stretched my wings out, away from my body. They spanned the length of the balcony, the silvery tipped feathers shining in the morning light. With a deep breath, I bent my knees slightly and launched myself into the air.

The cool wind nipped at my skin as I sailed straight up into a passing cloud. Sweat beaded on my skin, and I couldn't help the smile that crept onto my lips. Flying blind, I continued upwards until I was above the lower cloud line. Not but a moment later, I heard wing beats below me. I swerved out of the way heartbeats before Eden and Matea could slam into me.

"I don't know how you do this all the time!" Matea cried out, clinging to Eden tightly.

It stirred something in me at the sight of my sister clinging to my griffin. Maybe it was the insanity of the fact that I had a sister. Or maybe it was that even up here in the vast, pale blue sky again, I was to be able to see it. All I knew was that in that moment, something broke in my chest.

Tears sprung to my eyes, and I couldn't help but release the hearty laugh bubbling up inside my chest.

I spread my arms wide, angling my head towards the sun and clouds and sky beyond. My wings kept me steady as I laughed until my sides hurt. Matea eventually laughed as well, either at her own absurdity or mine.

After catching my breath and wiping my damp cheeks, I looked back towards Matea.

"I'll race you to the dens," I challenged her. Since Laurence took the time to bring Eden to us, the least I could do was ensure she made it back safely.

"Oh, you're *so* on," Matea responded, arrogance dripping from her words, seemingly covering her earlier nerves. "Let's go, Eden!"

Without warning, the two females sprang into action, Eden's wings beating so strongly they stirred the top of the clouds directly below us as the duo headed in the direction of the dens.

"Hey! We didn't even count down!" I called out. When they didn't stop, I shouted again, "Wait for me!" And with that, the three of us raced through the cloud-speckled sky over the Southern city of Cairnyl.

Chapter Two

"I believe it's a good sign. He's warming up to you," I told Matea as we crossed the gates surrounding The Haven.

"Yes, but most of the time he's so dismissive. I was surprised when he actually permitted me to enter your shared chambers this morning," she responded.

Apparently, she was under the impression that Byn didn't like her.

"Right, but he *did* let you. And anyways, can you blame him for being overprotective? My only other sibling seems to be a wild card of sorts."

Matea sighed, then nodded her agreement. "You're probably right. I'm likely over-analyzing the situation. It's just odd, to be so closely acquainted with my king after years of avoiding not only him, but *everybody*," she explained further.

Up until recently, Matea had been forced to be kept a secret from the world. With how protective—and, frankly, terrifying—my father was, our maternal grandparents had kept anybody from knowing Matea existed. They wanted to ensure it didn't become common knowledge that our mother had another daughter out there, even if she had been on the other side of the continent.

In all honesty, it sounded very isolating.

Though, with the way I grew up, I guess I didn't have it too much better than she did.

"That had to have been difficult," I murmured as we passed a set of guards, who immediately stood at attention when they caught sight of me coming towards them.

"It's what was necessary. I'm just happy that part of my life is over—living in that fear."

"I'm glad it is, too. I likely would still be in bed if it weren't for you," I responded as we walked through the front doors of The Haven.

The gargantuan structure made of a mixture of dark and honey-colored wood looked like it was glowing as the afternoon sun shone on it. The stone accents and towers broke up the sight of the wood, making the castle aesthetically pleasing to gaze upon. The glass panes of the window showed small glimpses of life and movement inside The Haven—so unlike the cold, distant, and empty castle I'd been raised in.

"There you two are," Quinn said, walking up to Matea and me. "Robyn's called a meeting of the Valwain—we have news from the border."

"You need both of us?" Matea asked the general.

"Robyn appreciates your continued support as of late, especially regarding his wife," Quinn responded, all too formally.

"I'm standing right here, you know," I chimed in.

Quinn smiled sweetly at me, her green eyes crinkling at the corners, though their usual shine had been absent the past month. The scar that ran vertically through her left eyebrow and down her cheek shifted with the movement. Without another word, she turned on her heels and headed towards the royal's private wing of The Haven, not waiting to see if Matea and I followed.

My sister and I shared a curious glance, then fell into line behind Quinn.

We passed guards and townsfolk alike as we followed the redhead, almost every one of them stopping to catch a glimpse at the three of us.

"An *Ashford*—"

"Married right before he *died*—"

"She just showed up out of *nowhere*—"

The whispering and murmuring about us grew overwhelming, but Quinn didn't falter. Her steps remained steady and unhurried as we made our way through the throng of fae surrounding us.

Soon enough, we reached the private wing, and I heard Matea let out a shaky breath, as if she'd been holding it in.

"I don't know if I'll ever get used to that," she said after rounding the corner and escaping the public's eye.

"You will," Quinn said simply.

As the first female army general in centuries, stemming from a family line of male generals, I could only imagine the atrocities Quinn had to listen to over the course of her life. And those that she'd have to continue to endure in the future.

Quinn knocked on a door to our left—three quick taps followed by two slower ones. After a soft rustling sounded from inside the room that I imagined was the movement of loose papers, Byn came to the door, opening it wide.

I didn't try to stop the hitching of my breath at the sight of him.

I feared he'd always be my undoing.

Today he wore a deep red tunic tucked into chocolate-brown trousers, all accented with gold threading, buttons, and details. The tunic's smaller details near his collar bones and buttons had a swirling pattern that reminded me of the markings on his right arm. The brown, loose markings spiraling up his hand and forearm symbolized his connection to his Titan Wolf, Atlas—who never seemed to be too far away.

The red of his top brought out the wine-red hues of his chestnut hair, which my fingers twitched to run themselves through. His freckles spread across his cheeks like tiny kisses overlapping, and the small scar on his jaw shone bright against his tan skin.

Each day I spent with him, I found myself only falling for him even farther.

"You too, Matea. If you'll have us, that is," Byn said, and I was suddenly hyperaware that he had been talking to us this entire time. I also couldn't ignore the mixed emotions radiating from my husband—toward Matea, it seemed.

Matea dipped her chin. "It'd be my honor, Your Majesty."

"Please, just Robyn. We are siblings by marriage, after all." Byn offered her a half smile.

Matea returned it with a hesitant smile of her own, and we all ducked into the room, where I noticed the rest of the Valwain—along with a couple others—had been awaiting our arrival.

Seated around a large oval table were Chess, Rayven, Teagan, and Callum, while standing on opposite sides of the room were Caelia and Laurence. The Ocrein Isle Princess was rarely very far from her brother—even now she stood near his chair, leaning against the closest wall with her arms crossed over her chest.

Callum and Caelia weren't members of the Valwain, which was made up of only those Byn—and now myself—saw fit. Since the Ocrein Isle royals had come to our aid almost a month ago, and had been helping us in this war ever since, they'd been permitted into almost each and every meeting we held.

Speaking of the Valwain, we had gained a new member recently. Laurence, the head librarian turned queen's bodyguard, had been overjoyed at the proposition. Laurence was my first addition to the group since I myself joined its ranks; all other members had been invited by Byn before I had ever stepped foot here in the South.

A week and a half ago there was a public ceremony in which both Laurence and I vowed to serve the South in any way we could, and to always be loyal to the Thorntier line. My vows had been slightly adjusted, as I was part of the Thorntier line now, by marriage, but we made sure the main point had remained the same.

We would live, and die, for the good of the South of Inphis.

I had technically been a part of the Valwain for a while by this point, but with everything surrounding the recent battle at Wittuck Woods—which had been named the Battle of Shadows, in honor of the Ocrein Isles—there hadn't been time for an official ceremony until recently.

Laurence and I had hugged after saying our vows to Byn, my husband, king, and partner in all things. I had been able to physically feel Byn's joy overflowing into my own body in that moment.

Now, Laurence met my eyes and nodded once, silently welcoming me to the meeting. As I settled next to Byn's seat, I noted Laurence shifting to stand slightly closer to my chair.

Always on guard, that one.

Matea took the seat to my left, Byn taking the one to my right, as I had assumed. Teagan sat to his right, flattening the papers before her and Byn, as though the two siblings had been looking over them together just moments ago.

"Thank you all for making it here so quickly. Teagan and I didn't think it wise to put this meeting on hold, with the new information we just received," Byn began.

"Get to the point, Thorntier," Caelia yawned, waving a hand lazily.

"*Caelia*," Callum reprimanded his younger sister. "Carry on, Robyn."

Byn's irritation rose in my chest like a wave, so I knew he must have been on edge if he was allowing Caelia to get to him so easily. I glanced down at the tattoo inked onto my inner left forearm, where the image of the Thorntier family line lay on my skin like a brand.

A wolf's head with the silhouette of the sun behind it.

In the same spot on Byn's body was a tattoo of the Heartshire family crest—a flared wing with a crescent moon behind it. My family's insignia, and also the symbol representing the entire North of Inphis. The tattoos had been embedded into our skin with a special sort of ink which allowed the two parties who shared the ink to feel each other's emotions.

Quinn and Ezra had used these special royal inks as well. The inks that had only ever been produced by one bloodline in the South—and whose final member had recently perished. The Mirthlowe family was no more, and they had taken the recipe for these special inks with them when they returned to the Stars. Whatever ink we had left was all that would ever exist.

And yet, Quinn and Ezra had gotten ahold of some.

I could only imagine the types of emotions she'd had to endure through the bond over the past month.

Since we had lost Ezra.

"We just received word that each and every corvid we sent with messages over the border into the North—they didn't make it. They were all found dead, necks snapped, in a pile just across our side of the border, the notes attached untouched," Byn said, diving straight into the meat of it, it seemed. "It appears the North does not wish to make contact with us at this time."

I couldn't help but notice the way Drayven's face dropped from across the table. As one of the main caretakers for our messenger birds, hearing about the death of so many corvids must have taken a toll.

"If the North decides not to answer, we have to assume Prince Dimitri—or possibly King Dimitri at this point—is going to continue on his father's work," said Quinn, who threw me a sideways glance as she spoke, but I couldn't be upset at the general. She was right, after all.

Though that didn't dim the bitter taste of disappointment left on my tongue at her statement.

"Right. We can't assume they will be peaceful if they won't answer a simple message," Callum agreed, nodding in Quinn's direction.

The room broke out in quiet conversation, with even Byn leaning over to ask Laurence a question behind me.

"I can go," a voice called out.

Teagan's voice.

"No way," I said in the same moment Byn stated, "Not a chance."

Even Callum threw a concerned glance towards Byn and me.

Teagan pinched the bridge of her nose before defending her case. "I'm our Northern Ambassador—this is quite *literally* my job and role to fulfill. I'll head to the border and deliver a message myself, since the North has deemed themselves too good to receive our corvids," she said, her voice unwavering.

Byn opened his mouth to argue further when Rayven cut in. "She's right," he said, his voice husky and deep.

All eyes shifted to him as he carried on. "This is her duty. Plus, if anybody were to cause any trouble at the border, she can defend herself. But she won't let it get that far, I'm sure of it. She'll play it smart, like she always does. It's not as though this would be her first time stepping foot into enemy territory."

"Exactly. I can handle myself. It's just a message delivery, after all," Teagan added, nodding her thanks to Rayven, which he returned with a slight dip of his head.

I supposed as the oldest two members of the Valwain—aside from Laurence now—they had to have each other's backs at times.

Byn glanced my way, and I knew he was looking to me for the reassurance he needed. After losing his parents late last year, he'd become very protective of those he cared about—his sisters especially. Teagan and Margo would forever hold a special place in his heart.

I reached out towards him through our bond—our emotions—and could feel his inner turmoil. Hesitation, doubt, and anxiety churned in his chest. In response, I sent a wave of calmness over them, like a hand covering the light of a flame. The flame didn't go out, but its radiating light dimmed just enough for Byn to see through his fog of emotions clearly.

Byn smiled at me slightly, and I knew it was a sign of thanks as he turned back towards Teagan. "Alright," he breathed, "but you're required to bring soldiers and guards with you. A small procession, led by you and Lychen."

Lychen, Teagan's Titan Wolf, would be happy to be back in action—even if it was just a trip to the border. The wolves' den seemed to be a little restless lately—Eden included.

"Deal!" Teagan exclaimed, and I could tell she was simply happy to have a mission to spearhead once again. She hadn't been given a true diplomatic mission to lead since she went to the North to try to bring peace to the entire continent.

"You and Quinn can hammer down the details of who will accompany you on this journey. But in the meantime, the rest of us need to prepare for our upcoming scouting missions, just in case Dimitri decides to not be as helpful as we hope," Byn said, his voice carrying the authority of the king he was.

"Right, so we're still planning to scout out Acrynd, Jackton, and Neokell?" asked Callum.

Byn nodded. "Correct, just as we discussed in our last meeting."

The day I'd met Matea was the same day we discovered our people were being kidnapped and taken prisoner, right out from under our noses, during battles. When we were trying to hammer down where, exactly, all of the missing fae were being held, we narrowed it to those three Northern cities: Acrynd, Jackton, or Neokell. Each one was on the east side of the Salic Mountains, and were mostly located on or near the flatlands.

We concluded that these locations were most likely where our missing fae were, due to the warmer climate compared to the snow-capped mountains. Along with that, transporting so many prisoners through the mountains against their will would likely be too difficult, and the cold would require more resources to keep them all alive.

Therefore, we had those three cities to scout—if Dimitri wouldn't simply undo the wrong our father did by taking them all in the first place, that was. I was hopeful that Teagan would be able to make progress with my twin on her mission—or at least figure out why they'd killed our corvids.

"When will Teagan leave?" Caelia asked.

"Tomorrow morning," Byn responded. When Caelia raised an eyebrow in question, I added, "It'll be a bit of a trek to make it to the border."

"Regarding preparations for the scouting missions, I'll be supplying everybody with an emergency healing pack to include in their bags," Chester, whom everybody called Chess, added. Always thinking like a trokav, it seemed.

Byn nodded his thanks to Chess, then looked to Teagan once again. "You have the rest of the afternoon and evening to prepare, sister. Come dawn, we'll see you off."

***

"You're worried about Teagan," I stated, scooping up a bite of pie and bringing it to my lips.

Byn nodded, then paused a moment. "I think I always will be. I understand she's the oldest, and she bears a heavy weight on her shoulders because of it—there was always a certain level of pressure on her from our parents. But being the only male, and the heir at that... it's a privilege, but also a burden at times. I simply wish to keep my sisters safe."

I hummed in response, allowing him time to add to his statement if he wanted to.

"Not to mention Teagan never shows or talks about how she truly feels. Sometimes I wish I could feel what she feels, just so I could better understand her." He sighed and laid his fork down, seeming to lose his appetite as he spoke.

Byn had requested a private dinner for just the two of us in our chambers tonight. We had a simple yet tasty dinner of some sort of small bird, fresh bread, wine, cheese, and now a small pie for dessert, and we were both content at this point into our meal. We talked about what we each needed to prepare for the possibility of scouting missions, and who would gather what. We decided to divide our tasks so only one of us—me—had to go into town tomorrow. Byn staying here at The Haven also allowed him to be easily accessible in the case that Teagan sent word early for any reason.

We talked about this morning, and how I felt a little better after flying with Matea and Eden, but that my heart remained heavy. That led to a discussion about Matea, and how much I had come to trust her in such a short amount of time. I explained how I felt around her—like I did when I was younger with Dimitri.

Safe.

Byn, on the other hand, expressed that he was wary of my half-sister. He explained that from his point of view, she had technically defied him by sneaking over the border and traveling into the North on her own. Even if her discoveries did end up helping us in the end, it still seemed to have left a bad taste in his mouth.

"I think Teagan feels as though she has to take care of everybody around her—Margo especially. She probably feels like her own emotions aren't as important because of it," I offered gently.

Byn sighed again "I wouldn't be surprised, but I wish it didn't have to be that way."

He glanced out of the stained-glass window next to the balcony, and I followed his line of sight, my gaze snagging on the crescent moon in the sky.

An arrow of pain shot through my heart as I thought about my twin brother, Dimitri. I couldn't help but remember who he was before our father began corrupting him. How the day I left my homeland, he told me any time I looked to the sky and saw the moon, that we'd be connected by it, as he would be gazing upon it, too. That I would always be a child of the sky, no matter how far from home I was.

Little did I know at the time, that I hadn't even found my true home yet.

"You miss him," Byn said softly, and I realized he'd been watching me as I stared at the moon.

"Every single day," I murmured. I was unsure if that ache in my heart would ever fully resolve.

"Let's get you ready for bed," he said as he stood from his chair and rounded the small table until he reached my side. Then, he held out his hand for me.

Always waiting, doing things on my terms.

Stars, I love him, I couldn't help but think.

Slipping my hand into his, he led me to our shared washroom. He gathered up my favorite sleeping attire—an oversized shirt of his and some silk pants he no longer wore—and placed them on the edge of the sink before us.

"May I?" he asked, gesturing between my current leather outfit and the clothes he'd just brought over.

My heart clenched at his offer. He wanted to help dress me for bed, even though I knew he had other things he should have been doing. Simply because he understood that sometimes the most mundane of tasks could be the most difficult.

"Please," he added softly before I could even object, and I knew I couldn't refuse him.

This was just one of the many ways he showed me he cared.

I nodded, my heart already beating quicker than before.

As soft as a feather, he unlatched each small clasp down the front of my torso that held my leather tunic closed. His breath hitched as he unhooked the last one and slid the two halves away from each other. He bent his head to place a light kiss on my chest, right above my pounding heart. Using his calloused fingers to push the tunic down my shoulders, he reached behind me and slipped the buttons on my upper back out of place, allowing the tunic to fall to the ground without snagging on my wings.

Now without a top, the cool night air nipped at my skin in an almost thrilling way.

Byn lightly took hold of my chin and tilted my face up to meet his gaze. His eyes were so deep and full of love, I felt as though I was melting into their pool of forest green. He planted a whisper of a kiss on my forehead, then dropped to his knees before me.

The King of the South.

Kneeling before me.

Not only that, but the warm love and adoration I felt in my chest radiating from him was a lifeline I clung to with my entire being.

I'd never felt so seen before meeting him.

He reached towards my waist, placing a hand on each hip, and pressing another kiss on my stomach. My hands began to shake slightly, so I intertwined them into his chocolate-colored hair, wrapping the waves around my fingers.

Soon enough he had undone the buttons on my leather pants, and I fear he had undone me, too.

Once the trousers were at my ankles, he carefully helped me step out of them. He reached up and grabbed the black silk pants on the lip of the sink, slowly helping me step into them and tying them into place at my waist. His fingertips grazed my skin, and it felt like every fiber of my being was lit on fire at the contact.

Rising from the floor, he slid the muted purple cotton shirt over my head. He paused to kiss the tip of my nose before the shirt was fully on, and I couldn't help but grin. He guided me in turning me around, so he could button up the top of my shirt where the holes in the fabric were for my wings to poke through.

Coming around my right side to stand before me, he pulled me to him and wrapped me in his embrace. He rested his chin atop my head, and I buried my face in the tunic covering his sculpted chest.

"I thank the Stars for you daily, Avi," he murmured, using the dead Northern language only him and I know, to say *my love*. His grip on me tightened ever so slightly as he spoke.

I pulled back to gaze up at him. "As do I."

Standing on my tiptoes, I grazed my lips against his in a feather-soft kiss.

"Your turn, my love," I said, heading into the wardrobe to gather his sleep clothes.

He didn't object, and the rest of the night was full of tender love and stolen kisses, until I drifted off to sleep to the rhythm of his heartbeat and the steady feel of his chest rising and falling beneath my head.

Chapter Three

The slight heel of my black leather boots sounded across the stone floor as I made my way, step by step, down the damp spiral staircase.

Click click click.

That was the only noise I could focus on as it filled the space around me while I hurried down all forty-two cobbled steps. Once I arrived at the large, mostly empty, open room at the bottom of the staircase, I paused briefly, fishing a ring of keys out of the pocket of my navy overcoat. The silver threaded coat was so long it nearly reached my ankles, but I didn't mind so much.

It was attire like this I'd seen Father wear so often during formal appearances, and even to simple meetings at times.

After all, it was his shoes I was trying to fill.

I made my way down the main corridor that acted as an artery to the dungeons below Gatlyn Castle, branching off in different directions. As I walked, I rubbed the edge of each key until I felt the groves of the one I was looking for against the pad of my thumb.

Having turned into the west-branching corridor, I quickly arrived in front of the cell door I had been seeking out without truly realizing it. I had found myself doing that often lately—ending up at this cell, trying to get answers to questions I had no hope of solving on my own.

Not allowing myself to hesitate more than a moment, I shoved the key into the hole in the cell door and flicked it open.

Sweeping into the small room, the foul odor always seemed to hit my senses first. Naturally, as a Northerner, my eyes rapidly adjusted to the dim light, making out the fae male's shape in the corner of the room.

When the prisoner seemed to let my presence go unnoticed, I ripped an unlit torch from the wall and called to the power that felt like pure fury in my veins. Blowing onto the end of the torch, fire sprouted and grew from where my breath had touched.

The sudden light drew the fae prisoner from his slumber.

"Dimitri," he breathed raggedly, dragging himself into a sitting position as his chains rattled with the motion.

With the alychite chains around his ankle being bolted to the floor, the male couldn't reach my side of the small, rectangular room—at least not without cutting off his foot first.

The alychite really wasn't necessary with this prisoner, from what I understood. He had no zirilium, according to the accounts, and from what I had gathered myself over the past few weeks—almost a month now.

Alychite was one of the most valuable minerals the North was home to. With its ability to cut off a wielder from their zirilium just by maintaining contact, it had been used for decades by my father to help maintain his control.

I glanced at the dark, heavy mineral in a rare moment of genuine curiosity. It was a wonder that the earth below naturally produced such a material. As if it always needed a way to keep us fae in check, just in case.

Fortunately for me, myself and those who had come before me mastered it before *it* could master *us*.

The prisoner slowly rose to his feet, his body stiff as he shielded his eyes against the torchlight. By looking at only his mud-colored hair, he could almost pass as clean; it was the white streak covered in dirt and sweat that fell into his face which gave away just how filthy he'd become in his time down here.

"Ezra," I responded, my voice flat, with a practiced sort of coldness to it.

Stepping farther into the room, I stopped next to the small table in the corner that housed a pile of different blades and other small devices. Shuffling through the various tools, my gaze snagged on a short, curved blade that reminded me of the crescent moon in my family's crest.

Selecting that blade for today's session, I realized it also somewhat resembled the claws of Ziana—my griffin—especially with the nearly black hilt that matched her feathers and fur.

"So," I said, turning back to face the prisoner, "you already know what information I want. You could make this much easier on yourself and tell me now." I slowly stepped closer to him.

To his credit, he didn't cower. He leaned his back against the wall, as if already fed up with the situation he had found himself in.

"I'll say it the same way I've said it before—I'd rather *die*," he said, his voice scratchy from screaming, but still unwavering.

Without missing a beat, my spare hand flew out and gripped his throat, pinning him in place against the wall. His hands attempted to claw at my arm, but his fingernails were just barely covering his nail beds again; they'd taken weeks to fully grow back.

Angling the claw-like blade in my hand an inch away from his eye, I said softly, "Maybe today you'll get your wish."

For the past few weeks, I'd been trying to pry out of him any weaknesses of the South's that I could exploit. Anything I could use to win this war and conquer them once and for all.

To my surprise, it was like he'd become a different person than who I'd heard about while here below the castle. I'd heard he was of the softest of the South's *Valwain*, and I figured that meant he'd be of the easiest to break. But despite some of my best efforts, he still hadn't given in.

Yet.

Baring my teeth at him, I took a step back, releasing him from my grip. His hands touched the now tender skin of his throat and winced.

Stalking back to the table, I placed the curved blade back onto the pile and ran a hand through my snow-white hair.

"Let's try something new," I suggested, turning back to the prisoner.

I called to the newfound embers of my soul, stoking them with the rage I felt at this individual, at this *Ezra*. He represented everything I had been taught to hate—as well as the people that turned my own twin against me—and against our father, too. Against our *nation*.

And Father's life had been the price.

But besides that, Aviva hadn't just betrayed Father with her acts of defiance—she'd betrayed me, too. She might not have left Hollis willingly, but she'd chosen to stay away all this time.

Or at least, that was what they wanted me to believe.

I knew my twin—I knew nothing would stop her from coming home, if she could help it.

I just needed to figure out what had happened—what had *changed*.

Using the anger I felt bubbling beneath my skin, sweat beaded on my forehead as I focused that energy in my hand, curling it into a fist.

The moment my hand ignited in flames, I met the male's eyes, and he had the decency to look fearful for once.

I took a step closer to him. "This time, I want to know what you and your *Valwain* did to my sister."

"*Did* to her?" he asked, as though he was truly clueless.

"What did you do to cause her to change so much, so *fast*? Was it another elixir—something that messed with her head? Did you torture her into being on your side? Into not coming home?" I asked, my flame growing stronger alongside my anger.

"What? Dimitri, *no.* She made her own choices—she put herself first for once. We didn't force her into anything. If you'd recall, it was your father that forced Aviva into things she didn't want to do."

Prowling closer, my flames burning bright enough to see the color of his light brown eyes, I whispered, "*Liar.*"

Faster than the prisoner could even process, I pulled my arm back and sent it sailing straight into the side of his ribs.

A vicious *crack* rung out at the same time a scream ripped from his throat, and he was thrown to the floor by the force of the punch. His dirty, sliced up shirt was being eaten away by small, residual flames stuck to it, but I didn't offer even a wing-beat of relief.

Pouncing on him, fist still alight with deep orange flames, I gripped him by the collar and continued to let the punches fly.

Over and over, I released my pent-up anger, hit by hit, until it started to die out. The moment my fury dissolved into embers once again, my flames banked, then winked out, leaving us in near darkness.

Frustrated that I couldn't even control a simple flame, I blindly threw another perfect punch—this time to his face—but he barely made a sound. It wasn't until this moment that I realized he had slipped into unconsciousness.

Releasing him swiftly, almost in disgust, I groaned in frustration. My hands caught in my hair, tugging at the roots as I retreated step by step to the other side of the cell.

Finally seeing the damage I'd done, eyes adjusting to the dim light, I realized I should feel something *more* than I did. I knew Aviva would expect me to.

And yet I didn't.

His clothes were barely held together by threads at this point, having been charred off or, in some places, melted to his skin. The bruises had risen to the surface almost instantly, his skin mottled in black and blue along the left side of his body, where my fist had made contact the most. His eye was in the process of swelling shut where I'd hit him last, his body reacting to the damage even when he wasn't conscious to.

The stone of the wall dug into my back and wings as I slid to the ground, my hands still tugging viciously at my hair.

Taking a breath so deep it almost hurt, I focused on that energy in my veins. It seemed to have calmed substantially after being given an outlet.

Interesting, I noted.

A soft knock sounded on the metal door next to me, but I didn't budge. There was only one other fae that had a key to this specific cell, anyways. Plus, nobody else would be stupid enough to venture this far into the dungeons.

"Enter," I said, my voice sounding distant and hollow in my ears.

I listened as he unlocked the door and slid it open, stepping into the room with a leather bag that was bursting at the seams with trokav supplies.

Hugo, who almost tripped over my extended leg when he stepped into the small cell, gasped when the smell of burned skin and flesh hit his nose. His white wings flared slightly in alarm, but his eyes were locked onto the unconscious form on the other side of the space.

"Has this session concluded?" the trokav asked, his voice thick with an emotion I couldn't quite place, not bothering to spare me a glance.

After I waved my hand lazily, feigning disinterest, Hugo crossed the cell to the prisoner's side and gently turned him onto his back. Moving much faster than the older male usually did, he flung open his bag and began sifting through the bottles and vials of various healing remedies.

I watched by the light of the torch as Hugo used his water wielding abilities to manipulate a foggy liquid out of a small vial, tugging it through the air closer to him and the prisoner. Hugo tilted the male's head back and swung his wrist, sending the entirety of the foggy liquid between the slightly parted lips of the prisoner's mouth.

Hugo paused, and I couldn't help but note how gently he handled those within his care.

Suddenly, the male before him gasped, flying into a sitting position, panting. He seemed to immediately regret the movement as he groaned, the sound pained.

"Shhh, you'll be alright. No, don't look, just close your eyes," Hugo said to the male, who had been tilting his head down to look at the damage done to him.

The prisoner's eyes searched Hugo's. He looked so vulnerable, so fearful, I couldn't help rolling my eyes at the sight.

The male must have found something in Hugo's gaze as he relaxed slightly, realizing Hugo was once again here to help him—not harm him. He hesitated, then closed his eyes and allowed Hugo to guide him back down to the floor.

In the following moments, I watched Hugo carefully tend to the male. It appeared as though Hugo only saw a patient, not a prisoner who needed breaking. That was one area in which the older male and I differed.

I didn't mind getting my hands dirty to do what needed to be done.

Soon enough, the male's skin had been cleaned and had begun healing from the ointments, and his bones had been set back into place by Hugo. He wasn't back to normal by any means—the affected skin was either scabbed over or extremely raw, and he groaned every time he moved, likely from his bones being set but not fully healed. Healing, even with the help of elixirs and spreads, took time nowadays.

Though the fae hadn't always been that way, it was our reality now, and that was all that mattered.

Plus, his slow healing benefitted me. He'd remember his lesson this time.

Having done all he could for the prisoner, Hugo packed his vials and such back into his leather bag, slinging it over his shoulder with care. To my surprise, instead of addressing Hugo, the prisoner looked towards me, meeting my gaze without an ounce of the fear I'd seen before in his eyes.

"I thank the Stars Aviva escaped you," he stated. It hadn't been said with hatred, but rather as though it were a simple fact.

As though that single sentence didn't add to the weight on my soul.

I grit my teeth to stop myself from flinching at his words, but something must have shown in my gaze. He looked satisfied with himself, as if he'd actually gotten to me.

The *audacity*.

I lunged for him, that fiery rage building in my veins once again, but was quickly pulled off course by Hugo, his hands around my arm.

"My pr-*king*, if you attack him again, you're allowing his words to get to you. *Snap out of it*," Hugo said—always the voice of reason.

The prisoner hadn't even flinched, hadn't moved at all despite the obvious threat.

He is likely right, I thought.

Forcing myself to breathe deeply to calm the energy buzzing within me, I nodded to Hugo. He dropped his grip on me, taking a step back in the process. He cleared his throat, then uttered the words I'd been dreading to hear from him.

"Your Majesty, perhaps we should discuss the possibility of you returning to the daily elixirs."

I froze, letting his words sink in. Ever so slowly, I turned my head to look at the older male with malice.

He flinched as his gaze met mine, averting his eyes to the floor instead.

"My apologies, my king. I simply am looking out for your best interests," Hugo said, his voice coming out breathy. I ignored the way his hands had begun to shake slightly.

"Do not *ever* suggest that to me again, Hugo," I said, my voice as calm and cold as I'd been trying to portray myself as to the world for so many years.

Hugo sputtered a quick, "Yes, Your Majesty," before slipping from the room without looking back at the prisoner.

Of course Hugo would suggest the elixirs. Him and Father had forced me to take them for nearly my entire life—why wouldn't that be his solution, now that him and Father could no longer control me?

When Father had been murdered and was no longer there to enforce the elixirs, I stopped taking them. The sickness I had endured afterwards was so awful, I considered Hugo's suggestion to just take them again. I almost believed him when he said I'd been born with a defect and *needed* them.

Turned out he was wrong.

Without them, I was *so* much stronger.

I had nearly smacked the older trokav for his misguidance, but he'd sworn on the Stars above he had only told me what my father had told him before.

Maybe I should have punished him somehow, after all.

I ran a hand through my hair, pulling myself from my thoughts, then said to the only male left in the cell with me, "I would instruct you to keep this between us, but you won't live long enough to tell anybody else, anyways."

Without bothering to glance at the male with the dirty streak of white hair, I took my leave from the cell, securing it behind me.

Chapter Four

"What about this one?" Matea asked, holding up a sizeable dagger—much too large for my hands, but perfect for Byn's—with the Thorntier insignia engraved on it.

I shook my head. "He has more than enough things with that sun and wolf's head on it, trust me."

Matea shrugged, then placed it back onto the table beside her and walked towards Margo and me.

The city of Cairnyl, which surrounded The Haven, was hosting its monthly creator's market that morning. It was my first time attending, but Matea seemed to know her way around. She had likely been coming for years, remaining unseen and slipping from shadow to shadow.

Caelia had also never been before, considering she'd only been in the South for a handful of weeks, so Matea—along with Margo—guided us from stall to stall. Matea was telling us everything about the market that she could, from an old vendor she missed seeing to the new ones she didn't recognize, as well as who had the best prices and highest quality. Margo, on the other hand, was quieter than usual. The same way she had been ever since we lost Ezra.

According to Matea, the crafters and creators of Cairnyl all did this once a month, each vendor showcasing their best items for sale. So far we had seen weapons, tools, jewelry, clothing, crops, pastries, paintings, and there were even more stalls we hadn't made it to yet. This market gave the lesser-known creators of Cairnyl a chance to show off their craft, since each stall was the same size and only so many items could be brought in to display.

It tugged on my heartstrings to see the community they had built here. Back in Hollis, we never had anything like this. People stuck to the same popular shops, monopolizing the industry and making it nearly impossible for new shops to pop up anywhere. Even when expanding the city by building new structures, the well-known businesses had their hand in the new real estate, controlling the entire market.

That same greed wasn't present here in the South. Sure, they weren't perfect—there were always going to be businesses that were more popular than others, and greed was always present to a degree—but they *tried*. With events like this, they tried.

"This one?" Caelia suggested, motioning to a knife with the swirling patterns of an Ocrein Isle tattoo on it. The tattoo was something they received once they were deemed a master of the shadows they wielded, from what Rayven had told me when I inquired about the ink adorning his right arm. Caelia and Callum both had the same ink on their right arms, the swirling pattern as unique as a fingerprint.

I shook my head again. "Considering Byn doesn't wield shadows, I think maybe not." I offered her a small smile, though, because at least the Ocrein princess was trying.

For better or worse, lately I'd spent more time with the princess than originally planned. She was the type that couldn't sit still, so she'd often joined one of the Valwain in whatever task they were doing that day. Several times over the past few weeks, she had tagged along with me. Whether it be checking on Eden, or heading into town, often Caelia asked to join.

Honestly, I understood. I'd needed to keep my mind occupied recently, too—or else the dark thoughts lurking in the corners of my mind would emerge once again. And, as it turned out, she wasn't *always* snarky and defensive—she could be caring and soft when it came to those she loved. I'd learned that she and Callum also had a younger sister and brother—Calliope and Cillian—and that Caelia and Callum both missed them dearly.

We were here at the market to gather any miscellaneous supplies we might need during scouting missions—missions which may or may not happen, but we were trying to be a few steps ahead, just in case. Since we were here anyway, I'd wanted to find something special for Byn. He'd given so much for me—*done* so much for me—I wanted to show my gratitude.

I glanced over at Margo, whose eyes had snagged on a jewelry and craft stall a few booths down from where we stood.

"Come on," I said to her, holding my hand out for her to take. She glanced at my hand, then up to my face, as though concerned I would retract my offer. When our eyes met, I smiled softly—encouragingly. She didn't smile back, but her caramel eyes softened ever so slightly as she placed her gloved hand into mine and we made our way over to the jewelry merchant together.

Teagan left for her mission to the border early that morning. While Margo wasn't privy to all the details regarding why her sister wasn't here, she knew Teagan was gone. The mission should only be for a few days, and we kept reassuring Margo of that, but the young female was still anxious beyond words.

Ever since Ezra had been injured and taken from us, she'd been this way. Quiet. Reserved. Far away, almost. Nothing like her usual giddy, upbeat self that I'd come to know in the past. She seemed haunted—of which I couldn't blame her for. She'd seen and experienced things that no child ever should.

"Take a look around! We have—" The female gasped at the sight of me and Margo, hand in hand, approaching her booth.

Margo was easily recognizable by the citizens of Cairnyl, with her short, curly hair, beads hanging from her ears, stunning eyes, freckles, and small golden circlet that matched her siblings'.

But if anybody was even easier to pick out, it was me. The giant, white and gray wings, mismatched eyes, white hair, and pale skin didn't exactly help me blend in.

The four of us at the market today had already been stopped multiple times. Some simply wanted to chat, some asked questions, and others took their time to thank me. They all knew I had a hand in the success of the Battle of Shadows, but it wasn't public knowledge exactly how I had helped. So I couldn't exactly fault them, despite the bile that rose to the back of my throat each time they expressed their gratitude.

"My queen! My princess! Thank you for stopping by my stall! Please, take your time looking at whatever it is you please," the female said. She was short for a fae—even shorter than I was—with black hair, olive skin, and beautiful curves. Her clothes, though, were well-worn, and the bags under her eyes were prominent.

"Thank you," I responded as Margo let go of my hand in favor of checking out some different types of beads and string for jewelry making.

Having nothing better to do, but wanting to stay near Margo, I stepped closer to the booth and ran my gaze over the section of rings.

"Did you know," I said to nobody in particular, "that the humans are said to have used rings on their left hand as a symbol of marriage?"

Margo glanced my way as I spoke, interest piqued, but returned to her shopping without saying a word.

"I didn't, actually," the merchant on the other side of the table said.

My eyes had just snagged on a set of matching rings as she spoke.

"What's your favorite piece here?" I asked her without looking up from the matching set.

"*Mine*, Your Majesty?" she sputtered, eyes widening in surprise.

I nodded, motioning for her to show me. She jumped into action, pulling out a delicate, gold chain necklace. Simple, yet stunning.

It would suite her perfectly.

"Here." I placed a small bag of gold coins on the table between us, then motioned to all the items I listed. "I'd like these matching rings, whatever the princess is fond of, and the necklace in your hands." I took a moment to slightly open the money pouch so she could see inside. It was double the price of what I was purchasing from her.

The merchant's eyes widened, almost brought to tears at the sight of the gold before her. "You're positive?"

"Absolutely… what was your name?"

"Tiff, Your Majesty."

"Absolutely, *Tiff*." I smiled.

Tiff, despite having to wipe at her eyes once or twice, quickly packaged up everything that I had bought. Margo's items took the most amount of time—beads, string, yarn, pearls, gems. It was nice to see her interested in one of her previous hobbies again.

"Here you are," Tiff said, placing the carefully packaged sack of goods in front of Margo and me.

I slid the sack closer to me and took out the smallest box—the box that housed the simple gold chain in it.

"This is for you," I said, sliding it back across the table to Tiff.

"No, Your Majesty, I couldn't possibly—"

"I insist," I said simply. And how could she reject her queen?

A stray tear slipped down her cheek as she bowed her head. "Thank you, my queen." She met my eyes. "If you ever need anything, my uncle—Henrey Dayfall—sits on your husband's council of advisors and oversees Breckshyre, to the southeast. He would be more than happy to assist you."

"Thank you, Tiff, I really appreciate that," I responded warmly, and the three of us females shared a moment of genuine smiles.

Tiff didn't allow us to leave her stall until Margo had acquired even more crafting materials, and we left with two packs full of items from that singular booth.

"Stars, did you buy the entire market?" Matea asked as Margo and I approached her and Caelia.

Margo's little ears flushed red, but I laughed the comment off. I knew Matea meant no harm.

"Almost," I responded fluidly. "It looks as though you two ended up with a good haul, too." I motioned towards the smaller pack Matea was carrying, and the two Caelia had in her arms.

We swept through the market one last time, picking up a few more various items along the way, before heading back towards The Haven.

"Do you miss your home?" Margo asked Caelia while walking. It was often that I wondered what my little sister by marriage thought about.

Caelia took a breath before responding, "Yes and no."

Margo, large sack in her arms, looked towards her expectantly.

The Ocrein Princess sighed, but continued explaining as we walked. "I don't miss the pressure. Sure, there's pressure on Callum and me here, too, but there's also more freedom. Our parents aren't breathing down our necks and we aren't constantly entertaining those around us. Yes, we're still on display here in the South, but in a different way than back home. We can sort of... create our own image of ourselves here, while back home our image was honed and crafted to perfection by our parents since we were very small." She nodded towards me. "I'm sure Aviva gets it."

I could feel Matea glancing at me, but I took a moment to think about it before responding.

It was true, the pressure and control kept on me back in the North was intense. Here, sure there was still pressure and expectations, but it wasn't the same as when I was growing up. Caelia was right—here, I got to create my own image. I was able to be my own person.

"She's right, Margo," I said after a handful of thoughtful seconds.

Margo nodded, looking as though she didn't expect this answer. "I think I'd miss it here, if I ever left," she said quietly.

Shifting the pack I was carrying into one arm, I used my free hand to ruffle her unruly hair as I said, "Good thing you never have to."

***

I stood in front of the door that led to my original chambers; the door itself being the newest one in the long hallway I was hesitating in.

Steeling myself, I inhaled deeply, then knocked four times on the wooden door.

The room beyond was silent and still, from what I could tell. Despite my turbulent emotions recently, my ability to wield my zirilium had only strengthened. The sun and moon stones helped me focus them through the conduits, instead of solely being connected to my emotions, as they had previously.

Even with the desire to stay in bed most days recently, getting out and using my abilities in *some* way was still necessary, at least a couple times a week. Otherwise, I realized they would get backed up quicker than when I was taking my elixirs. I supposed the elixirs not only hid everything about me that was Southern, but also helped keep my zirilium from regularly overflowing.

Or, maybe it was simply the fact that I had been using them more often recently, due to not being forced to hide that part of myself any longer. Like a muscle that grew in strength over time, my zirilium seemed to grow with me, too.

"Aurora, can we please talk?" I asked through the door.

She'd been staying in my old chambers since she arrived here in the South with Eden, my griffin, a month ago now. And though I was beyond happy she was somewhere safe and had made it out of the North alive, she didn't seem to view the situation the same way.

Despite having been here for some time now, Aurora would still only speak to me. She refused to even *interact* with a Southerner. She also wouldn't agree with my reasoning that I was, indeed, Southern as well, so they can't be all bad. Her understanding still was that the South was the enemy to any and all Northerners, as they had been for centuries. I tried introducing her to the Valwain, but she'd refused to utter a word. I had even asked Laurence to try speaking to her, but we made the mistake of introducing the two of them on a day where Laurence was helping out in the library. Though he had a Northerner's blue eyes, the dark green robes the library helpers wore had her immediately closed off to him. She had called him a traitor, and I had quickly dismissed my friend and personal bodyguard after that, not wanting him to have to relive any of his past trauma.

Now, I stopped by frequently, trying to get through to her and help her see reason. I did my best to be understanding—her having to learn to accept that the North was forced to remain in the dark was difficult. But it was also necessary if she ever wanted to start building a life here in the South.

I sighed, then focused on the sun stones adorning the knuckles of my right glove. Using just one, I shifted my feet slightly wider than they were and threw my awareness into the earth below me.

The corridors of The Haven were all made of wood flooring—except for the private, royal wing. The royal wing—which I'd learned had been an addition to the original structure of the castle—had stone flooring, which was, technically, a type of earth.

Through the stone below me, I could feel the female who was once my closest friend pacing the length of the room just on the other side of the door. She did well to step lightly enough so her footsteps remained unheard, but she couldn't stop the tiny vibrations that were sent through the earth with each step she took.

"Aurora, I know you're in there. I checked the library *and* gardens for you—this is the only place you could be. Plus, I can feel you pacing in there. You only do that when you're stressed or anxious." I leaned my head against the door. "Please let me in."

Having never dropped the connection I had with the stone below, I felt her pause. I imagined her in there, hesitation and caution written across her features.

Then, she moved. The door swung open so fast I had to catch myself on the doorframe in order to not fall into the female suddenly standing there.

The female before me was different than I had come to know her as over the years we'd spent together. Her soft, blue eyes no longer sparkled as they once had, such as when she'd learned something new during her trokav training with Hugo. Her face had grown slightly slimmer in her time here, as she often refused the food I brought her. Her light blonde hair, which used to appear as delicate as silk, had lost its shine.

I couldn't understand it. She was *safe*. She'd made it out, and now we had each other. Wasn't that better than nothing?

"Hi," I said, a bit dumbfounded, before clearing my throat. "Care for a walk?"

Poking her head out into the corridor, she glanced up and down the length of the hallway. "Maybe we can chat in one of the lounge rooms?" she asked.

Thinking of the meetings we'd had lately, and the different rooms housing different documents and plans, I shook my head. "They're... occupied. But we could walk into town, if you pleased. It's a beautiful day out," I replied hopefully.

At that, her expression hardened. As though she had pulled up the drawbridge that she had dropped between us, even if it had been briefly.

"What is it this time, Viva?" she inquired, getting straight to the point.

"I just..." I hesitated a heartbeat, before deciding to bare my heart to her. "I miss you. I miss our friendship. I thought you would end up adjusting, but you haven't, and I'm not sure what I can do to help."

Aurora's eyes softened a degree, but not by much.

"I don't belong here, Viva," she sighed. "I'm happy you feel as though you've found your place here—even if I disagree—but this isn't *my* place. And I won't fall for their tricks. They may act welcoming and kind, but that doesn't change everything we were taught back home. Deep down, they're still *monsters*, Viva."

It was so frustrating to hear that after all she'd seen firsthand while in the South, she still didn't believe them to be the good ones in the war. And yet even if she couldn't do that, couldn't she believe in me, and what I had to say?

"They aren't monsters, Aurora! You don't have to trust them, but why can't you trust *me*?" I cried out, wings flared slightly, and tears threatening to spring to my eyes.

At that, her tough demeanor cracked and fissured. She reached for me, placing a hand on my shoulder, and for just a moment I saw the female I had grown up with again.

"I'll try, Viva. I'll try," she said softly, as though whispering a promise.

Though I wasn't completely sure I believed her anymore.

It seemed like I wasn't the only one who had changed during our time apart.

Chapter Five

The moisture in the air was so thick and dense, it was beginning to stick to my fair skin, and I'd only been down here a few moments. The condensation on the stone walls surrounding me ran down in rivets, like the sweat I'd surely begin producing if I didn't get out of there soon.

The tunnels below Gatlyn Castle wove together like the stitching of a handcrafted blanket, overlapping with twists and turns that were nearly unpredictable.

Unless, like me, you'd grown up roaming them until you got lost.

Nobody could hear you from down here, so you had to walk until you found your own way out.

So, that was what I did. I learned. And I adapted.

As I had with everything in my life.

Taking a sharp left, I headed towards the wing of the castle I hadn't dared to venture to in over a month.

The ruler's wing, which *usually* was home to whoever was currently on the throne.

My advisors—which I'd inherited from Father's reign—had encouraged me to take Father's chambers and the rest of his wing for myself.

I'd quickly declined.

Father had been the only fae I'd ever known to use that wing of Gatlyn Castle, and I couldn't stomach the thought of erasing him like that. Not just erasing him, but also building on top of it for myself...

The thought made me sick.

Another bout of random turns, and a few minutes more of listening to my boots sound against the stone beneath me, and I'd finally arrived.

At a dead end.

Well, it would look that way to anybody else, anyways.

I reached out a hand and pushed one stone out of place in the wall, then shoved against it with my full bodyweight. And with that, the hidden opening I hadn't used in what felt like ages slowly swung open.

Shutting it behind me, the other side of the hinged wall looked fairly ordinary. This wing housed multiple pieces that my grandmother had painted. I'd never met her personally, but sometimes I liked to imagine I could catch glimpses of her in the paintings she'd left behind.

They were all brightly colored, even the ones in snowy scenery—there'd be a patch of flowers, or a house, or an animal of sorts that drew the eye. It seemed as though she knew how to focus mostly on the positive elements.

How foolish, I couldn't help but think.

I was stalling, I realized with a start.

Sighing lightly, I turned away from the wall of paintings and headed a few doors down on the opposite wall. There were seventeen doors in the hallway that made up the ruler's wing, but there was only one I was looking for right now.

Every door in this wing was identical. They were a deep, rich brown wood so dark it was almost black, having been harvested from the surrounding area, and made up each door, with silver accents and handles.

Steeling myself, I reached into my pocket, feeling for the right key. Once found, I slipped it into the lock below the handle and turned, unlocking the door with a soft shifting sound. I gripped the silver handle and pushed down. The door squeaked as it opened in on itself, echoing down the silent hallway and reminding me of how long it had likely been since anybody had been in this particular room—besides myself, that was.

Mother's private study.

It was a fairly small space—likely the smallest in the entire corridor—but Mother had made the most of it. Floor-to-ceiling shelves lined nearly every wall, overflowing with books and nicknacks of all sorts. It was as though she'd crammed her entire life into this one room.

And it had been left almost entirely untouched.

Except by me.

I imagined if Aviva had ever dared to venture into Father's part of the castle, she'd have become emotional to know that so much of our mother still existed inside the same building we occupied. Yet my twin did her best to stay out of our father's way at all times, overpowering her curious nature. Besides, we'd both been told all of Mother's things had been given away or donated after she'd *passed* all those years ago.

The discolored rug on the floor was covered in layers upon layers of dust—just as everything else was—and had only been disrupted by my coming and going before the recent battle in Wittuck Woods. I rounded the desk towards the back of the room and blew the majority of the dust off of the chair before taking a seat. Drumming my fingers against the top of the wooden desk before me, I found myself becoming lost in my thoughts.

A couple of weeks before the latest battle, when I had just learned that it was going to happen so soon, I approached Father. I'd argued that if we went forward with his plans to spring an attack, the South very well may hurt Aviva as retaliation against us. They were said to be barbaric, after all—there was no telling what they'd do to her.

Sending her away was supposed to have been an act of peace—one that Father had initiated—and yet there he'd been, trying to ruin it all.

I hadn't care much about the battle itself, only what it would've meant for my sister.

When I hadn't let it go, Father snapped. He had been under a lot of stress due to planning the details of what was originally supposed to be a surprise attack, and I likely shouldn't have pushed, but with what I thought was Aviva's life on the line, I couldn't let it go.

Then, Father had made a bargain with me.

He'd take me to see his *favorite prisoner* if I cooperated.

I couldn't agree to a deal I didn't know all of the specifics about, so at first I had declined.

That was, until Father told me who he was speaking of.

Who was still *alive.*

My mother.

Father had vaguely and with little detail explained that despite him telling me almost my entire life that Mother had died of a vicious, mysterious illness that had taken her in her sleep, he had been lying the entire time. He had said due to *unforseen circumstances*, she had to leave the castle, but that she hadn't passed.

That was when he'd finally told me everything. Or at least, what I thought everything was, at the time. I had to learn about Aviva's abilities on my own.

Father had revealed that we were to spring a surprise attack on Cairnyl, which then lead to the Battle of Shadows. He'd then told me all I needed to know about the encampments, and what exactly it was they were mining for—including the fact that what the alychite they were mining for was then used against them.

He'd told me everything except where Mother was.

And now he was gone, that knowledge lost with him.

Unless I could find something that would point me in the right direction.

I opened every drawer in the desk, shuffling the old, decaying papers inside and searching. For what, I wasn't sure. I just needed *something*.

Finding nothing in the desk before me, I began shifting things around on the bookshelves, searching high and low for a sign or a clue—anything that might lead me to Mother.

After long moments passed without finding a thing, I sighed, pacing the short span of the room.

Suddenly remembering the gift I'd given Aviva, I circled the desk once again and shoved the chair out of the way, dropping to the floor.

Tapping lightly on a specific small stone in the floor, I was reassured that I'd found the right one.

The one with a hidden compartment under it.

Pushing and tilting the thin stone, it lifted just enough for me to pull it out of place.

Underneath housed various objects that must have been sentimental to our mother. Pulling each object out one by one, I first pulled out the pouch of coins, placing it on the floor next to the hole in the ground. Next, there was a box with two golden rings in them—one for a male and one for a female. There was a dagger, one that was slightly bigger than the one I'd given Aviva, but matched it all the same. The daggers both had the same engravings, and the same colored gems at the hilt.

Sliding the second, bigger dagger into an empty sheath on my belt, I reached for the last thing in the compartment.

A small, slightly torn portrait on a thin sheet of paper.

The portrait consisted of three fae. Mother, who had a glow to her that I never remembered her having, along with a male with dark olive skin that I didn't recognize. Between them, being held by Mother, was an infant.

One that looked much too similar to Mother and the mystery male for my comfort.

But looking at Mother… I saw my twin in her.

If I could get Mother back, maybe I could get Aviva back, too.

Folding the paper and sliding it into a pocket, I tossed the other objects I'd pulled out back into their hiding spot, and I slid the stone back into place before getting to my feet.

Securing the door to Mother's study behind me, I headed towards the room I'd been avoiding the most.

Father's chambers.

I went to unlock the door, only to find it already so.

It made sense. Nobody would dare mess with Father or enter his chambers without permission. I wasn't surprised he'd left it unlocked.

Though, it did show his arrogance.

Determination set in my bones, I entered the quarters, which were much too quiet for my liking. There was a large lounge area to the left, a private desk and multiple shelves to the right, and in the middle was a giant four-post bed. The large room was perfectly themed and accented, floor to ceiling, to match the Northern flag—blue and silver. Father even had one of said flags hanging over his desk, as though while plotting war schemes he had needed a reminder of what he was fighting for.

The room, unlike Mother's study, had hardly any dust. It truly hadn't been *that* long since Father had last been here, in his chambers.

I picked at the skin around my nails as I walked deeper into the room, trying to dull the feelings that swelled up simply by entering the space.

And the surge of energy those emotions brought with them.

I'd hardly been inside the space before, as Father rarely took company here. There were a handful of occasions, though, where he'd invited me for small things—to share tea, or to give me personal tips about my combat skills, or to simply sit in front of the fire together during the rare instances that the cold became too much, even for us.

Oddly enough, it was small moments like that which I found myself missing the most.

Heading over to the lounge area, I imagined if he were trying to hide anything about Mother, he'd have it within reach. I sat in Father's favorite spot—the left side of the long, navy couch—and searched. A small table with drawers stood to the left of me, but they housed nothing of importance. The low-lying table in front of me had no place to hide items, either. Standing, I even went as far as to lift the couch cushions, my desperation becoming more and more potent as time went on.

Not finding anything in that area, I checked his desk and shelves, but came up empty-handed there, too.

Sighing, I took another moment to think.

My eyes lingered on Father's bed. It looked as though he'd only ever slept on the right side of it, even after Mother was gone. The left side was untouched, nothing on the bedside table, while the right had a slight dip in it, and the table beside it was covered in papers and trinkets.

I approached the large bed, and within moments had checked the entire thing, as well as the top of the bedside table. Nothing under the mattress, or in his pillows, or anywhere in between. The papers and trinkets atop the table also didn't aid in my search.

But it did still smell like him—the fresh smell of the calm after a storm—and the strike of grief that hit my heart felt like a physical blow.

My blood sang with a power that wanted to escape, but I pushed it down, determined to find something. *Anything*.

I noticed the top drawer of his bedside table was slightly ajar, as though Father had left in a hurry, and yanked it open. I shuffled through a few pens, papers, daggers, and other random, useless objects.

Slamming it, my anger sparked when it didn't shut all the way, still slightly sticking out from the rest of the wooden piece.

Great, I thought. *I broke it.*

Bending to fix it, I pulled it open and peered towards the back of the drawer when something shiny caught my eye.

Heart racing, I pulled the drawer out of its place and put it on the ground next to me, then blindly reached for whatever it was I had seen.

My hand met leather, and I pulled the object out slowly, my hand shaking just barely.

It was a journal—and a very elegant one at that. It was black with a silver pattern all over the front and back cover. The pattern had no rhyme or reason, but it was pleasant, nonetheless.

Loosening a breath I must've been holding, I lowered myself to the floor with my back and wings against the edge of the bed. Balancing the journal on my knees, I cracked it open.

It was almost completely full of Father's tiny, nearly impossible to read handwriting. As I flipped through, I noticed only a few pages at the end hadn't been filled yet, as though he'd not had enough time.

Technically, I supposed he hadn't.

Though, I couldn't help but notice that on every page, multiple times, he'd written about somebody he called *prisoner fifty-one*. Stopping to read on a random page, I could tell this was somebody Father must have been studying, or was important for some other reason, for he saw them far too often for somebody who was also running an entire kingdom.

Flipping towards the beginning, I noticed Father had sketched out a small map of the encampments he'd mentioned before the recent battle.

My eyes were drawn to a star on the top left side of the page, where he'd circled what looked like one of the stone towers multiple times.

Slamming the journal shut, I had to remind myself to breathe.

Father did *nothing* without reason.

I just had to put the pieces of the puzzle together.

Chapter Six

"So shadow wielding doesn't originate from within the South?"

"Correct. The South only obtained shadow wielding through integrating closely with the fae of the Ocrein Isles for centuries," I answered Aurora, who was peering at me from the other side of my usual table in the library.

The library had quickly become a place of peace and comfort for me during my months here in the South. Bright red granite with dark crystal inclusions made up the floor and pillars of the large space. The walls and bookshelves were crafted of varying dark shades of brown, making the inclusions in the floor stand out even more. The Haven's library took my breath away each time I stepped inside, and I wished to the Stars that never changed.

The small enclave I had claimed as my own—which the public seemed to also acknowledge and avoid when I was present—currently housed Aurora and me, along with stacks of books. They ranged from the existence of Titan Wolves, to the zirilium of the South, to the ties the South had with the Ocrein Isles in the past. If Aurora was to stay here in Cairnyl, I wanted her to at least have a clearer view of what was true and accurate about the South and its people.

"But... you're able to wield shadows, right? How did that come to be?" Aurora questioned, and I could tell her curiosity was piqued. Even the tense demeanor she'd worn since the moment of her arrival had relaxed a fraction.

"Well, apparently, my mother was—"

"Your Majesty!" Laurence called out from the main sector of the library, cutting off my explanation.

"Laurence?" I stood from my chair as my friend and bodyguard slipped in through the closed curtain separating this enclave from the remainder of the library.

"There you are! We need—" He halted when he realized I wasn't alone today, and I stole a glance at Aurora.

Her relaxed demeanor had vanished, replaced then with tense muscles and a scowl. She picked up the book we had been reading from together and proceeded to ignore Laurence and me completely.

My wings and shoulders caved in slightly, disappointed. I thought I had been making progress with her.

Sighing, I turned back to Laurence and refocused. After motioning for him to continue, he cleared his throat and carried on. "The Valwain needs you, my queen. I can accompany you to the meeting room."

I narrowed my eyes slightly at the male before me. I could tell there was more he wasn't willing to say, but with how hostile Aurora had acted toward him before, I couldn't blame him for being hesitant around her.

Nodding, I faced Aurora again.

"It's alright, Aviva. I get it. You have more important matters to attend to," she said before I could even utter a word to her.

"No, Aurora, it isn't—"

"I said it's alright," she said sternly, her wings curling around her instinctively—something I knew she only did when she was upset.

"Your Majesty..." Laurence urged, and I could hear from the tone of his voice that it was pressing.

Picking at my cuticles viciously, I said to Aurora, "We'll catch up later, alright?"

Aurora didn't bother to even spare me a glance as I hooked arms with Laurence and let the curtain fall behind us. The heaviness I felt in my heart didn't dissipate even as we exited the library, arm in arm.

"What is it, Laurence? You have that look on your face," I said softly, so only he could hear.

"It's Teagan," he said quietly. "She's returned."

"Already?" I questioned, the shock I felt reflected in the way my eyes grew wide. It had only been two days since she'd left.

Laurence cast me a look that confirmed, but that also caused my anxiety to spike.

The two of us sped through The Haven, crossing over into the private royal wing, where most of the Valwain stayed—upon Byn's insistence. Laurence came to a stop in front of one of the first meeting rooms in the long hallway, and I could hear chatter beyond the door.

Nodding my thanks to Laurence, my hands met the door, pushing it open and stepping inside. My bodyguard was a step behind me, shutting it to the outside world.

My ears perked up at the sound of Byn's voice, and I searched for him in the midst of our Valwain, along with the Ocrein royal siblings and, to my surprise, Matea—whose gaze found mine almost immediately.

"I understand, but did you—"

"Byn, I did everything I could! I can assure you of that," Teagan responded, her voice raised louder than her usual soft attitude. "They weren't letting *anybody* over that border."

"Alright, alright. This simply isn't the response I was expecting." Byn sighed heavily, his shoulders sagging in defeat.

Stepping farther into the room, I asked, "What happened?"

All eyes landed on Laurence and me at the sound of my voice. I rounded the table and lounge area to Byn's side, gently brushing his form with the tips of my feathers as I passed. I watched as his tense shoulders relaxed a fraction at the innocent contact. I could feel his building anxiety ease as I came up next to him.

Once I'd found my place, Teagan leveled her gaze at me as she explained, "I got to the border, but was swiftly told to turn back around and return home, unless I wanted trouble to befall me. From what I could tell, for some reason, Dimitri didn't make it public knowledge in the North *who* killed King Horace, but tensions are very high right now. The soldiers there were outright hostile, threatening not just me and Lychen but the guards I had with me, too," my sister by marriage said. "They didn't offer any clear explanation about the corvids we found, either. I have a feeling they simply had their way with our birds. I tried to stay and reason with them, but I feared if I had stayed any longer, they'd have attacked."

"So... what do we do now?" Chess asked, his tall form looking smaller than I'd seen it before as he sunk into the lounge chair he rested on. Sometimes it was easy to forget that he was just a couple of months younger than I was.

"We try again, right?" Quinn asked, sitting on the edge of her seat.

Teagan shook her head. "I don't see how that would benefit us."

The room broke out into multiple smaller conversations, each fae trying to find an alternative solution to our current predicament. Even Byn had decided to ask Teagan another series of questions.

I felt Matea's presence behind me before I saw her. I shifted in my seat to look at her, eyes holding a level of determination that I admired. She nodded slightly, letting me know I had her support in whatever I decided to do.

And I had decided.

"I'll go," I said loudly, in order to be heard over all of the chatter in the room.

"Absolutely not," Byn said almost immediately.

"Your Majesty, you can't," Laurence agreed.

"Aviva... is that such a good idea?" Chess asked.

All three spoke one after the other, each one meaning well, but not truly understanding.

So I'd help them understand.

"You misunderstand me. I won't be going to the border and talking to the soldiers there. I'll be *crossing* the border and finding my brother myself. With the help of the shadows, of course."

At this, the room erupted into a chorus of different agreements and arguments. Byn reached out a hand and gently took mine into his. I could feel his anxiety returning, bubbling up like a geyser about to burst. Meeting his eyes, I could see the pleading there. The silent begging for me not to go through with this.

Gently, I cupped the side of his face in my hand and murmured so only he could hear me, "I can do this."

He pursed his lips together tightly, worry etching every feature, when he slid his kingly mask back into place and faced the rest of the room once again.

If I couldn't feel his emotions in my own body, that move would have shut me out completely. He appeared calm, almost at ease.

But I knew him better than that, and I could feel the distress he was emitting.

"We'll put it to a vote," he announced. "There's a reason the Valwain functions so efficiently, and I don't plan on changing how it runs now."

"All against Viva's proposition?" Byn asked.

Chess and Laurence's hands shot up, and a second later, Byn's followed.

I wasn't exactly surprised, but a small pang of disappointment rang out through my heart at the sight. I knew it didn't stem from a lack of trust in my abilities—I'd more than proved myself a few weeks ago. He was simply scared of losing more people he loved; that fear had taken root in his chest, and as a result, in mine.

But he couldn't protect me forever.

"And all those for it?" he asked, and I could already see him deflating at the outcome as my hand shot up, along with Rayven's, Quinn's, and Teagan's.

As guests, and not true members of the Valwain, the Ocrein royals and Matea didn't get a vote. But even if they did, I was still fairly certain I'd have overruled Byn.

I watched as Byn's shoulders sagged as he looked around the room, his eyes snagging on his sister for a moment, then meeting my gaze.

"The floor is yours, my love," he said after a moment of silence. I knew this was something we'd have to talk about, but right now, we needed a plan.

And I just so happened to have one.

***

We took hours hammering out the details of my plan. It was more complicated than simply storming Gatlyn Castle—we needed a route to get there, we had to pick the right people to join me, and we debated on how to handle Dimitri as a whole once we arrived.

It was difficult doing all this planning and plotting without Ezra and his seemingly endless well of knowledge. It took Laurence and me to map out the majority of Hollis, and Laurence and Matea to map out the best route to get there once we crossed the border.

Getting to the border wasn't the problem. It was crossing it, then going beyond it without getting caught, that was the issue.

Next came the debate about who would accompany me.

Matea, as the only one in our makeshift group that had experience crossing the border, was an obvious pick. Byn, despite coming to trust her more recently, had suggested taking some *official* members of the Valwain instead. Quinn had volunteered, and her determination to find Ezra was a fantastic motivator, but I argued that we needed shadow wielders on this journey. Besides, we weren't entirely positive that Ezra was being held in Gatlyn Castle, anyway.

In the end, the selected group was kept small—only Matea and Drayven would accompany me on this mission.

The three of us could shadow wield, which was a huge plus. Besides that, Matea knew how to get to Hollis and back, I could navigate inside Gatlyn Castle, and Rayven was an expert on handling missions like this without being seen. In theory, we could've used more hands and eyes on this journey, but in reality, it wasn't practical. The energy it would've cost us shadow wielders to carry an extra fae with us for what could be days on end wouldn't have been worth it.

Quinn had insisted she was necessary on this mission, but Byn had to gently shut her down. He'd explained that she had too much personal investment in the outcome of this mission, and we couldn't put a loose cannon on the playing field right now.

Because we weren't just going to talk to my twin. If we could manage it, we were going to search for Ezra, too, and rescue him if we came across him.

If there was anything left to rescue, that was.

I had quickly shut down the conversation on how to handle Dimitri once we got there. He was *my* brother and *my* duty. I wanted to talk to him one on one—to try one last time to help him see reason.

If it didn't work this time...

No, I thought to myself, *it won't come to that.*

I looked around the room at the people I'd grown so close to. Even Callum and Caelia had stayed and helped us plan, giving us tips on shadow wielding and how to conserve energy for the journey.

Quinn stood suddenly, squaring her gaze on me, Matea, and Rayven. "Bring him back to me," she said. Her features softened a fraction, and my heart ached for her when she added, "*Please.*"

"I'll do my very best," I promised. I watched as Rayven placed a fist over his heart—a vow to do the same. Quinn mimicked Rayven's motion, took a deep breath, then excused herself from the room.

I stole a glance at Byn then. I couldn't imagine the lengths I'd go to in order to get him back—or how much self-control and trust Quinn must've had in order to leave this mission in our hands.

Her husband's *life* could be on the line.

"I appreciate how open you've been with us, Robyn," Callum said as he stepped forward, Caelia right behind him.

Byn nodded. "Of course. We owe you, both of you, after the recent battle."

Turning to me, Callum said solemnly, "May the Stars watch over you all."

At that, he and his sister saw themselves out of the meeting room. It wasn't until then that I noticed the sun outside had begun to set, and night was nearly upon us.

"I'd like a word alone with my wife, please," Byn said to nobody in particular.

The room paused for a brief moment before Matea awkwardly said, "I'll... go pack for the journey." Then she departed with Rayven following behind her, likely to do the same.

Teagan caught my eye as she stood and flashed me a look that said *good luck*, before she and Chess left the room, Laurence a few steps behind them.

Laurence stalled by the door, and didn't leave until I reassured him I was fine, and that he should get some rest. That I'd see him in a few hours, before Rayven, Matea, and I left for Hollis, and the rest of the group saw us off.

When the door shut behind Laurence, and it was finally just me and my husband, I said softly, "Speak your mind, love."

Byn sighed, causing me to look his way. He had his chin resting in his hand, propped up on the table before us as he shook his head.

Turning my entire body his way so he knew he had my undivided attention, I said, "Please, Byn, talk to me. You're safe."

"Yes, but *you* might not be. What was that, Aviva? Aren't we to be a team at times like this?" he asked, looking up at me, distressed.

Shifting to sit on the table before him, I took his face into my hands with tenderness. "Yes, we are. We *still* are. Just because we disagree doesn't make us any less of a team. We aren't always going to agree—we're two different people with two different, messy histories. It's how we react that determines the rest," I said gently, my mismatched blue and green eyes peering into his forest-green ones.

We lapsed into a moment of silence as his gaze met mine. I took this opportunity to reach out emotionally—down that bond that rested between our souls. I gently touched the anxiety welling up inside of him with my determination and certainty; there wasn't an ounce of doubt in me at that moment.

Something changed in his gaze then. It was as though I could see as he finally grasped just how sure of this I was, and that this truly wasn't an impulsive or rash decision on my part.

He let out a shaky breath then, wrapping his arms around my waist and laying his head in my lap. My wings wrapped around our forms and my hands brushed through his hair in calming strokes as he meekly said, "I can't lose anybody else, Avi."

"I know, Byn. I know," I murmured.

I knew I didn't have to say more than that. He could feel the hope radiating from me—the hope that we'd retrieve Ezra, and the hope that I'd get to talk to my brother in a calm manner. Monarch to monarch, twin to twin, brother to sister.

Buried beneath all of that, a small part of me was excited to see my homelands again. To be in the same city, the same castle I'd grown up in.

I breathed deeply. *This isn't about me*, I reminded myself.

Quinn had still been having vague feelings through what she was certain was her bond with Ezra. None of us dared to doubt her—we all *wanted* to believe her, anyways.

It was easier that way.

Byn and I stayed like that, finding comfort in each other's close company for a while before night had fully taken hold of the sky and I insisted he help me pack. His worry wasn't fully gone, but it had been soothed, almost as though my confidence and hope had been a balm to his turbulent emotions.

Roughly two hours later—which was past the meet up time, but thankfully wasn't mentioned—the Valwain, along with Matea, stood on the outskirts of Cairnyl, along the border of Wittuck Woods. We had all talked and laughed the whole walk here, but now, the somberness had set in. It hung like a mist in the air, settling solely around our little group.

Rayven stood with Chess and Quinn ten feet away, likely talking strategy and swapping last minute tips. Teagan had stayed behind with Margo, and Matea and Laurence stood closer to the trees, their heads bowed and voices hushed as they spoke. Then, there was me and my husband.

He was still dressed in his formalwear—pants that hugged just the right places and a silk button-up shirt. He seemed to have lost his overcoat along the way, during the stress and planning of the day.

"You haven't even left yet, and your mind is already wandering to places I can't reach," Byn said, slipping a finger under my chin and tilting my face up towards his.

Sometimes, I didn't mind the height difference so much.

"You're always on my mind," I reassured him, smiling cheekily.

He rolled his eyes playfully at my attempt at humor, but he couldn't stop the small smile that crept its way onto his full lips.

Unable to help myself, I fisted my hands into his shirt and I pulled him down to my level. Our lips met half a heartbeat later, the desperation and need ruling over everything else.

He nipped at my bottom lip, but the moment was interrupted when somebody cleared their throat.

Loudly.

"They need to get going, Byn," Quinn said, her arms crossed over her chest. My cheeks flushed bright red, but Byn didn't take his eyes from me.

Instead, he cupped the side of my face and kissed me all over again.

This one was softer, more meaningful. I could feel as he reached toward my emotions with his—love on love, warmth on warmth, adoration on adoration.

Stars, this is all I want in life.

All too soon, he broke away and stood straight, his arm still around me as he addressed the other two who were about to depart with me.

"Drayven, I know this goes without saying, but this is a stealth mission. Get in and get out without drawing too much attention, got it?"

I watched as Rayven nodded. "Got it."

Byn turned to Matea next. The softness he had held in his face for Rayven hardened, turning much more serious.

"Matea. We haven't known you very long, so this mission is an act of trust in you on our part. Do *not* fail us, or me," he said sternly.

"I won't fail *Aviva*, my king," she said confidently, somehow managing not to cower beneath the power of his gaze.

I felt the surprise he held at her response, but shockingly, it was laced with pride.

"And my wife," Byn said, turning to me. "Come back to me *whole*."

That, I feared, may be the most difficult part.

Chapter Seven

"At least I don't have a stupid scar running across my entire face," Matea snarked.

"At least I have my mastery tattoo," Drayven quipped back.

"Well, at least my whole personality isn't shaped around being broody and mysterious," Matea responded without missing a beat.

"What is the matter with you two?" I snapped, pinching the bridge of my nose in frustration. They'd been at this for the past day, and I was fed up.

Honestly, I'd come to expect this kind of attitude from Matea. It seemed to be how she defended herself and kept at arm's length from those around her. But what I didn't expect was Rayven allowing her to get under his skin so easily. I was accustomed to him being much more... unbothered. It was a sight to see, but it was also getting on my final nerve that afternoon.

We'd been traveling a little over two and a half days, having avoided the Salic Mountain-range for as long as we could. Rayven and Matea weren't accustomed to the severe climate and elevation of the mountains, so we were attempting to take it easy. We didn't want to wear ourselves down too soon, so we traveled by foot often, to not solely rely on our shadow wielding. This was extra beneficial for me, as somebody who had yet to master her shadow wielding abilities. It had taken a few tries in the beginning, but the shadows were slowly becoming friends of mine.

Crossing the border had been easier than we'd thought, as we'd taken a path that was rarely used, and therefore hadn't been guarded. Since then, our little trio had been heading northwest that whole time, and now we were about a ten-minute trek away from the outskirts of Genisyn—a smaller Northern town—which was the first and only town to stop in during our journey, besides Hollis itself.

"If I'm correct, we're almost upon Genisyn now," I said, turning to Rayven, who was carrying the map with our route marked on it. He'd just set his pack on the ground beside us. We'd started heading into the mountains this morning, and I could already tell it was going to be a rough trip from here on out for these two Southerners.

"Right, we should be there and back with enough time to set up camp for the night." Rayven nodded as he held out the map between the three of us. "We're about right... here," he said, indicating to just south of Genisyn, within the base of the mountain-range.

We had just found a small cave carved out of the side of one of the smaller mountains outside of the town, and had decided it was going to be our spot to re-cooperate and check in on each other and our location before carrying on. Fortunately, the inside of the cave was lined on almost every surface with moist moss, which stopped our voices from echoing too much.

"Well, I'm short on rations. I forgot just how hungry wielding so often makes me," Matea said. I couldn't help the quiet chuckle that rose from my throat. "What?" she asked, crossing her arms over her chest as Rayven rolled the map back up.

"Nothing, nothing," I said, though I couldn't help but think about how differently we must have been raised, simply by the difference in mannerisms and bluntness.

I caught my sister rolling her eyes, but she didn't press further.

"I'm low too," Rayven admitted, slightly sheepishly. It was the first time I'd seen him embarrassed about something before.

I sighed. "So I have to make a pit-stop in Genisyn for you hungry fools. Got it."

"*Hey!*" Matea exclaimed.

"Why did you make it sound as though we won't be going with you?" Rayven asked, both of us ignoring Matea's outcry.

"Because you won't be," I said simply, shrugging.

"Wrong answer," Rayven said, while Matea raised an eyebrow as though to say, *as if.*

"Stars," I cursed, exasperated. "Look, only one of us is going to blend in around here. You two don't have wings, remember?"

"Oh right, I forgot. Thanks for that reminder," Matea said flatly.

Before I could respond, Rayven jumped in, "I think what she's trying to say," he glared at Matea, "is that you don't exactly blend in, either. The hair? The two-toned wings? The eyes?"

"Alright, alright, we get it," Matea said, side eyeing the male.

"He's right. But," I paused, pulling out a small vial from one of my various pockets, "I've got that covered. For the most part, anyways."

Matea, without warning, snatched the vial from my grasp and popped off the cork.

"Wait! It isn't edible!" I exclaimed before she could knock back the dark, murky liquid.

She tilted her head, then asked, "What is it?"

"It's a concoction that Chester made me! I'm supposed to smear it on my wings and hair, and it'll help darken their color temporarily. It's like ink, almost. He said the main ingredient comes from some part of a fish he collected back in Echen Bay, so I can't imagine it would taste, or smell, very good."

Rayven shot me a quizzical look, causing me to explain further.

"Back during the battle at Wittuck Woods, the ash and soot washed off my wings far too easily. You were there, Rayven—you know I'm telling the truth. If things were to go awry, and a weather or water wielder came at me, the soot would wash off again. This time, I wanted to feel more secure about my identity being hidden if need be. *Thoroughly*," I said. "Chess even made me a special cleansing oil that will help get all of the ink off when we're done."

"How did you know we'd need this?" Rayven asked as Matea put the cork back into place.

"I didn't," I said lightly, "but I wanted it, just in case."

Rayven, seeming to find that answer sufficient, nodded.

Matea held out the vial towards me and said, "Here."

"Actually, keep it. You have to help me put it on."

I set my pack on the ground, then started unbraiding my waist long hair, freeing it of its plait.

"I can—" Rayven started.

"No," I quickly interrupted. "Not this time, Rayven. I know you can, and I appreciate the offer, but it has to be Matea."

Rayven shot me another questioning look, but before I could explain, Matea reached out and softly brushed a hand along the top of my left wing.

Chill bumps immediately broke out across my skin, the feathers sensitive to the touch.

The spy, finally realizing what I had meant, had the decency to look embarrassed before saying he was going to fill up our water skins and dipping out of our little cave.

Once it was just us females, Matea muttered, "About time. I thought I would never be able to get rid of him."

"What's your problem with each other?" I inquired.

"He's just so..." she trailed off, making a nasty face towards the entrance of the cave where we last saw Rayven.

"Oh, yes, because that answers *all* of my questions," I sighed.

Matea cleared her throat, then changed the topic. "Shouldn't we get this gunk on you?"

One at a time, I stretched my wings out as much as I could inside the relatively small cave. Matea and I passed the vial back and forth, applying a thin layer of ink-like liquid to every feather on my wings. We used strips of an old cloth shirt to apply the liquid, so as not to stain the skin of our hands with it. With every pass we made, my white and gray feathers turned a gray so deep they were nearly black.

The sight reminded me of Father, and once we were finished, I pulled my wings in close to my back and refused to look at them.

I wanted to be nothing like him, and yet here I was—looking the part of *his* daughter.

Picking at my fingers, I couldn't help but hate the way it made me feel.

"Viva?" Matea said, waving a hand in front of my face.

I jumped, but her expression softened slightly when she saw that I'd been messing with the skin around my nails—something I couldn't help but do when anxious.

"Come." Matea gestured to the stone ground in front of her as she took up a spot with her back against the wall. "Sit, and let's cover up your blindingly white hair."

I couldn't stop the sad smile that lifted my lips.

As I sat with my back to my older sister and her fingers slid into my hair to deposit the ink, I was reminded of Mother.

The way she would have me sit at my vanity and stand behind me to do my hair every morning.

I used to wonder why she insisted, when we both knew a servant could do the task, but now I got it.

It was an escape for us both—a moment to *breathe*.

A swell of warm emotions filled my chest as I realized how much I missed her, but the feeling quickly turned sour.

I hadn't realized just how little of Byn's feelings I could still sense until now. But the moment I became aware, it felt like a gaping hole had been opened up inside my chest. As though I was no longer complete, like I was missing a part of my own soul.

Is this what Quinn has been feeling for weeks?

I could still sense the bond between us, like a rope leading from my soul to his—as though I could use it as a way to get back home.

To him.

Home.

Yet, with each step I took farther away from him, the tauter that rope became—as though he were on the other end of it, trying to pull me back to him.

Stars, did I *ache* for him.

Even now, with kingdoms and distance and time standing between us, I ached for him with every fiber of my being.

My power sang in my core at the very thought of him and that soul-bond we had somehow found ourselves with.

Shaking my head slightly, I rubbed at my chest as though it would ease the aching pain I felt there.

"Hey, be careful or this will stain your pretty face."

I was snapped back into the present moment at the sound of Matea, and I realized she was now massaging the liquid into the ends of my hair; she was almost done.

A moment later, she handed the completely empty vial back to me.

"We needed every drop, but I think it looks great. Here, turn around and let me see," she said.

Getting to my feet, I turned to face her, doing my best not to let my wings into my direct line of sight.

Before Matea could do more than open her mouth to speak, a whistle came from the front of the cave.

"You almost look like one of us, Aviva," Rayven commented.

I dropped the hand that had already been reaching for my nearest dagger.

"She *is* one of us, you idiot," Matea responded, crossing her arms over her chest.

"Of course, I didn't mean—"

"I know what you meant, Rayven, don't worry," I said, throwing Matea a scalding glare and taking a step towards the spy.

"Can I use your cloak? I have an idea."

Soon, I'd donned Rayven's cloak, pulled the hood up to help hide some of my face, and took a deep breath.

This next part was where the concentration came in.

I reached out with that shadow zirilium that felt like pure darkness in my veins, searching for a small piece I could latch onto and keep.

It didn't take long for the deep shadow of a small rock to form a connection with me, and I tugged it towards me.

The shadow raced across the cave ground towards me, and I flung out a hand to direct it to where I wanted it.

A few heartbeats later, the small shadow hovered over my right eye—the green one—and remained there. It felt warm and cool against my skin at the same time, but this shadow was quiet. It didn't whisper against my skin like some of the others seemed to do.

It was waiting, following *my* lead.

I reached up and shifted my bangs to help conceal my right eye, too, and once I was satisfied, I looked back towards Rayven.

The shadow made my vision slightly darker, but I adjusted fairly quickly, likely thanks to my Northern blood.

"Well?" I asked when Rayven didn't immediately say something. "Did it work? Can you tell about... about my eyes?"

Rayven, whose jaw had fallen slightly ajar, quickly recovered and said, "Yes, it most definitely worked. You can't even tell, and if you keep your head down, it'll blend in perfectly with the shadows of the cloak hood."

Matea, who had come to stand beside me and Rayven, nodded her agreement. "Plus, that was a crazy cool move for a newbie to pull."

Smiling slightly at my welling pride, I took a second to be grateful the two of them were at least agreeing on something for the first time this entire journey.

"We're going with you, but it'll be just like what we did during the battle, alright? We'll stay in your shadow, and we won't intervene unless you give us the signal," Drayven said.

Before I could utter a word, Matea added, "Don't argue, because we'll just follow you into Genisyn no matter what you say."

Sighing, I knew there was no way I was going to be able to shake them both. Plus, it would be comforting to know that if I needed them, they were there.

"Alright," I agreed. "Then let's get moving."

***

The breeze blowing down the dirt road I walked along caressed the feathers of my wings like an old friend. As if the wind and sky were asking, *Why are your feet still on the ground?*

I didn't have an answer.

I longed to give into the urge to launch into the sky and fly freely, but this wasn't Hollis, the Tower City, where each winged fae flew to where they needed to be. It was Genisyn, which I was ready to call the *city of mud* as the slight heel of my boot sunk into the ground below me with almost every step.

Genisyn, or at least the section of the outskirts I'd found myself in, was nothing like the North's capitol. Where Hollis was all cobbled roads, towers, and pristine buildings, Genisyn was the opposite. Made up of uneven dirt paths and stout, seedy looking structures, every hair and feather on my body was standing on end.

I'd never left Hollis growing up—I had been fortunate if I were allowed to leave Gatlyn Castle. I had no idea that so many of my Northern people were living in such conditions. I'd never given it much thought, what the North was like outside of my hometown. I'd always imagined each Northern city was like Hollis.

Oh, how wrong I had been.

The fae here matched their surroundings—unclean and sad. Some, I found, were even underweight with sunken in faces and hungry expressions.

Was the entire city like this?

Hollis was rich in more ways than one, and my father had been wealthy enough beyond his wildest dreams.

So why were my people suffering to this extent?

Did Dimitri know?

Overwhelmed with the guilt I felt for what I could only assume was my father's greed and inability to supply his people with bare necessities, I bent my knees and leaped into the skies for a better look.

I felt Matea and Rayven leap with me, sticking to the shadows of my cloak and wings, but they knew this hadn't been the plan. Rayven had given clear instructions to not draw any attention to myself—and in a city where almost nobody else was making use of their wings, I most definitely stood out.

Not to mention that without my naturally light-colored wings—which were now stained so dark they looked nearly black—I stood out against the sparsely cloudy sky. Not only that, but true black wings were fairly rare in the North, my father having been one of the few with that precise coloring. White, gray, and brown wings made up the majority of the population.

Once I was high enough over the nearby buildings, I could finally see the city as a whole. It was large, I'd give it that—it simply stretched on and on, nestled here within the rocky mountains.

From what I could see, it appeared that the closer you got to the center of the city, the better the living conditions were. There, the buildings grew cleaner, taller, and more sturdy looking. Some of the pathways were stone or cobbled instead of only packed dirt, and there was at least one fae flying into the town, from what I could see.

A small part of me took comfort in knowing that not the *entire* city was living in unclean conditions.

But it did little to ease the guilt.

Taking a deep breath, I refocused on why I was here in the first place. We needed a supply refill.

Since I was already in the air, I decided to make a small circle of the area. It was as I was doing so that I heard it. Carried on the breeze, the hustle and bustle of a market met my ears.

The sound of people bartering, grumbling, and yelling out advertisements.

Perfect, I thought.

Following the sounds of the people, I descended, landing at the edge of the market. A market that was so close to the edge of the city, it might as well have been outside of the settlement.

It wasn't a terribly large gathering, but there would be more than enough supplies there for myself, Matea, and Rayven.

Loosely tying the hood of my cloak into place, I double checked that the shadow I had taken from the cave was still in place over my eye. Satisfied with how I could only assume I appeared, I reached into the shadows near me until I felt Matea and Rayven—who were sticking as closely as they could.

Heading down the dirt road with my head down, dozens of makeshift booths made of scrap wood lined either side of me, each with their own vendor, shouting about their latest deal. The items themselves being sold reminded me of other markets I had been to—baked goods, fabrics and clothes, weapons, dried meats, and gems.

It was as I was heading over to the dried meats, following their smell, that I nearly tripped over the leg of a small fae female.

At first, I thought she might've been a child. It wasn't until I righted myself and went to apologize to her that I noticed she wasn't—she was simply malnourished. She was likely a few years younger than me, maybe fifteen. Her clothes were in tatters, her skin was ashen, and even the brown feathers of her wings looked dull.

When her eyes searched my face, I couldn't stop the way my heart cracked a bit for her.

Kneeling next to her, I reached into the inside of my cloak and pulled out as many silver coins as I could grab in one go. Taking her hands into mine, I passed them from my hands to hers.

"Take care of yourself," I said softly.

Her sunken, gray eyes widened, and she began to tear up as she looked at the coins in her hands. There was a mixture of disbelief and hope that danced in her eyes at the sight.

"Who... who are you?" she asked, her voice hoarse.

"Somebody who will come back to help someday. I promise," I vowed, forcing my own emotions down so as not to get choked up.

"Hey! You there!" a gruff voice called out over the sounds of those around us. The market seemed to still and go silent at the sound of this male's voice.

Before turning to face the male, I locked eyes with the female before me. "Run," I whispered.

Her eyes widened as she clutched the loose coins close to her body.

Slowly standing and turning on my heels, I did my best to keep my head down. "I-I don't want any trouble," I said to the male.

It wasn't the various weapons strapped to his body that made him scary, or even the menacing scars that littered his arms and face. It was his expression that had my stomach dropping. His eyes, so full of jealousy and hate, had my heart racing.

What had I just gotten myself into?

"Is that right?" the male asked, his shoulder-length blonde hair swaying as he took a step forward. "You go around *my* market flashing coins like that, and you don't expect a little trouble?"

The chuckle he let out sent a chill down my spine.

At that sound, I felt the female behind me turn tail and flee.

"Hey!" The male turned to another fae a few feet away and motioned towards the fleeing female. "Get her!"

The second male nodded, but when he made to follow her, I stepped into his path, giving the malnourished female more time to escape.

Even though I knew it might cost me.

"You seem to think you're so tough. I think it's about time we teach you a lesson," the second male said, while the first grinned wickedly.

It was in this moment that my panic began to overcome me. I came to this market on a simple mission, and just wanted to help one female. How did that spiral out of control so quickly?

Was I truly about to fight two of my own people?

The moment the first male unsheathed one of his many blades and I felt Matea and Rayven stir, my racing mind cleared. I signaled subtly to the two shadow wielders to stand down.

A crowd had gathered around us at this point—all the fae who had been at the market to shop today had come to watch whatever was happening. There were dozens of citizens, so I had to play this safe.

But that didn't mean I couldn't defend myself.

I tilted my head up slightly, just enough to see part of the blue sky from in between the clouds. Sliding my left hand into my cloak pocket, I tightly gripped the gloves Byn had gifted me. In a matter of seconds, I secured my connection with the moon stone I wanted.

Then, the sky began changing.

Often, I found it easier to shape the elements around me when I moved my body along with whatever I was wielding. It was a display of incredible power and control to be able to wield and connect with the world around you without moving.

And right now, I wanted to show that side of myself.

As I willed the clouds to darken and come together overhead, I worked on strengthening my connection to the weather. I imagined it as a cord between me and the sky above, the power thundering through my veins.

As the second male gasped at the shift in the sky, I took a step forward.

"Maybe," I said with gentle malice, "I should teach *you* a lesson instead."

As my connection with the weather doubled, then tripled in strength, the wind picked up, stirring the dirt below our feet and whipping my cloak in the wind.

"You don't scare me, *crid*," the first male said just before he lunged, blade raised.

Instead of dodging, I bent my knees slightly, holding my position. I caught his wrist before he could get too close, then twisted swiftly, causing him to release the knife.

"Perhaps I should," I said, and with that, the rain and hail began pelting us.

At that point, the majority of the crowd ran for cover, and merchants frantically packed up their goods so as to not to ruin them.

I pushed the male back, releasing his wrist and putting distance between us. Though, it seemed instead of instilling fear in him, I'd simply angered him even more.

It wasn't until then that I noticed the second male had slipped behind me, and I was now stuck between the two of them.

"Oh, you're going to regret that," the first male spat.

"I really don't think I will," I responded flatly.

Still gripping my gloves in my pocket, I focused more energy into one of my sun stones, forcing a connection with more than one stone at once. With that sun stone, I could feel through the ground below as the male behind me began to charge.

With just enough of a warning from my earth wielding, I quickly manipulated some of the hail on the ground to wrap around the second male's foot and ankle. He cursed as he found himself unable to take another step forward.

"You're... a multi-wielder," the first male breathed.

"And you're a greedy, selfish bully of a male," I said, matter-of-factly.

The effort it took to maintain solid connections to multiple different elements at once was beginning to get to me as my hands began to shake in my cloak pockets.

"I think we're done here," I said with a wink, hoping my faux confidence was enough to hide the exhaustion overcoming me. "Follow if you dare."

Before the anger could return to the scarred male's face, I did to him what I'd done to his lacky, freezing him to the ground below. At the very least, I'd get a head start in my escape.

Before he even had time to curse at me, I launched myself into the sky, dropping the connection I had on my earth wielding and replacing it with a swift bond to my air zirilium. I used that burst of energy to swoop down over a food cart, grabbing an arm-full of snacks and dried meats.

It would have to be enough.

Using the air around me to create a solid protective bubble around me, I flew back up and into the heart of the storm, two shadows sticking close to my wings. I tried my best to ignore the way they both seemed restless. I couldn't imagine they were very happy with me.

As my wings carried me straight into the storm, I knew myself and my zirilium well enough to know I was safe.

But the males below did not share the same comforts.

Once I was far enough away, I let go of my connection with my ice zirilium and the shadow over my eye, but I wasn't worried about the males following. They may have been bullies, but they didn't seem stupid enough to fly into my storm.

As I headed back to the small cave we had set as our base earlier, I couldn't help but wonder what else I didn't know about my homeland.

Was each Northern city in such unfortunate conditions?

Could I even do anything to change things?

Chapter Eight

The instant I landed, my feet barely scraping the lip of the cave, I felt Matea materialize next to me.

"What was *that?*" she asked loudly, shoving my shoulder and causing me to fall back a step.

"Hey! Back off," Rayven responded after appearing next to me and resting a hand on my shoulder gently, as though to stabilize me.

Shrugging off his hand, I regained my step forward.

"*That,*" I said, "was me doing my best! You both saw how they're living out here. I couldn't stand by and do nothing!"

Matea looked stunned, but a moment later, she began laughing. "Do you really think that handful of silver is going to help? You're delusional, Aviva."

My heart sunk at the thought. I knew, realistically, that the coins wouldn't make a dent in the kind of help the fae of Genisyn needed, but I had thought it was better than doing nothing.

"You don't truly mean that, Matea," Rayven said. "I was there, I felt your shadow *itching* to help her when those two males showed up. You aren't upset with Aviva for wanting to help that female—you're upset with her for putting herself in harm's way." He stepped up to my side again. "Or does that hit too close to home for you, little wielder?" He nearly sneered the last part.

The amount of emotion written on his face as he spoke shocked me. The spy was always so calm and collected, but Matea got to him *so* easily.

Turning on her heel without another word, my sister ducked into the small cave, hopefully to cool off.

Watching as she disappeared from view, I couldn't help the creeping feeling of helplessness that snuck into my mind. What could *I* do for my people?

In the South, I'd gained power and I'd had a say in what happened, what moves we made. But in the North, I didn't have those privileges—my twin did.

I wished to the Stars that Dimitri didn't know the state that the North was truly in. And if he did, that he was doing what he could to fix it.

Before my mind could spiral any farther as I began to think about my brother, Rayven stepped into my line of sight, pulling me from my thoughts.

"Hey, Your Majesty? I think we're safe now. You can let go."

"Let go?" It wasn't until that moment that I realized just how utterly exhausted I had become in such a short amount of time. And how windy it had become.

"The storm, Aviva. Let go of the zirilium, before you lead them to our location," Rayven said, firm but gentle.

I gasped as realization hit me, and my face tilted up to look at the gray clouds that had followed me all the way here. Thunder rumbled, and I could see the rain and hail not far off from where we were hiding out.

Panic began to eat at me as I thought about the last time I'd created a true storm—back at Echen Bay—and how I'd needed Byn's help to release the hold I'd had on my zirilium.

This time, I didn't have him.

It was just me.

I'm here, a tiny voice inside me whispered. *Always with you.*

Even with so much distance between us, and the emptiness in my chest, I could still pinpoint where my soul met Byn's.

And that would have to be enough.

Closing my eyes, head still tilted toward the sky, I focused on that tiny glow of green buried deep in my chest. I used it to center myself around, keeping myself grounded to the present moment and not letting my zirilium overpower me, but the other way around.

Weather zirilium felt like thunder in my veins—like pure power. I took a deep breath and swiftly severed the connection with it before the urge to use that power got the best of me.

The thunder ceased instantly, and as I opened my eyes, I watched as the clouds began to disperse within moments.

I was smiling to myself with pride when the first wave of exhaustion hit.

"Hey, Rayven?" I asked, my eyelids drooping.

"Yes?" he responded, turning away from where he had been looking at the sky above.

"Catch," I said, right before the next wave of bone-deep exhaustion hit, taking me into its dark abyss with it.

The sensation of falling followed me into my dreams.

***

I slept until late in the evening.

When I awoke, Matea and Rayven were—once again—arguing. Only this time it was over how much rest I needed in order to carry on, since we were on a bit of a time crunch.

Once I'd diffused the situation between them and reassured them both that I was fine, that I had just pushed myself too hard, too quickly, we focused on what our next steps were.

We were less than a day away from Hollis now, but if there were patrols at the border, we reasoned that there were likely more around the North's capitol, too.

With this in mind, we divided the last of our rations, covered any traces of us we left in the small cave, and headed toward Hollis in the dead of night. We traveled by foot while it was dark and hopped from shadow to shadow during the day. There had been a number of patrol groups surrounding the outskirts of Hollis, but none of them seemed to be looking toward the swift, dark shadows gliding by in the edges of their vision.

As we neared the edges of the town, I could feel the energy waning more and more in my sun stones. I could only imagine Matea and Rayven were feeling it too. Not to mention, my moon stones were nearly depleted after the storm I'd wielded yesterday.

My theories were confirmed once we reached the very far edges of Hollis, where we materialized and paused in a rundown, abandoned looking griffin stable.

"We'll have to charge them now, before the sun sets," Rayven said, slipping his left glove off and setting it on top of a rock in direct sunlight.

Matea and I followed suit, sliding our sun stone holding gloves off and setting them next to Drayven's. Mine held five stones, while Matea's held three—shadows, crystals, and plants, if I remembered correctly.

All nine stones were dim, drained of their color and so unlike the usual golden stones I was accustomed to seeing. Sun and moon stones didn't require a charge too often—it depended more on how often they were used. But even the moon stones on my other hand were dull without their silvery sheen.

"We'll have to stay a little while after dark, too," I mentioned while motioning to my moon stones.

"Right," Rayven agreed, nodding.

I looked towards Matea, who had not yet said a word since we arrived, and noticed she was looking toward the tavern in the distance.

"Is that it?" I asked. Tammy's Tavern—the place where my sister had seen a portrait of our mother after being told for years that she had died in the war.

The portrait that changed everything for her.

Matea nodded, and I could tell by her expression what it was she needed.

"Let's go," I said softly to her.

At that she turned to me, a quizzical look on her face.

"I want to see it, too," I clarified.

"I'm not sure this is a good idea..." Rayven said hesitantly.

"Stay or go, it affects me little, Rayven. But *we* are going." I looped my arm through Matea's and headed out of the stable.

I heard Rayven sigh, then felt his shadow clinging to me a moment later.

It wasn't that wielders *needed* their sun or moon stones to wield, or to even sense the elements around them. The stones simply helped with control and strength over what zirilium a fae wields. And as shown by his mastery tattoo that snaked over the skin of his right arm, Rayven was an expert in shadow wielding—with and without his sun stone.

Matea and I crept our way to the edge of the tavern, standing along the back wall of the building. There was a small series of windows, thin but tall, that Matea waved me over toward. Following her lead, and wishing to the Stars that she knew what she was doing, I met her next to the first window, where we both crouched into the shadows of the slanted roof overhead.

Rayven stirred, then quickly departed—he stayed near enough that if we needed him, he'd be there, but he seemed to understand that we would need a private moment.

Matea, deliberately ignoring Rayven's departure, peered into the window, her hazel eyes instantly catching sight of what we came here for.

Coming up to the other side of the glass panes, I followed my sister's line of sight until I, too, saw it.

Father and Mother's portrait was hung near the fireplace on the far wall, closer towards the entrance of the tavern. They were both dressed in royal attire—crowns, multiple layers of clothes made of silk and satin, and both had a broach pinned to them with the Heartshire family crest on it. What stood out the most, though, was their expressions. Father didn't look quite as harsh as I remembered him—as though being in Mother's presence put him at ease, to a degree.

The opposite could be said for Mother. I always remembered her as relaxed and calm, but next to Father, she looked like she'd rather chew her own arm off than stand beside him. She looked anxious, on edge, and knowing what I knew today about how Father was, I couldn't say I blamed her.

After a few moments of us both silently studying the portrait from afar, Matea asked softly, "What was she like?"

I wasn't entirely stunned by the question, but I still took my time answering.

"One time, we had a wild female griffin show up just outside of the castle grounds. Her and I found it while playing in the forest behind the castle. It seemed violent at first, but upon closer inspection, we found that she was in the early stages of labor—she was about to welcome her grifflings to the world. Mother immediately set off to help. She sent me to gather a small list of supplies—stuff that nobody would notice went missing—and she stayed for hours, helping the griffin in any way she could. Mother constructed a small home, dug out from the ground, for her to give birth in, and stayed for hours even after she'd had all her babies.

Meanwhile, she kept me busy with small tasks, so I could feel helpful, too.

"Mother wasn't Northern—she had no connection to our griffins, and even then, she'd never met this griffin before that moment, anyway. But she saw another living creature in need, and she stepped up. She did that with everything and everybody she came across—she stepped up and helped in any way she could." I paused. "She's who I thought of when I gave those pieces of silver to that female. She was gentle, and kind, and so, *so* caring. Even after whatever happened to her for her to end up as the Queen of the North, she didn't lose those qualities. And I aspire to be more like her each and every day."

By the time I finished speaking, a single tear had streaked down my sister's cheek.

"I'm sorry, I didn't—"

"Thank you," Matea said, cutting me off and meeting my gaze. "For sharing that piece of her with me."

She reached out and lightly gripped my bare hand in hers before standing and carefully making her way back to the abandoned stable.

I watched her go as the sun began to set, then looked back toward the portrait inside.

I wasn't sure how long I'd been crouched there, but eventually, as twilight set in, Rayven materialized next to me. He slowly, as though giving me the opportunity to stop him if I so pleased, poked his head into the frame of the window and peered toward the portrait.

Looking back to me after a moment, he said, "If your sister is right, and she really is still out there, we'll find her."

"I know," I agreed. "I won't stop until we do."

A little while later, we found ourselves back at the stable. The three of us had once again adorned our gleaming sun stone gloves, while my moon stone one took their place. And while my moon stones gained energy from the moon above, I gained energy from the determination settling into my bones. With each of our next steps we planned, my resolve solidified.

I'd find my twin soon.

And that interaction would change everything, one way or another.

Chapter Nine

The release of zirilium I received after sessions with the prisoner was so addictive, it was becoming a necessary ritual of sorts. Each time I left his cell, I could think clearly again. Otherwise, I felt like my newfound abilities were trying to devour me from the inside out.

I found that it was not exactly a *pleasant* experience.

I tossed the small, bloodied dagger onto the table in the corner and listened as the prisoner slumped to the ground, his breathing wet and labored after all I'd done to him.

Hugo had healed him too well after the last time I'd visited, so I'd wanted to make sure he'd remember who he was dealing with after today. He had needed a more permanent reminder.

I tossed the dismembered tip of the prisoner's finger in the air, catching it and tossing it over and over casually as I turned back to where he lay, clutching his bleeding finger at the base.

"Maybe next time you'll remember this, and you'll have some real answers for me." I spoke quietly, my voice low.

He did little more than painfully grunt in response.

Doing my best to not let my facial features give away any sort of emotion, I refrained from rolling my eyes at the pathetic creature before me.

He looked worse for wear nowadays—he was thin and pale, but as he slowly tilted his head up to meet my gaze, that spark in his eyes remained.

"You won't make it out of this war alive if you carry on like this, Dimitri. We'll make sure of it," he croaked.

I couldn't stop the laugh that slipped past my lips.

"You and who, *Ezra?* In case you haven't noticed, nobody is coming for you," I hissed, his name sour in my mouth.

He flinched slightly at my words, his form deflating quickly as he paled further—likely from the blood loss. The remains of his shirt had completely charred off after this session, and the bruises and burns were even worse than last time. Honestly, I was surprised he had stayed conscious this long.

Too soon, I thought as I watched his eyes shut and his form slump back to the ground, his body giving out and succumbing to unconsciousness.

I sighed, waiting for Hugo to burst in at any moment to fuss over the male before me.

Yet as time went on, the older trokav never showed up.

This isn't like him, I thought.

Hugo was very detail oriented, always on time and prepped with extra supplies, just in case. If something was holding him up, it had to be something important.

Well, it had better be, anyway.

Exiting the cell and locking it securely behind me, I walked down the long corridor, still tossing the prisoner's fingertip into the air and catching it repeatedly.

It wasn't until I was halfway down the corridor that I heard a soft grunt from far away, in the direction that I had been heading.

Suddenly on edge, I crept down the corridor, placing my feet deliberately so each step was perfectly silent.

I knew I had connections with more zirilium than just fire, but I hadn't quite figured out how to bend them to my will just yet.

Right then, I wished I had taken more time to learn how to do so; other zirilium likely would have been helpful in that situation.

Fortunately, despite my lack of control, I was still aware of the earth surrounding me and the shadows whispering when I walked by.

And *that*, I had learned, I could use to my advantage.

When I made it to the end of the long corridor, I paused and did my best to focus on what I felt not just physically, but also with the zirilium running through my bloodstream.

Feedback from my zirilium came in waves, the pictures unclear in my mind's eye, but I could at least decipher through the stone below me that there was nobody waiting to ambush me in the dungeon entryway I was about to step into.

With renewed confidence, I headed into the large room before me and moved for the stairs, knowing I needed to figure out what I had heard a few moments earlier.

I had only made it halfway through the rectangular room when I felt it.

Like a prickle on the back of my neck, I slowly turned on my heels to look to my left. My eyes snagged on the shadows in the corner of the room, but it took a wingbeat for me to realize why.

These shadows didn't whisper to me like the rest of them.

Without a second of hesitation, I drew a dagger and threw it flawlessly towards the small group of shadows.

Just before the tip of the dagger made contact, the shadows *scattered*.

They raced toward me, and only once they were positioned in a half circle around me, blocking off the exit, did they materialize from their shadow forms.

And the sight knocked the breath from my lungs.

Before me was my sister.

My twin.

My better half.

Aviva.

The female matched my features exactly. We had the same white hair, the same dual-colored wings, and the same pale skin.

And yet her eyes, the blue ones I had known all my life that mirrored my own, had changed. Now, one was green—the only physical mark our mother seemed to have left on either of us. I had convinced myself maybe it had been a trick back at Wittuck Woods—but it seemed it wasn't. Aviva truly held the only Southern distinction our mother had left to us.

Besides our zirilium, that was.

Despite that physical difference, when I looked into her eyes, I could still see *her*. The hope and love in her gaze hadn't changed.

Sighing a shaky breath of relief that I might just have a chance at getting my sister back, I took a step towards her.

Immediately, the two figures to the left and right of her, both who had cloak hoods obscuring their features, took a step in front of my sister. It was a protective move, and one I was shocked to see.

Who were these strangers to try to keep my twin from *me*?

Who were *Southerners* to protect my sister?

Who were they to defy a *king*?

Yet before I could respond to their disrespect, Aviva finally spoke.

"Stand down."

The two hooded figures returned to her sides silently, their loyalty unwavering.

Deciding to solely focus on my twin, I held my hands out in front of me and softly spoke her name.

"*Aviva.*"

Her gaze flickered to my hands, but snagged there before they flickered back up to my face.

It wasn't until that moment that I realized what I likely looked like right then.

"Don't worry, the blood isn't mine," I reassured her, taking another step forward, my hands still outstretched. Suddenly, the prisoner's blood coating my skin made me feel suffocated. Dirty, even.

My twin looked toward the tall, broad figure to her right, and he looked towards her a second later. She dipped her chin in what I could only imagine was a sort of signal between the two of them. In response, yet without a word, he vanished into shadow and speared off down one of the long corridors into the dungeons.

Now, with just my sister and me—along with her second lackey—I could finally convince her to come *home.*

"Aviva, I—"

"What's going on, Dimitri?" she asked, cutting me off before I could make my case before her.

Before I could even greet her, or let her know just how much I had missed her.

"What are you—"

"Our corvids? The ones you had killed? Dimitri, we even sent Teagan, our ambassador, to try to talk to you. You have soldiers stationed along the border to keep us out. So I'll ask again—*what* is going on?" she said, her voice more stern than I'd ever heard it before.

"Are you..." I stumbled over my words. "Aviva, are *you* upset with *me?*"

I had never convinced the prisoner to admit to how the South had gotten my twin to turn against the North—against *me.* And in that moment, I began to doubt that there *was* anything for the prisoner to admit.

"*Upset?*" she asked, a laugh creeping on the edge of her voice. "Dimitri, I did what I did to Father that day for *you.* I wanted you to be *free,* so you could make better decisions than those that came before us. But instead, it seems like you're carrying on in their footsteps! Which means it was all for *nothing!*"

I watched as her eyes watered, her emotions always getting the best of her. That was something I'd always admired about her—how freely and how strongly she felt things.

It was something I wished I didn't share even a fraction of with her. If I could have erased the complicated mix of emotions whirling around in my chest, I would have in a heartbeat.

"Aviva," I said gently, trying to calm her down, while also working to keep myself composed—there was still hope. "I understand there's a lot going on, but surely we can work things out between us. I can *help* you."

"Help me?" she questioned.

Dumbfounded and confused, I said, "I can help bring you *home*, Viva."

A heart-wrenching feeling I didn't understand shot through my chest as I watched that hope I'd seen earlier in her eyes go out as I spoke.

"Oh, twin," she said softly, almost with a hint of pity. "I found my home. And it isn't here."

Maybe the prisoner had been right.

Maybe they hadn't done anything to Viva to turn her against me.

Maybe she'd done this willingly.

And if that was the case, then she truly couldn't be saved.

Finally realizing how differently we were approaching the situation, but not knowing how to make her see my side in the moment, I slipped into my usual, cold indifference.

Letting that numbness sweep through my heart and mind was the only reason I remained upright.

"You've... *changed*," I stated slowly, trying to wrap my head around this new reality—the reality that my twin wouldn't be coming home.

Viva nodded and took a small step forward. "Yes, Dimitri. And you can, too. It doesn't have to be this way forever. We have the power to fix things." She paused. "You and me, brother."

My eyebrows furrowed as I thought about what she was saying.

What did she think was so messed up? What could be fixed, anyways, if she wasn't willing to even *try* to return home?

"We can put an end to this war," she said softly, and I realized she was trying to keep me calm, as though *I* was the one that needed convincing.

She genuinely didn't understand.

I could tell by the look in her eyes that she wasn't joking, or pulling some cruel prank on me. She truly believed what she was saying to be true. Whether they'd brainwashed her or not, this was her new reality.

And there seemed to be no going back.

At the end of the day, she truly was lost to me.

And I wasn't sure anymore if I could get her back.

But until I could figure it out, she was one of *them* to me.

With that truth in mind, my emotions swelled—anger, hurt, grief. Using that to fuel me, I conjured a ball of fire to my hand and aimed to strike.

"There is no *we* anymore, Viva," I said with cold malice.

Then, I let the flames loose.

Chapter Ten

Acting purely on instinct, and ignoring the shock, I planted my feet and called to the stony earth below us.

Just before the fireball could make contact, I caused a thick slab of stone to jut out of the ground in front of Matea and me, serving as a shield for us both.

Not wanting to drain my energy too fast, especially with how much I'd used the past few days, I dropped the stone back into place a moment later when the fire dissipated. I looked toward Matea, who was glaring straight at my twin with hatred in her eyes, but was fortunately unharmed.

Before he could form another fireball, I quickly asked, "Dimitri, you're a wielder?"

"Feeling less special now, aren't you, twin?" he taunted. "Seems like Father had us keep a lot of secrets from each other over the years."

"Like what truly happened to Mother?" I asked, careful to keep distance between the two of us. I drew comfort from having Matea so close.

"Exactly," he said as another ball of fire began forming in his hand, purposefully slow. "Though I'm sure she'd say hello if she could."

"*Where is she?*" Matea said viciously, throwing her hood back and stepping forward with more courage than I had ever felt at once.

Dimitri's jaw fell ajar at the sight of Matea, realization and vague recognition washing over his features, when I felt Drayven's shadow self quickly approaching the end of one of the many corridors.

He materialized at the mouth of it, still partially shadow, and made an unlocking motion.

The keys.

I wasn't sure why Rayven couldn't shadow wield his way past whatever lock he was facing, but I wasn't about to question him in these circumstances.

Flicking my eyes to Matea, I knew she'd seen his signal, too. Now, the three of us were all on the same page.

When I looked back at my brother, he was still staring at Matea in shock. I wasn't sure where he'd seen her before, but he obviously recognized her from somewhere.

On the other hand, Matea looked ready to gut him, if that was what it would take.

"I vouched for you, Dimitri. I really thought we could handle this peacefully," I said, a hint of sadness in my voice. "Instead, you've proven me wrong and left us with no choice."

"And what choice would that be?"

"To win this war," I responded nonchalantly. "But right now, you have something I need."

With that, I drew the condensation off a nearby wall and quickly shifted it into an icicle, using it as a small spear and throwing it straight toward Dimitri's shoulder.

He dropped, dodging it, and used his fire to melt it before hopping to his feet again and coating his clenched fists in flames.

"If you wanted a fight, Viva, all you had to do was ask," he said with a false level of innocence in his voice.

We fell into a rhythm as we circled each other, my fists now coated in water and ice I'd wielded to myself from the floor and walls.

"I didn't *want* a fight, but you've left me no other option." I swiftly dodged a flaming punch he threw at my face and coming up behind him, prepared to kick him to the ground.

This time, he was ready—unlike our previous veltik khan, which was supposed to be a fight to the death between two Northerners.

Father's life had been the price.

Dimitri spun and caught my boot seconds before I could make contact. His fire burned so hot that it began to melt the leather of my boot, the shoe starting to cave in on itself. The heat quickly seeped into my skin, causing me to panic. I yanked my leg back the same moment he pushed and let go, making me collapse to the floor in a heap.

Landing on my back, the breath was knocked out of me, my wings pinned between my body and the floor painfully. Gasping, I scurried to sit up just as Dimitri prowled closer, malintent in his eyes.

Though before he could strike, a length of shadow looped around his ankle and tugged, causing him to stumble. His warrior training kicked in swiftly as he righted himself, but not before the shadow slid up his form and looped around his key ring. By the time he noticed something was amiss, the keys were midair, caught in Matea's shadow grasp.

The moment the keys were in her hand, I motioned to where we'd last seen Rayven and yelled out, "*Go!*"

As we locked eyes, I watched the internal struggle in her gaze as she debated between being loyal to her sister or being loyal to her queen.

In the end, she chose both.

Faster than I'd ever seen a shadow wielder move, she vanished and reappeared next to me, helping me to my feet and sliding one of her extra daggers into my hand. Her eyes examined me head to toe, then dispersed into shadow again, heading to where we'd last seen Rayven before I could scold her.

It wasn't until I turned my attention fully back to Dimitri that I noticed he'd intensely watched the entire interaction.

And he was *livid*.

But behind the anger, I could see the hurt.

"You've replaced me already, sister?" he asked, his voice nearly shaking with unrestrained anger.

"I could never, Dimitri," I reassured him. Despite everything that had happened, I was still holding onto a sliver of hope that I could save him. That he could change for the better.

Because if I was wrong, what was it all for?

Both of our heads snapped toward the corridor that Matea and Rayven had disappeared down, having heard a scuttle.

"You can have him," Dimitri said after a beat of silence. "What's left of him, anyway."

Ever so slowly, I turned my face to look back at my twin.

"What did you do?" I said slowly, almost scared to hear the answer.

Dimitri smiled, and when he did, Father's face flashed in my mind.

They shared more than the Heartshire throne. They shared their wicked smiles, too.

Then, Dimitri pulled out of his pocket the dismembered tip of a finger, cut off at the top joint.

A fingertip that I could only assume was Ezra's.

"Dimitri..." I clasped a hand over my mouth as I asked again, this time with horror in my voice, "*What did you do?*"

"What needed to be done." He shrugged, as though this was a casual interaction. "Unfortunately for me, he's a tough nut to crack."

It was in that moment that I finally accepted the truth standing before me.

This wasn't the twin I'd come to know and love throughout our lives together.

Something had fundamentally broken inside of him back in Wittuck Woods. And if what Aurora had said was true, it likely started before then.

Father had broken him even before the Battle of Shadows.

But then I couldn't help but think, *If Dimitri is capable of this, what else did he do to Ezra?*

Innocent, kind, caring Ezra...

The more I considered how much pain and suffering my friend must have endured, the more my anger bubbled up inside of me.

From far away, I could feel Byn's calm trying to lend itself to me, but the distance between us wouldn't allow it. It wasn't powerful enough.

And that was exactly what I wanted.

"There she is," Dimitri said, reading the pure fury in my expression. I watched as his hand ignited into flames again, burning the fingertip to ash before my very eyes within a matter of seconds.

I'd felt the crystal bundle in the earth beneath me earlier, but I had hoped I wouldn't need it.

Now, with little thought about what I was doing, I called to it. The connection solidified almost instantly, reacting to my heightened emotions and the control I'd learned to have with Quinn through the stones adorning my gloves.

Stones Dimitri had failed to notice thus far, thankfully. I couldn't imagine how he'd react if he noticed all ten of them.

With the connection solidified, and fueled only by my anger for what Ezra had likely gone through, I let loose.

And I *exploded*.

The crystal bundle shot from the earth to my hands, shattering outward. Shards flew in every direction except mine, and I watched as Dimitri reacted purely based on instinct. He pulled a chunk of stone from below us and used it to cover his head and torso just before the crystals made contact, the gems shattering into splinters on impact.

When he dropped the earth a fraction to reveal his face, he was grinning wildly.

And that only further fueled my rage.

Did he think this was funny? Or a game?

Letting my connection with my various zirilium guide me, I dropped to the ground and placed my hand on the stone. Within heartbeats, thick vines wrapped around my twin's ankles, holding him in place. Then, focusing on the water the plants held, I froze the vines, further solidifying their hold.

Dimitri, who was still smiling like a madman, looked down, unphased. He called to his fire and melted the frozen vines with more control than I thought he'd had.

But that little trick had just been a distraction.

When he looked back to where I had been standing, he found I was no longer there.

I reappeared to his right and slightly behind him, using the water still on the ground from before and quickly shifting it into ice, coating his right wing in it. The sudden weight imbalance caused him to stumble, and I took the opportunity to throw a strong, focused air current at the backs of his knees, making his legs collapse in on themselves.

He ended up kneeling before me, all in a matter of wingbeats, and I quickly drew the dagger Matea had given me, holding it to his throat as I stood closely behind him.

The anger dying out of me with the energy I'd expelled using my abilities, I said quickly, "I'm sorry about Father. I live with that weight on my soul every day, Dimitri. But I truly believed you'd be a fair and just ruler that would help me put an end to this war."

With tears threatening to well in my eyes, I spoke quieter this time. "I just want my brother back."

I watched as his hands curled into fists at his sides—the only indication of his rising anger.

"You're right, twin. I *will* be a fair and just ruler. But I will rule all of Inphis, not just the North. Even if you are rightfully the heir, this was Father's dying wish, and although that obviously means nothing to you, it means everything to me." He lifted his chin. "And I *will* succeed, or die trying."

With those final words, Dimitri dissipated into shadows for just long enough to escape my grasp. He reappeared facing me, and with no hesitation, I watched as he pulled a small throwing knife from his sleeve and tossed it with such force at me, I barely have time to react.

I dropped as quickly as I could, but not fast enough.

A scream was ripped from my throat as the blade embedded itself in my left wing.

Gasping, I stumbled a step as deep red blood dripped onto my shoulder and down my arm. Dimitri pulled another one of those knives out, and it was at that point I realized just how exhausted I'd become.

Yet, a wingbeat before he could throw it towards my other wing, Matea's shadow speared out of the darkness of the nearest corridor, wrapping around the blade and throwing it down, straight into Dimitri's foot, pinning him there.

"Matea, wait!" I yelled out before she could cause further damage.

I watched as her shadow form paused, and while she was hesitating, I grasped a small vial I had hidden in my pocket.

I'd hoped I wouldn't have to use it, but it appeared that was not an option anymore.

I observed Dimitri reach down and yank the blade out of his foot, grunting in pain. But when he straightened, I was there, and so were the contents of the vial.

I blew the powder the vial had been holding directly into my twin's face, and though he sputtered and backed away, the effects were nearly instantaneous.

He backed away so much that his wings hit the wall, and he slowly slid to the ground, his eyes glossing over.

As it turned out, Chess knew more than how to heal people. He knew how to incapacitate them, too. And that trokav bag he'd packed was filled to the brim with not just things to fix fae, but things to break them, too.

"What—" Dimitri said, trying to form a sentence and failing.

I came to stand beside him, knowing he was no longer a threat, and watched sorrowfully as his form slumped fully to the ground.

The last thing he did before unconsciousness took him was meet my gaze.

And the pure hatred in his eyes nearly knocked the breath from my lungs all over again.

It conveyed everything he was unable to say.

Then, his eyes closed, and the darkness took him.

Matea came to stand beside me as we both looked down at my twin.

"Why didn't you use that earlier?" Matea asked, shifting her gaze to look at the fresh blood running down my wing and arm.

"I thought..." I trailed off, unable to express myself fully.

The emotions in my chest were so jumbled, I couldn't think straight as I kneeled next to my brother and gently swept his hair out of his face.

"I'm so, so sorry," I whispered to him as tears flooded my eyes.

Was this what it was like to grieve somebody that was still breathing?

He looked so peaceful now—nothing like the angry, hurt male that had stood before me just moments earlier.

Before the tears could escape, Matea placed a gentle hand on my shoulder.

"We found Ezra, but we need to go," she said. "He has to stay in a shadow state with Rayven until we get out of here, though. He's... really been through it."

My heart sunk as I thought about leaving Dimitri like this, and about the state Ezra must be in to need to stay a shadow.

Leaning over my brother, I studied his face. The beauty marks that he'd always hated, the straight nose that matched mine, his long lashes, and especially the look of tranquility on his face.

That was how I wanted to remember him.

"Viva..." Matea urged softly.

"Alright, alright," I said. Hesitantly, I brushed my lips to my twin's cheek in a feather-light kiss. "Until next time," I whispered to him.

Then I slipped my royal mask back into place. I pushed the complex emotions weighing me down deep into myself, somewhere I wouldn't have to deal with them for a while.

Steeling myself, I stood, avoiding Matea's gaze.

I felt Rayven, and who I assumed was Ezra—whose energy felt weak—shoot into the large room, Rayven's grip on the male tight.

"Let's go," I said to Matea. I could see the concern written on her face from the corner of my eye, but I let the shadows conquer me before she could address any of her concerns aloud.

A handful of moments later, the four of us slipped through the cracked walls of Gatlyn castle, doing our best to blend in with the darkness of the night.

As we raced for Tammy's Tavern again, our rendezvous point, I couldn't help but think that if we weren't at war with Dimitri before, we sure were now.

Chapter Eleven

Once we arrived at the abandoned stable behind the tavern, I dropped the connection with the shadows as though I'd touched something hot. Immediately, my wing resumed bleeding, the thick red liquid streaming down the length of my body.

The pain radiating from my wing was sharp and prominent, but I pushed it aside in favor of helping Ezra.

He and Rayven appeared a moment later, the spy laying the male down on a bed of hay in the corner, under a part of the roof that hadn't collapsed yet.

While Rayven settled an unconscious Ezra onto the hay, I headed for the corner that we'd left our bags in, partially hidden under some hay.

Except Matea had beat me there, and our bag's contents had been ravaged.

"You've got to be kidding me," I heard my sister say as I rushed over.

"What happened?" I asked as I watched her crouch down.

"Must have been looters that came through." She rummaged through what was left. "They took nearly everything..."

"Not the kits Chess gave us, right? Please say it isn't so," I begged the Stars as I kneeled next to Matea.

She checked her bag and shook her head, indicating there was no trokav kit in it, nor anything else of use. She reached for Rayven's bag next, while I grabbed my own.

"Nothing in this one either," she said, throwing the second empty bag to the ground.

"Please," I whispered to the Stars before peering into the last of our three bags.

And to my relief, a small wooden box sat at the bottom, the image of a vial carved into the top.

"I got one!" I spoke loud, excitement edging in my voice.

I pulled out the only trokav kit we had left, then looked up at Matea.

Instead of being relieved, though, she looked beyond worried, her brow crumpled with concern.

"We only have one, but two of us are harmed..." she trailed off as she glanced towards my wrecked wing.

"Every bit of this is going towards Ezra. Do not try to convince me otherwise," I nearly demanded before standing and heading over to the corner the two males were residing in.

Rayven had propped Ezra's head up slightly, though I didn't understand why until I drew closer and heard the ragged, heavy way he was breathing—as if his airway was partially obstructed.

Likely internal bleeding, I thought. *Not a good sign.*

It wasn't until I was that close that I noticed just how badly Ezra was hurt.

There were places on his bare chest where you could see his ribs had been cracked and were slightly displaced, but you could only notice *that* if you looked past the extensive level of burns and cuts and bruises littering his skin from head to toe.

It looked as though he used to have a shirt, but now pieces of it were charred to his skin, the rest likely ash underfoot somewhere at that point.

Even his white streak of hair was filthy, like the rest of him, coated in blood.

I almost looked away as fresh tears threatened to escape.

"Aviva, we can't stay. We need to keep moving," Rayven said, and although it seemed like an uncaring request, I knew he was doing his best to keep all of us safe.

Before I could respond, Matea was at my side. "How heartless of a friend can you be, Drayven?" she asked harshly.

"*Matea,*" I scolded.

"I mean, Ezra obviously needs time to heal! Plus, Aviva is wounded, too. Did you even notice that part, *master wielder?*" Matea mocked.

"*Matea!*" I glared at her. "Go get me some water so I can get to work on Ezra."

"I'm not leaving you—"

"*Now,* Matea," I said sternly, then added softly, "Please."

Matea's mood shifted, likely realizing her stress and concern were showing itself in a negative light. Huffing, she snatched up an empty bucket from nearby and headed out of the stable.

Sighing, I turned my attention back to the males in our group. "Sorry about her. I don't think she's used to dealing with her emotions like this," I said to Rayven.

"It's alright, we all have to learn at some point."

"What is it with you two and your endless bickering, anyway?"

"Honestly, I don't know. I don't think she does, either. I just know she gets under my skin like nobody else ever has," he explained, then sighed.

"Well, try to keep it together, please. For mine *and* Ezra's sake."

Rayven agreed, and I began inspecting the extent of Ezra's wounds.

And Stars, were they *bad*.

The burns were all at least a second degree, and the bruises were varying shades of purple and blue across his creamy skin. His skin had split in multiple places, likely on impact, but I couldn't bring myself to think any further on how this had all come to be.

Soon enough, Matea returned with a bucket of cool water. Taking a small cloth from the trokav kit, I got to work cleaning Ezra's wounds.

"Could you hand me a cloth, too, Drayven?" Matea asked. Her tone sounded calmer now, which I appreciated.

"I need pretty much all of them, Matea," I warned.

"I'm going to clean *your* wound, little sister," she said, and I could tell this was a hill she was willing to die on.

Sighing, I knew my wing needed it, so I nodded slightly to Rayven, who then handed a cloth to Matea.

"Only one," I said firmly.

With that, we set to work cleaning wounds. I even assigned Rayven to sit on Ezra's other side and clean what he could over there, just to make things go by a little faster.

I did my best not to flinch each time Matea's cloth touched my wing, but the pain was doing its best to bubble up out of that deep spot I'd pushed it down into. But if it escaped, so would my complicated emotions, and we simply didn't have time for me to process all of that.

So I pushed it all down further and got to work.

Rayven didn't have any formal trokav training, but I soon learned that Matea knew a thing or two. I knew she was a plant wielder, but apparently, Billie—our shared grandmother—had trained as a trokav for a while, and taught Matea what she knew. I'd spent enough time with Hugo growing up whenever I was bored—which was often—that I knew the basics, too.

After she'd finished tearing small strips of her cloak to wrap my wing with, she insisted on helping me with Ezra. We fell into a rhythm of sprouting small herbs, using things from the kit Chess had given me, and doing our best to apply our combined knowledge to the unconscious male before us.

We ebbed and flowed well together, and soon enough, we'd done all we could for Ezra.

I still wished I could've done more.

Now, Ezra had varying bandages and wraps made from strips of our clothing tied around him and his wounds. By morning, he should be alright enough to discard some of the wraps.

"I'll keep watch," Rayven offered. Before I could object, he added, "Please. I won't be able to sleep, anyway."

I watched as his gaze slid over to his friend's unconscious form, and I understood. I was worried about Ezra, too.

He may heal physically, but how was he besides that?

Only time would tell.

"Alright," I said, nodding. "Thank you."

It didn't take long after that for Matea and me to find a dry section of the stable and a bed of hay. We curled up next to each other, and with the wing that she didn't wrap, I covered her shivering form. It was obvious she wasn't accustomed to the weather here in the mountains.

"Thanks," she mumbled, and soon afterwards her breathing leveled out in a way where I knew she'd fallen asleep.

I laid on my back for moments afterwards, staring up towards the Stars through a crack in the roof above.

Please get us home safely, I wished to them before I allowed sleep to overpower me.

***

Heavy breathing and a horrified yell woke me while the sky was still dark with night.

Drawing in my wing that had been draped over Matea, I quickly sat up, my eyes adjusting faster than I could process what I was seeing.

Rayven was whispering something to Ezra softly, obviously trying to keep him calm, but Ezra was outright panicking. Sweat slicked his skin and stuck his hair to his forehead, and he had begun to hyperventilate.

"How did I get here? How did I get out?" Ezra asked Rayven, frantically looking around. As I got up and slowly moved to Rayven's side, I watched as Ezra flinched at the sight of me.

I must've looked so much like Dimitri to him.

"Ezra," I said gently, kneeling next to him. "Breathe. Part of our mission was to search for you, and once we found you, we couldn't leave you behind. You're safe now."

"No, I feel the chill in the air. We aren't safe anywhere near them." He shook his head. "How do I know this is real? That I won't wake up and be back... there?" he whispered, his eyes boring into mine now, searching for answers he wasn't sure he'd find.

"Listen," I told him. "You can hear the crickets out in the tall grasses nearby, and the wind shifting through the roof of this stable."

I drew a small amount of water from the bucket we'd used hours before to clean him and froze it into a small sphere.

"Hold this, and focus on the cold while you listen. It'll help ground you." I held the ice out to him, moving slowly so as not to spook him.

He stared at the ice for a moment before letting me drop it into his hands, our skin not making contact even briefly.

Taking my advice, he held the ice tightly and tilted his head to hear the wind better.

"Also, if you look through the holes in the roof, you can see the Stars twinkling. I bet they're welcoming you back to their presence,." I said, looking up. He followed my gaze.

"You can also smell the hay all around us, if that helps, too," I suggested.

He looked around then, his eyes clearer than they had been before, and his breathing beginning to steady before it could get too bad.

Then, he saw Matea. His eyes widened, but before he could panic again, Rayven and I both tried to explain.

Our sentences ran together, and Ezra looked back and forth between us wildly.

Finally, I pinched Rayven just hard enough for him to gasp. In the break between his words, I quickly jumped in to explain.

"You've missed a lot, but you can trust her, I promise," I reassured him. "She helped get you out."

At that, his gaze softened. He looked up again at the Stars, then met my gaze.

"How long has it been?" he asked.

"Over a month, brother," Rayven said, guilt lingering at the edges of his gruff voice.

"I... I've really made it out?" Ezra asked after a beat of silence, tears welling in his eyes as he stared into my mismatched ones for confirmation.

"Yes, Ezra. We've got you now," I responded softly.

Finally accepting this reality, the tears spilled over onto Ezra's cheeks and his chest was wracked with quiet sobs.

Unexpectedly, he looped an arm each around Rayven and me, pulling us both into a fierce hug. Tears brimmed my own eyes, and even in Rayven's as we hugged our friend back, gently so as not to disturb his wrappings, but solidly enough so he knew we were there.

"Thank you," he said between sobs. "Thank you for not forgetting me. For coming for me."

"I'm *so* sorry it took us this long," I responded remorsefully.

"Me too," Rayven added.

Ezra let go and looked at us both as he replied, "I'm just happy you came."

He looked past us then, toward Matea. "Thank you, too," he said to her.

She dipped her head respectfully, then added, "Any friend of Aviva's is a friend of mine."

Rayven shot me a skeptical look that almost made me laugh, but then I heard a twig snap outside, and the laugh died in my throat.

"Since I doubt any of us are going back to sleep, why don't we get going? We have a long trek back home," I suggested.

"*Home,*" Ezra murmured, and I could tell by the look of love in his eyes he was talking about more than Cairnyl.

He must think of Quinn the same way I think of Byn.

As home.

"Good idea," Matea said, and Rayven nodded.

Considering we no longer had any bags to pack and take with us, we simply covered any sign that we had been there before stepping foot outside.

Ezra, to my surprise, could walk better than I'd expected. Yet, I was drained, and I hadn't slept enough to recharge my energy.

With that factored in, we began our journey back to the South under the blanket of the night sky, every step we took bringing us closer and closer to our destination.

Home.

Chapter Twelve

Drip, drip, drip.

The sound of dripping water echoed in my head over and over as my senses slowly returned to me.

My eyelids were too heavy to lift at first, so I worked on regaining control and the feeling of my body as I thought about how I'd gotten here.

I worked my way up physically, wiggling my toes and fingers, and then flexing my arm and leg muscles from bottom to top until I was once again aware of my form. Once I did that, I realized just how much my foot hurt.

It took a moment, but then the *why* came rushing back.

Aviva.

Her lackeys.

The prisoner escaping.

A knife to the foot.

Dust blown in my face.

And then it was all dark after that.

At that last thought, my eyes snapped open, quickly adjusting to the darkness of the dungeon entry room I'd found myself in. I groaned as I sat up, my body stiff.

How had I let this happen?

How had I let myself be bested—and by my original student, no less?

The zirilium in my blood grew in strength as my frustration and anger rose. The more I recounted what had happened, the worse my mood became, and the more questions I had that were left unanswered.

Rising from the cold ground, I leaned against the wall beside me as my head spun. I waited for the dizziness to pass, then began the trek up the spiral stairs.

All forty-two steps.

But with each step I took, the more solid my resolve became.

It was time to move on.

I could stay in denial no longer.

It had become clear to me by now that Aviva had not only betrayed me by staying in the South, seemingly not against her will, but she'd also already replaced me. And with who I could only assume was our half-sister, no less!

The name *Matea* had been scribbled on the back of the portrait I'd found with Mother's things—though it seemed my guess had likely been correct, anyway.

By the time I reached the top of the stairs, I practically burst through the heavy metal door, only to find my guards passed out on the ground before me.

As I had been moments earlier.

Reaching down, I ripped off the Heartshire family crest pin both males wore over their heart. I pocketed the pins, taking note to dismiss each and every guard that had failed to stop my twin and her companions.

I tried to ignore the way the sun was already creeping over the horizon, meaning I'd been out since last night.

It would only serve to anger me further.

Doing my best to ignore the power surging within me, I left the two males there and simply started walking.

I was so stuck inside my own spiraling thoughts of abandonment and grief that I didn't realize where my feet were taking me until I'd arrived.

Right in the middle of Aviva's chambers.

The air had grown stale inside, but it still held the sweetness of the floral soaps she used to cleanse her hair with. The smell should have been a comfort, but instead it only stoked the embers I felt heating inside my chest.

Aviva had always been my better half. The one that could feel so strongly, even for those she didn't know personally. The one that had the free spirit, and enjoyed doing things just for the fun of it. The one who was always trying to better herself, whether it be through knowledge or experiences.

She had just been... *better*.

Somewhere along the way, it seemed she had lost all of that.

Out of the corner of my eye, I caught a glimpse of myself in Aviva's vanity mirror. Unable to help myself, I turned to face my reflection.

I nearly cringed away from what I saw.

My hair was grimy, my clothing wrinkled. I had heavy bags under my eyes, and various layers of dirt and ash on me from the fight and the night on the dungeon floor.

But under that, I could almost *see* my twin looking back at me. The twin I had known, the version of herself she was before she left.

Almost.

It was still too close for comfort.

Fury striking hard and fast, I swiped everything off the vanity in one swift motion. I watched as the mirror fell and broke, the shards reflecting pieces of me back to myself as it shattered on impact.

With that act motivating me, I marched over to the wardrobe next, yanking out the priceless dresses Father had bought her and tossing them onto the floor, ripping some as I went.

Next, I stomped over to the bookshelf. Her books and tomes had meant so much to her—some more priceless than all her gowns combined.

I couldn't have cared less as I grabbed them all, starting one by one and working my way up to armfuls of them, and throwing them all across the room. I tore pages out as I went, or ripped the covers and bindings apart.

It wasn't until I was panting heavily from the energy exerted that I realized my hands had been aflame that entire time.

And I had set fire to everything I had touched.

It was as though *I* had been the embers of a weak fire, and my emotions had been the spark it needed to return to life.

The room filled with smoke quickly, but I had nothing left in me to care with.

Seeing the wreckage I had caused, I dropped to my knees in the middle of the space, the fire fleeing from me, doing me no harm.

Finally, I yelled out.

I screamed until my voice gave out, tears streaming freely as my anger and frustration and hurt and grief became too much to bear. It was too much to hold inside, and so I was letting it out the only way I knew how.

The entire room was ablaze around me by the time my tears ran dry. I lay there, curled up in a ball, trying my hardest to not exist as I listened to the fire and embers crackle around me as it ate what connections I had left to my twin.

All the while, the fire had not come within a foot of where I lay.

Chapter Thirteen

With each step we took that brought us closer to Cairnyl over the next four days, I could feel more and more of Byn's emotions returning to my chest.

It was a relief—a comfort—to feel that again. Ezra and I talked quietly about it at least once a day when we stopped to rest or eat. He could feel Quinn the same way I could feel Byn, and he'd had questions about it. Somehow, despite his time away, he hadn't lost the spark inside that made him... *himself*.

By the second day, I couldn't hold on to my shadow form anymore. Matea picked up my slack, shifting us both into shadows as we traveled, while Rayven did the same for Ezra. Not only did this help us stay hidden and unseen during our journey, but it dulled the pain both Ezra and I felt.

We didn't stop in Genisyn this time. Rayven decided to put his survival skills to the test by hunting or fishing instead, depending on what was available. He had felt bad asking me to cook whatever he caught with my fire zirilium, but lighting a normal bonfire could have drawn too much attention to us, and I understood that.

We stopped and ate twice a day, but with each stop, the length of time we remained in one spot grew longer. All four of us were exhausted beyond belief. Even with recharging our sun stones—and my moon stones—we hadn't had the time to recharge ourselves.

On the rare occasion when we traveled by foot, Rayven, Matea or I lent a shoulder to Ezra for him to lean on. He was weak, nearly skin and bones from his time in the dungeons, and had the least amount of energy out of the four of us. I'd given him what was left of my cloak that first day, since he hadn't had a shirt, and I used my wings as coverage over my bare arms and to help keep me warm—despite the pain it took to move the injured one. Though, I didn't mind it much, as I was the most accustomed to the colder weather.

Fortunately, by day three, we'd snuck back over the border into Southern territory—which now had even more patrols than before—and were in the home stretch.

Now, on the morning of our fourth day, we were nearly home.

We'd all decided to set out early that morning, our relief about being so close to home palpable. But as we soon learned, Rayven and Matea were nearly drained by that point in our journey, too. We had no choice but to set out on foot.

As we made our slow trek through the last stretch of Wittuck Woods, I couldn't help but be grateful that Matea—who had a big hand in the route we'd taken to and from Hollis—helped us avoid anywhere near the place where the Battle of Shadows had taken place.

I wasn't sure I could have stomached it, being back there.

I knew she'd picked this route on purpose, and I appreciated her even more-so because of it.

"Are you ready to see her again, brother?" Rayven asked Ezra, drawing me from my thoughts.

Ezra, who was currently being held up by Rayven and Matea while taking slow, steady steps together, sighed lightly at just the mention of his wife.

"It'll all have been worth it once I see her again," he said, his voice full of unyielding love.

My heart ached for Ezra and all he'd been through. We'd patched him up the best we could, but we had no more bandages or medicines left from the trokav kit. He'd likely scar in some places because of it, but at least he had made it. On the other hand, my wing pained me each time I moved it, so I'd been avoiding doing so.

"She speaks highly of you, you know," Matea says, breaking the silence we'd fallen back into.

Before Ezra could muster the strength to respond, his head snapped sideways to look at me, his eyes frantic with... *excitement*?

"Do you feel it?" he asked.

"Feel wh—" I stopped when I finally understood his reaction.

Byn.

He was close. I could *feel* him—*sense* him, even.

Which had to mean that Quinn was close, too.

Faster than I could process, Ezra shrugged off the two shadow wielders, attempting to run ahead out of the edges of the forest on his own. He didn't make it more than three steps before he stumbled, but Rayven and Matea were instantly there to catch him before he could fall. Together, the three of them broke out into a run—slow enough so Ezra could keep up—bursting out of the edges of Wittuck Woods after having spent what felt like weeks inside of it.

Before I could process what I was doing, I was tumbling forward, my feet moving faster than my thoughts as I, too, came bursting out of Wittuck Woods to stand outside of Cairnyl.

I nearly ran right into my companions as I crossed over into the harsh sunlight, now unobstructed by the lack of trees overhead. Coming to stand next to them, I paused.

Ezra and I were simply *feeling*.

Sensing.

The bonds we shared with our spouses went deeper than the ink in our flesh.

They were soul bonds.

One that proved not to fail us then as suddenly, from one of the dirt roads leading out of Cairnyl, came two figures.

Two fae who were running like their very lives depended on it.

As the first came into view, I knew I'd recognize her bright ginger locks anywhere.

Quinn, who despite being substantially shorter than the second figure, was multiple yards ahead of them, her legs carrying her faster than a thrown dagger.

Ezra stumbled forward at the sight of his wife, out of the reach of the two shadow wielders, doing his best to meet Quinn halfway.

I wanted to watch the reunion, to help Ezra reach her, but my eyes caught sight of something I wanted more than anything else in this realm.

The second figure.

Robyn Thorntier.

My husband.

My love.

My very heart which beat outside of my chest.

And when I saw him, I couldn't help it.

I *ran*.

It didn't matter that it had been less than two weeks—I ran.

I cursed the Stars for the pain in my wing stopping me from flying to him, but running would have to do.

Before I realized what I was doing, an air current was there, pushing me forward, faster and faster until Byn's features became clear—exactly as I had memorized them to be.

It all came bubbling up swiftly—everything I'd been trying to push down. The physical pain, the emotional wreckage, the mental fractures of what I thought I knew to be true. It wasn't until then that I realized in doing that, I'd been blocking Byn out to a degree, too.

And now he was back, full force.

His anxiety, love, concern, hope, and relief all flooded into me in a wave of forest green as he grew nearer.

And then, like an eclipse of the sun and moon, we collided.

His arms were around me, and mine around him, and he was close, but never close enough. I'd leaped, my legs locking around his waist as he held me so tight it felt like he was trying to merge our very beings into one.

I would have let him.

I didn't realize I was crying until the sound of Byn saying one word over and over grounded me back into my body.

"Avi, Avi, Avi…" he murmured repeatedly, stroking my hair and being my source of comfort, even when he didn't know exactly why I'd needed it. Even his familiar scent—sweet magnolia blossoms and fresh rain—was a comfort I hadn't realized I'd missed.

If I hadn't been absolutely exhausted, I was confident my zirilium would have acted up somehow.

"I've missed you," I said, my cries turning to sniffles.

"I know, my love. I've missed you, too." He sighed. "Saying I simply missed you doesn't do the feelings I experienced justice. I yearned for you, *ached* for you, every moment you were gone. When I could hardly feel you anymore, Teagan practically had to drag me back to The Haven by my ear," he said, causing me to let out a surprised chuckle.

"You know, for somebody that hasn't slept in a real bed in nearly two weeks, you still manage to take my breath away," Byn said after pulling back to look at me, that handsome smirk of his quirking up his mouth on one side.

I rolled my eyes, then teased, "Shut up and kiss me, Thorntier."

And that was all the encouragement he had needed, his lips crashing into mine a split second later. It was a hungry, devouring kiss full of claim and need and desire. I finally understood him when he said he burned for me—I felt so many things at once for him, I wouldn't have been surprised if I broke out into flames just outside of town.

Just outside of town.

I gasped, pulling back and locking eyes with my husband, my cheeks flushing pink.

"I was just getting started," he complained, but I could hear the playfulness in his voice and feel his delight in my chest.

"Another time, love," I said, untangling myself from him and standing on my own two feet again.

"So..." Byn said, looking over my head. "You three were at least somewhat successful."

I turned, following his gaze until my eyes landed on Quinn and Ezra.

They were kneeling before each other, Quinn holding her husband's face as they simply marveled at each other. They were so close, I knew they'd already been wrapped up in each other, and I was just catching the tail end of the interaction.

Byn slipped his hand into mine and began the walk over. But once we got near, my heart cracked at what I heard.

"I didn't break, Gem. I thought of you, and I *knew* deep down that I'd see you again. I knew I couldn't live with myself if I broke, so I thought of what you would do, and it worked. I *didn't* break. I *didn't break. I didn't break.*"

Soon, fresh tears were rolling down Ezra's face, and Quinn pulled him close, as though if she held on tight enough, she could undo all the hurt that had befallen him.

"I wouldn't have cared if you had, Ezra. I just wanted you home safely." She pulled back and cupped his face again, her own eyes welling anew. "And you did that. You made it. You survived, Ezra."

Ezra laughed then, as though he could barely believe it himself.

He caught sight of Byn then, his focus shifting for just a moment as he said, "Thank you for not giving up on me."

"Never, my brother," Robyn said, his voice cracking slightly as he leaned over to place a hand on his shoulder and squeezed softly. I could feel the joy radiating from Byn so strongly, and it reminded me of the fire he wielded.

I knew Byn wanted to speak to Ezra more, to hug him and make sure he was alright, but he was also aware that Quinn had him now. And that was reassurance enough.

I watched as Byn turned to Rayven and Matea. On making eye contact, Rayven placed his fist over his heart and bowed his head. Byn smiled, mimicking his friend's hand movements. The look of respect and appreciation that passed between them was something I was grateful Byn had. It seemed like a whole conversation had passed between them, without a word needing to be said.

Facing Matea, Byn dipped his head to her and said, his voice full of appreciation, "Thank you. Whatever you need or want, it's yours. Just let me know."

It wasn't just the appreciation in his voice that I noticed, though. I could feel the mixed emotions he'd harbored before unraveling as he softened toward my half-sister. Now all he seemed to be feeling towards her was gratitude.

Matea, whose eyes were full of pride for her accomplishments, waved a hand dismissively and responded, "It was nothing."

Her utter nonchalance caused Byn to laugh. I smiled, his laugh like flawless music to my ears.

Oh, how I've longed for him, I thought.

He headed back over to my side after making sure Matea truly knew he was there if she needed anything, then slipped his hand back into mine. It was as though he couldn't stand not to touch me in some way.

"Let's go get you into some fresh clothes, wife," he said, then added, "And checked out by Chess. Don't think I didn't notice."

He looked pointedly at my left wing then, letting me know he, indeed, somehow was aware.

"Who snitched?" I asked as Ezra and Quinn slowly got to their feet, too, with Ezra leaning into Quinn's side.

"Rayven," Byn said easily.

We all laughed—mostly from the hysterics—as we made our way back to The Haven.

And with my hand in Byn's, finally, I was home.

Chapter Fourteen

Calling to one of the softest of my zirilium, I brushed my fingertips up the stem of a nearby flower, causing the drooping plant to straighten and puff out its petals.

"There you go," I murmured to the sprouting flower. "Looking better already."

I looked around at the dozens of other flowers I had already nurtured back from the brink of death, all surrounding the Thorntier thrones.

The Haven throne room stood in the very center of the giant structure. There was no solid roof overhead, and portions of the sky could be seen between the gaps of the trees.

Yes, *trees*.

The throne room was more of a giant courtyard—the same courtyard Byn and I were wed in—with grass and earth underfoot and exposed to the elements above. There were many Southern wildflowers, trees, shrubs, and other greens spread about the space.

Though the thrones themselves were the highlight of it all.

Having been shaped from the growing trunk of giant trees, each throne was breath-taking. I could only imagine they were crafted with plant zirilium, having the two trees grow and bend into the perfect shape for their king and queen. They sat towards the back of the open space, but I could feel their roots running in every direction in the earth below. Their backings were nearly as tall as Atlas—Byn's Titan Wolf and one of his closest companions—making me feel tiny as I sat on the ground in front of them.

Reaching out a hand again, I breathed life back into another flower, this one a soft yellow.

Apparently, the fae that usually maintained the plants of the throne room had fallen ill. I'd overheard Giles, Byn's assistant in nearly everything court-wise, mention it, and had offered to lend a hand today. Giles had been beside himself and tried to softly talk me out of it, but I thought it'd be good for me.

Ever since facing Dimi recently—and seeing the lengths he was willing to go to get what he wanted—I'd spiraled into my own dark thoughts again. The day after we returned, I hadn't left mine and Byn's chambers even once. The following day had been a bit better, but there were still shadows lurking within the depths of my mind.

Today, though, I *wanted* to be in this courtyard. Not only did it keep me occupied, but because we'd been so busy since I'd arrived in the South, I'd only taken my place on the throne once—when we appointed Laurence into the Valwain and he'd vowed to serve the Thorntier line with all he was. I'd also been appointed that day, but I had simply stood and made my vows to Byn, instead of kneeling before the thrones, as Laurence had.

Besides that, I hadn't *needed* to be in the throne room—other than the day Byn and I had gotten married.

It made me feel... appreciation. That was where Byn's parents had sat and ruled from, where they'd led not only their people but their family. Their children.

And Stars, did it seem like they did a fantastic job.

I knew the Thorntier siblings grieved still, and likely felt differently about seeing the thrones without their parents sitting in them, but it also made *me* feel blue, oddly enough. I wished I had been able to meet them, under different circumstances.

And thank them for raising the male I couldn't live without so incredibly well.

"Your Majesty?" I heard Laurence say, his voice gentle and soft as always.

Tilting my head to look away from the lively flowers now surrounding me, I caught sight of my guard and friend heading towards me from the main throne room entrance.

Looking back towards the thrones, I couldn't help but say, "I feel like I can see them in Byn and Teagan and Margo."

"See who, Your Majesty?" Laurence asked as he neared.

"The previous King and Queen of the South. I've seen their portraits on the walls, and heard the siblings talk about them briefly, but here I feel like I'm able to appreciate them more. To connect."

I ran my hand through the soft soil below mindlessly, bright green grass sprouting from under my palm upon contact.

Laurence watched, subtle awe on his face as the native grasses grew.

"They were kind, like King Robyn," Laurence said, crouching next to me and gently cupping the yellow flower in his hand.

"And thoughtful, like Teagan. Queen Genevieve was creative like Margo, and King Orus was stubborn like her. They were two sides of the same coin, using their strengths to work together the best they could for their kingdom and those they loved." Laurence raised his brows at me. "Much like you and King Robyn."

A few moments passed in a comfortable silence before Laurence asked, "How's the wing?"

"Feeling much better, thanks to Chess." I flexed my left wing out, then pulled it back in to prove my point.

After Rayven, Matea, Ezra, and I had all arrived back to The Haven a few days ago, Byn had insisted the group's first stop would be the infirmary. Mostly for Ezra, but I had felt my husband's worry about my wing, too. Considering at the time my own blood had stained my clothes, I couldn't exactly fault him.

Chess had gone right into trokav mode upon seeing Ezra, and although he was obviously relieved to see his friend, he couldn't hide the concern on his face. He'd asked one of his helpers—a female on the smaller side—to care for me, who patched up my wing with ease, despite never having worked on wings before.

Now, it would only need a few more days of ointments and bandaging, and it would be nearly back to normal.

The same couldn't be said for Ezra.

What Matea and I had done hadn't been enough. While we treated the outside, the inside of his body had been damaged, too. Broken bones, internal bleeding, a slightly punctured lung, the list went on. He was nearly beyond repair, according to Chess. But ever since getting back to Quinn, Ezra had been fighting even harder than before. I could see the effort he was putting in to get better, day by day.

And Quinn was there for it all, every step of the way.

"I'm happy you're healing well," Laurence said, lightly placing a hand on my shoulder and drawing me from my thoughts.

"But you came to find me for a reason, I suppose," I speculated, looking up at the older male.

He nodded. "King Robyn asked me to take you to him."

"Is he alright?" My stomach dropped as I instinctively reached for Byn through our connected emotions.

My expression relaxed in relief before Laurence could even respond.

"All good things, my queen," he said with a smile. "He's prepared a surprise for you, I believe."

I couldn't help the excitement that rose within me. I'd hated surprises all my life, but Byn always seemed to know exactly what I needed.

I trusted him.

I brushed dirt and blades of grass from my cotton pants as I stood from the ground.

"Lead the way, Laurence."

***

"There you are!"

The sound of my husband's voice graced my ears, stealing my attention away from the light conversation I'd been having with Laurence.

We'd just stepped outside and onto the path that led to the royal gardens, but it seemed Byn had gotten antsy and came to find us.

"I can take it from here, Laurence. You should probably get some rest, anyway," Byn suggested.

That's right, I thought, *we'll be leaving again soon—almost all of us this time.*

After we'd arrived back home, Matea, Rayven, and I had a meeting with just Byn. He said he would talk to Ezra at a later time, but that he wanted to know how the trip went, from start to finish, while the details were still fresh in our minds. He acknowledged it was a heavy task to ask of us, but the three of us understood. So we sat for hours, recounting what had transpired over the past nearly two weeks.

That was when I'd learned of the alychite.

It would figure my twin would be using such a material that made it so Rayven couldn't wield around it—hence why he'd needed the key to Ezra's cell. Dimitri had always been so much more intelligent than others had viewed him.

My chest felt as though it caved in slightly at the thought of my brother.

"Yes, my king." Laurence bowed, then turned to me, pulling me back to the two males before me and away from the one that was a kingdom away. I dipped my chin slightly, signaling that he was free to depart. He didn't smile, but his eyes still shone as he looked at me, then headed back inside.

"You truly believe we're ready to go back out there?" I inquired as Byn linked our arms together, leading me towards the gardens.

We would be heading out in a matter of days, into Northern territory once again. Though this time, we'd be taking a different approach.

"I believe we don't have another choice, unfortunately. Not if we want to find our missing fae." His expression darkened for just a moment, but the second we walked through the green arch leading into the gardens, I could practically see the stress on his features brighten with excitement.

Laurence had mentioned a surprise, but I wasn't sure what could have gotten Byn so giddy.

"What's got you so excited today, love?" I asked.

"Why shouldn't I be?" he laughed. "I've got the most beautiful female in the realm on my arm. Any male would be excited—mark my word."

My lips tilted up in a smile as we continued to walk through the gardens, past various flowers I didn't know the names of, until we ended up standing in front of a tall, thick wall of shrubbery.

"What are we—"

I was cut off as Byn gently let go of my arm and stepped forward. I watched as he used his plant wielding to create an opening in the shrubbery. In one step, he was through. He reached a hand back through to me.

"Do you trust me?" he asked.

"Always, Thorntier." I placed my hand in his and, in one large step, I was on the other side.

And what I saw took my breath away.

The shrubbery—which was even taller than Byn himself—wrapped around the small area in a square with no natural openings to walk through. It was completely closed off to outsiders—private. But that wasn't what had stolen the breath from my lungs.

In the center of the small space stood a gazebo. Its pale wood contrasted the dark roof and black stone base, and countless vines of moon lilies surrounded it.

They draped down from the roof, climbed the pillars holding the structure up, and wrapped around the sides. It provided additional privacy, hanging down even over the entrance, but it was also the first time I was seeing moon lilies in Cairnyl and on a vine.

Additionally, the flowers were scattered throughout the rest of the small clearing, like the stars scattered the night sky.

I gasped at the sight of them and their silvery and white petals with a soft purple center.

Mother's favorite.

And mine.

"How did you..." I trailed off, unable to complete my question.

"I might have studied them a tad back at Echen Bay. I could tell how much they meant to you there, and I wanted to know how to grow them so you could have them here, too," Byn said softly.

It spoke to his control over his zirilium—to have only had a short period of time to study a specific plant and recreate it from nothing more than the earth below.

I blinked back the tears threatening from behind my eyes at the sight of them.

"Come on," he said, linking our arms again and leading me to the gazebo.

He parted the moon lily vines for me to duck through, and I paused in my tracks once I stepped inside.

It was the most perfect picnic I had ever seen.

There were multiple small dishes of Northern food—along with a few of my favorite Southern ones—spread out on a dark purple blanket. Multiple sizes of white plush cushions covered the space. There were jugs of water and wine already near the food, and the way the setting sun peeked through the vines made it look as though I'd stepped through the pages of a fairytale.

Without looking away from the astounding set up, I grabbed his hand and squeezed.

"Let's eat," he suggested, his voice quiet. He led us into the middle of the setup, atop the plush cushions, before lowering to the ground and gently pulling me down with him.

The next moments were full of food, laughter, wine, and quiet chatter. Here, we weren't the King and Queen of the South. We were just Robyn and Aviva—two fae who were madly, sickeningly in love with one another.

Once Byn had fed me the last of the strawberries—so slowly it was antagonizing, to my dismay—I picked up a napkin to wipe my mouth with, but he beat me to it. He gently cupped the side of my face, using his thumb to wipe away the tiny droplet of juice that had rested near my lip.

But he didn't stop there.

"You know," he said as he slowly ran his thumb against my bottom lip, "I believe... I'm still hungry."

My eyes flicked up to meet his, and the desire in his gaze made my core run hot. I could tell he wasn't hungry for more food.

And if he was hungry, I was *ravenous*.

Picking up on the desirous shift in my emotions—emotions that matched his own—his grip on my jaw tightened as he tugged me closer to him and brought our lips a breath from each other's.

My breathing hitched at the nearness, but our lips failed to meet.

I cracked my eyes open, meeting his hungry gaze as he murmured, "I plan on *worshipping* you tonight."

My core tightened at just the thought of such a thing.

Then his lips were everywhere but on my own. He left a trail of kisses down the column of my throat, which I gladly exposed to him. When he made it to my shoulder, he looked at me for confirmation—of which I happily granted—before tugging my shirt off, undoing the buttons on the back for my wings as he went.

Then, without my shirt, he gently laid me on my back while being mindful of my injured wing. He carried on his trail of kisses, stopping every few to leave small purple marks. When he reached my waist, he paused to look up at me.

"May I?" he asked.

"Please," I responded, breathless.

I couldn't ignore the smirk that made his dimple pop as he looped his fingers into my waistband and tugged.

He tossed them away mindlessly before beginning another trail, this time on the opposite side of my body as before, of kisses and marks. He moved excruciatingly slowly, taking his time to taste me on his lips.

By the time he reached my shoulder again, I groaned impatiently.

"You're such a tease," I said, my heart racing at the close contact—yet not close enough.

He chuckled, but made no effort to quicken his pace. I lifted a hand and fisted it in his hair, my patience wearing thin as I tugged him up and crashed my lips into his.

It was as though we were trying to devour each other through a single kiss. It was all lips, teeth, and tongues as we explored territory we both knew by heart at that point.

I pulled back moments later, panting, as I lifted his shirt off over his head, exposing his toned and golden torso.

"I want all of you, Byn." I ran my hands over his soft skin as I peered up at him.

"Your desires are mine, Avi—I want all of you, too." He tucked a stray lock of hair behind my pointed ear. "Your mind, your emotions, your body, your soul—all of it. You're *mine.*"

I leaned into his touch as I agreed, "Yours."

With that to set the tone, the rest of the evening was, indeed, full of worshipping. Not the Stars, as some had the custom, but each other.

That might not have been our first time, but it was one of the most meaningful. As our bodies melded into one form, that bond tying our souls together became one, too. His feelings were mine, and mine his, and we didn't need words to know exactly what the other needed.

We moved together in perfect harmony, our essence like that of an eclipse.

Skin met skin.

Emotion met emotion.

Soul met soul.

Chapter Fifteen

The cold stone of the throne felt as though it was seeping into my very bones after so many hours of sitting upon it. The small band of string musicians played on a platform in the middle of the grand open space that made up the throne room. The music they played wasn't horrid, but it echoed throughout the open room, making my head throb relentlessly. That, and the hundreds of people that crowded the normally empty space.

Recently, my advisors insisted on opening the castle gates to nobles and civilians alike for a grand coronation ball. Since my coronation had been rushed due to Father's untimely demise, we hadn't held a public ceremony with the fae of Hollis. The event I had found myself stuck in for the evening was to make up for that, supposedly.

I watched and waved a hand dismissively at each fae that approached the throne and offered their congratulations. Hugo had mentioned that they were all well-meaning, but I couldn't seem to understand how that could be. Didn't they realize it ran deeper than congratulating me on my accension to the Heartshire throne?

Didn't they realize what we'd lost—and for my gain?

I couldn't stop the creeping feeling that if Father were here, he'd have been disappointed. There I was, wasting time on a useless ball when there were still larger problems at hand that needed to be addressed.

The thought made my blood run hot, and I had to clench my hands in an attempt to control the swell in my zirilium that matched my emotions.

I desperately needed to get a handle on them.

Or to find another outlet, a voice that reminded me of Father's said quietly in my mind.

I shook my head as the sound of his voice echoed in my thoughts, and abruptly stood from the solid onyx throne. The four guards on either side of me stood slightly straighter at my sudden movement.

"Relax, soldier. I'm just in need of refreshments," I said, looking toward the nearest male. He bowed his head, then offered to send somebody else to grab me a glass, so I could remain where I was.

The thought of sitting still a moment longer made me feel sick to my stomach.

"That's alright. I shall return in no time at all," I assured the guard, then walked off the throne's platform before he could attempt to persuade me further.

Sliding my way through the crowd with my wings tucked in tight, I brushed off anybody who tried to stop me for a chat. Sweat began to bead on my forehead, right under the silver Heartshire crown that sat atop my temples.

Father's crown.

A moment later, I reached the far wall and made my way around the long buffet style table, so I could stand on the less crowded side. I came to a stop in front of the wine, grabbing a goblet of the deep red liquid and taking a heavy swig, then another.

My skin was slick, my head was throbbing, and my heart had begun to race.

But at least there was wine.

It had to help.

Right?

Just as I went to take in my third mouth-full of liquid, a voice rang out nearby.

"A wise fae would likely suggest that you slow down."

Shifting to see who had just spoken, I found myself mere steps away from a female.

Her short hair was a soft yet rich brown, her eyes a striking blue, with a small beauty mark dotting her left cheek by her eye, similar to my own. Her wings were an ashy gray, and she wore the classic Northern colors of blue and silver—but a soft blue, not the usual navy one saw all over Hollis. Her creamy skin appeared soft, but the calluses I noted on her hands as she reached for her own goblet suggested she did some sort of manual labor, too.

So there was more to her than met the eye, it seemed.

"Fortunately, I would not consider myself wise," the female said, the corner of her mouth tilting up into a sly smile.

Any other male would have drooled at the sight of her—relished in her attention. Yet to me, she just appeared slightly... *off*.

Her hair was *too* dark, her eyes *too* intense. Her lips, while plump and pink, were not the ones I had imagined kissing so many times before. The ones I still thought about as I fell asleep some nights, and had for years.

The claim to that part of myself belonged to one female, and one female only.

Someday, anyway, I wished to the Stars.

"I fear your efforts will be wasted upon me, m'lady," I said over the rim of my crystal goblet. "I am spoken for."

"Our king has a special lady?" she gasped, placing her spare hand over her heart in an act of dramatics.

When I didn't react, she chuckled, dropping her hand back to her side and smiling slightly.

"You can't blame a female for trying." She shrugged. "You are the most powerful fae in the room right now, after all."

I narrowed my eyes at her, examining. Analyzing.

Indeed, there seemed to be much more than met the eye when it came to the fae standing before me.

"What is your name, stranger?"

"Valenia, or Val, Your Majesty. At your service." I watched as she curtsied perfectly, even with the glass of wine still held in her hand.

She dressed the part of a perfect lady, and could even act as one, and yet there seemed to be more to her. Aside from the calluses, I could also see soft muscles rippling beneath the skin of her upper arms and the faint outline of a small blade hidden in her top.

She had the tellings of a sort of warrior—not that of a noble, like her attire suggested.

Slowly, so as not to concern her with any sudden movements, I took the goblet from her hands, placing both hers and my own on the table next to us.

"Care for a dance?" I glanced toward the dance floor as the current song came to a close.

"Your Majesty?" Her voice gave away her surprise at my sudden offer.

"Don't you trust me?" I asked, meeting her gaze and quirking one side of my mouth up into a smirk. I held out my hand.

"Not in the slightest," she responded in the same breath as she placed her hand into mine.

My smirk grew at her response as I led us out into the middle of the floor, close to the musicians. The crowd parted as I walked through, all eyes on Valenia and me. The whispers and chatter began almost immediately, so I stole a glance at the female beside me.

To my surprise, her face gave away nothing of what she felt beyond confidence. She almost appeared comfortable.

Wordlessly, we took our place on the dance floor and listened as the crowd overcame their shock when the next song began. This one was slower than the last, and called for close contact to perfect the moves.

Her hand found mine, placing the other on my shoulder. I looped my other arm around her waist, resting my hand on the small of her back as I pulled her close to me. With our bodies nearly flush, we began our dance.

"So, little warrior," I said into her ear over the music playing so close. "What brings you to my castle tonight? Because I know you're not here just to chat and dance."

I felt the way her breathing hitched at my accusation while in such an intimate position. My zirilium pounded through my veins, but I did my best to block it out. Nobody there besides Hugo knew I even possessed any abilities—and I intended to keep it that way.

Besides, I had to focus.

I needed to know why she was there.

She drew her head back to meet my eyes, her expression showing a hint of the surprise she must have felt. Her grip on my hand faltered, but I held on tight.

"How—"

"You're not as slick as you may think you are," I offered, not deigning to explain further, though I could only assume she'd come here with bad intentions.

As we spoke, we moved in time with the music, performing one of many traditional Northern dances. To my surprise, Valenia knew every step to take and did so at the exact right moment. Whoever she was, she was impressive.

I spun her, our arms outstretched, before pulling her back to me, forcing our bodies flush against one another again.

"Alright," she responded, ever so slightly breathless. "You've caught me. Now what?"

"Now, you have a choice to make." I dipped her as the melody called for, arching her back away from me while keeping what parts of us I could pressed together.

Once I'd pulled her up in one elegant move, she met my gaze and arched an eyebrow—a question without having spoken.

"You can abandon your old life, including whatever brought you on your mission here tonight, and tell me everything you know while serving at my side..." I took a breath, letting the weight of my words sink into her. The type of dedication I was asking for.

"Or?" she pushed, continuing to step and move in perfect rhythm with me and the song.

Dipping my head so my lips barely brushed the shell of her ear as they moved, I purred, "Or, I can out you right here, right now. Don't worry, I appreciate your confidence—I'd tell them to make it a swift death. You wouldn't even get to see the inside of Gatlyn Castle's dungeons."

I smiled as I felt her shoulders stiffen ever so slightly—the only reaction I noticed, besides the defeated, angry glint in her eyes when I pulled away.

The song tapered off as the melody came to an end in a single, drawn-out note.

"So?" I inquired softly a heartbeat after the song ended, the crowd clapping all around us.

I watched, fascinated, as she subtly studied her surroundings. When she finally seemed to realize just how badly she'd failed whatever her mission might have been, she sighed heavily.

Then she kneeled.

She looked up at me expectantly, although I had been bargaining on having to watch her die tonight.

When I cleared my throat loudly, what little of the crowd's attention that wasn't already on us shifted our way at the sound.

Choosing my wording for this next part carefully, I finally spoke.

"Do you, Valenia of the North, vow to serve me for the remainder of your days and protect me with your life, until one of us returns to the Stars?"

If I was to keep an eye on this beautiful stranger, this was the best way to do it. She'd be vowed to me, unable to harm me, and she'd always be nearby.

For that reassurance, I could drown out the sound of my doubts and anxieties.

Valenia, whose shoulders had been squared back and her dress elegantly pooled on the floor around her, responded strongly and with that unwavering confidence I knew I could mold. "Yes, my king. I vow this."

I smirked as I listened to her speak. It seemed the old tradition of vows was still well known, as gasps and chatter rang out from the crowd. That, and the old standard of not having females in a place of power.

"Then rise, and take your place as my Right Hand," I commanded.

The female kneeling before me bowed her head before rising to her feet and taking her place by my side.

Now, she was *mine*. If she were to ever break her vow, it was death on sight—no questions asked—by the hands of any Northerner that could get their hands on her. Only the ruler of the North could excuse her—and we both knew I wasn't doing that.

Though I felt sure it wouldn't come to that.

"Anybody who needs to speak to me now goes through Valenia of the North first. She shall be as my spoken word and my action." I looked out at the disgruntled, enraged faces in the crowd. "And if anybody believes they'd be a better fit for her position, please, feel free to try and take it from her."

Chapter Sixteen

"We should be right about... here," Laurence said, pointing toward a spot on the map before us, his finger resting on the outskirts of the northern part of Wittuck Woods. The Northern border patrols had lessened slightly, but we'd still decided as a group to pair up and shadow wield across while it was dark out—just in case. The section of the forest we stood in was across the border that separated the North from the South.

A border that I had—once again—crossed.

Sometimes I found it difficult to believe that I had, at one time, never wanted to leave Hollis. I'd still only seen a portion of our world so far, and yet I couldn't imagine going back to having such a narrow view of life and our realm as a whole.

"We're almost to our rendezvous point," Rayven added, motioning to a small dot just above Laurence's finger that signified where we would be setting up our collective group meeting place.

We'd left Cairnyl about a day ago. Quinn had stayed behind to care for Ezra—with very detailed instructions from Chess, of course. Besides Quinn and Ezra, we were also missing Teagan, who had stayed behind to not only keep an eye on Margo, but to hold down the fort while the rest of us were away.

The remainder of us—Callum, Caelia, Rayven, Matea, Chess, Laurence, Byn, and myself—were going to find our own clues about our missing fae.

No matter what it took.

Just then, a dark form flew out of the shadows of the thinning trees, heading straight toward our group.

We all looked up from the map we'd spread out on the soft grass toward the shadow, watching as Caelia took on her physical form.

She got back from scouting the path ahead super fast, I thought.

"You were *all* incorrect," she said matter-of-factly. "We're closer than you all thought. The spot we're heading towards is straight ahead, not even a ten-minute walk."

Laurence and Rayven turned to look at each other, looking sheepish, before Rayven cleared his throat and folded the map.

"Lead the way," the spy said to Caelia.

Caelia, whose hands rested on her hips, smiled, revealing a false level of innocence before melting back into the shadows and leading the way.

I shook my head, but couldn't help the small smile that played on my lips as I felt Byn drawing nearer. A moment later, my hand was in his, and our large posse was racing to keep up with Caelia, who suddenly seemed to think it would be funny to travel as fast as she could.

"How's the wing feeling?" Byn asked as we cleared a fallen tree.

Flexing both wings equally, I responded, "Good as new. Chess would have chewed me *and* you out by now if it was anything less than. We both know how strict his herbal routine has been."

Byn chuckled, then looked toward the blond male up ahead, who was doing his best to keep up with the crowd, even though his multiple trokav kits seemed to weigh him down.

It had surprised me when the trokav had insisted on joining us on these scouting missions. While he could fend for himself, Chess was a creature of kindness and empathy; if it came down to it and we were caught, I wasn't sure he could do what it took to get himself out alive.

I believed he felt some level of guilt for not being there sooner for Ezra. I wished to the Stars nobody got harmed that badly on these missions, but Chess seemed to be taking no chances.

I found that I admired him for it.

Soon enough, our group reached the small, hidden opening in the side of a short rock wall. The terrain had become more and more rocky as we'd walked farther North—closer to the Salic Mountains. That worked in our favor, though, because we could set up camp in caves like the one we'd just walked into.

That specific cave, still being a part of the edges of the forest, had a plush, moss-covered floor and some sort of winding vines running all over the ceiling and walls. A small trickle of water could be heard from somewhere within, making the air warm and wet. And if one really searched, the roots from the trees outside could be seen in between the vines overhead.

Callum whistled at the sight, then said softly, "Maybe I will miss the continent just a little, once all is said and done."

"I won't," Caelia, his sister, said without missing a beat.

Rolling my eyes, I walked toward one of the far crevices in the rock, setting my bag down.

"Alright," Byn said, after placing his pack next to mine. "Let's go over this one more time."

"We've already gone over this six times," Caelia groaned.

I watched as Callum snapped at his sister, causing her to quickly clench her jaw shut.

"We *do* remember, my king," Laurence stated reassuringly.

Chess, seemingly wanting to prove himself, added, "We'll break off into pairs to scout out Acrynd, and if we find nothing there, we'll break off into two groups from here. One will go to Neokell, and the other to Jackton."

"And what's the most important part?" Byn asked, looking out across our small group.

"Do *not* engage. We have no backup, and we have no idea what we'll be walking into. We're here to scout, study, and report back. Nothing more," Matea spoke up.

Byn nodded. "Correct."

Matea met my gaze and winked playfully, obviously proud of herself. I couldn't help but smile in return.

"Alright then," I said, clasping my hands in front of myself. "Let's break off into pairs. Remember, make sure at least one of you has shadow zirilium."

The group began dividing themselves up, Callum heading over to Laurence and clasping forearms. I wanted to watch to see who would be paired with who, but Matea's form blocked my view as she marched over to Byn and me.

"If I get stuck with *him*," she pointed toward Rayven, "I'm going to start screaming."

I met her gaze and, realizing she was completely serious, I didn't know if I should laugh or scold her.

In the end, I simply sighed and shook my head. "You and I can go together—on one condition," I said, holding up a hand.

"Anything."

"I get to give you a nickname. More specifically, Matty," I offered.

"No," she said, her voice an octave higher than usual. "Anything but a stupid nickname."

Now, I couldn't help but laugh at how easy it was to get under her skin.

"She's paired with me, anyway," Byn said, having been watching our conversation play out.

"I'll start screaming in three... two..."

"Alright, alright!" I laughed. "Byn, I'm sure Rayven would be more than happy to have you."

My husband sighed dramatically, slumped his shoulders, and looked at me with puppy eyes I had previously thought only Margo could pull off.

In response, I hopped up onto my tiptoes and pressed my lips to his. I felt as his emotions swelled at the contact, but just as he reached for me to pull me closer, I stepped back.

"Later, Thorntier," I reassured him when a playfully hurt expression passed over his features.

And with that, we headed out, stepping further and further into enemy territory.

***

Everything was dirty.

It was like a perpetual layer of either mud or dirt covered every surface in that part of Acrynd. The city itself was much closer to sea level than Genisyn had been, resulting in more storms rolling in off the Anvali Ocean to the east. Because of these extra storms, it seemed as though the packed earth underfoot never fully dried out—meaning mud and dirt everywhere.

Fortunately, I had seen earlier that only the sector of Acrynd that Matea and I had been assigned to was like that. It seemed we drew the short end of the stick, having to once again explore the poverty-stricken area of the city.

Matea and I had already been there for about two hours, slinking from shadow to shadow, determined to remain unseen.

We were simply observers.

That was, until somebody caught my eye.

"You *don't* understand—I need that lead!"

I tugged on Matea, our shadow forms linked, pulling her to a stop at the mouth of a dark alleyway. The space was full of overflowing trashcans, and unsurprisingly, more mud and dirt. Piles of it, oddly enough—as though somebody had tried to clear a nearby path and left the remains in that alley.

"I understand well enough. You can't pay for what you *claim* to need, so I shall give it to the next highest bidder."

Moving closer, I could make out that the fae who had just spoken was a fairly short, older male with hair the same color as the mud below—and wings to match.

But in front of him was the female in distress.

She wore a scarlet cloak with the hood pulled back to reveal lovely, deep blue eyes and short hair that was a soft, nutty brown. She was built like a fighter, and by the way her hands were slowly clenching into fists, I knew that to be true.

"I have to find him," she said sternly, then weakly added, "He's all I have left."

I watched as the male's face softened a degree. Then he sighed.

"Remind me again what happened."

"I had been... away. I shouldn't have left him to fend for himself in Hollis, but I needed to take the job—we needed the money. By the time I came back, he was gone, and all of our stuff had been moved out or thrown away. I asked our neighbor what happened, and she said he'd gotten into trouble with the guards. That they'd had enough of him, and had taken him to the camps. The *camps*! He's only *ten*!" Her voice grew louder with each word she spoke, her panic and concern so genuine it hurt to listen to.

"Quiet down, would you?" The male pinched the bridge of his nose. "I can give this to you, but you owe me one. And I *mean* it this time."

The female began nodding and softly thanking him repeatedly.

"I... got a new job, so I might not be as easy to find. But when you need me, you'll know how to get ahold of me," she stated after taking a small group of folded papers from him.

"*Bah!* I've always known how to find you. Now, if you're done blubbering, I have to be home for dinner," he said to her. There seemed to be a deep level of familiarity between the two of them, which struck me as odd.

They shook hands, said their goodbyes, and then the male departed. Walking out of the alley after making sure the coast was clear, he breezed right past Matea and me.

Before Matea could try to stop me, I shot forward towards the female, making my form smaller to not be as noticeable as I moved. I tried my best to catch a glimpse of what the contents of the papers held, but I couldn't seem to get a good look.

Something deep inside told me I needed to know. I didn't know if it was my unending curiosity, or a small push from the Stars, but I knew in that moment that I needed to find out.

After all, each life was like a string of silk, and together, the people of Inphis made up a giant web—paths overlapping, intertwining, and all of it for a reason.

Maybe that was my string overlapping with the string of the female's before me.

That was what I told myself, anyway, as I stepped out of the shadows and stood directly behind the female, Matea seething at me from within the safety of my shadow.

"Hello there," I said calmly, trying not to startle her.

It didn't work.

She nearly jumped out of her skin, spinning on her heel and immediately throwing a punch straight at my face.

I ducked and shifted over a step swiftly, holding my hands up in surrender. "I just want to talk."

She looked shocked that I had evaded her attack, taking a step back as she clutched the papers close to her chest.

"I heard everything," I started, speaking quietly. "And I want to help, if I can. But I have questions first."

"Who are *you* to help *me?*" the female questioned.

"A powerful ally, if you'd have me." I conjured a small ball of fire to my palm and watched as her eyes grew at the sight. I knew she had seen my wings and had assumed me a Northerner. Now, I met her gaze, letting her see with my abilities and my eyes that I was not *just* Northern.

"You're—you're like *him*," she stammered. "The king, I mean. There have been rumors of his abilities. And considering your complexion... you're our lost princess."

"Queen of the South of Inphis, now. But yes, I was once Princess of the North," I clarified, trying not to let the mention of my old life sting. "Now, can I ask those questions or not?"

She nodded slightly, seemingly unable to speak.

"Great. Who are you so concerned about?"

"My nephew. He's the only family I have left and... I didn't do a good enough job in taking care of him." She hung her head.

"I'm sorry," I offered genuinely. "What are *the camps* you mentioned before?"

At that, her head snapped up. "You don't know?"

I shook my head and motioned for her to continue.

"More rumors, I suppose, but I swear there's more to it than that. They say that's where they send people that are too much trouble to deal with, or that they need to simply get rid of. People just... *vanish* nowadays. No trace left behind—and trust me, I've checked. The thing is, we don't know exactly where it is. Or the people who do either aren't alive to talk about it, or are so loyal to the crown that they'd die before they spill the crown's secrets."

My mind whirled with the possibilities.

That had to have been Father's doing—if not generations before him, even. Especially considering how far back our records went when it came to missing fae.

But why would Dimitri still be letting this go on if he knew about it?

Because he isn't the same brother you knew, a small voice whispered in my mind.

Shaking my head to clear the voice, I asked, "Are these papers a lead? Or a clue? I'm... looking for these camps, too. It's why I'm here, even though I shouldn't be."

The female clutched the papers tighter, gazing into my eyes as though she could peer right into my soul—and I let her. I wanted her to help us willingly. I wanted her trust. Besides, there was a kid at risk here, too. One that was not much older than Margo.

Slowly, she released her grip on the papers and held them out to me.

"They're makeshift maps, I think. And one is, I believe, a rough sketch of part of the place. I was hoping to be able to pinpoint the location from it, and put the map together enough to be able to use it to guide me in and out. But... I'm sure you heard I took on a new job recently. It requires me to be in Hollis, and I can't spend all of my time investigating anymore."

She paused as she watched me flip through the papers. She was right—there was a sketch along with seven other papers with vague markings, but just enough detail to try to piece them together to make one big picture, maybe.

"The Stars led you to me today," she said suddenly, and looking into her face, I could tell she believed it with her whole being.

Like she *needed* to believe it.

Like she needed to believe in *something*.

Anything.

My heart ached for her.

"Please, if you're looking for the camps anyway... *please*. Find my nephew. Take him back to the South with you, *anything*. Just find him and keep him safe until I can make it to him." Her eyes were welling with tears. She'd drawn closer, and her expression was so incredibly open, it almost hurt to look at her. Her anxiety, concern, self-doubt, disappointment, and guilt. She looked as though it was so much to bear, it would make her sick at any moment.

She'd lost her nephew.

And I'd lost my brother.

Despite our differing circumstances, I understood her.

I shifted to face her fully and pulled the female into a tight embrace. She stalled, as though not accustomed to being touched. But within seconds, she gripped me back, just as ferociously. Her chest shook with a single sob before she seemed to hold it all in again—another female forced to remain strong when facing extreme difficulty.

"I'll find him. I promise he'll be well taken care of," I said softly.

We pulled back, putting distance between us, before her mouth opened, seeming to remember something. She produced a tiny, well-loved portrait on soft paper of who I could only assume was her nephew. The small boy had black wings—differing from her medium gray ones—and black hair, but bright eyes. I couldn't help but notice that one of his wings hung lower than the other. At the bottom, the name *Kaison* was written.

"This is him?" I asked. "Kaison?"

"My Kai." She nodded, then held it out toward me. "Take it. It's the only way he'll know I sent you, and to trust you."

"I couldn't—"

The female grabbed my hand, swiftly placing the now folded portrait in my palm and curling my hand into a fist.

"Please," she nearly begged.

I met her eyes again and could see the determination and hope that shone there now.

I nodded.

"Thank you," she breathed, her relief palpable. "I have to go. I must get back to Hollis as soon as possible."

I watched as she headed toward the mouth of the alleyway.

"Wait!" I called out, causing her to pause. "What is your name?"

She poked her head around the corner of the rundown building to her right, checking to make sure the coast was clear for her to slip away.

But before she did, she looked back at me one more time to answer my question.

“Valenia.”

Chapter Seventeen

By the time Matea and I slinked through the opening of the rock face and into the cave we'd set up camp in, night had fallen.

The moment our shadow forms entered the cave, Byn's head snapped our way, his eyes scanning the darkness. He couldn't sense shadows like some of the others could through their zirilium, but he could sense *me*. Rayven, who he'd been speaking to, also looked our way a moment before we materialized.

Byn started walking our way immediately, but I noticed Rayven looking over not just me to see if I was unharmed, but Matea too, his eyes lingering on her.

I tucked that small bit of information away.

"Are you alright?" Byn questioned as he approached. Once I confirmed I was, he looked toward Matea. "And you?"

"Me?" Matea asked, a hint of surprise in her tone.

"Yes, you. You are, technically, family, after all." Byn smiled softly, his dimple popping.

Matea returned his smile with a timid one of her own before nodding. "Yes, I'm well, too. But you should talk to your wife about making better decisions."

With that, she walked deeper into the cave, looking back at me only to wink.

I groaned and quickly added, "I couldn't help it!"

Byn quirked an eyebrow. Then, seeing my helpless expression, shook his head. "Come on," he sighed. "Let's make this easier by having you tell everybody at once."

I hung my head dramatically, following behind my husband as we headed toward the center of the space and the group slowly gathered around.

For the next half hour, Matea and I sat in the middle of the gathered group and relayed what had happened and what we had found—moment by moment. I even pulled out the papers and laid them out before everybody, in the order I assumed they'd gone.

The only thing I left out was Valenia's name, and the fact that I had promised to help find her nephew. The portrait of Kai sat in my internal cloak pocket, its weight heavier than the earth I wielded.

Once the group was up to speed on what had taken place, I let Matea answer questions they had as I grabbed Byn's hand and discretely broke apart from them. Byn didn't question what I was doing—he simply allowed me to guide him.

Moments later, we were outside in a small clearing within the sparse forest around us, only a short walk away from camp.

"I didn't tell the group everything," I admitted after dropping his hand and walking a few paces forward, beginning to pace.

"I know," Byn said, gently tugging me to a stop by my shoulders and facing me to look at him. "Tell me," he encouraged.

I let out a shaky breath, the weight of what I had promised to a near stranger feeling like a boulder resting on my chest.

"The female I mentioned—we talked more than I let on. Her name is Valenia, and she *did* have her own reasons for obtaining those leads. She believes that when we find the encampment, we'll find her missing nephew—Kaison." I paused, my hands beginning to shake. "I promised her I'd find him. That I'd take care of him for her until she could get to him."

I watched as Byn's eyes widened as his mind whirled with what this meant, and the weight he must've now understood that I felt.

Gently, he took my shaking hands into his.

"Together, Avi. We do this together. *We* will find Kaison, and *we* will keep him safe until we can reunite him with Valenia," he reassured me.

"You're... not upset?"

"We are already looking for the camps—what's one more task?" He smirked, his dimple making an appearance and his calmness helping to ease my anxiety.

"You make it sound so easy," I stated, standing on my toes to place a kiss on his dimpled cheek.

"Anything is easy if we take it one step at a time and do it together," he responded, his hand coming up to grip my jaw and throat.

He tilted my head back, grazing his lips against mine as he said, "Your empathy is a strength, my love. Use it like one."

Unable to help myself, I lifted myself higher, pressing not just my lips to his, but our bodies together. He let out a small breathy sound at the contact—a sound I wanted to hear again.

And again.

And *again.*

By the time we made it back to camp to instruct the group on our next moves, my lips were swollen with kisses, and Byn's hair was heavily mused.

And both of our eyes shone brightly with the love we held for each other.

How this overwhelming amount of love can fit inside of my physical body, I thought as I gazed sideways at my husband, *I do not know.*

***

The first half of our group left the night before us; they'd needed the extra time to get a head start on their journey to Jackton. It had taken a little time to sort out, but in the end, the Ocrein royal siblings, Callum and Caelia, headed to Jackton along with Chess and Rayven. Jackton, which was situated on the farthest northeast corner of Inphis, was about a day's journey from our rendezvous point outside of Acrynd, while my group—Byn, myself, Matea, and Laurence—was heading to Neokell.

We had agreed to meet back at the lush cave in roughly three days' time.

North and slightly west of Acrynd, Neokell sat higher up than Acrynd, but lower than Genisyn when it came to elevation. I'd seen artist's renditions of all the other cities of the North in books growing up, so I knew when we arrived roughly what to expect—rocky terrain with a city nestled against the mountains.

After traveling the day before, then resting at our latest hiding spot, we'd finally made it.

But despite all I had tried to prepare myself for, what I did not expect was the *smell*.

I couldn't pinpoint exactly what it was coming from, whether it was simply the city or terrain or something more, but each time the wind blew, it brought gusts of foul air to throw us off guard.

We would not let it.

We ended up using our cloaks to help shield the lower portions of our faces as we had walked the last stretch toward the outskirts of the city. We'd then set up our meeting point and split into pairs once again to scout and see if we could find any leads. Needing a shadow wielder per pair, I brought Byn with me while Matea took Laurence. My sister and guard both had such stern expressions before they dissipated into shadows, I worried for anybody they happened to run into.

Now, we'd all been scouring the nooks and crannies of the mountain city, all without finding a thing.

We'd found nothing, and the sky had grown dark.

We had lost an entire day—and for *naught*.

Frustrated, I shadow wielded Byn and myself to the top of a high building, only letting go and materializing us once we were safely in the middle of the roof.

"*Ugh!*" I groaned, my emotions beginning to sizzle in my veins, courtesy of my zirilium.

"I know it's upsetting not to find anything, but maybe Rayven and Callum found something over at Jackton. Maybe they aren't here, Avi." Byn's voice carried just a hint of sadness, and I could feel that he was disappointed, too.

"It's just... what am I if I can't do this one task? I couldn't help my own people. I thought maybe I'd redeem myself by finding yours, but..." I trailed off as I slowly slumped to the ground, my wings splaying out behind me on the rooftop.

Byn came to kneel next to me, gently cupping both sides of my face to get me to look at him.

"They're both *our* people now, Avi. And we haven't failed yet."

Drawing strength from his confidence in us, I took a deep breath.

It was time to start over.

Pulling out the papers Valenia had given me, I laid them all out in random order—minus the sketch, which I handed to Byn. The sketch had been of what I assumed was the inside of the encampment, showing a handful of buildings and structures, which would only be helpful *after* we found its location.

On the papers, the only contents consisted of lines and dots. I didn't quite understand—until I did.

I had been giving my eyes a break from looking at the confusing papers when it hit. "Wait..." I murmured. Byn stayed silent, letting me think without interruption.

Tilting my head further up, I stared at the Stars overhead.

I'd looked at these pages more times than I cared to admit, but it didn't click until that moment as I gazed at the Stars.

That was the key. The *Stars*.

"Byn!" I said suddenly, excitement in my voice. "That's it!"

"What's it?"

"The Stars! That's what we've been missing! Every time before when I looked at these sheets, we were either in a cave, under trees, or it was daytime. But do you see—" I pointed to a small cluster of dots on the page closest to me, "these?"

"The dots? Yes, I see them."

"They line up with the Stars! Look, this one is the dove, right there." I pointed to a group of the Stars to the east that followed the same pattern as the dots on the page.

"And this one..." I carried on, unable to stop now that I'd begun. "This one is the vine, and—look! The griffin! They all match!"

I frantically rearranged the sheets of paper in front of me, matching them to reflect the constellations overhead. As I did, the lines came together to vaguely make up a sketch.

A sketch I had an idea about—but one I wasn't sure about just yet.

"I'll be right back," I said, hopping to my feet and leaping into the air.

Byn caught my hand before I could fly off without a second thought. I whipped my head around to look at him, only to watch him press his lips to my knuckles.

"Be careful," he advised, then released his grip on me.

I stalled a moment, wishing I had Eden here with us so he, too, could see what I was *so* confident I was about to.

I nodded to him, then shot straight up into the sky.

Taking my husband's advice, I covered my form in shadows but remained solid. If anything, I would look like a blur or a trick of the light to anybody below.

When I got high enough in the air, I pumped my wings at the perfect pace to hold me steady. I tried not to relish too much in the feeling of the wind in my hair and feathers again as I looked down at the city of Neokell.

And a spark of hope lit up inside of me.

The shape of Neokell's city borders almost perfectly matched that of the lines on the papers.

And there just so happened to be an outlier on those papers.

One I was willing to bet was put there for a reason.

Within a moment, I was landing on the edge of the roof and rushing toward Byn. Kneeling next to him in front of the papers, I pointed to the outlier.

"They're here. I'm sure of it."

"It could just be a random marking, but it doesn't hurt to go check it out. We've already come this far, after all." Byn rested his hand on my shoulder and squeezed. I could feel his pride for me radiating through my body.

"On Laurence's map, that outlier is roughly where the old Northern mineshaft is. Maybe it's not a coincidence." I tugged a small piece of charcoal out of a small bag on my hip. Using it, I marked the papers, so I'd be able to place them in order again promptly if needed.

"We need to find—" I was interrupted by a shadow spearing towards us from the far corner of the roof.

A moment later, Matea appeared a few feet away, holding up a sick-looking Laurence.

"Where have you two been? We waited at our spot for over an hour. There's nothing here," Matea stated.

Laurence groaned as he slumped to the ground, his hand clutching his stomach.

"Oh, stop being dramatic, old male. Shadow travel isn't *that* bad." Matea rolled her eyes.

"I beg to differ, my lady," Laurence panted.

"Is he—" I started to question, only for Matea to say quickly, "He'll get used to it."

I patted my friend on the shoulder, then tugged on Matea until she was sitting beside me before the map of papers.

"There's nothing here because they aren't *in* the city. They're *outside* of it, hidden in the mountains," I explained.

The next few moments were consumed by catching Matea and Laurence up on my discoveries and theories. By the time we were ready to head out toward the southwest—the direction the map's outlier was in—Laurence, fortunately, no longer felt like getting sick.

I felt guilty for asking him to travel by shadows once again, but it became necessary the further southwest we traveled. The amount of Northern soldiers subtly patrolling the forested area only solidified my confidence.

We had found them.

I was sure of it.

The smell from before had returned full force by the time a giant stone wall came into view through the sparse trees. No matter what we did, the smell invaded our senses. But with the wall in sight, I could hardly care about the stench.

That had to be it.

The wall was made up of giant pieces of the surrounding mountains, with wood and metal spikes at the top, and it seemed like smaller versions of those metal spikes stuck out of the sides like small thorns. Every so often, there were towers built into the wall, making up what I assumed were watchtowers.

Oddly enough, though, the closer we got to the dark wall, the weaker I felt. My connection to my zirilium seemed to wane, and in the short seconds we'd been in our solid forms, it seemed like even the sun and moon stones adorning my gloved hands weren't glowing as brightly.

Soon, I couldn't hold Byn and myself in shadows any longer. Pausing in the thin forest's darkness, not far off from the wall, I dropped my connection with my zirilium.

"Something's wrong," I panted. "I can't hold the connection any longer."

Matea and Laurence stepped out of the shadows a heartbeat later, Matea looking rattled with a furrowed brow, and Laurence a sickly shade of green.

Byn held out his hand, and a small spark lit in his palm as quickly as it went out.

"Something is blocking our zirilium," Matea observed, saying aloud what I had been too scared to.

Curiously, I tried to redirect the soft breeze that had just graced my face toward Laurence, hoping it would work and make him feel slightly better.

To my disappointment and confusion, that didn't seem to work, either.

"Whatever it is, it's affecting my Northern zirilium, too," I noted, reaching for my Northern abilities within me and feeling them weakly pulsing within me.

Just like my Southern abilities.

If there hadn't been so much riding on the four of us in that moment, I'd likely have begun panicking.

Byn shook his head, obviously trying to refocus our efforts.

"Alright. We still have to find a way onto that wall, at the least. We need to make sure we're in the right place," Byn said—ever the logical ruler. "Any ideas?"

"Check for weak points," Laurence groaned softly, "in the wall."

"Good thinking." Byn nodded, then tilted his head as if considering something.

"What is it?" I questioned quietly.

"I think you two," he looked toward Matea and Laurence before us, "should stay here. We're less likely to be spotted or caught if there's not as many of us slinking around."

"Respectfully, my king, we shouldn't be sending both of our royals off, either. Let me accompany my queen," Laurence suggested, though he was still struggling to regain his composure.

"He's right," Matea sighed. "But it should be me and Aviva. Aviva found this place, and she has the most zirilium, so maybe she'll be able to find a weak point easier than the rest of us could."

"And why should it be her and *you?*" Byn raised an eyebrow in question.

Matea looked at Laurence, whose complexion was still green. Then she looked back to Byn—to his temples, where his casual circlet usually sat.

Byn, having followed her gaze to both and gave the impression he understood, seemed to deflate slightly.

Matea didn't even need to utter a word to get her point across.

Byn's hand found mine in the dark and squeezed, causing me to look over and meet his gaze. I focused on our emotions within me and tried to imagine wrapping my confidence in my assignment around his anxiety.

A small smile played on his lips and I knew he could feel the difference, especially as his anxiety seemed to fade ever so slightly.

"Be careful," Byn said to me for the second time tonight. "And remember you only have a couple hours until sunrise."

I nodded once, steeling myself as I stood from our place on the ground to take my place next to Matea.

After checking on Laurence briefly, Matea and I began our trek around the wall.

***

"Maybe we should head back to where we saw that weird bug."

"There's got to be a weaker point than that somewhere," I replied to my sister in a whisper.

We'd already spent the better part of an hour—maybe two, for all I knew—creeping around the perimeter. We had to stop more often than we'd liked due to passing patrols, but progress had been made.

I had felt a small surge in my zirilium near an iridescent beetle we'd seen, but it didn't seem like enough of a surge to make use of the spot.

"But if we don't find one, we've wasted all this time," Matea argued.

"I understand the risks, *Matty*," I teased, but I couldn't hide the sharp edge in my voice that displayed how serious I knew the situation was.

We continued walking in silence. One of my hands made contact with the wall at all times, dodging the metal spikes that threatened to make me bleed every few steps. Fortunately, I *could* avoid them, thanks to my Northern ability to see better in the dark. Matea walked on my other side, doing her best to keep an eye out not only on the trees and mountain-scape surrounding us, but on the wall and in the sky above us.

A few times, we'd had to duck for cover when a patrolling soldier walked across the top of the wall, or flew overhead.

Each one we'd seen had been armed as though they were ready for a battle to break out at any given moment.

Part of me didn't doubt they were.

I focused intensely on the way my zirilium felt within my veins with every step I took.

"I really think we should go back to—" Matea started, but was interrupted as I shushed her, coming to a pause.

Looking up at the wall, I realized we were standing below the largest watchtower built into the structure that I'd seen thus far. With that, there were larger supports to ensure the watchtower would remain upright on the rocky, uneven terrain.

Which meant less room for the odd metal spikes that dotted the outside of the wall.

For whatever reason, that area with less metal sticking out of the wall seemed to make my zirilium surge in strength. It wasn't like my usual flow of power, but it also wasn't *nothing*.

"Here," I breathed, ushering Matea over. That was when I realized the sky had lightened just a shade or two.

Before she could take more than a step forward, we heard wing beats in the distance.

Then nearby.

And soon, all above us.

We sprinted towards the closest copse of trees, taking cover as dozens upon dozens of Northern soldiers and guards flew over the wall and out of view. These were likely all the ones we'd seen around the area—along with the ones we *hadn't* seen.

They all wore the same navy material, and all had multiple weapons strapped to them in various places.

But were they working to keep fae in, or keep them out?

Or worse—both?

"It must be shift change, with dawn coming so soon," Matea observed.

I nodded my agreement, taking a step toward the wall again once I could no longer hear wing beats coming from the other side.

Matea tugged me backwards, whisper yelling, "What are you doing? We need to go back!"

Shocked, I pulled free of her grip, turning back to face her.

My expression must have been more angry than shocked, though, because the realization of who she was talking to seemed to pass over Matea's face.

"I am not leaving here without confirmation," I said through clenched teeth.

Approaching the structure again, I placed my hands on the stone before me and reached my power out, feeling what I could with any zirilium that would respond.

To my surprise, it felt as though they were all reaching for me, too. Like they were trying to remind me that they were still there—still with me.

I picked earth wielding first and used it to check our surroundings without moving a muscle. It was like I could sense not only the earth below, but anything touching it or made of it. I could feel the vibrations of the winged fae landing on the ground inside the wall, as well as the *lack* of vibrations within the watchtower above.

Gasping as I dropped the connection, I turned towards my sister, who had drawn closer.

"Now," I said urgently. "We can shadow wield up the watchtower, but we have to go *now*."

A look of uncertainty passed over her face, but quickly vanished.

"Alright," she responded. "I'm trusting you."

Without warning, she grabbed my shoulder and suddenly, we were dissipating into what almost felt like nothingness. Within seconds, we were slinking up the crevices of the watchtower, using the still semi-dark sky to our advantage.

After a swift check of the top of the watchtower, we stood in the middle and materialized.

As I lifted my head to look inside at what the North was so *desperately* trying to hide, I felt as though the breath had been knocked out of me.

Stumbling toward the edge, I couldn't believe my eyes.

That was most definitely the place we had been looking for. *Encampments* didn't seem like a harsh enough word for what I was seeing, though.

I watched as navy-clothed figures walked into wood and stone structures—which I could only assume were where the captive fae were being held. But it seemed they didn't have enough room inside, since there were also countless groups of prisoners huddled together outside. More blue soldiers rallied those groups, too. Every captive wore shackles or cuffs and was being roughly tugged to their feet or outside of the buildings before the sun could even rise. They all seemed to know the drill, though, as they filed themselves into lines and began heading up a gravel trail into the mountains.

But why...

I gasped as it dawned on me.

This wasn't just an encampment for prisoners.

This was a labor camp.

A small commotion drew my eyes back to one of the nearest houses—if you could call it that.

Then I fell to my knees as I watched the soldiers drag children out of the grasps of their parents and put them in a separate line from the adults.

Tears flooded my eyes, and without realizing, I felt my wings spreading, as though I was preparing to leap into the skies.

Matea quickly wrapped her arms around me, tugging me back down to my knees.

"We have to go, Viva."

A sob tried its best to claw its way up my throat, but I swallowed it down harshly.

"We have to *do* something," I reasoned, my voice hoarse.

"We'll be back for them," Matea promised. Our eyes were both on the line forming of children—children with and without wings. Northerners and Southerners alike.

"Each and every one of them," I swore, looking up toward the Stars as I spoke.

I'd tear the Stars from the sky if that was what it took to rescue these fae.

I'd tear *myself* apart if that was what it took to succeed.

Chapter Eighteen

The pain hummed through every fiber of my being.

The zirilium I still couldn't control very well wanted—no, *demanded*—an out.

I didn't have much time left.

For better or worse, the putrid smell surrounding the outskirts of Neokell finally hit my nose after flying since early that morning. I held back a gag, though part of me knew this was a good sign.

It meant we were close.

I'd only been here twice before with Father, but not a single detail could ever escape my mind.

Instead of the pain, I focused on the way Zaina's form moved under mine. Each beat of her wings, each inhale of breath matching my own. We'd always been synced like that—griffin and rider. And tonight, she seemed to understand my sense of urgency.

I just need to make it to the camps...

In the sky behind me, I could faintly hear Valenia and the griffin she supposedly *borrowed* from the royal stables, Dax. I had told her to stay behind, that going to the camps was something I'd needed to do alone, but alas—there she was, disobeying direct orders.

I had a feeling that wouldn't be the last time she would do so.

Once I noted the mountain peak that told me I'd arrived, I directed Zaina to dive—without warning Valenia. I could hear her shout from behind me, but the wind and sky swallowed up whatever she said as Ziana's black wings tucked in, our forms free falling together toward the earth below.

Just above the tree line, Ziana's wings flared out, halting our descent and carrying us forward, over the thick stone wall covered in spikes and into the heart of the encampment.

Fortunately, I'd remembered to have Hugo dose me with the alychite nullifier before I left Hollis. I'd only been there twice with Father, so the process wasn't all routine just yet. Valenia, who seemed to be taking her job as my Right Hand very seriously, had gotten a dose, too, since she almost never left my side. Thanks to that nullification, my zirilium still simmered in my veins—unlike the abilities of the prisoners kept inside the camps.

Ziana landed near the soldier's barracks, which was blessedly close to where the worst of the prisoners were held.

And that was exactly where I needed to be.

Handing Ziana's reins off to the closest guard, all of whom were standing straighter now that they'd seen who had just arrived, I headed for the dungeon doors.

The doors opened to a stairwell that went straight down into what would have been pure darkness if it weren't for the gift of Northern sight. I heard Valenia racing to catch up, and I looked back just as she was swinging the doors closed behind us. If I hadn't known better, I'd have said she looked rattled to be there.

"Move faster," I hissed to her, my veins and muscles feeling as though they were being burned from the inside out.

"My king?" a guard asked as we made it to the bottom of the stairs. I grit my teeth, my hands curling into fists at the sight of not one, but two soldiers down there.

From the corner of my eye, I caught Valenia looking my way. Seeming to somehow understand the pain I was in, and maybe even *why*, she straightened her spine and stepped forward.

"Dismissed, soldiers. Wait on the other side of the doors, up the stairs," she demanded, her voice assuming the authority I had bestowed upon her.

The two guards exchanged a glance, but when I didn't interfere or correct her, they obeyed. Slowly departing, I couldn't ignore the way they stole looks at me. Maybe I looked worse than I had assumed.

I bared my teeth in warning as they passed.

Once their steps quieted and we heard the echoes of the doors up top being firmly shut in place, I was on the move again, though in a more sluggish manner than I'd care to admit.

Valenia, taking initiative, headed straight for the doors the soldiers had been guarding and flung one open for me to cross into the dungeons. The smell was just as strong down there, but that was the least of my worries at that point. Most of the fae being held down there were huddled in the back of their cells, curled in on themselves, likely trying to stay warm. Torches were placed between cells, out of reach of prisoners, but the light glinted off the alychite cell bars in a way that had my temples throbbing.

I was almost out of time.

I came to a sudden stop, one that made my head spin, as a prisoner became brave enough to stick his leg out through the bars and into my path—all in an attempt to trip me up.

"Valenia," I said through gritted teeth, summoning her to my side with a single breath.

When she'd taken her position beside me, I motioned toward the prisoner to my left—the one that had tried to stumble me.

"Grab him and follow me."

She did as I ordered, quickly acquiring the keys to that cell and dragging the male by the dark alychite chains behind me.

By the time I made it to the end of the long hallway, I had nearly collapsed in on myself.

So close...

At the end of the corridor laid the torture chamber. When we stepped inside, the smell of old and fresh blood alike was so strong, the stench from before was barely noticeable. All six surfaces in the rectangular room were made of stone inlaid with alychite.

No wielder would be breaking out of there—not without the nullifier.

Behind me, I heard the door slam shut after Val and the prisoner—who was actively resisting and whimpering for mercy.

That word alone made me see red.

Valenia hooked the male up to the chains hanging from the ceiling, so that he stood on the tips of his toes, his arms stretched out above him.

He shook like a mouse—one that had just realized it was checkmated.

And if he was the mouse, then I supposed that made me the snake.

Unable to utter a word through the pain, I sunk into a crouch, my muscles spasming and limbs shaking. I was vaguely aware of Valenia attempting to check on me, but I sternly pointed to the door without a word.

And only when she finally left, only once it was just myself and my prey, did I let my hold on my zirilium loosen.

But in giving my abilities an inch, they swiftly pushed through the grip I'd thought I had on them. They burned through my body, starting at my core and down my limbs, until bright streams of fire erupted from me.

I could feel the flames lapping over every inch of me, though not a single hair on my body was singed. I could only imagine what I looked like.

I supposed I likely appeared as the sun—the same one who had cursed me with these *gifts* when the moon had neglected me altogether.

I didn't realize I was screaming until I couldn't anymore, and with that burst of energy having taken the edge of the pain off, I got to my feet and approached the prisoner—who seemed to have already soiled himself.

I didn't need blades of any kind tonight, like I had with Ezra.

No. Tonight, I would gain my control back, piece by piece.

No matter how many prisoners I had to burn my way through.

***

Their screams had been like a balm to my aching muscles.

Their begging had been like a bandage that held me together.

And their tears? Those had only fueled the power I felt simmering inside.

Four male prisoners laid in various parts of the chamber, their forms too still to mean anything other than death. The first prisoner looked, objectively, the worst—third-degree burns covered the entirety of his body. I'd barely touched him before the fire covering me had leaped to him—and engulfed him.

Compared to the three that had followed, his death had been swift.

He had begged for mercy, after all.

I sat there in the center of all my destruction, my white and silver wings wrapped around me as though they could block out the voices circling in my head.

I'd taken these prisoners' lives.

Four of them.

What was I becoming?

Stronger, a voice reflecting Father's echoed through my mind.

A monster, a voice that sounded—to my horror—like my twin's whispered in my thoughts.

"Shut up," I mumbled, digging the heel of my palm into my temple.

The pain and pressure to my head wasn't a large enough distraction, though, the words *monster* and *stronger* circling the inside my skull.

"*I* rule *you*," I reminded the voices that haunted me as I tugged on my hair.

These prisoners were Southern. They are thc enemy. They are evil. I didn't do anything wrong. I had to.

I repeated these five sentences in a soft whisper, over and over, until it was all I could hear echoing in my brain.

Slowly, I released my hands from my head and placed a palm on the floor. I couldn't seem to tap into the earth to bend it to my will just yet, but it didn't completely elude me, either.

I could feel Valenia pacing back and forth just outside of the door. I wasn't sure what her life had been like before vowing herself to me, but she seemed... sensitive.

It was something we'd have to work on.

After some long moments, she finally approached the door. She knocked as she cracked it open gently, keeping her eyes downcast. We both knew she'd seen what I'd done tonight. She had been the one to bring me the other three prisoners, after all.

"My king? Might I enter?" she requested, her mannerisms refusing to be shaken.

Gingerly, I folded my wings back against my body and nodded, not uttering a word. My throat was still a tad raw.

My Right Hand came and elegantly positioned herself on the floor next to me, not seeming to care about the drops of blood seeping into her maroon riding leathers, the silver accents reflecting the dim light in the room as the alychite bars had earlier that evening. She hadn't had time to change out of her riding attire once we'd arrived.

And she wouldn't have a chance anytime soon, either.

"How are you feeling now?" she questioned, her voice giving away none of the anxiety she must have felt in order to cause her to pace just a moment before.

My muscles, which no longer felt like they were being shredded from the inside out, flexed as I held my hands out in front of me. They were covered in blood from all four prisoners, along with ash and burned bits of... something.

Clenching my fists and relaxing them again, I looked up into her eyes when I responded.

"Powerful."

Using my zirilium felt... *enthralling*. Each time was better than the one before. It reminded me of training—how you built up endurance, muscles growing stronger after being used so often. Maybe zirilium was like that—a muscle that needed training.

Now that my abilities were within my control again, I couldn't have felt any better.

But as I remembered what I held in my coat pocket, I still wanted to try to beat that feeling.

And maybe solving one of my father's numerous mysteries would do that.

Tugging Father's journal out of my internal coat pocket, I cracked it open to the page I had folded the corner of. As I flipped through, I tried to do my best not to smear blood over any important bits. I could feel Valenia watching intensely, her curiosity seeming to peak.

"Here," I said, pointing to the entry labeled *prisoner fifty-one.* Running the finger with the least amount of blood on it over the page, I searched for the parts I had read before.

It mentioned that this prisoner had been special to Father, but not why. They had never been named, only numbered. To refresh my memory, I slid my eyes over the bottom half of the page.

That was where it noted that the prisoner was held in the tallest tower within the camp walls, held at the very top of the structure.

I slammed the book together suddenly, startling Valenia—who I realized with a start had been peering at the contents of the journal as well.

It was a good thing that she was vowed to me. Other wise, I'd have to kill her, too

Though, when the thought didn't bring me any type of positive emotion, I frowned. I barely knew her—was I already beginning to enjoy her company?

Or did she just remind me of the female I might have let slip through my grasp?

Shaking my head, I looked towards Valenia, who caught my gaze and quickly schooled her face into neutrality—but not before I saw her quizzical expression.

Deciding that I'd have to trust *somebody*, at least a little, I sighed. At least if I told Valenia, I knew she couldn't turn against me.

With those thoughts in mind, I decided to risk it.

"This is the late king's journal," I explained.

As I stood, my body feeling stronger than ever, I added, "Don't look inside of it again."

She nodded, hopping to her feet beside me. As her hair brushed her shoulder when she moved, I couldn't help but catch the scent of roses.

And I couldn't deny the spark of desire that lit up, hidden deep within.

"So, where's the tallest tower?" she asked, heading for the door and reaching for the handle.

"I said—"

"You said don't look inside *again*," she interrupted. "I had already seen that part."

I pinched the bridge of my nose as I sighed, knowing she had a valid point to argue with.

"Most of the towers are in the eastern part of the camp. We'll head that way. I don't want anybody else trying to direct us or to even know what we're looking for, understand?"

"Yes, Your Majesty," she said, her voice dripping with something I couldn't quite place.

She tugged the chamber door open as I approached. I lead the way to the doors at the other end of the hall.

Not a single prisoner tried to trip me that time.

Once we were on the other side of the dungeon doors, I noted a bucket which was catching drops of water that dripped down from the ceiling.

Walking over to it, I went to crouch down to wash the blood and bits off my hands. But before I could reach for it, the water moved unnaturally. Then, in a gentle stream, it was lifted out of the bucket.

My head snapped toward Valenia, who now had a hand raised and was directing the water stream through the air toward herself.

I watched as she coated her own hands in the water and stepped toward me, holding her hands out.

"May I?" she asked.

My mind flashed to another time, another moment in time where a female I had cared about did the same thing with water, for the same purpose—to cleanse.

Slowly, I held my hands out toward her, though they shook ever so slightly.

Using her own water-covered hands, she rinsed off the gunk from my skin. As my hands became cleaner, it appeared as though hers were becoming filthier.

Like she was taking my sins upon herself.

"You can trust me, you know," she offered gently without looking up from her task.

"That's still being proven," I said quietly—but there was no venom in my voice. No malice, no defensiveness.

If I was being honest, I wanted nothing more than to trust somebody again.

Yet each time I did, it seemed to come back to bite me.

And I refused to be the mouse.

With that thought alone, the walls I hadn't realized I'd been lowering went right back up.

I tugged my hands from hers, ignoring the small parts that hadn't come off, and cleared my throat, ignoring how startled she looked.

"We should go." I took a step backwards, toward the exit.

Valenia's expression, which had seemed open just a moment before, was carefully blank again. I watched as she funneled the now dirty water back into the bucket, her own hands just as clean as before.

As we headed up the stairs that lead outside, I couldn't help but think that maybe sins couldn't be transferred so easily.

It seemed my sins would be remaining my own, after all.

***

"Step aside."

Valenia had taken up her position in front of me, as though her smaller frame could hide mine from the gazes of the four guards that stood in front of the tower door.

The moon was to be setting soon, but after leaving the dungeons, we'd wasted no time flying up to the towers within the camp and figuring out which of them was the one we were searching for. So there we stood, so close to solving one of Father's big mysteries—yet we were being held up by *crids*.

"Who are you, that we should listen to your orders?" one of them spat—the one with light brown wings.

It appeared that Valenia had been appointed as my Right Hand so recently that the news hadn't spread to every corner of the North just yet. So until they understood who she was, I'd make sure they made no mistake in disrespecting her.

"She's *my* Right Hand," I said, placing my hand on Valenia's shoulder as I stepped up to stand to the left of her. "And she will have your respect, soldier."

All four of the males looked momentarily stunned, but they were well trained. They quickly moved out of the way, allowing us to approach the door.

When Valenia tried the door, though, she found it was locked.

I looked toward the male with the soft brown wings and raised an eyebrow in question.

"The... The late king didn't allow anybody inside. He said whoever was in there was too dangerous to ever see the full light of the moon again," he said, avoiding my gaze while he fidgeted anxiously with the keys.

"Are you trying to say that I, as the *current* King of the North, am not permitted inside? And that if I was, that *I* would be in danger?"

"No, Your Majesty, I just—"

"Hand me the keys." I held out my hand.

Within a heartbeat, the keys were in my palm.

The soldier's eyes widened as he noted the crusted blood on my skin.

Forcing myself not to roll my eyes at him, I tossed Valenia the keys without looking her way. When I heard her catch them and unlock the door, I gazed upon the four males before me.

"Let nobody else inside, *ever*, besides myself and my Right Hand. Make sure everybody that takes this shift knows it," I instructed, then followed Valenia into the dark.

Shutting myself and Valenia inside, my eyes adjusted quickly to the near pitch-black interior. Valenia stood on the bottom steps of the stairs—which seemed to be the only thing inside.

I followed the stairs with my eyes, looking up, and up, and *up*, until I couldn't see anymore—even with Northern sight. It was one giant staircase within the tower that led up, likely hundreds of feet in the air. But what it would lead to, I wasn't sure.

There wasn't enough room to fly up—the tower itself was narrow. The entire thing seemed to be made of the same material the dungeons had been made of—stone inlaid with alychite. I also noted how there were no windows, only small holes every so often to allow for a bit of airflow.

After pushing past Valenia, it took what felt like ages to make it up the spiral staircase, but it gave my body something manual to focus on. And Valenia didn't complain once, to my surprise. She walked silently behind me, her steps light and her breathing as steady as could be.

Yes, there was definitely more to her than I'd originally thought. She appeared to be well trained.

When we finally made it to the top, we came to a small landing before an ornate metal door, which I could feel the presence of alychite radiating from.

I almost went to knock before Valenia handed me back the keys we'd gotten from the guard.

"Right," I breathed quietly, selecting the key that seemed the fanciest. Its weight was slightly heavier than the others, and it felt as though its metal had been engraved with swirling patterns, while all the others were plain and smooth.

Sliding the key into the door—a perfect fit—I looked back at Val and instructed her to stay here and be on her guard.

With a simple nod, she took a step back and tilted her head toward the stairs watchfully.

With a deep breath, my heart pounding, I cracked open the door and stepped in to the threshold.

The first thing I noticed was how cold it was inside. Then I noted how the small heels of my boots seemed to click against a type of metal—as though the floor was made of it. Oddly enough, though, it seemed like the room was empty. There were no windows within, either, but there were a small series of holes in the ceiling that showed just a few stars through them. I imagined if it stormed, not much would come through. Not enough to bother anybody, anyway.

I gasped as a form I hadn't noticed on the far side of the space shifted, the distinct sound of alychite chains rattling as they moved.

Not empty, after all.

"Who goes there?" I asked, reaching for one of the many blades I kept on me at all times.

The prisoner continued moving until they stood just under the holes in the ceiling, so the dim light of the rising sun shone down on their face.

And at the sight, I stumbled back a step.

I yielded, just for a moment.

The shade of her brown hair was duller than I remembered, and her skin was much paler—even her freckles seemed faded. Her face was gaunt, but it was her eyes that solidified my understanding of why Father had hidden this fae away so thoroughly.

I had seen that exact shade of green before.

Specifically, in my twin's right eye.

The one thing she'd inherited physically from our...

"Mother?"

Chapter Nineteen

My mother blinked a few times, as though she was processing, or simply couldn't see well. But within seconds, recognition flashed across her face.

"*Dimitri,*" she said, though it barely came out as a whisper, her voice hoarse from what I imagined was disuse. "My boy."

I watched as her eyes filled with tears that threatened to spill over onto her cheeks. But there I stood, just barely inside of the space, rooted to the spot like a century-old tree.

"I—I thought for so long that you were *dead,*" I stammered, my voice cracking as I tried to wrap my head around this new reality.

For months before Father's demise, he had danced around the idea of Mother still being alive—but he'd never provided a legitimate answer to any of my questions. I'd begged and bartered, but Father loomed the possibility over my head the way you dangled a treat in front of a griffin—just out of reach.

I'd done the same to Aviva, right after our veltik khan. I'd had no proof about Mother then—I'd just wanted her to hurt the way I had.

As a child, I was told Mother had died in her sleep. Peaceful, but extremely sudden. It was said she'd gotten sick, and the illness had taken her out swiftly.

That was what I'd always been told, anyway.

The older I got, though, the less that explanation had made sense. But since there was not a single trace of any wrongdoing or proof of foul play, there was no way for me to disprove what Father had told me. So although it bothered me, I'd learned to live with it. To accept it as factual.

But in that moment, what I thought had been my reality shifted.

What else had Father lied about?

"Everybody believes that," Mother responded softly.

My hands began to shake, and I couldn't seem to stop the barrage of words flowing from my lips, my mind whirling.

"Father kept hinting at you being alive, but I'd thought he was bluffing just to get to me—I didn't think until recently that he was *serious*. But he wouldn't have kept mentioning it unless there was some substance to it, so I kept digging. When I found Father's journal entry about *prisoner fifty-one*, I didn't exactly know what to expect. I just knew whoever was up here was special to him."

"Is that how you found me?" Mother asked, her voice still soft. Soothing, as I'd remembered it, despite the rasp in it.

I nodded.

"He'll be furious when he finds out about this, Dimitri," she said, concern etching itself onto her face.

My brow crinkled. She didn't know Father was...

"Father is... he's..." I stuttered, trying to say the words aloud, and failing. My eyes watered, the reality of his absence hitting me full force in the presence of my mother. I'd been keeping myself busy for weeks, all so I wouldn't have to face the fact that was now sitting like a lump in my throat.

Father may not have been everybody's favorite, but he'd been a rock in my life. Something solid, something unyielding.

Until the very end.

"Oh, my son," Mother said, her expression sullen—empathy and compassion radiating from her like the heat of an undying flame.

I listened to the alychite shackles and chains rattle as she slowly opened her arms towards me.

I didn't know what to think at first. I wasn't sure why Father had hidden her away, and the soldiers at the tower entrance had claimed she was dangerous.

But in the end, the fae before me was still my mother.

The same female I used to cry for as I fell asleep—after she'd *died*.

The one that used to sing to me when I was upset until I calmed down.

Somebody I didn't realize I'd missed so intensely until that moment.

But there she was. Her arms were outstretched, ready to comfort me like she had all those years ago, despite her own current circumstances.

She was still exactly who I'd remembered her to be.

I wasn't sure if I ran or flew, but within heartbeats I had closed the distance between us, sliding to my knees and throwing my arms around the female before me.

Her chains were longer than I'd thought, as she had no issues wrapping her arms around me in return and tucking me into her much smaller, thinner frame. My chin rested on her shoulder, and I couldn't ignore the way a few stray tears rolled down my face as I took comfort in my only parent that, as it had turned out, had not yet returned to the Stars.

"I missed you," I said through clenched teeth—an effort being made to hold in the sobs I could feel threatening to escape my lips.

"I missed you, too, my Dimi," Mother responded as she ran a hand up and down my back, right between my wings. A soothing motion she'd done many years ago—yet it felt so familiar then, it could've been as recent as yesterday.

Once I'd calmed down enough to think clearly again, I slowly released my hold on her and sat back, still very near to her, our knees almost touching. She watched my every move, her eyes sharp despite her time locked away. Her gaze was soft, though, as she waited for me to collect myself.

"How... How are you alive?" I finally asked, curiosity gnawing at me.

"What did your father tell you had happened when I disappeared?" she responded with a question of her own.

A crease appeared between my eyebrows at the response and her choice of wording, but I answered anyway.

"He said you'd gotten sick suddenly. That you got very bad, very quickly. And then one morning, he said you'd died in your sleep. That it was swift and peaceful, at least. We... never saw you again."

Mother let out a breath that easily could've been a soft laugh. Almost like she couldn't believe what she was hearing.

"That doesn't surprise me in the slightest," she responded.

"So... what actually happened?"

Mother sighed. "Your father had an opportunity to erase me, to remove me from the playing board—so he did."

I tilted my head and asked, "But why?"

"Horace... He caught me and your sister, Aviva, practicing her zirilium." Her eyes softened a degree at the mention of my twin, while mine felt as though they'd hardened. "I'm sure you know by now that she was born with both Northern and Southern abilities—a gift from the Stars. She got her Southern abilities from me, of course, as I'm also sure you've figured out. But despite Horace's infatuation with me, he wanted his children to be like him—not tainted by my bloodline's zirilium. When he found me practicing with Aviva that day, well, things got out of hand."

I watched as she rolled up her tattered shirt sleeve to reveal two child-sized handprints scarred onto her upper arm. The skin was warped and discolored; scars like that, which obviously hadn't healed properly, were either extremely bad wounds or weren't treated afterwards the way they should've been. Or both in this case, if I were to guess.

I couldn't stop the slight grimace that flickered over my features.

"Your sister didn't mean to. She thought she was helping. It was the first time she'd accessed her fire zirilium and I discovered the hard way that her fire burned so hot it was *blue*. But the pain was too much, and I passed out. When I woke again, I was here, in this tower. And I've been here ever since."

I'd already known Aviva possessed abilities from the North and the South, but that was a relatively recent discovery. On the other hand, I'd guessed that our mother wasn't Northern for most of my life—though I kept those thoughts to myself, so as to not upset Father. She didn't have wings, and her coloring was all wrong for a Northerner. Once I'd noticed those qualities about her, I couldn't unsee them.

I couldn't unsee how Southern she looked in my foggy memories.

My own abilities were also a recent discovery, though, as well.

I wonder...

"Did you know that I also had taken after you? That I, too, possessed Southern zirilium?" I asked tentatively.

Her lips tilted up in a small smile, then she nodded. "You hadn't displayed any solid evidence of it yet the last time I saw you, but I felt the shift in you. Aviva had been a *very* early bloomer, but it didn't surprise me when I realized you would be, too," she noted. "You must be a master of your craft by now. Which abilities were gifted to you?"

I pressed my lips together tightly, the tips of my ears burning with shame.

She was right—I *should* have mastered my abilities before now.

Yet I hadn't even known about them until a handful of weeks ago.

Another thing Father had managed to hide from me.

"What is it?" she prodded gently.

"Father… He had me drink these elixirs every day, without fail, that seemed to hide my abilities—even from myself. I started taking them right after you… *disappeared*. I guess my zirilium hadn't surfaced just yet. I don't know if Father knew they'd have surfaced soon, or if it was just a precaution. It wasn't until the past couple months that I realized the elixir hadn't just been for me—Aviva had taken them too, and it had done more than just hide abilities. It seemed to erase any trace of Southern from her, too. I didn't even remember she had two different colored eyes until after she left," I explained.

I wasn't sure how Father had managed to terrify both me and my twin into never telling the other about our individual elixirs. Though, I *did* know that Hugo had been a part of it; he'd always created the elixirs, and he was there to provide them when Father couldn't be.

At that, Mother's eyebrows shot up.

"Your twin left?" she asked, drawing her brows together.

"Well, kind of," I said hesitantly. Then I simply dove in headfirst.

I shot right into a detailed explanation of everything that had led to me finding Mother here. How Father had arranged for Aviva to go to the South, how she'd left me and her best friend, Aurora, behind, and how it turned out months later that it had all been a setup. How Father marched over the border with as many troops as he could muster up and how we were ambushed before we could make it to Cairnyl. Leaving a select few details out, I carried on to explain the veltik khan Aviva and I had fought—and how it had ended with Father's death instead of one of ours. I briefly summarized how the past month and a half since that battle had been—how I'd ascended the throne and how I'd found Father's journal, which had led me to the tower we then sat in.

After my explanation tampered off, we sat in a still silence for a few heartbeats. Then Mother let out a shaky breath.

"I'm so sorry you've gone through so much, and I wasn't there." She looked down before carrying on. "But... he's truly gone?" she asked quietly.

Slowly, I nodded, unable to utter the words aloud once again.

A sort of relief seemed to flood her gaze, though she tried to hide it—along with another emotion I couldn't seem to place. It was like a spark had re-entered her eyes, one that hadn't been there before. I didn't quite understand, but maybe I didn't know the full story just yet. If Father had taken away my abilities just to force me to fit into his mold better, what had he done to my mother in their time together?

"You said you hadn't been able to access your zirilium until recently?" she questioned.

Shifting, I struggled not to turn tail and run out the door, but I still nodded.

"If you ever would like some help, I'd be happy to help train you, Dimi. It'd be my honor to do my best to pick up where I left off in your life all those years ago."

She reached out then, gently grasping one of my hands in both of hers.

The contact seemed to ease my anxieties. That was until she looked down at our joined hands.

Clocking the dried blood remaining under my fingernails, she stilled. Even her breathing seemed to cease as her eyes locked onto the crusted blood on my hand.

Once I realized what she was looking at, I ripped my hand from hers and swiftly got to my feet. Before I knew it, I was across the space from her, my back against the door.

"Dimitri," she breathed, her gaze on my face, searching and trying to read me—the way only Aviva had ever been able to.

My breathing sped up as guilt and anxiety overpowered any amount of comfort or relief I had felt before in the arms of my mother.

Without another word, I slipped out of the ornate door and locked it behind me, the sound echoing in my ears.

I would lock her away the same way I locked up the anxiety and guilt of what I'd done—at least until I figured out what to do next.

Chapter Twenty

That day marked the third of our group's journey to Neokell. If we didn't get back to our rendezvous point soon, the other half of our posse would start to worry.

That thought, among many others, kept me from completely breaking down.

But we'd been going for days straight with little to no rest, and my body felt as heavy as my crown did.

We'd been switching between walking and shadow travel all day, but the exhaustion was starting to catch up to me. Not just physical exhaustion, but emotional, too. It all felt like too much. So much so, I thought it might be better to feel nothing at all.

We zoomed by trees and rock and even some animals, all in a rush to make it back to meet the others before the sun set. If I was reading the sun right, we'd make it with time to spare—but only a little.

Despite that, when we materialized next to a crystal-clear creek for a quick break, I couldn't help but itch to *be* the water. The creek didn't have to think about its next moves—it always knew exactly where to go.

And right then, I wanted to be one with that.

Or at least as close as I could get.

As Laurence, Matea, and Byn all crouched—or stood, in Laurence's case, as he could water wield—next to the creek to refill our water skins, I didn't stop walking at the water's edge.

Fully clothed, I walked into the frigid water, barely registering the temperature of it against my skin. The water filled my boots and soaked through my pants within heartbeats, as though it was welcoming me to be a part of it—exactly like I'd wanted.

"Love, what are you doing?" I heard Byn call out as I passed him.

Without responding, and with the water finally up to my waist, I dove forward into what I could tell was a deeper part of the creek. Being that it wasn't a large body of water, it didn't go as deep as I'd have liked to go, but I'd make do.

I kicked my feet a few times, keeping my wings wrapped around myself to preserve heat, and approached the rocky bottom. There, I laid with my back against the rocks and my face toward the sky. I could still feel the kiss of the sun on my face, but just barely.

I used just a touch of my zirilium to move the water in a way that held me in place. And each time my breath nearly ran out, I reached for bubbles within the water around me and guided them into my lungs. A couple times, I reached far enough to take fresh air from above the water.

Down there, with the weight of the water all around me, I didn't have to think about everything that was riding on our success—on *my* success. Down there, it was just me, the water, the rocks, and a few tiny yet curious fish.

And if a few salty tears mixed with the fresh water surrounding me, well, nobody was the wiser.

My hair floated all around me, and I was just beginning to feel at peace with the absence of my usual thoughts and anxieties, when two large arms wrapped around me and tugged me back towards the surface.

My eyes flew open as I slipped out of the trance I'd been in, only to see Byn pulling me up.

Within seconds, and no time to fight against him, we'd broken the surface of the water. I listened as he gasped for air, while I hadn't needed to.

"What were you thinking?" I reeled on him, my emotions returning full force.

"*Me?* What were *you* thinking?" He threw his hands in the air, his soaked hair falling into his face.

"I wield water *and* air, Byn! I was fine down there!" I reasoned.

His concerned expression faltered slightly, seeming to understand that he might have made a mistake.

I looked toward the shore, only to see Matea and Laurence heading into the forest. Giving us privacy even without being asked.

Stars, did I appreciate those two.

"I'm sorry, I wasn't thinking clearly," Byn said softly after I looked back towards him.

I sighed, but before I could respond, a cool breeze licked at my skin, sending chills down my spine. The two of us were still standing in the creek, the water up to our thighs.

"Come on," I said softly as I walked toward the shore.

Once we were both back on dry land, I closed my eyes and focused. Byn didn't speak as I did so, seeming to understand that whatever I was about to do, I needed to concentrate.

I reached into myself, searching for the zirilium that felt cool to the touch. Not freezing, but refreshing.

Once I'd reconnected with my water zirilium, I slowly moved my hands in a motion that looked like I was grooming Eden—large swipes in the air in front of where I knew Byn was standing. With those motions, I slowly collected the entirety of the water that clung to him, holding it in the air until I had every last drop. Shifting my hands slightly, the water moved to be over the creek again, where I funneled it back into the stream we'd gotten it from.

I couldn't let my husband freeze to death.

Nor myself, I supposed.

A moment later, I too was completely dry. The cool air coming off the mountains still slid over my form, but it was more of a comfort than anything.

Like a small piece of what I used to call home.

Now, my home stood in front of me.

Looking more anxious than ever, actually.

"What was that?" Byn asked as he gently took my hand, guiding me to sit on the ground in front of him.

"I just... needed a break. From the thoughts."

Byn's gaze softened, and I could feel through our soul-tie that he truly understood what I was saying.

"I know what you mean. But... a quick heads-up next time would be greatly appreciated."

I nodded, stating that I would warn him if there was a next time, before we lapped into a comfortable silence.

"*We need more,*" I said softly, Nolvym slipping off my tongue.

"More of what, Avi?"

"More soldiers. More wielders. More trokavs. More willing to fight. More *numbers,*" I said, the anxiety slowly trickling back in. "We don't have enough right now. Not after the latest battle. Not enough to fight *and* defend the number of captives I saw in there."

Byn sighed, running a hand through his unruly hair, but he didn't answer immediately like he usually did.

I shifted my energy inwards, towards the place I had come to find his presence at inside of me, and felt. Then realization washed over me.

"You have an idea already," I stated, looking up to lock eyes with him.

Slowly, he nodded. But the next sentence out of his mouth did little to ease my anxiety; if anything, it made my anxiety spike.

"I do... but I fear the asking price might be more than we can afford."

***

The sun had just slid below the distant horizon when the four of us barreled into the lush cave that served as our rendezvous point.

Rayven's head snapped toward us as we materialized from our shadow forms. He was in front of us a few heartbeats later, with Chess and the Ocrein royal siblings fast on his heels.

As Matea and Laurence appeared first, I couldn't ignore the way Rayven's eyes slid over my sister's form, checking to make sure she was in one piece.

His attention shifted quickly, though, as Byn and I appeared next to them. Rayven was immediately before us, his loyalty to his king and queen apparent.

"Are you two alright? We were concerned when you four weren't back before us. I was just saying we should start looking for you all." Rayven subtly looked us over, checking for wounds and the likes as he spoke.

"We're fine, brother. Don't worry," Byn said, resting his hand on his friend's shoulder.

"We didn't find a single thing in Jackton. It was a waste of time and resources," Callum informed us as he stepped closer toward Byn and me.

I took a deep breath before my next statement. "That's because we found them."

I watched as the royal siblings shared a concerned look, and Chess's face blanched. Rayven met my gaze, his expression stony.

"What did you find?" Rayven asked, his voice cold.

Byn, Laurence, Matea, and I all took turns speaking as we filled in the other half of our posse on what we had discovered. And as we spoke, even Caelia, who rarely displayed her true emotions, had a look of horror on her face.

It was how we all felt, by the end of the discussion.

"So… we don't know what caused this lack of zirilium?" Callum asked, obviously still processing everything we'd just divulged.

"I… think I do," I spoke up.

All eyes in the cave shot over to me, and I could even feel Byn's surprise. But I locked eyes with Matea from across the space, and she nodded slightly.

Her encouragement was all I needed.

Slowly, I reached into my internal cloak pocket—where the map and sketches from Valenia had been, which were now on the floor before us. When I pulled my hand back out, I held a tiny metal spike in my palm—no bigger than the length of my finger.

The spike I had taken from the wall.

I had it placed on a small strip of cloth so it wouldn't touch my skin. I held it out before me for everybody to see.

"Whatever this is made of did it, I'm pretty sure. When I first ripped it off the wall, before Matea and I went back to find Byn and Laurence, I held it in my hand, and it touched the skin of my fingers. And when it touched my skin, it was like… nothing I'd ever felt before. It's like it zapped the zirilium from me, like it completely cut me off from them." I shuttered as I remembered what that felt like.

"I think, even though we weren't making contact with the metal when we were near the wall, the sheer amount of them so close to us cut off our zirilium. Aviva and I were only able to shadow wield to the top of the wall because there was less of this material in that area," Matea added, nodding toward me when speaking my name.

"May I?" Callum asked, his gaze on me and the spike.

With precision, I tossed it to him from across the cave. I watched as he caught it with one bare hand.

Then I watched as his face paled.

"I can't... I can't even feel my zirilium," the prince said, concern and frustration in his voice.

"We know," I said gently, then held my hands open. He tossed it back, and I caught it in the cloth, folding it back up and sliding it back into my pocket.

"That's..." Callum shuttered, "terrifying."

Matea nodded her agreement, but didn't speak. The grave expressions of those around me matched how I felt about it, too.

"That looks like the same stuff Ezra's cell in Gatlyn Castle's dungeon was lined with, and that his chains had been made of. It made it so I couldn't wield past it," Rayven added, staring at the last spot he'd seen the shard—my pocket.

How could we fight against something like *that?*

"So... what do we do now?" Chess spoke up, his eyes wide.

Byn, who had been unusually quiet these past few moments, looked up at that. "Now we pursue the only option we have left. Aviva and I talked about this, and she made a devastating point." He paused before adding, "We need more numbers."

I watched as a few heads bobbed in agreement, and couldn't ignore the way Caelia looked towards Callum—like she knew what Byn was about to say.

"Now, we get ready to head to the Isles."

Chapter Twenty-One

I swung my feet back and forth in the open air, looking out at the mixture of forest and private royal gardens I could see from the balcony of mine and Byn's room. I'd hopped up on to the railing that enclosed the balcony and sat with my feet dangling in the open air. I knew if I somehow managed to fall, it'd be as easy as one wingbeat to pause my descent. If anything, sitting there was relaxing. The wind was blowing softly, which brought the sweet scent of the flowers below up to my nose.

For the first time in a while, I smiled—despite being alone.

It was easy to smile around those I cared about. It was when I was *alone* that the thoughts attempted to eat me alive.

And that was why I'd come out here. I'd needed to get out of bed, even if it was simply to rest on the balcony.

I didn't want to fall back into the funk I'd found myself in after Father's... *demise*.

Just as I had closed my eyes to enjoy the feeling of the wind sliding between my feathers, I felt a small disturbance in the shadows at the edge of the balcony.

In all our traveling to and from the North, I'd learned how to stay connected to my zirilium without using too much energy.

With how much we had needed to rely on shadow wielding, it felt almost natural to stay connected to it now.

And those skills I had learned were exactly why I was able to pick up on the change in energy nearby.

"You can come out, you know. It's just me here right now," I said without looking over, my feet still gently swinging.

I made an effort to lift my wings and tuck them in, rather than having them splayed out behind me.

I was still only comfortable letting my wings touch the ground around Byn.

Old habits were difficult to shake, I supposed.

After a beat of hesitation, the shadow slinked out of its hiding spot and curled in on itself near me. Then, from out of it, stepped my sister.

"You're aware that you could always knock, correct?" I asked jokingly.

She stood next to me, her arms resting on the railing I sat on. Her freshly cut hair sat a width above her shoulders instead of brushing her skin as it had before. And instead of a cloak and all-black attire, she actually wore some color today. Her pants were still black, but her top was a dainty, royal purple blouse with half sleeves that touched her elbows. The royal purple was broken up in a pattern of black flowers, and I realized they were velvet.

Sometimes I forgot her grandparents were nobles.

Our grandparents.

Stars, I hadn't even seen them outside of meetings since I learned Matea existed.

Another thing to add to my list of things to do—and my list of anxieties.

"What are you thinking about?" Matea asked gently, and I realized she'd been observing me.

At the question, I chuckled under my breath.

"I'm trying not to think at all, if we're being honest."

"That doesn't mean you've been successful at it," she countered.

With that response, my smile faltered.

I turned to look back out at the world below as I told her, "You're right."

Matea stayed silent, looking at the trees and flowers with me—giving me the space and time I needed to decide to let her in or not.

"Honestly?" I sighed. "So much has occurred over the past handful of months, with so little time to process it all. My entire life and what I thought my future would be shifted right before my eyes. I discovered hidden secrets about myself, my family, and the war. Not to mention I feel like I'm grieving a brother that's still alive, while also grieving a father that was never there—who *I* saw to his end. Do I even deserve to grieve them? And Stars, Father isn't even here anymore, and his influence still reigns strong, especially over Dimitri. Now, I'm stuck with the consequences of the choices that Father made, and that my twin is continuing to make."

After a beat of silence, I added quietly, "It all just... begins to feel heavy, after a while, is all."

Slowly, Matea released a breath, letting what I'd said hang in the air between us.

"And here I thought *I* had problems," she said. I couldn't stop the small up-turn of my lips at her ability to cope with humor. "That does sound really heavy, Viva. But I think sometimes you need to remember that you aren't alone anymore. You've lost a lot, but you've gained even more than what you had. Yes, you left behind a corrupt family, but you made a loving one for yourself here, in this very castle. That's something to hold on to—and to utilize." She gently nudged me with her shoulder. "And don't you dare forget that you have me now, too. And if you'd give them a chance, you have our grandparents as well. I know they'd love to get to know you in a deeper way than you simply being their queen."

She paused before adding, "That's part of why I came here today, actually."

Turning to her, I watched as she pulled a small slip of paper out of her pocket and slid it across the railing to me.

"Nan and Pops—Billie and Geoff, I mean—would be honored if you accompanied us for dinner later tonight. Don't say no just yet! You have all day to consider it."

I unfolded the paper to peer at the contents, which turned out to be an address that I could only imagine was the Ashford's estate.

Folding it in on itself again, I tucked it away.

"What was the other part? Of why you came?" I asked curiously, trying to avoid giving her an answer right away.

At that, Matea looked slightly sheepish as her eyes darted around before she answered. "I just wanted to check in on my... my little sister."

A smile crept its way onto my face as I listened to her, but I knew she wouldn't want me to make a big fuss over this—even if I was beaming on the inside.

"If you'll have me, that is," she added when I didn't respond instantly.

"I always wanted a sister. I thought I'd found that with Aurora, but... well, you see how that's going." I met her gaze. "It would be an honor to be considered an Ashford, you know."

"You already are one." Matea wrapped an arm around my shoulders and squeezed me into her side. Though the contact was brief, I relished in the affection she *did* show.

"Where is your Robyn, by the way?" she asked, pulling her arm back to her own side.

"He's with some of the others, preparing for the journey and mapping the route out for the Ocrein Isles."

Matea raised her brows. "Were you not invited?"

"I'm always welcome." I shook my head. "But I needed some time to myself this morning."

She nodded her understanding, then straightened so she was no longer leaning against the balcony railing.

"Think about dinner, alright?" Matea took a step back toward the shadows.

"I will," I promised her, just before she dissipated into darkness before my eyes.

And just like that, I was once again left to tend to my own thoughts.

***

A new weight on the edge of the couch I was lounging on stirred me from my dozing. I almost panicked until I felt Byn reaching out through our connection. He felt calm, content—even joyous.

I cracked my eyes open to see him sitting next to me on the edge of the cushion.

I must've slipped into a light slumber while I was soaking up the sun above. If the position of the sun in the sky was any indication, I'd only been out for roughly an hour.

"Hey there, my gorgeous wife," he murmured, then leaned down to kiss the top of my head.

Pulling myself out of my sleepy haze, I sat up abruptly. "How did the meeting go?" I asked as I rubbed the sleep from my eyes.

Instead of answering right away, he repositioned himself on the couch so he was lying next to me, instead of sitting nearby. There was more than enough room to stay side by side, but before I knew it, we had melted into each other. I rested my head against his chest, my pointed ear listening to his heart beating strong. Our legs intertwined, and his arms held me like I might slip through his fingers at any moment. I draped an arm over his waist and slid my hand up his shirt, softly running my hand up and down his back in soothing motions.

To anybody else, we probably looked like we didn't have a care in the world. But when I reached inwards, towards Byn, I could feel the anxieties that troubled him—and to get there, I had to pass my own.

After some moments of allowing him to relax after what I could tell was a stressful meeting, he finally answered in Nolvym.

"*The route to the Isles has been laid—down to where we shall camp each night. But we have to leave as soon as we feasibly can. We can't wait for even our fastest corvids to fly there and back with a message, simply hoping for the best. Plus, we can negotiate better in person. We'll just have to hope that they decide to greet us with open arms.*" He sighed.

"*That's... not very reassuring. What did Callum and Caelia say about it?*" I asked, also responding in the dead language that rolled off our tongues with ease.

"*Callum will stand with us against his parents. He's their heir, so he holds some weight with them. But from what I remember, they're stubborn fae, Avi. Even with Caelia, who is allotting to follow her brother into whatever he does, I'm not sure we have enough to offer them.*"

With that, the air felt heavier.

Not having enough to offer them simply wasn't a choice.

"*Who is going on the journey?*" I asked, running a nail up and down his spine. I watched as small chills rose across his skin at the contact.

"*I was thinking the same ones who went on the scouting missions with us, but that isn't final yet. Obviously, Callum and Caelia must go, but I'm unsure about the rest of the Valwain just yet.*"

"How is Ezra?" I asked quietly, trying to soften the blow while switching back to the modern language.

I could feel the guilt radiating from him at the thought of his best friend. His brother.

"He could be better, but he's doing as well as can be expected. It's going to take time for him to put muscle back on, and he's resting a lot, but he's mostly just happy to be back with Quinn. Surprisingly, she allowed Rayven to watch over him for the evening. She's behind on her duties since Ezra's return, but at least she seems to know she can only put them off for so long." His eyes drifted to the distance, as if thinking. "He's started asking what he missed while he was gone, and what kind of trouble we've been getting into since he was here last. Quinn hasn't allowed anybody to fill him in, though. She says he needs more time."

"Hmm," I hummed, contemplating what he'd said as he ran a finger up and down my side, pushing my shirt up slightly with each pass to make more contact with my skin.

"How are *you*, my love?" he asked, raising his hand to cup my face gently, tilting my head up to look at him.

"I've had worse days. But..."

He raised an eyebrow, but waited patiently for me to gather myself.

"Matea visited earlier. She invited me to dinner with... *our* grandparents. Tonight."

Byn's eyes widened slightly. "What will you do?"

"I don't know," I admitted. "I've lost all the family I've ever known, in one way or another. Now I seem to have another chance—but what if I end up losing them, too?" I met his gaze once again as I asked, "What do you think?"

His emotions felt warm yet sad at the same time. A lot of love was there, but the sting of grief and regret hung heavy over it.

"If I had gotten the chance to get to know my extended family—the fae who raised and loved my own parents—I'd have done so in a heartbeat. Because I imagine it would be like getting to know my parents all over again." His lips tilted up into a sad smile as I could see him imagining that exact scenario. "Love doesn't always have to hurt. If you have an opportunity here to learn that, you should take it."

I slowly let out a shaky breath.

"You might be right. Despite what Matea believes, it's been a decade and a half since anybody has seen my mother. There's no guarantee we'll find her among the others we rescue. This... could be my only chance."

He nodded his agreement, and I could feel his pride in me.

"You know, I do have some time to spare before I have to go check on everybody over at the den this afternoon," Byn said, slowly reaching an arm behind me and stroking the inside of my wing.

I bit my lip to stop the sound that tried to escape my lips, but I couldn't stop the way my toes curled at the contact.

A second later, his nose was gently nuzzling into the side of my neck, then his lips met the soft skin there, and I melted.

As we spent the rest of the late morning in each other's company, we shared kisses, our skin met, and our emotions flowed freely between our bound souls.

Just as I was coming down from the high of being with Byn, I couldn't help but think that despite not knowing what I'd been getting myself into with our tattoos, our souls didn't meet by happenstance. Because being in my husband's arms, our bodies and souls bound as one? That was exactly where I was meant to be.

Chapter Twenty-Two

All too soon, the sun reached its peak in the sky, and Byn had to depart to carry on with his tasks for the day. He'd invited me, but I'd told him I had something else I needed to tend to before the dinner tonight with the Ashfords. He'd asked no questions, his trust in me apparent; he'd simply pressed his lips to mine in a loving, gentle kiss before walking back towards the main part of The Haven.

Sighing, I headed back inside, leaving the balcony, flowers, and sunlight behind me. Pausing, I looked at what had become of our space.

When I'd first arrived, right after our wedding ceremony, I'd entered to find that Byn had swapped everything he could to reflect that of the North and what I was used to. The bedspread, the curtains, even the hardware on the doors and on the wardrobes had been swapped from gold to silver.

Now, it was a mixture. I wasn't the same terrified female I'd been that night. Byn and I had begun to grow together—and I could see that development in the different gold and silver, green and blue hues throughout our shared space.

Smiling at the realization, I headed toward the wardrobe. I shuffled through the clothing I had—an interesting combination of my older Northern attire and my newer Southern clothing. The difference was striking, but I found it fun to try to mix the two cultures when it came to clothing.

With what I wanted to wear already picked out in my mind, I shuffled through the different items of clothing until I found what I wanted and donned it all, one piece at a time.

For the base, I picked a soft blue dress, the hue light to match my left eye. It just barely brushed the floor as I walked, and the flowing sleeves rested just off my shoulders. On top of the dress, I laced up a brown under-bust corset—one that was made mostly of leather and had an elegant floral pattern lightly carved into it. Thanks to its flexible boning, I'd still be comfortable throughout the remainder of the day. To match the corset, I slid on a pair of brown leather boots that went almost up to the knee, and were only visible when seen through the slit in the bottom half of the dress.

Aside from that, I decided to wear my silver circlet—something I was still trying to get accustomed to wearing casually—atop my braided half-up hairstyle. The crescent moons at each end near my temples faced each other, as though enjoying a conversation only they could hear. I wore the silver chain around my throat that my moon stones had once hung from—the chain now bare, but still lovely. I buckled on a belt that held a sheath for a single dagger. There weren't enough places to hide my usual dozen in this sort of attire, and I didn't imagine I'd need them today, anyway.

Besides, I was becoming a weapon myself.

Into the sheath, I slid the dagger that Dimitri had supposedly found in our mother's things. I still questioned in the back of my mind just how my brother had found it, and what the second crest on it meant. I knew one side was engraved with the Ashford family insignia—but I'd never discovered whose was on the other side.

Or what it meant.

And I imagined if anybody were to know more about Mother's past, it'd be the Ashfords.

Pausing to catch a glimpse of myself in the mirror, a small smile found its way onto my lips. I had a glint in my eyes I hadn't possessed a month ago.

As I ducked out of our chambers, I tucked the gloves with my moon and sun stones into the pockets of my dress. But as I walked, my smile slowly fell as I thought about what I needed to do before dinner.

It was time to check in with Ezra—and to make a decision.

We'd been back from our scouting trips for a couple of days at this point, but the Thorntier royal advisors were not happy with Byn for leaving them once again. Teagan staying behind while we went on our recent scouting missions had helped, but the advisors were very demanding. So immediately upon returning, we'd been thrust into meetings where we'd filled them in—albeit vaguely—on what we'd discovered while away, and where we planned on going to next. Teagan had attended these meetings, but we'd made an effort to pull her aside afterwards and fill her in fully with details we'd left out. With that keeping us busy—so busy that I hadn't even gotten to see Margo outside of brief meals—today had been our first day since our return that we'd had to catch up on ourselves and our general tasks.

Now that I had a moment to breathe, I desperately wanted to check on Ezra. And provide him with what was being kept from him—if need be.

The walk across The Haven was quieter than usual—as though everybody had settled down for lunch all at the same time—though I didn't mind it. It meant less fae would see where I was heading.

While Quinn used to stay on the top floor of Cairnyl's barracks, that now solely served as her office. She and Ezra had picked out their own quarters there within The Haven, just before the Battle of Shadows, apparently. I wasn't sure where Ezra had stayed before that, but now they were situated near the library for him, but also down the hall from the closest exit to the barracks for Quinn.

The two worked well together.

As I neared the door I'd been told was theirs, I *almost* hesitated—but instead of giving into my anxiety, I knocked without letting myself think twice. If my information was right, somebody from the Valwain—besides Quinn—should've been with Ezra right now.

Having used the familiar series of knocks I'd picked up from the Valwain to signify the person knocking was also of the Valwain, Rayven appeared relaxed when he answered the door, leaning against its frame. He was never the most expressive of us, but even I could tell the calm on his face was forced.

It looked like Rayven was following what Quinn had told all of us.

Which was to tell Ezra *nothing*.

We all knew she meant well for her husband; Chess had said Ezra needed minimal stress. But if I knew Ezra at all, he was likely losing his mind being holed up in their chambers while he healed. And when I'd said exactly that, well... Quinn hadn't exactly gone easy on me.

I guess I didn't learn, though, if my presence at Ezra's door meant anything.

Rayven's eyebrows lifted at the sight of me.

"What can I do for you, my queen?" he asked, his voice low—likely so Ezra wouldn't hear from farther inside.

"I volunteered to sit with him for the next couple of hours until Quinn got back, but I think I have to cut it a tad short. Can you return just before dusk?" I requested, trying to keep my voice light.

"Aviva, I'm not sure this is—"

"I'm just checking on my friend," I reassured Rayven.

He crossed his arms over his broad chest, not moving from the doorway.

"*If* I get in trouble, I won't tell anybody you let me in," I sighed.

"*When* you get in trouble with Quinn, I'll be by your side," he said, reaching out and gently resting a hand on my shoulder.

Shocked at his words, I looked up to meet his eyes, searching for the trick or lie there.

But I found only genuine concern in his gaze.

"I don't think her stance on this is right, either, but she's my peer. I don't want to overstep any boundaries. But supporting my queen, especially when she's doing something I believe is right? That's something I can—and *will*—always do."

With that, he stepped past me, allowing me to take his spot just inside of the doorframe.

In an act of respect and gratitude, I placed my fist over my heart as I faced him.

He mimicked the motion, then bowed slightly.

"Before dusk," he promised, then dissipated into wisps of shadow, disappearing from my sight before I could utter a response.

Loosening a breath, I shut the door behind me and made my way down the short corridor that led into the chamber's main space. They had decorated it in warm colors—shades of gold, red, and orange covered the space and made it feel inviting—though I supposed the small flame in the fireplace could have something to do with that, too. Their bed was tucked into the far corner, thin drapes hanging from the top of the four posts and blocking most of it from view. Toward the front of the main room was a comfortable lounge area, and in the opposite corner sat what I imagined was Ezra's desk, as the surface was completely covered in paper, books, and what looked like maps.

"Aviva?" I could hear the pleasant surprise in his voice as he called out, having just walked out of the washroom, the door sliding closed behind him.

He looked better than I'd been expecting. There were no gaping wounds on his skin from what I could see, but I knew most of the wounds he'd been dealt had been in places he could cover up. He had on some loose cotton pants and a button-up shirt colored in cream and deep orange stripes, and his hair was wet as though he'd just taken a bath. The white streak running through his strands was bright again—not dirty and bloody, like it had been when we'd found him.

He *appeared* put together. But I knew wounds didn't have to be physical for them to still hurt.

"Hey there," I responded, a soft smile on my lips. I slid my hands into my pockets to stop from picking at the skin around my nails, but before I knew it, Ezra was crossing the lounge towards me.

Swept up in his arms, I gasped at the sudden contact as he squeezed. I wasn't sure he'd be feeling up to a hug, let alone whatever *that* was.

I wrapped my arms around him in return, though I wasn't exactly sure what was happening. I'd been expecting him to abhor any kind of physical contact, not initiate it.

When he pulled back, resting his hands on my shoulders, and saw my puzzled face, the beginnings of a small smile haunted his mouth.

"I don't remember much from when you three rescued me, or much from the days we traveled—Chess has had me on tons of herbs and medicines—but I do remember snippets. I... I can still see it in my mind, the image of you facing down Dimitri—your own *brother*—for *me*." As he spoke the last sentence, his voice cracked and tears rushed to flood his eyes. "*Thank you* doesn't feel like it quite cuts it, but I can't think of anything else to say," he expressed softly, the gratitude in his voice thick.

"Ezra... You don't need to thank me—or any of us, for that matter. You're one of us. And no member of our Valwain will be left behind." I looked him right in the eyes as I spoke, so he knew I meant every word I said.

I listened to the shaky breath he let out, then he released his soft hold on me and took a step back. I hadn't noticed it until then, but he had a very slight limp as he walked, and he focused more of his weight onto his left side.

Before he could see the guilt flooding my expression, I plastered another small grin on.

"I love what you two have done with the place," I said, motioning to the surrounding chambers.

"That's right! You haven't seen it yet! Well, welcome. Here, come sit and make yourself at home." He moved a few cushions from the longer couch and motioned for me to take a seat.

Instead of tucking my wings in tight, I sat with my back to the far arm of the couch and let my wings hang over the side. Still close to me and not touching the ground, but more comfortable than squishing them against the back of the seat.

"I... should've thought about that." He scratched the back of his neck.

Just before I could open my mouth to tell him not to worry, the fire on the other side of the lounge from us sputtered and went out.

"I've got it!" Ezra proclaimed, suddenly hopping from his seat and making his way over to the fireplace—but not before having to pause and regain his balance, as though the sudden motion had made him dizzy or lightheaded.

Raising a hand toward the fireplace, I said, "Ezra, I could just—"

"I can do it!" he insisted, gathering a few logs from a perfectly arranged pile nearby and placing them inside, where the flame had just been. I watched as he struggled to hold the small flint device in order to create a spark, and at that point, I could no longer sit back and watch.

Crossing the space, I put a gentle hand on his shoulder and guided him backwards so he wasn't so close. Then, with a single flick of my wrist, I managed to conjure and toss a small ball of fire into the center of the small logs.

The wood crackled as it caught fire, casting a golden glow across our faces.

Ezra seemed to cave in on himself, leaning backwards until he sat on the floor with his long legs spread out in front of him.

"If I can't manage to light a stupid fire, what use am I to anybody?" he asked, the fight seeming to drain out of him as he spoke, his eyes glued to the flames.

Slowly, I positioned myself to be sitting in between him and the flames, pulling my wings in tight to my body.

"I'm all ears," I reassured my friend softly.

He pressed his lips together for a moment, his expression contemplative. Then, he sighed shakily, and just let the words flow.

"Everybody is treating me like I'm going to break at any given moment. They're coddling me, and at first, it was sort of nice. I couldn't move or do much without feeling pain, so I appreciated their efforts. But I thought it would've stopped by now. They keep walking on eggshells around me, Quinn especially. But none of them seem to get it—I *want* normalcy. I want to be useful again, Aviva. I want to be *me* again. And I want to know what's really going on, because I know what I went through was only the beginning. The North will stop at nothing, and Dimitri might truly be the key to making them successful. And yet, I'm positive Quinn has threatened the entire Valwain into keeping their lips sealed around me, because nobody is filling me in. I understand that they want to protect me, but this should be my decision to make. And I've made it." His voice was raw as he spoke, his eyes beginning to water the more he let out. "They don't seem to comprehend that if I were going to break, I would've broken while I was being actively tortured. But I *didn't.*"

His hands shook as he rung them out before him. His expression was sullen, like he'd nearly given up.

But he deserved better than that after all he'd been through. And I'd let him know it.

"You're right," I said softly as I reached out and placed one hand on top of my friend's.

It was then that I noticed the first finger on his right hand was shorter than it should've been. For a moment, I thought it was a trick of the light, but no. The tip of his finger was completely gone, cut off at the top joint, below where the nail once was.

My stomach dropped as I remembered what, exactly, my brother had been tossing around when I'd last seen him.

Without letting Ezra notice what I'd observed, I carried on, though the thought that he'd endured that and *worse*—and at the hands of my twin, no less—was like a knife to the heart.

"You deserve better than how everybody has been treating you," I clarified when he looked up at me, seemingly shocked at how I'd agreed with him. "I'm here to fix that."

"You'd... You'd do that?" Ezra asked quietly.

"I can deal with Quinn later." I nodded. "Plus, Rayven agrees with me and will have my back."

"I don't want to cause a divide..." He hesitated, though I knew this was what he wanted.

"There already is one, Ezra. Quinn loves you dearly, but she's going about this the wrong way. And like you said, this should be *your* decision to make. If you truly want to pick up where you left off, there's no reason for me not to fill you in."

At that, he looked down at the tattoo on his left arm. It appeared as a crystal wrapped in flames—Quinn's family crest, and the tattoo that tied his entire being to his wife's, just as my tattoo tied my soul to Byn's.

Slowly, he raised his gaze to look me in the eye as he made his next request.

"Tell me *everything*."

And so, I obliged.

***

The sun was nearing the horizon by the time I'd caught Ezra up on everything he'd missed. What I had thought would take no more than an hour ended up being multiple as he pulled out maps and books, wanting to know the exact details of what had transpired in his forced absence.

It was like he was working to make up for lost time, and while my heart still hurt to see it, a spark had re-entered his eyes. It was as though he had a purpose again. And it brought me great joy to know that I'd been able to give that to him.

Ezra had been the driving force that made me feel welcome during the beginning of my time here in the South. If it weren't for him, I wasn't sure I'd be where I was today. I was indebted to him, whether or not he knew it.

"And after that, we all rushed to get back here, to Cairnyl, so we could plan our next moves. *That's* everything," I concluded as I placed my finger over Cairnyl on the map before us, after pointing out the end of the route we'd taken to get back.

Ezra whistled as he stared at the map of the continent, and I imagined his mind was moving faster than he could talk. I'd taken the time to answer each in-depth question he'd asked, so I knew he was processing a lot.

"Alright," he said after a few beats of silence. "What can I do?"

My eyebrows raised at the question. I knew he wasn't the type to back down, even if fighting wasn't his forte, but I was still a bit surprised he wanted to jump right back in like that.

"After everything I just told you, you still want to be a part of this?" I inquired.

He nodded. "If my friends, my *family*, are facing all of this, then there's no reason for me to stay on the sidelines when I have the ability to help."

My admiration for the male before me only grew with that statement.

"If you're sure... Our next move is traveling to the Ocrein Isles. We can't take on the North by ourselves when they have something that steals our zirilium from us. We're hoping that with help from Callum and Caelia, the king and queen of the Isles will come to our aid," I explained.

Ezra sucked his teeth, then added, "And I'm sure the asking price will be as steep as they come."

I nodded my agreement, then we lapsed into a moment of comfortable quiet.

After some seconds of building up courage, I asked, "Besides everything Dimi did... how was he?" Then, realizing that might be a horrible thing to ask, I began apologizing profusely.

"It's alright. I understand that you still care for him. Our hearts are tricky like that," He smiled slightly. "He seemed... lonely. Lost. As though he couldn't find his way back to whatever or whoever he was before."

Tears prickled at my eyes, but I forced myself to hold them back, taking slow and deep breaths until they subsided.

"One more question, if you're up for it," I said.

"M'lady?"

"Why? What's driving you to keep going, even after the horror you've been through?" I asked gently. I couldn't quite understand it.

And for some reason, I realized I *really* wanted to.

He sighed lightly. "It's a mixture of things, really. Besides wanting to be content with myself and how I decide to live my life, I also want to make those I hold dear proud. Quinn, Robyn, even my parents—despite them having returned to the Stars already. I want to follow their lead—and I know this is something they'd do." He looked toward his desk. I couldn't see exactly what he was looking at, but something over there must have reminded him of somebody he loved.

I tilted my head. "Your parents? I thought you were orphaned."

"Robyn never told you?" he asked, surprise written all over his face as his jaw dropped.

I shook my head, motioning for him to carry on.

"Orus and Genevieve were Robyn's parents, but also mine—at least in every way that counted. You're right, I was orphaned. At the ripe age of three, as a matter of fact. I can't remember the fae who created me, and I likely will never get to know them. It's something I've come to accept. But because The Haven sometimes takes in orphans in exchange for some sort of service, I had somewhere to live besides on the streets. I was too young at three to be of much help, though, so I would often end up wandering the castle, since those who were in charge of me often had many tasks to handle at once. Usually one of the older kids, Finn, would watch over me as I roamed. One day, I ran into Queen Genevieve and Robyn. Like a moth to a torch, I was drawn to them—and them to me. Finn says Genevieve scooped me up and carried on with her tasks, simply claiming me from that moment on." He smiled as he spoke, the love in his voice and expression strong.

"But... you're not a prince," I pointed out.

He shook his head. "Orus didn't mind me being around, if it made his wife happy. She'd always wanted a big family, and this was long before Margo was born. But formal adoption hadn't been done in the Thorntier line before. If something had happened to Robyn, Teagan, and Margo, then the kingdom would've had me as its last heir—but because I'm not Thorntier blood, and I possess no zirilium, Orus and Genevieve's advisors forbade it. They had no choice but to stop their pursuits, but I was still raised as close to them as I could be. I took classes with Robyn and sometimes even Teagan, and joined them for meals and on family outings. Genevieve and I were as close as a parent and son could be. She gave me the family I hadn't realized at such a young age I'd been missing, and the brother and sisters I wouldn't trade for the world."

He looked at my shocked expression, then gently added, "They would've loved you, you know."

I smiled sadly. "I wish I'd gotten to meet them. They sound lovely."

Ezra opened his mouth to respond, but before he could, a Valwain member knocked on the door.

I looked toward the far window, then cursed as I realized I was going to be late to dinner.

"*Stars,*" I whispered. Before I could even consider leaving without saying goodbye, Ezra pulled me into a fierce hug.

"Thank you," he pulled back to meet my eyes as he added, "my sister."

I smiled, honored to hold such a title to him.

"I'll see you soon." I headed for the door, calling out over my shoulder, "Don't worry about Quinn, by the way. We'll handle it."

Ezra didn't respond, but I could hear papers rustling—like he was already immersing himself inside the books and maps again.

On the other side of the door stood Rayven, who immediately asked, "It's done?"

I nodded once.

"Quinn has a late night tonight, but I hope you're ready to deal with her. She's going to be furious," he advised, rubbing his stubbled jawline.

Brushing off his concerns and telling him not to worry, I slid past him into the corridor.

Rayven shot me a skeptical look, but shook his head and sighed. "You should hurry up. The sun will dip below the horizon any minute now."

"So stop distracting me!" I stuck my tongue out playfully over my shoulder, then broke out into a run.

As I ran down the long hallway, I could hear Rayven's soft chuckle in my ears, and couldn't help but smile myself. Despite the backlash I was sure would come, I felt a little lighter. It was nice to have Ezra back—and nice to know that Rayven would stand with me, no matter what, so long as I was doing what I believed was right.

Most times, I didn't feel as though I completely fit in when I was in the South, and I hadn't exactly belonged in the North, either. But I'd found that when I was with the Valwain, when we were supporting and caring for each other the best we could, maybe that was the feeling of belonging I'd been seeking after all.

Chapter Twenty-Three

The warmth of the sun-soaked wooden railing of the balcony seeped through my clothing and into my skin as I sat. I'd watched as the sun had made its descent in the sky, the moon taking far too long to arrive in its place.

Though my hatred for what the sun represented to me persisted throughout my life and into adulthood, I couldn't see the moon as an escape as I once had. Now, it reminded me of the promise I'd made to who I'd thought was my better half, all those months ago.

I'd promised Aviva that so long as we were both looking at the moon at night, we'd be connected through it. That she'd never truly be alone because of it.

How foolish of me, I chastised myself.

I could hear the last of the servants behind me placing the final few dinner dishes on the solid onyx table.

Tonight, I had a purpose.

As the sun kissed the horizon, I realized it was almost time.

This evening, I wanted to see the extent of my new Right Hand's training. Her calluses gave her away as not being nobility, but were they from manual labor or something more interesting?

It was up to me to find out.

With that thought in mind, I spread my wings and jumped into the air. A moment later, I found myself perched on the edge of the roof, which overlooked the balcony I'd just been sitting on.

Valenia and I had come to the Heartshire's Neokell Estate right after visiting Mother. I still had yet to tell Valenia why I'd needed space from the encampments—or more specifically, who I'd found to be there—but she'd quietly obeyed, following me to the Estate.

The Heartshire royal family had an estate in each city in the North. Apparently, those of my lineage used to travel between the different cities quite often. For what, I wasn't sure. Father had simply selected different advisors to oversee each Northern city instead, obtaining the majority of his intel from them. He rarely left Hollis, and when he did, it was purely for business.

At the thought of Father, I felt a void in my chest. I ran a hand through my hair, pushing each strand out of my face in an effort to distract myself.

The estate we were currently at was crafted mostly of a desaturated, dark wood blend, along with onyx accents scattered throughout where necessary, such as to make up certain floors or staircases or supports. Stained glass windows lined the walls, made up of hues of blue, gray, black, and some purples. Those had become my favorite part of the Neokell Estate, especially with how the moonlight lit them up at night.

As the sun finally disappeared from sight, and the sky began to rapidly darken, I lifted the hood of my black cloak over my head. I secured it in place the best I could, though it was oversized enough that I wasn't exactly worried.

Before the sun had begun its final stretch below the horizon, I'd taken ground-up charcoal and smeared it all over my feathers, making sure to thoroughly cover up the white and gray-silver colors I'd been born with. I'd given myself a small scare when I'd walked past a mirror inside; the charcoal had made my wings resemble my father's exactly.

The idea of disguising my wing color was, unfortunately, not one that I could take credit for.

Before I could finish that thought, I noticed a shadow stretching across the balcony, approaching from inside the estate.

I tugged my hood forward a final time, mostly to reassure myself it was still where I'd placed it. With my features obscured, I then bent my knees slightly as I prepared to jump from where I'd placed myself above the balcony.

I held my breath as I waited for my target.

And the moment she was directly beneath me, I stepped off the edge of the roof.

Landing directly behind my Right Hand, I allowed myself to continue my descent as I dropped into a crouch. Though I hadn't made a sound, Val was good—she'd felt *something* shift. But despite how quickly she turned on her heels to face me, it only worked in my favor as I kicked out her legs from under her.

To my surprise, instead of falling, she *arched*. Stretching herself backwards, she got her feet back under herself swiftly and pushed, flipping herself over and farther away from me.

It was a smart move, I had to admit.

Unfortunately for her, I'd prepared for everything.

It only took a few long strides to reach her before she could fully gather her bearings. Before she could orient herself, I threw a solid hit to her stomach, causing her to double over and gasp for breath. I made sure to use a flat hand and not a fist, though. I couldn't have her in too horrible of a condition.

Pathetic, I thought as I looked down at her.

I took a step back, somewhat disappointed. I had thought she'd put up more of a fight than that.

It wasn't until I gained a different perspective that I noticed her hands weren't clutching her stomach like I thought they were.

She was working through a series of movements I wasn't sure I had seen previously.

Before I could stop her or let her know I wasn't a true threat, I heard a cup from the table not too far off clatter to the ground.

My head snapped up just in time to see what Valenia had been focusing on.

An attack.

The spear of water hit me square in the chest, causing me to stumble backwards. I grunted at the pain, slowly standing straight again.

Valenia had gotten to her feet and was standing a healthy distance from me now. She began to move her hands again, this time in a sort of tugging motion—like she was pulling one end of a rope towards herself.

With that motion, I noticed the water at my feet—and the water that soaked me—was collecting together and rolling back towards her in large droplets. I watched in subtle awe as she did so, though envy nipped at me.

Wielding abilities like that were supposed to be *mine*.

Instead, I had been *cursed*.

But if I was cursed, I would make it my life's mission to ensure that the Stars regretted even thinking of punishing me.

She finished drawing all the water to her, the streams of it flowing around her like a snake wrapping around its prey. She placed her feet firmly apart and looked toward my covered face.

"Let's do this," she said, raising her fists, which she'd coated in water as well.

A small smirk grew slowly across my face at her words.

I flicked my wrist once, causing a great ball of flames to come to life against my skin. The light from the fire lit up my features, and I could see the confusion written across Valenia's face as she tried to process what she was seeing.

"Gladly," I responded, then lunged for her.

Now that Valenia was more prepared—unlike when I'd snuck up on her—her skills weren't bad at all. Some moves she used reminded me of ones I'd learned while growing up in Gatlyn Castle and being taught by some of the highest ranking noblemales and warriors in the North. On the other hand, though, there were a few moments when I could see her true nature coming out as we sparred. She was scrappy—resilient. She wasn't afraid to play a little dirty if it meant she could win.

I liked that very much.

As we flitted around the balcony, lunging and dodging and throwing punches, I continued to study her. The way she kept her hair partially up at all times so it couldn't be used against her, just in case she did find herself in a situation like her current one. I enjoyed watching the way she moved, which was much like the water she wielded. She ebbed and flowed just like it, always ready and willing to adapt to what she needed. And her eyes—they were constantly so sharp, so attentive. I felt like she could have seen right through me if she really wanted to.

Though I admired the way she presented herself, I was also greatly enthused by the way the two of us seemed to complement each other as we moved around the balcony in a dance of sorts.

But that was a thought for another time.

"Come on, little warrior, is that all you've got?" I taunted her, though my voice came out softer than I'd intended.

Valenia's eyes met mine, and to my surprise, I thought I saw true fury resting there.

With that, she raised a hand and directed it at me.

Expecting another water spear to be thrown my way, I held my arms out, inviting her to do her worst.

The rage in her eyes remained as her hand began to produce sparks.

The surrounding air electrified in an instant, and that was when I realized just how much my Right Hand had truly been holding back.

Lightning wielder.

Despite the threat I was up against, I didn't feel fear. If anything, the chaos of the situation made me feel more at peace than I had in a long while.

I kept my arms open and spread out, as if daring her to strike.

Though I could see her hesitation in her body language. Her eyes were still like two flames in her skull, alit with that fury she must have kept buried deep inside.

I knew what that was like, after all.

After a moment, I closed my eyes and waited for the pain of the strike to hit me. I heard the buildup of the lightning, the crackle as it split the air in such close quarters. My vision went white as it passed through the air between us. Though, to my surprise, the pain never came.

I slowly peeled my eyes open to look at Val. Her hand was still raised in my direction, but her aim had been adjusted so her lightning must have gone up and over my shoulder, off to the side.

Realization dawned on me as I thought of how she truly could have ruined all of my plans just then—but didn't.

"Why?" I asked softly, letting my arms fall back to my sides after pushing the cloak hood back away from my face.

"I am vowed to you," she said, though suddenly, she wouldn't meet my gaze.

"Valenia, it was just supposed to be a test. A stupid test, one meant to examine your fighting abilities—your abilities in general." I took a step in her direction. And while she didn't back up, she didn't step forward, either.

"You can just *ask* me things, Dimitri!" she snapped, but quickly covered her mouth with a gasp. "Your Majesty. I apologize." She dipped her head, looking toward the ground.

In all honesty, I didn't care much what she called me. I didn't solely want to be her king anymore, anyway.

I slowly crossed the space between us, allowing her time to move away if she so pleased. When she didn't, I reached out and took her hand in mine.

"Dimitri is fine, Valenia," I reassured her.

"Val." She looked up at me—*finally*. "It's just Val."

Her eyes, which were no longer rage-filled, were just as breathtaking in that moment as they had been the night we'd met. They were such a deep blue that they reminded me of the water of Cynth Bay.

"Val," I breathed softly, trying the nickname out on my tongue.

A wingbeat later, she cleared her throat and took a step back, our hands falling apart because of it. To my surprise, I found myself disappointed at the sudden distance.

"What sort of things were you testing me for?" she asked, and it was like I could see her carefully crafted walls going back up around her.

Why did I find myself wanting to tear them down?

Shaking my head, I sighed. "I just... wanted to get to know you better. How a fae fights says a lot—especially you, being a female in the North," I explained. "The fact that you know how to fight at all says all I need to know."

"Oh?" she said, her interest piqued. "And what did you learn?"

"Well, mostly this confirmed what I'd already thought—that despite how you appeared back at the ball, you don't have a purely noble background, if at all. And you've obviously been well trained—though by who, I haven't a clue. The lightning was a pleasant surprise, though."

At that last comment, she looked slightly pleased with herself.

"You knew I wasn't of the noble class, even the night of the ball?" she asked.

I nodded.

"And yet you still allowed me to vow myself to you," she continued.

"Nobody has ever been brave enough to try to harm me—or spy on me, or whatever it was you were up to—within the walls of my own castle before. You... intrigued me, is all." I ran a hand through my hair, the white strands insisting on falling into my face.

We'd lapsed into a moment of silence when she blurted out, "I meant it, you know. I'd rather you be upfront and ask me things, instead of randomly being tested."

I pressed my lips together to hold back my wince. I guess it had been a sort of odd plan, to say the least.

"So, you're not of the noble class. Were you at least raised in Hollis?" I asked her, taking advantage of the moment while I could.

"Yes." She nodded, taking a seat on the railing of the balcony. "My older sister and mother raised me in our cottage, on the outskirts of Hollis. My father died in the war when I was an infant, so I never knew him. Mother and my sister, Nat, did their best to keep me out of trouble, but I suppose it didn't work very well in the end."

"What—"

"My turn," she corrected, holding up a hand. "Can you only wield fire?"

A question for a question. I supposed that was only fair.

"It's the only one I have some control over, but I can... *sense* the earth below, as well as its shadows. I know I can wield them, too—I just haven't figured it out yet." I looked down, my cheeks and the tips of my ears heating up slightly with shame.

Val nodded, then motioned for me to go ahead.

"What kind of trouble did you find yourself in?" I asked, taking up a spot next to her on the wooden railing, sitting closer than I knew I should've.

"All sorts," she sighed. "It started with me just hanging out with the wrong crowds, but one thing led to another until I was tied up in some shady organizations. That was where I was trained to fight—in hand-to-hand, and with my zirilium. I was the only one in my family that could wield lightning after Father died. My family... didn't know what to do with me."

I'd always known there were organizations flying under the radar in the North. Most of the time it was about petty crime, but I'd heard whispers about bigger goals.

Like taking what was mine.

"How is it possible that you still can't tap into all of your zirilium? You're far past the age for it," she questioned next.

How could I explain without making Father sound bad?

And why did I still care about that?

"My father and our royal trokav found a way to nullify anything Southern about me—as well as my twin. Neither one of us were free of his grasp until recently. And there isn't exactly a line of Southerners willing to train me, so I'm doing my best to figure it out on my own."

Val looked at me thoughtfully, and I could see the wheels spinning in her head, ready to ask her next question already.

"The organizations you mentioned, they're why you were there the night of the ball, correct?" I inquired.

"Yes, but it was a setup. Even within those groups, I was never fully welcome. There was always somebody trying to trip me up. Despite my best efforts, they got the best of me that night. I was supposed to get close to you, but not close enough for this," she motioned between the two of us, "to happen."

"Hmm," I hummed, processing each crumb of information she was feeding me.

"It must have been your mother that was Southern, then? Do you know where she is, and could she train you?" Val asked, leaning forward slightly to draw closer to me. I seemed to have piqued her curiosity; she was looking at me like I was a puzzle she could piece together.

"Yes, my mother was Southern. My whole life I thought she had returned to the Stars, but now..." I trailed off, thinking back to the top of the tower.

And who resided inside.

Val studied me for a moment, searching my face and body language for answers. Only Aviva had ever been able to read me so thoroughly, yet there was Val, doing her best to figure me out.

I wasn't sure how I felt about that.

"The tower." Her eyes widened. "Tell me your mother isn't up in the tower. You acted so oddly afterwards, I wasn't sure what could've been so upsetting, but..."

I shifted my gaze to look at the ground far below us. The estate was on the edge of a large piece of land, scattered with small streams and tall trees. I took a moment to collect myself before quietly admitting to Val what I'd been terrified to voice aloud.

"I don't know what to do."

We lapsed into a brief moment of silence.

Stupid, I screamed internally. *Now you've screwed it all up and—*

"If I had the chance to see my father again, I'd take it," Val said quietly.

She stretched out one of her wings and gently brushed it against my own in a comforting motion. The contact sent chills down my spine, spreading across my skin in an instant.

"What happened to the rest of your family?" I asked after a moment.

Val pursed her lips together hesitantly before responding. "They're all either dead, dead to me, or out of reach. Doesn't really matter much now, does it?"

Those words rang out like bells in my mind.

Dead.

Dead to me.

Out of reach.

"No," I responded quietly. "I guess it doesn't."

As Val and I headed to the table to try to salvage what parts of dinner we could, those words kept circling in my head like a cyclone.

Father was dead.

Aviva was dead to me.

The female I'd pined after for years was out of reach.

But Mother? She wasn't dead, or dead to me. And she didn't *have* to be out of reach if I didn't want her to be anymore.

I'd *found* her.

And it was about time I did something about that fact.

Chapter Twenty-Four

Looking up from the note Matea had given me, I stared at the estate before me.

It sat on the western outskirts of Cairnyl, a sprawling estate that rested at the top of a small, lush hill. Tall trees speckled the area, and tall hedges along with metal fences covered in vines edged the property, boxing off the Ashfords' little sector of the world.

I had flown most of the way there, rushing to make it on time, but now as I walked through the metal gates that I could only assume had been left open for me—I couldn't help but slow my pace.

The walkway up to the front door was made of large flat stones, and every couple of paces the path was framed on both sides by long, raised flower beds. Each small bed consisted of a different type of flower, as though whoever planted—or grew—them were displaying them like trophies. Some flowers I even recognized as herbal, not solely decorative.

Yes, I thought, *whoever looks after these knows how to love them accordingly.*

The house itself was a structure made of mostly wood on the outside, which had been stained a pale brown—while the accents were made up of a pale marble that had a copper hue mixed into it.

As I got a few wingspans from the front door, though, my gait stopped completely. I knew I was in the right place—I'd followed the scribbled note Matea had left me exactly; no, I wasn't anxious about being in the wrong place. It was much larger than that.

Tonight would be the first time I'd spent genuine, one-on-one time with my mother's parents. They'd likely have questions I wasn't sure I knew how to answer. For me, tonight was a step toward getting to know them. But what was it to them?

My hands shook slightly as I stuffed the note back into my dress pocket, right next to my gloves. Though I tried to convince myself that everything would be fine, my hands continued to shake, my mind whirling with everything that could go wrong tonight.

Just as I was beginning to consider turning tail and running, I felt a weight on the earth behind me that hadn't been there before.

I spun around, already reaching for the dagger resting on my hip, when I realized it was just Matea.

"Stars, you nearly scared the life out of me!" I exclaimed, dropping my hand back to my side. Matea snickered lightly in response, obviously proud of herself for having snuck up on me.

"You know you can come inside, right?" she asked, a hint of sarcasm revealing itself through the tone of her voice.

"I was just about to knock," I stated, crossing my arms over my chest.

She cocked an eyebrow at me. "You've been standing out here for so long, I thought you'd forgotten how."

"I was building up the courage! And really, I was just about to!" I said, lying straight through my teeth.

"*Right...* That's why you looked like you were about to turn around, right? Stars, our queen can face down our enemies head on, but don't ask her to visit for dinner!" Matea mocked, placing a hand on her hip.

I gasped at her audacity, my eyes widening. "Watch *this*." I turned on my heel and marched right up to the front door of the house. On instinct, I knocked the way all members of the Valwain do, then took a step back as I waited for somebody to answer.

My heart skipped a beat as the door swung open, expecting to come face to face with either Billie or Geoff—only for my eyes to land on Matea.

"What—" I looked over my shoulder to where she'd been just a moment before, seeing only empty space there now.

Realizing what she'd done—managing to keep me from running away from what I had found scary—I turned back to face her.

"You are a thorn in my side," I said quietly, lightly punching her shoulder.

"I haven't the slightest clue what you're talking about." She grinned innocently, though her eyes gleamed with mischief. "Come on inside! Dinner is nearly ready. We've been working on it for hours."

"You all made it yourself?" I asked, surprised but also honored that they'd go through so much effort for me.

"Indeed. We dismissed the estate staff for today. I imagine Nan and Pops wanted some privacy—just the four of us."

Taking a deep breath, I stepped past Matea into the foyer and listened as she shut the door behind us.

The small heels of my boots clicked against the marble floor—which was the same color and pattern as the marble pillars outside—as I walked further into the foyer. The lighting inside was warm like the sun, and the smell of baked goods overtook my senses in a way that made the entire space feel cozy and welcoming. There was a small chandelier overhead that had the golden light sprinkling throughout the entryway, and I realized then that at least one fae in the house must be a fire wielder, as I doubted they regularly climbed up to light each wick of the chandelier by hand.

"Matea, dear, was that the door I heard?"

Looking up in the direction of the voice I'd just heard, I watched as Lady Billie rounded the corner of the hallway to the left of us.

She still had on an apron, which was spotted with flour in random places. Her hair, which was mostly the same shade as Matea's—aside from her gray roots—rested atop her head in a neatly braided bun. At the sight of me, she gave pause, her gaze lingering on my face, as if she could see the remains of her daughter there.

Seeming to suddenly remember herself, she bowed and said, "My queen. Thank you for honoring us by coming tonight."

I forced myself to not outwardly cringe as she did so. I wasn't sure I'd ever get used to that, but if I was hoping to start building something more meaningful here, then we had to start with that.

Crossing the space between us, I gently rested my hands on Lady Billie's shoulders and guided her up from her bow.

"Please," I said softly, "call me Aviva. We do share blood, after all. There is more to me than simply being your queen."

When her eyes met mine, I could see her searching. Whether she was searching for her lost daughter, or simply wondering if I was attempting to trick her, I wasn't sure, but I held her gaze unwaveringly.

After a few heartbeats, she let out a heavy breath. Her green eyes—the same shade I remembered Mother having—still peered into my mismatched ones.

"I feel her in you," Lady Billie said, her voice shaking slightly. "The same way I feel her in my Matea. Despite recent events and discoveries, she lives on in you two."

When she mentioned Matea's name, her gaze slid to my half-sister, her expression softening tenfold.

I smiled gently as she looked towards me again, then reassured her, "She lives on in you, too. I see her in every piece of you. Despite what happens from here on, it doesn't change the past. It doesn't change that I'm deeply sorry for the pain you've endured."

Lady Billie's eyes began to water, but she lightly shook her head before any tears could fall. "Goodness me, we haven't even made it past the entryway and I'm already emotional," she laughed softly.

"I told you that you wouldn't last longer than halfway through dinner!" Matea chimed in, coming to stand beside us. Lady Billie lightly nudged her and playfully glared at her granddaughter, but the smile on her face remained.

"Right this way, my qu—*Aviva*. We'll be having dinner in the private dining room this evening." Lady Billie led the way as she began walking down the corridor she'd come from, leaving Matea and me to follow.

As we walked leisurely toward the dining room, Lady Billie rattled off different dishes they'd spent the day preparing. They ranged from venison, to fruit I hadn't even heard of before, to a dessert croissant that Lady Billie *swore* tasted like it was sent from the Stars themselves.

As we stepped foot into the private room, the first thing my eyes were drawn to was the numerous dishes that spanned the middle of the round table. There was everything Lady Billie had listed and more—platters of food in nearly every color, the aroma of it all causing my mouth to water. Above the table, hanging in the center of the space, was another chandelier, like the one in the foyer, but on a smaller scale. It, too, had already been lit, making me endlessly curious who there could fire wield—and what else they could control.

It wasn't until I turned toward the small fireplace on the far-left wall that I noticed the painting that hung above the fire.

There hung the largest, most detailed portrait of Mother I'd ever seen.

Her skin was tanner than I remembered, and there was a glimmer in her eye that I'd never seen before, but it was most definitely her. Her silky brown hair, the green of her eyes, the heart shape of her face—it was all *her*.

Back in the North, the only portraits I'd been able to find of Mother—which were already difficult to come by—had all been painted in shades of gray. No color had graced the canvas, which I assumed helped Father hide the fact that she was Southern for as long as he did.

"I... probably should've mentioned that was in here," Matea said, her tone apologetic.

I shook my head slightly, breaking out of the haze I'd found myself in.

Lady Billie, realizing what I'd been staring at, gasped softly. "I wasn't thinking. You have my deepest apologies, my queen." She hung her head.

"No, no, you misunderstand," I said, stepping farther into the room, towards the two females before me. "I haven't seen a portrait of my mother in full color, well, *ever*. Father ensured they were all in gray-scale, likely to help hide her origins, if I had to guess. I just... was surprised, is all."

Matea and her grandmother shared a skeptical glance, but before they could respond, I added, "And it's just *Aviva*."

At that, Lady Billie smiled slightly and nodded. "Aviva it is."

Just then, a whistling tune could be heard approaching from behind a closed door on the other side of the room. Through it came Lord Geoff, also adorned in a flour-spotted apron, holding what I could only imagine were the dessert croissants. Somehow, he'd even managed to get just a bit of flour in his chocolate-colored hair, too. When he saw the three of us standing near the entryway, he paused, his whistling coming to a halt.

The silence stretched on as his guarded brown eyes settled on me. His expression shifted through different emotions, ranging from regret to relief.

"Well, what are you ladies waiting for?" he asked as he placed the dish on the table, breaking the silence heartbeats later. "Let's eat!"

Matea, who hadn't left my side, lead me to the table and gently motioned to where I should sit, taking up her spot to the right of me, with Lady Billie on my left and Lord Geoff directly across. I watched as Lady Billie and Matea both prepared to serve the food, but I acted before they could.

Standing, I grabbed for the utensil Lady Billie had been reaching for.

"It'd be my honor to serve you all tonight, if you'll allow me," I offered, though my tone was firm. Confident.

"Oh no, please, allow me," Lady Billie gasped, standing from her chair and holding her hand out, waiting for me to pass her the serving spoon.

I smiled at her softly and instead placed my hand in hers.

"If we were under normal circumstances, I would be considered your youngest grandchild. It's tradition for the youngest of the family to serve the others when they're old enough—at least in the North." I squeezed her hand. "Please, let me."

The older female hesitated for a moment, but slowly withdrew her hand from mine and returned to her chair.

The next few moments were full of light chatter as I took each plate, starting with Lady Billie's to my left and making my way around the table, filling each one with a little bit of everything. When I wasn't sure what something was, or what a specific ingredient was, Lady Billie or Matea were quick to fill me in. They didn't laugh that I didn't know—they just filled in the gaps.

The venison had been glazed with something that had a pink tint to it. When I asked what it was as I served a large piece to Lord Geoff, he was the one to explain that it was a mixture of honey and pinkthumb—a type of flower native to the South, and one that was often used to spice up a meal.

That was the first time he'd spoken since he sat, and I made sure to respond positively. It appeared he would take a longer time to come around and warm up to me, but I had a feeling it'd be worth the extra effort.

Now, we all had plates full of a variety of delicious foods. Having served myself last, I sat toward the edge of the chair, trying to keep my wings from pressing against the back of it too much. Matea looked my way as I shifted for the third time in a matter of a few minutes, and the realization of my discomfort flickered across her features. Though before she could do or say anything, Lady Billie chimed in.

"So, *Aviva,*" she started, trying out my name on her tongue. "What is it like up there? In the North?"

I chewed thoroughly, buying myself another moment to think before responding.

"If you had asked me that before the past few months' recent events, I'd have said it was a lovely place. Cold most of the time, but bursting at the seams with music and food and life."

"And now?" Lady Billie inquired after a beat of silence.

"Now that I've seen more of the world than just the inside of Gatlyn Castle? Than just Hollis?" I sighed. "I'd say it's all fake. They all put up a good front, but nobody seems to know true happiness there. Not to the extent the people of the South do, anyway."

Lord Geoff nodded slightly, as if silently agreeing with me.

Lady Billie hummed at my response, then clarified her question. "What was *your* experience like? Were you happy?"

I refrained from letting a scowl pass over my face, thinking back to my life in the North.

They don't know, Viva, I thought to myself.

"Up until recent events, I believed my entire life that I killed my own mother as a child in a crazy accident. My father neglected me because I was something my twin, his *favorite*, was not. Father did not permit me to leave the castle grounds but a handful of times in my life—though I learned to escape sometimes, anyway." I took a deep breath, willing my emotions to subside and for my zirilium to remain leashed. "But I did have my brother, and my best friend, and my griffin. I still had meaningful relationships, even if they were few and far between. So while I had been caged like an animal since birth, I still managed to learn how to fly."

I watched their eyes widen as I spoke, especially when I mentioned Mother. I supposed without much context, I likely sounded insane. But where could I even begin?

Matea, to my surprise, cleared her throat to break the deafening silence.

"You should tell them everything. Tell them your story, Viva," she encouraged me.

Not even Matea knew all the details, but she knew more than her—*our*—grandparents did. I supposed this was part of coming to know them—even if it was painful to recall.

"We're all ears," Lord Geoff said, his voice the most tender toward me I'd heard it thus far.

"Well..." I began after a beat of hesitation.

And the rest poured out of me, like a dam had been broken within.

I began with a story involving a flash of blue light from a decade and a half ago—one I'd tried to forget for so long. About how I'd killed Mother—or so I had thought. Because despite what Matea believed, we still didn't know anything for sure.

I spoke of how Father treated Mother that day, and how he'd never laid a hand on his children, but that didn't mean he hadn't hurt us in other ways.

Leading from that, I recalled how I'd been forced to take elixirs each day of my life, and what we had discovered they were suppressing in not only me—but in Dimitri, too.

I told them about how what I had known all my life had been uprooted so quickly after that first time I'd met Teagan, and the love that had blossomed because of it. Not just with Byn, but with each member of the Valwain, in one way or another.

I explained, from my perspective, what had happened since I'd arrived in the South. Discovering *all* of my zirilium, Aurora showing up, the battle that followed, and what I did during said battle.

I ended it all by summarizing what had happened since the battle, including the scouting missions. I made sure to refrain from telling them exactly what we had found during our time sneaking around in the North lately, and when Matea and I shared a look as I spoke, I knew she was grateful I'd done so. I assumed she didn't want to worry them even more than they likely already were.

"That's as simple as I can make it, I think," I finished. Our stomachs were all full at this point, and I wasn't sure I'd ever enjoyed food before the way I had tonight.

"That is..." Lady Billie trailed off.

"A lot to digest," Lord Geoff finished for his wife, the double meaning not lost on me after such a satisfying meal. Lady Billie cast her husband an appreciative look, their gazes full of love for each other.

"I know this is more than you asked for, and I apologize. I just—"

"Aviva," Lady Billie interrupted, though her voice was soft and steady as she spoke. "You forget—our family has served the Thorntier line for generations. We are accustomed to war and loss and tragedy. We are just sorry that all of this has happened to *you*. And in such a short period of time, too!"

I dipped my head slightly so they couldn't see me blinking back the stray tear attempting to make its escape.

"So..." Matea cleared her throat. "What's next for us, Viva?"

I lifted my gaze to look her way. "Us?"

"I've gone this far. I'm with you 'til the Stars fall from the sky, *sister.*" Matea smiled slightly, her hesitation obvious, but it was apparent that she was trying.

My chest ached with gratitude for her.

Sitting straighter in my chair, I carried on. "Right. Well, we plan to seek allies next."

Lord Geoff's eyebrows furrowed. "What allies?"

"The Ocrein Isles."

His eyebrows shot up, and I watched as he and Lady Billie shared a look of genuine concern.

"Are you all sure that's the best idea?" Lady Billie asked.

"It's our only option, I can assure you," I responded.

"The Isles haven't been out of this war for very long, in the grand scheme of things. They may not want to be looped back into all of this so soon, if ever again," Lord Geoff warned gently.

"We know, Pops." Matea nodded.

"Trust me, if you'd seen what we've seen"—I glanced at Matea as I spoke—"you'd understand why it's necessary. We've weighed our options, and this is the best path forward. Plus, we have the Ocrein heir on our side—as well as one of their princesses."

When the two older fae *still* didn't look completely convinced, I added quietly, "We've got this. I promise."

Lady Billie slowly released a breath she seemed to have been holding in, then looked towards her husband. A silent sort of understanding seemed to pass between them before she focused back on me and nodded.

"We trust you. Not only as our queen, but as our granddaughter... if you'll allow us the honor, that is."

My heart raced at the thought. I'd only ever known Dimitri and Father as my family, yet in such a short amount of time, I'd lost a father and gained a sister. Now I was to gain a set of grandparents, too?

It was almost overwhelming, the thought of allowing the Ashfords officially into my life. There was already so much riding on me and the Valwain when it came to the war—would the offer before me only add unnecessary weight?

Though I knew deep down if I didn't let them in, I'd end up regretting it. At the end of the day, they were a connection to my mother that I hadn't had before. Aside from that, I had a feeling they'd prove wise to have around.

"It'd be *my* honor, Lady Billie," I assured her.

She barked out a surprised laugh at my formal response. "Please, *at least* drop the titles from our names. We've agreed we're all family, after all." Her smile grew before adding, "And maybe someday we'll be Nan and Pops to you, too."

The bright grin she wore was so infectious, I couldn't help but smile in return.

"Billie it is, then," I agreed.

"Before you go, you have to try the dessert croissant!" Geoff exclaimed, picking up the plate of said treats and passing it around the table.

As the rest of the evening carried on, I found myself feeling more joyful than I had in a while—outside of being with Byn. Being with the Ashfords felt so... *easy*.

And when the night came to a close, and I stepped outside into the midsummer air, I could've sworn I felt a cool breeze from the North kiss the skin at the back of my neck.

If I were to let myself dream in that moment, I'd have said maybe that was a gentle caress from Mother, letting me know she was with us—even when she wasn't.

Yet, a tiny, hopeful voice inside of me whispered.

She wasn't with us *yet*.

***

Matea and I walked back to The Haven under a moonlit sky. We made small talk about how dinner had gone as we walked, which we decided together was an overall success.

As we approached the open gate leading into The Haven, I waved toward the two guards that were on duty. They each rested a fist over their heart in return.

After Matea and I had passed through the main gate, I came to a slow stop, making sure we were out of earshot of the guards.

Matea, realizing I was no longer next to her, turned around, puzzled.

"I said I'd walk you to the door, Viva. We're almost there," she commented.

"I... want to show you something," I said, motioning for her to backtrack to where I stood.

Raising an eyebrow, she approached me, then crossed her arms over her chest. "Let's see it."

I swallowed forcefully, then slid the dagger I'd been gifted by Dimitri out of its hiding place and into my hand. The same dagger I hadn't gone anywhere without since I'd received it. I made sure to hold it in a way that covered the Ashford family insignia on the side of the hilt, facing up.

"Dimitri gave me this right before I left the North. He'd said he found it in Mother's things, and at first I didn't believe him, but the family crest matches up with the Ashfords'." I slid my fingers away to reveal the insignia of the deeply rooted willow tree with a small bird on one of its many branches. The green gem embedded below the carved image sparkled as though the sun had shone on it at that moment.

"I have a feeling," I flipped the dagger over to reveal the other side, "that it should belong to *you* instead."

The other side was carved with an image of a great ocean wave. There were stars over the wave, and a blue sapphire embedded in that side of the hilt.

I'd been thinking about it lately—how Mother had come to own a dagger with an unknown crest on it, along with her own. There had only been one explanation that made sense to me.

And my sister's reaction told me everything I needed to know.

Upon seeing the second insignia—the one I'd never been able to identify—Matea gasped.

Quick as the lightning I wielded, Matea snatched the dagger from my hands. She tilted it toward the dim light coming from torches near the guards we'd passed, but as she shifted it in another direction, it dawned on me that she didn't have the gift of Northern sight.

Lifting a hand, I conjured a small flame to rest in my palm and held it closer to my sister to light up her surroundings enough to see whatever it was she was searching for.

Shifting her weight to lean closer to my flame, she lifted the dagger to the light, her eyes scouring over every detail.

"Do you care to fill me in on your findings, or am I to guess?" I questioned, becoming a tad impatient at her lack of an explanation.

"You're right—the first side is the Ashford family crest. But on the other side... that's my *father's.*" My lips tilted downward as her voice cracked on that last word.

Her father. Ethan.

I didn't know much about the male, and I wasn't sure how much Matea herself knew, either. She'd likely heard stories of him and our mother growing up, but stories weren't the same as knowing somebody—or having a piece of them.

"Matty, I—"

"I have to go," she stated, abruptly turning tail and dissipating into shadows, the dagger disappearing with her.

"Wait!" I called out, taking a step toward her shadow form, but she was already through the main gates and out of sight.

Well, at least I'd guessed correctly, I thought.

Sighing, I decided to let Matea have her space. Even if I chased after her, there was no way I'd be able to catch up now. Plus, she'd lived in Cairnyl her entire life. She could likely shake me from her trail in a matter of seconds.

After letting my flame go out, I carried on into The Haven. There were very few fae milling about at that hour, as I'd stayed at the Ashford estate longer than I'd intended to. I headed for the royal wing of the castle, not paying much mind to my surroundings—I was just ready to be in my husband's arms and recall our days together.

My daydream was rudely interrupted, though, as I turned the corner into the royal wing and ran directly into something hard, causing me to stumble back a step.

Lifting my gaze, I came face to face with Quinn.

She was only a little taller than I was, though in that moment it felt as though she was looming over me. Her eyebrows creased in anger, and her green eyes reflected the torchlight on the walls in a way that made it look as though the flames were framed in that emerald green.

The fire seemed to suit her current mood, though, as before I could even open my mouth to speak, she *erupted.*

"How *dare* you," she hissed. "He was not ready to be thrown back into all of this. You've been off scouting and such, and the *moment* you get back, *you* feel entitled enough to throw a hammer into *our* plans? He's still in pain—and I don't just mean physically. He was *tortured*, Aviva. Tortured and mutilated and then healed just enough to do it all over again the next day. *That's* the kind of family you have. Fae who would do that to another—and an innocent, no less. You better wish to the Stars that I don't ever meet him on the battlefield, because he *will* be going down for what he did. But you? Oh, it's obvious it must run in your *Heartshire* blood. The Ashford blood couldn't cleanse you of that."

She practically spat the name Heartshire, and the venom dripping in her voice almost had me taking a step back.

I knew Quinn could be harsh sometimes, but I'd *never* heard her like this.

"Quinn, I didn't—"

"Yes, you did, Viva! You messed it *all* up! *He was not ready.*"

"Was it him that wasn't ready?" I asked, my voice as soft as one of my feathers. "Or was it you?"

At that, Quinn took one step back, her expression flickering to show all the pure shock and distress she must have felt due to what I'd just asked.

Quinn quickly slid on her mask of fury again—which was, I imagined, the only thing she knew how to feel on a large enough scale that must've blocked out the pain she was feeling.

Before either of us could utter another word, I suddenly realized there was an additional weight on the ground below, just behind Quinn. A weight that I had been too busy arguing with Quinn to realize was there—for how long, I didn't know.

Slowly, I stepped to the side of Quinn, resting my gaze on the small figure standing there.

Rubbing the sleep from her eyes, Margo asked, "Who are you two talking about?"

Chapter Twenty-Five

After gently greeting Margo and being met with more and more insistent questions, I instructed Quinn to take the young female into the closest lounge room in the wing. To my surprise, the general did exactly that without saying a word.

Then, I went to get Byn.

As it turned out, he was already slipping on a soft cotton shirt and heading to the door to our chambers when I opened it.

"I felt a shift in you," he explained before I could even ask what he was doing. "Are you alright?"

"I will be, but..." I hesitated, unsure how to explain how careless Quinn and I had been only moments ago.

Byn closed the space between us, placing a finger under my chin and lifting my face to meet his.

"Tell me."

And so I did, leaving not a single detail out.

Moments later, I found myself in the lounge with Byn, Teagan, Quinn, and Margo. Quinn, Margo, and I sat on plush chairs and sofas that felt much too comfortable for the amount of discomfort in the room.

Byn and Teagan stood near the bookcase on the other side of the space, whispering furiously to each other. They obviously disagreed about how to handle the situation, and they weren't exactly doing a good job of hiding it. I could feel Byn's urge to protect his younger sister at all costs rising within him.

"Why is everybody being so weird?" Margo asked me, shifting to sit closer to me on the sofa, then leaning over to rest her head against my arm.

Thankfully, the sofa we sat on was one of the larger ones in all of The Haven, allowing me enough space to stretch my wing out just enough to wrap it around Margo, drawing her closer to me.

"Sometimes we have different ideas of how a certain situation should be handled," I explained, my voice just above a whisper. "I think, right now, your brother and sister are figuring out how to work past that."

Margo looked over at my wing around her, then up to meet my gaze. I stared back into her big, caramel-colored eyes, trying to let her know without a word that everything was going to be alright.

"I'm telling her, with or without you, Robyn," Teagan finally said, her voice rising to a normal level.

"Teagan, wait—" Byn reached out a hand to try to grab his older sister as she walked toward us, but she was out of reach before he could stop her.

"Tell me what?" Margo whispered to me.

"I guess we're about to find out, aren't we?" I whispered back, watching as Teagan came and sat on the low table in front of the sofa, directly before Margo.

I felt Byn deflate before I saw it, his resolve crumbling.

I knew he just wanted to protect Margo for as long as he could, but she was a curious one. She would have found out eventually.

I envisioned myself running a soothing hand along the bundle of emotions of his that sat in my chest—the ones that seemed to shine a forest-green color in my subconscious. I just wanted him to know he wasn't alone.

I felt a hint of his gratitude at my small act as he took a deep breath, then crossed the space and perched himself across from me on the table next to Teagan.

I shifted my leg slightly so our knees touched, trying to help ground him through the anxiety I knew he was feeling. Though I could feel his appreciation, outwardly, his attention was purely on Margo.

"Margo, there's something we've been keeping from you, but I think it's about time we tell you," Teagan began, her voice somehow light but firm.

She'd make a great mother of her own, someday—if she so chose.

"Now, recalling some of this might hurt a little, but know that we're all right here for you, alright?" Byn chimed in, leaning in slightly closer to his sisters.

It was an intimate moment—one I was incredibly honored to be a part of as Margo slid her little gloved hand into mine. Though she didn't look my way, I knew just holding her hand in mine was a comfort for her in itself. She needed to be grounded, the same way her brother often did.

And I was happy to be that for both of them.

"You... remember the most recent battle, correct?" Teagan began.

Margo shrank back into my wing, which was still loosely curved around her small frame. But despite her obvious discomfort with the topic at hand, she murmured a small, "Yes."

"I know you remember what happened to Ezra—you're still having nightmares about it," Teagan said, her voice the gentlest I'd ever heard it. Her usual firm tone had vanished. There was no room for that side of her right now.

My heart ached as Margo's bottom lip jutted out into a sad pout, and I could tell she was trying her best not to cry. Even so, she nodded.

"Well..." Teagan glanced at Byn one last time before revealing the news to their little sister. "When the group went back for Ezra's... *body*, after the battle had ended, it... wasn't there."

At that, Margo's eyebrows furrowed, her expression shifting from sad to confused in a heartbeat.

"That's who Quinn and Aviva were talking about, in the corridor," Byn added, his voice as soft as Teagan's.

At that, I glanced toward Quinn, who had moved toward the far bookshelf at the front of the room, obviously giving us space. Though *talking* had been an understatement.

Teagan took a deep breath before finally saying, "Ezra didn't die that day, Margo. The Stars know he's been through a lot, but he lived."

Margo's eyes widened, and I could see the questions beginning to bubble up like a geyser about to erupt.

Before she could begin asking what I could only imagine would be an overwhelming number of questions, the door to the lounge creaked open. The torchlight from the hallway illuminated the silhouette of a male, though I couldn't tell who until he began to speak.

"Quinn, are you in here?" Ezra said quietly as he slowly pushed open the door. "Are you coming to bed soon? I—"

Ezra paused after entering the room, the door having swung open at his touch. His gaze found Quinn first, closest to him, then flickered over to where we Thorntiers sat in the main lounge area.

At hearing his voice, Margo stood up swiftly, rounding the table her siblings sat on and standing at the edge of the sofa. If I could barely make out his frame in the doorway, I imagined her view was even worse.

But there was no mistaking that voice.

"Ezra, what are you—" Teagan began asking at the same moment Byn said, "We were just—"

The two looked at each other, their uncertainty about the situation written all over their faces. I could feel Byn's panic rising slightly as the scene before him unfolded faster than he could control.

Seeing Teagan and Byn's hesitation, Ezra's gaze met mine.

Despite the spike of emotions coming from my husband, I still felt calm. I knew Margo needed this just as much as Ezra did.

I let Ezra see the certainty in my eyes as I slowly nodded to him. A small signal, telling him to go ahead.

This was between Ezra and Margo now.

He may not have been blood to her, but I'd learned the past few months that not all family had to be. Blood wasn't what made another family to you.

Love was.

"Margo, I can explain, if you'll let me," Ezra said, taking a step farther into the room slowly, as if approaching a wild beast.

I watched as my own little sister began to shake.

I bit my lip to keep it from wobbling as her knees buckled and she made her descent, sliding to the floor.

My eyes began to water as Ezra, who must have known what was coming, was there in a second, catching her before she could bruise a knee.

And in the next heartbeat, I listened as Margo's sobs errupted.

"It's alright, I'm here," Ezra said over and over as she clutched at him—her brother, her mentor, her friend. Tears streamed down her face endlessly, and her breathing had become ragged as she gulped down air in between her cries.

"I thought—I thought—" Margo stuttered between sobs, unable to complete her sentence.

"I know, little wolf, I know. I'm so sorry," Ezra murmured, resting his chin on top of her head and rocking the two of them back and forth gently.

I couldn't tell the difference anymore between my pain and Byn's inside of me. I reached out and took his hand in mine anyway, giving a light squeeze to let him know I was there, though my eyes remained on the duo on the floor.

I'd *always* be there. However I could be.

As the moment stretched on, it seemed to become apparent that Margo was having trouble calming down.

Ezra seemed to pick up on that fact first and acted on it without a word to anybody else.

Right then, it was just him and his little sister in his eyes.

Ezra sunk all the way to the floor as he pulled back slightly, Margo resting in his lap. Her breathing hadn't slowed—if anything, it had quickened.

It dawned on me then that I'd run into that before.

With Byn, just before battle.

She wasn't just crying anymore. She was panicking.

Coming to that realization in the same moment, Byn took a step in their direction. But the look in Ezra's eyes… I knew he could handle it.

I tugged on Byn's hand so he wouldn't take another step forward.

This wasn't about him—despite how much I knew he wanted to help his sister.

Right now, she needed her other brother.

"Margo, *you're* alright," Ezra said as he took her hands in his. Ever so gently, giving her all the time in the world to pull away, he unclasped one of her gloves at the wrist and slid it off.

Underneath, the skin of her hands was slightly lighter than the rest of her, signifying just how much she wore her gloves. Why, I still wasn't sure—though right then wasn't the time to ask.

"*I'm* alright," Ezra reassured her softly as he clasped her hand in both of his.

Unprompted and still having trouble breathing, Margo shook off his grasp and lifted her hand until it rested on Ezra's bare cheek.

Her gaze bore into his, but Ezra didn't balk. He rested his hand atop hers against his face and stared back, his expression as open and clear as I'd seen it since his return.

"*We* are alright," he said finally.

With that, Margo's breathing eventually began to slow. Her gaze shifted from Ezra's face to focus on the air around him, almost as though she could see something the rest of us couldn't.

Out of the corner of my eye, I noticed Byn and Teagan share a look, though I was still so focused on the scene before me that I didn't stop to read into it much.

"I'm sorry," Margo said once she caught her breath. "I didn't mean to get you hurt. I didn't—"

"I know, Margo. But you have to know that I don't regret a thing, alright?" Ezra replied.

"You look..." Margo hesitated as she dropped her hand from his face, finally taking him in fully for the first time.

She didn't have to finish her sentence for us all to know what she meant.

He was much better than how he'd arrived, but he was still far too thin. He looked frail, and his skin appeared sunken in after losing all its color.

He looked sick—and in a way, I supposed he was.

Though, not physically.

"I'll get better," Ezra reassured her. "But you know, all that matters is that in here? I'm still me." I watched as he pointed to his chest, right over his heart, as he spoke.

"You're still you," Margo sighed, her relief palpable.

"That's right. You can't get rid of me that easily," he joked, gently nudging her.

At that, Margo smiled slightly, then jumped into Ezra's arms again in a tight hug.

Finally, I tore my eyes from the duo and looked towards Byn.

He quickly used the back of his free hand to wipe a stray tear before looking my way.

His gaze met mine, and he looked as though he wanted to explain, yet no words passed his lips.

Fortunately for him, he didn't need to.

I felt it all.

Chapter Twenty-Six

The light from the rising dawn outside made its way through the small slits in the stone tower just often enough to become annoying as it repeatedly blinded me. Squinting, I continued up and up and *up* the steps of the tower I'd found Mother in just a few days ago.

Val and I had stayed in Neokell longer than I'd intended, and now I was paying the price. My advisors back in Hollis had sent word through a series of messengers over the past few days, practically demanding me to return home. It seemed the longer I allowed them to stew over our recent loss in the war, the more they wanted revenge.

Not that I was *against* plotting our next moves—I just had other things that needed my attention at the moment, too.

The stairs leveled out below me as I came to the small landing before the ornate door at the top of the tower. I looked down at the tray in my hands, which was nearly overflowing with different fruits and pastries and meats. I wasn't sure Mother could even make it down to the bottom of the tower in her condition—she was beyond thin and weak—let alone the journey back to Hollis, *if* she chose to accompany me.

Keeping my steps light, I approached the door. With the tray in one hand and the keys in the other, I realized I should've been excited to see my mother again, who laid just on the other side of the door.

But instead, I hesitated.

In that moment, I wished Father were still with me. He'd likely have an explanation as to why he'd done this to his wife.

Instead, I was being forced to navigate the situation myself—with Father's vague, mostly irrelevant journal entries to guide me, and nothing else besides my wretched heart.

Steadying my breathing, I slipped the key into the door.

Stepping into the space, I used the heel of my boot to crack the door behind me. My eyes adjusted to the dim light inside, quickly spotting Mother sitting against the far wall.

"Good morning," I said, feeling a tad awkward.

"Dimitri," she responded, though she made no effort to draw closer.

Cringing internally, I slowly made my way over to her. "For you," I said as I placed the tray of food on the cold ground before her.

When she hesitated, eyeing it suspiciously, I sighed and sat in front of her.

"This is the food I was served this morning. I brought it straight here—it hasn't been tampered with." I leaned over and plucked a berry off the tray, popping it into my mouth. "See?"

Mother waited another moment before also picking up a berry and biting into it. She groaned as the flavors hit her tongue.

"I see they bring you the best of the lot," she said, picking up a slice of meat next.

"I would hope so. I am their king, after all." A faint smile tugged at the corners of my mouth.

"Of course," Mother agreed, and we lapsed into a semi-comfortable moment of quiet while she ate to her heart's desire.

"You know, I thought I'd scared you away for good. It's been a few days." Mother gently pushed the tray back a bit, signaling that she'd eaten her fill. It hadn't been much, but if we were going off how skinny she appeared, then I imagined she didn't get fed as often as she should've been in her time locked up.

It would take time for her to adjust.

"I just... needed a little time to think, is all." I ran a hand gingerly through my hair, pushing it back.

"I hope that helped," she said, sounding genuine.

I nodded, but didn't say anything more.

"Have you considered my offer? To train you?" she asked after a moment, her tone as gentle as I'd always remembered it being.

It was difficult, trying to convince my mind that this was the same female who sometimes visited my dreams at night. She spoke and acted how I remembered, but she looked worse for wear. Not to mention, there had to be a catch at some point. She'd been locked away and forgotten about for nearly a decade and a half—there was no way that hadn't begun to affect her after a while.

Despite my skepticism, she was still my mother, though. And some bonds were not so easily broken.

I had to *try*.

It wasn't like I had anything more to lose, anyway.

"Yes," I responded, "I have."

"And?"

At that, I stood and began to pace the small space, my anxiety obvious.

"I have some requirements," I said, not looking her way.

She sat up straighter than before. "Let's hear them."

I curled my hands into fists at my side to keep from wringing them together as I paced.

"I would like for you to do more than train me," I started. When she didn't object, I carried on. "I would have you leave this tower and join me at Gatlyn Castle. You would remain there, but unseen and unheard by almost everyone. You'd be a shadow, if you will. I would keep you clothed, fed, and healed, but you *must* remain hidden. Also, aside from training my zirilium, I'd like to consult you *whenever* I please about *anything* I please. You would act as an advisor of sorts. I imagine you must know more about the South and their weaknesses than I, so together, we will defeat them once and for all."

I paced as I spoke, the possibilities in my mind becoming endless.

Yes. That would work.

It *had* to.

When Mother deigned to answer, I paused my steps and cast my gaze towards her.

Her expression had been carefully crafted into neutrality, as though it was a look she'd practiced often. Eventually, her shoulders sagged slightly, and she loosened a soft breath, as if she'd already come to terms with her fate.

"So?" I inquired.

I wanted to know what she was thinking.

It was times like these that I wished I'd had my twin's gift of naturally being able to read fae as easily as the books she'd loved so dearly.

Ever so slowly, she got to her feet and stood, pushing off the wall so as not to lean on it. The alychite chains around her ankles clattered together as she moved, but she didn't seem to notice as she tilted her chin up to meet my gaze.

And when she finally spoke, she said exactly what I'd been hoping to hear.

"When do we leave?"

***

Dusk fell over all of Neokell swiftly. The sound of hammers and pickaxes hitting stone echoing off the surrounding landscape quieted as the encampment's residents made their descent down the mountain.

Each day, they repeated the same routine.

They woke up before dawn and ate before the sun rose, headed up the mountain that housed the old mineshaft, labored the entire day away by collecting the very material used to trap them there, trekked back down the mountain for their second puny meal of the day, and then they were sent to the cabins and the surrounding areas to rest for the night.

And then they rose the next day, simply to do it all over again—adults and children alike.

It sounded fairly miserable, but considering the vast majority of the fae kept at the camp were Southerners, I couldn't find it in me to care all that much.

Though, I didn't feel guilty for the Northerners forced into that camp, either. They were solely ones that had done something wrong and got caught—from petty crimes to murder. Each Northerner who was there had also had their wings clipped to stop any escape attempts from happening. After that, there was no chance of them flying to their freedom.

I caught sight of the moon through the tower's slits, realizing that most of the encampment's inhabitants had hit the hay after their long day of labor already.

Which meant it was time to get going.

I looked down toward the final stretch of the spiral staircase within the tower, careful to keep a firm grip on Mother—just in case. She was still weak, and the tower was extremely tall; the stairs had been a challenge in themselves for her to get down in one piece.

Once we stepped onto level ground again, Mother let out a soft *huff*, as though relieved. Val stood next to the only door that led in or out of the structure, guarding it exactly as I'd ordered.

Val and I had both dressed in riding leathers. Mine were so black I realized I'd blend in against Ziana with ease, while Val's had been colored a dark shade of maroon—the same as before, but with no brown in her outfit that time. We both had various weapons strapped to us, and if all had gone as planned on Val's end, both of our griffins should be right outside with the rest of our things.

My Right Hand's eyes widened slightly at the sight of my mother, but I didn't have time to attempt reading into her expression. We needed to get going.

Still gently holding onto Mother, I guided her towards the exit. The clinking sound of the alychite cuff still around her ankle echoed throughout the space, but I did my best to block it out. I wanted to trust Mother, but Father's voice haunted me from the corners of my mind, causing me to still be a tad hesitant. With the alychite still touching her skin, at least I knew I could get her back to Hollis with little to no disruptions.

When Mother caught a glance of Val in the dim lighting, she said softly, "Thank you."

Though they hadn't officially met, I'd filled Mother in on who Val was, how we'd met, and her newfound position as my Right Hand. With that fresh in her mind, Mother didn't need an introduction to know who the female before her was.

Nor did Val need one to know exactly who I was helping to hold up.

Val dipped her head in response, though I wasn't sure Mother could make out the movement with so little light. As we came to stand beside Val, she slipped out of the tower to ensure we could get out of there without causing a commotion.

I didn't want to be present when the guards realized their most *dangerous* prisoner had gone missing.

Besides, I'd left a note.

Good enough, I thought.

It wasn't as though I owed those fae anything, anyhow.

"Did everything go as planned?" I directed my question towards Val.

"Yes." She nodded. "The griffins were easy enough to slip out of the stables, and we should have another few moments before the next set of guards shows up. After that, nobody should enter the tower until after the sun rises. By that time, we'll be well on our way back to Hollis."

"Perfect." I kept one arm around my mother as I guided all three of us out of the tower for the first, and last, time.

Outside in the brisk mountain air, Mother and I stuck to the shadows as we made our way over to Ziana. Looking back briefly, I noted that Val was diligently on task as she secured the door to the tower so it looked as though we'd never been there.

A few feet from my griffin, though, Mother paused, her feet no longer helping to carry her forward. Just as I was about to express how important it was that we keep moving, I saw the look on her face, which was pointed up towards the sky.

"Mother?"

"I wished to the Stars every day to see them again," she said, her voice shaking. "I guess they heard me after all."

I swallowed thickly at her words, pushing down the emotions I'd been avoiding since the last time I'd seen my twin.

Clearing my throat after a moment, I murmured a soft, "Let's go," and continued walking Mother toward Ziana.

By the time I'd gotten her settled onto the back of Ziana's saddle, Val was heading our way.

"We're all set to head out," she said as she approached.

"Good. Let's get flying, then. There's nothing left for us here, anyway." I turned to face Ziana, but when I didn't hear Val moving to mount Dax, I turned back towards her.

I was correct—she hadn't moved. She was looking back over her shoulder, in the direction of the tower and the cabins beyond it. Her expression appeared sullen, though I couldn't be sure why.

"*Valenia,*" I hissed suddenly, causing her to jump as whatever trance she'd been trapped in was broken by the sound of my voice.

"My apologies," she responded quickly, shaking her head slightly as though the movement would help her refocus on the task at hand.

With that, she made her way over to the griffin she'd borrowed from my castle stables back home and hopped up into the saddle.

As I did the same, Mother looped her arms around my middle and held on firmly despite her thin stature. Her face was still tilted toward the sky, and a small part of me was a bit excited that we were about to be airborne, so she could be that much closer to the Stars she seemed to adore so much.

"Hold on tight," I advised Mother, then dug my heel into Ziana's flank, causing her to leap into the air and soar upward.

I knew the journey would take longer than it usually did, as I assumed Mother would need more frequent stops than I was accustomed to. But the resounding awe in her watering eyes each time I looked over my shoulder seemed to make it all worth it as I watched her rediscover the world that had missed her for over a decade.

Chapter Twenty-Seven

The only thing keeping me calm was the sound of the water gently lapping against the ship as we sailed the Sisrym Sea.

As well as the knowledge that if anything went wrong over the next few days, I was the only one of the Valwain who could simply fly away from their problems if I so pleased.

I huffed a small chuckle at the thought.

As if.

"Aviva, are you listening?" Caelia questioned sternly, forcing me back into the reality of the present moment.

"I believe you'd just begun listing the ninth generation of the Rividian royal line, no?" I responded with a sigh.

For over a week now, Caelia and Callum had been trying to drill into me everything I *might* need to know for what we were about to walk into.

Apparently, before the sun set today, we'd be greeted by King and Queen Rividian of the Ocrein Isles.

I just wished to the Stars above that they would warmly greet us.

All of us—the entirety of the Valwain, along with Margo, Matea, and the royal Ocrein siblings—had set out on this journey to the Isles, leaving Cairnyl behind about eleven days ago. Byn and

I's advisors had been anything but pleased, but once we, along with Teagan, gave them a vague rundown of why we needed to do this, they seemed to finally understand we were leaving, whether they liked it or not.

Byn had been hesitant to bring Margo along, but since he didn't trust anybody outside of the Valwain to care for her for an extended period, we'd had no choice. She, too, had been getting lessons from Caelia and Callum on how things worked in the Isles.

Aside from that reasoning, Margo had also been drawn to Ezra's side the way a bee was repeatedly drawn to spring flowers. There hadn't been a day since they reunited that Margo didn't visit him, if she didn't spend her entire day with him. It was obvious she had desperately missed her friend and brother. I imagined that simply *seeing* him with her own eyes had helped ease her anxieties, too.

None of us dared to say it aloud, but Ezra was a large part of the reason as to why the journey had taken a day longer than it should have. He was doing much better than before, of course, but he was still healing and rebuilding the strength he'd lost. We'd often had to pause our efforts so he could rest, or so Chess could tend to him. His muscles seemed to lock up painfully when he rode on horseback for too long, meaning he and Chess would often have to ease the aches out of his muscles.

I knew he hated that he was slowing us down, but we all knew he'd hate it more if we'd left him behind. Plus, his vast knowledge could always come in handy.

Aside from that, I'd considered asking Aurora to join us. I'd done so mostly so that she wouldn't have to stay in our wing of the castle all by herself in our absence, but she'd still been cold toward me recently. It was weighing on me more than I cared to admit. I couldn't wrap my head around the switch that seemed to have been flipped inside of her. Instead of asking her to come with us, I'd decided to take this journey as an opportunity to clear my head, so when we returned, I could approach the situation with a clear and calm mind. Before we'd left The Haven, I'd simply asked Aurora if she'd check in on Eden for me while I was away. She'd agreed, thankfully; I felt horrible having to leave my griffin behind, but Callum had warned me that in the Isles, a griffin was a symbol of death and destruction. And since Byn and I didn't want to overstep more than we already were, we'd had no choice.

I had my father and ancestors to thank for that impression of the sweet creatures, I supposed.

"The *tenth*, actually. Now pay attention—this is important," Caelia corrected me with a scowl.

"Honestly, is knowing your entire generational line necessary? How bad can your parents be? I am Queen of the South, after all. Shouldn't there already be some kind of mutual respect?" I groaned, feeling frustrated and fed up.

I'd memorized everything I could about the Isles in the past week and a half. That included each major city and town they had, and which of the three main islands each one resided on. I'd learned the past four generations of Rividian royals by heart, even going so far as what zirilium each of them had wielded. I'd practiced the most common of the traditional Orcein Isle dances—just in case Queen Rividian decided to throw a last-minute surprise ball while we were present.

Now, with us already having left the Southern coastal town of Fallaine, sails high as we headed toward the largest of the Isles, Caelia and Callum were trying to force even more knowledge into my head.

"She's right, Lia," Callum finally chimed in, causing Caelia to spin around to face her brother—partially due to him disagreeing with her and partially for the use of the nickname, I assumed.

Throwing his hands up in a mock surrender, Callum added, "Aviva is going to have to earn Mother and Father's trust in her own way. Plus, they're out of touch—they don't know the status of the war, or even if we won the battle that we originally came to assist in. There will be so much to catch up on when we arrive, my hope is that they'll overlook what exactly we've brought to their doorstep."

A quick, nervous glance passed between Caelia and Callum, though I wasn't sure of the root of their anxiety.

A small tug in my chest had me looking around the dock for the origin of the feeling. Looking toward the front of the ship, my eyes first found Ezra and Quinn. They'd had so little time for themselves since they got married in secret before the most recent battle. It appeared they were trying to make the best use of their time now that they had each other again. They sat at the nose of the ship, a blanket under them and a bowl of fruit at their side. I watched as Ezra lifted some sort of berry to Quinn's mouth, gently feeding her. Quinn, always one to take charge, looked up into her husband's eyes, then fisted her hand in the front of his shirt and pulled him toward her. Their lips crashed together, and I looked away as the couple melted into the embrace.

My cheeks would surely begin to ache if I kept smiling the way I was.

It was so nice to see them both happy, despite everything they'd gone through.

Swiveling my head the opposite way, I caught sight of the warm chocolate head of hair I'd been searching for.

Byn sat with his sisters, with Margo placed between her two older siblings as Teagan read a story to her aloud. I couldn't hear from my position what story was being told, but I could tell from Margo's expression that she was thoroughly enjoying it. Atlas and Lychen—who had been hesitant to board the ship in the first place—were staying near their respective bonded riders, the duo a few feet from the siblings. And while Margo and Teagan were focused on the book before them, Byn was looking right at me.

I could feel a small swell of his emotions rising in me, concern radiating from him.

In all honesty, I *was* nervous. All my life, I'd planned on Dimitri being the one taking the charge of a nation—not *me*, not in the *South*, and definitely not in any way that required me to *sail to the Ocrein Isles*.

And yet, there I was.

Just when I began to think I had everything figured out, the Stars seemed to have something else planned for me.

I allowed all of those mixed emotions to simmer within me, knowing Byn would feel each one. Though, he seemed to be more concerned by what I was feeling than I was, as he started to rise from where he sat with his sisters without taking his eyes off me.

I shook my head and motioned for him to stay. I offered a soft smile instead—the ship was too large for him to hear me from where we were each situated—and hoped that conveyed enough of my thoughts to calm him.

I had somebody else to check in on, anyway.

I stood from the wood of the deck, brushing my black leather pants off as I did so. My sapphire blue top matched the ribbon that held back my thick mess of wavy white hair perfectly, though the sleeveless top had a mix of silver and gold accents stitched into it. To finish the outfit, I had donned my gloves as well as the circlet Byn had given me a couple months back. I'd grown much more comfortable wearing it recently, the weight a sort of protection to feel atop my head.

Caelia and Callum had headed to the far railing, their heads dipped close together in what seemed like an intense conversation. Behind me, I could hear Rayven helping to train Laurence in some of the more advanced Southern fighting moves the spy knew. The older male, despite having been in the Northern army, had needed to brush up on his Southern battle skills. Plus, extra training would only do the males good in order to blow off their pent-up steam.

Though I still didn't see who I was looking for.

Heading below deck and into the belly of the ship, I headed for the corridors of small cabins. Passing by the kitchen on the way, I said a quick hello to Chess, who was currently dictating to the kitchen staff to help him stock up on elixirs and such.

Poking my head into each unclaimed cabin, I finally found her tucked away in the second to last room in the narrow hallway.

"Matea?" I called out softly once I finally found the space she was occupying.

A shuffling sound came from within before my sister responded, "Here, Aviva. Come in."

Slipping inside, I shut the door behind me before gently perching next to Matea, who sat on the edge of the thin bed that occupied the majority of the slim space. She was peering out of the small circular window, looking up toward the sky.

"I should've known I couldn't hide from you," she said, though her gaze remained on the clouds above.

"Never," I joked, gently nudging her with my shoulder. "What's ailing you?"

"Is it that obvious?" Matea sighed.

"How do you think I found you? I could smell the sorrow wafting off you from down the hall."

At that, Matea barked out a surprised chuckle.

We remained like that for a few quiet moments, listening as the waves hit the side of the ship, spraying up and wetting the window we were peering out of. I'd learned that my sister wasn't the type to be so easily forthcoming with her emotions, so I remained silent, giving her the space and time she needed to express herself—if she so chose to.

After a few more waves hit the side of the ship, she finally revealed what was bothering her.

"You know, this is the closest I've ever been to where my father is from."

Ah, I thought. I had been curious about how visiting the Isles would affect her, but she'd insisted on not leaving me to do this without her by my side.

"And how are you feeling about that?" I asked, treading lightly on the subject. Matea still held onto the hope that both her father *and* our mother were somehow still alive. And I didn't have any plans to take that faith from her.

"I'm not sure," she sighed, sounding resigned. "I always dreamed of coming here with him. He'd show me all his favorite spots, take me to where he used to live before he met Mother and relocated for her. But he didn't have any family he left behind—at least that I know of—so is there even anything for me here?"

"Sometimes, those we care for live on through the things they loved," I offered. "If you get a chance to sneak away while we're here, by all means, go explore. Do what you need to do, Matty."

She looked my way and narrowed her eyes slightly at the nickname, though she remained silent for another moment before nodding.

"I'll see what I can do."

"Good." I made to stand up, but before I could, Matty's hand wrapped around my wrist to pause me.

"I have something for you," she stated, releasing me in order to reach into her cloak.

I watched with eyes full of curiosity as she pulled out two stunning bejeweled brooches. They were identical, both depicting the beautiful tree of the Ashford family crest.

"Nan and Pops got them made for us," she explained. "You're a part of our family now, remember? They figured you should have something official to show for it."

"I..." I stared at the brooches in her hand, my emotions a jumbled mix of gratefulness, joy, belonging, and sorrow.

"Don't get all emotional on me now, Viva." She motioned to the right side of my chest. "May I?"

I nodded, still a bit stunned at the generosity the Ashford family continued to show me.

My family.

Matea reached over, gently pinning the brooch to my shirt. Though it was somewhat large, it seemed weightless, sitting snuggly in place against my chest.

I watched as my sister looked down at her own chest and pinned the second brooch in the same spot she'd put mine. She pushed her cloak to be behind her shoulders, resting on her more as a cape than a cloak, so the brooch wouldn't be covered.

Looking back toward me, a small smile took over her lips as she took me in.

"Look at you. You have the features of a Heartshire, you wear the circlet of a Thorntier, and now you're adorned with the crest of an Ashford."

I took a quick moment to bask in the feeling of belonging that rose in me at her words. The weight of the circlet and brooch were light but ever-present. I'd never imagined I would be more than my father's daughter, and yet there I was.

Not just a Heartshire, but a Thorntier and even an Ashford, too.

And as our ship docked on the Ocrein Isles, I made a promise to myself and to the Stars that I wouldn't let any of them down.

***

If I remembered the geography correctly, we'd just arrived in Regis. Regis was the small town that had served Southerners as the main passageway in and out of the Isles for ages, being positioned on the largest Isle, nearest to Fallaine back on the continent.

The Islanders below were obviously confused, and maybe even a tad concerned, as they hovered around our ship on the docks, trying to steal looks at us.

I stood with Byn and Matea on the deck, watching as the ship's staff managed to lower the gangway and secure us an easy way back onto solid ground. Teagan was speaking with the captain on the opposite end of the ship, likely to ensure we'd have a way back to the mainland once our business here on the Isles was through, but all the other members of our group were nearby. Even Margo, who stood with Ezra and Quinn, was close enough to the edge of the ship to peer back at the Islanders below.

Once the staff motioned that it was clear to head down, I heard Byn take a deep breath before stepping forward. As King of the South, it only made sense for him to lead us into whatever it was we were about to face. I fell into place behind him as he made his way down the gangway, my wings tucked tight and my chin held high. I even rolled my shoulders back once I glimpsed a few Islanders gawking at me.

I needed to look the part of queen—now more than ever.

We were halfway through our descent when a female's voice rung out through the air.

"*Stop at once!*"

Running toward our ship were half a dozen soldiers, each dressed head to toe in black—including the chain-mail armor covering their chests.

It didn't surprise me much this time to see females as guards and soldiers; not like it did when I first interacted with the South.

Though I couldn't ignore the way Byn's anxiety spiked in my chest—and stayed that way.

"State your reason for coming to these lands!" the head of the soldiers ordered us as she neared. Her sword had already been pulled from its sheath, and a wisp of shadows wrapped around her arm and down the blade in a fiercely protective manner.

"I *said*—" She was cut off as we all watched two shadows breeze between each of the members of the Valwain and down the path back to land.

The duo of shadows stopped at the very edge of the gangway, not quite crossing onto the Isles and their property, when they materialized side by side to reveal Callum and Caelia.

The Ocrein Isles heir and princess.

"My prince," the lead soldier gasped, then deeply bowed. "And my princess. Welcome home."

"Thank you, Niki," Callum responded, and a weight I hadn't noticed before seemed to settle on his shoulders as he stepped onto the docks and back into his homeland.

"I know this looks... *odd*, but we need to see the king and queen," Callum said.

"*At once*," Caelia impatiently added, stepping down to take up her place at her older brother's side.

"Of course, my prince. Princess." Niki dipped her head toward each sibling respectively, then turned back toward the five other soldiers that were with her, directing some of them to go ahead of us and ready the king and queen, while others helped clear the docks of the fae crowding around.

Cautiously, we filed off the ship and down onto the docks. Callum and Niki lead the way, their voices low as they spoke, though Niki would occasionally look our way as we walked. Caelia stayed near them, though she seemed intensely focused on our surroundings, rather than on her brother's conversation.

Though, I couldn't say I blamed her. The Isles were *stunning*.

The landscape reminded me of our time at Echen Bay. The water was slightly more blue than teal, but the sand was the same near-white. Overhead, flocks of colorful birds flew, squawking to one another—very different compared to the griffins I'd been raised around. Past the sandy shore and small coastal town laid a dense forest—one that we seemed to be heading toward.

Once our group, along with the Titan Wolves—who supposedly refused to be left behind—reached the outskirts of the forest, we paused. It wasn't until then that I noticed the new group of soldiers that had trailed behind us.

"Alright. From here on, everybody needs to grab onto one of the soldiers," Caelia said, turning back to face us.

"Why would we do that?" Quinn questioned.

"Some shadow wielders have what we call hastened shadows. They can maneuver through shadows so quickly that it cuts the time it takes to travel by shadow into a fraction. These soldiers have this ability, and will help us get to the castle much faster," Callum explained, though he looked as though it pained him to divulge this information to us. Based on the murmurs that arose from our group, I felt it was safe to assume Callum looked that way because the mentioned ability wasn't common knowledge.

Tilting my head to look at my husband, I raised my eyebrows in a silent question.

He gave me a cheeky smile, then ever so slightly dipped his head toward Rayven.

Ah, I thought. *Of course our very own shadow wielder would have that ability.*

Because a shadow wielder could only shift one other person besides themselves into their shadow forms at a time, it took a few moments to pair everybody up with a soldier. Everybody except the wolves, who would be waiting here in the small ocean town with a few of the soldiers until we returned. Callum had noted that the castle we were heading to wasn't equipped to house the giant creatures, anyway.

Atlas and Lychen didn't appear too pleased, but once some of our group started taking on shadow forms, they seemed to understand a bit better.

Intelligent creatures, those wolves.

Teagan and Byn seemed put off by the fact that their wolves wouldn't be nearby if needed, their muscles tensing when they heard the news, but we weren't exactly given another option.

Byn paired up with Callum, and Caelia with me. They wanted to present us to their parents themselves, they'd claimed. Rayven refused a soldier, and I noticed that when Matea turned to find a pairing, he headed her way instead.

Teagan had talked softly to Margo for a few moments, trying to calm her sister, but nothing worked. That was, until one of the female soldiers headed over and made a flower bloom behind her ear. Margo seemed slightly more at ease with that soldier after seeing her produce the plant, her shoulders dropping at the sight. Maybe she'd just needed to be reminded that the Islanders weren't so different from her and what she knew, after all.

Once we were all settled, I gave Byn a quick kiss on the cheek, then grabbed Caelia's hand.

In an instant, we took on the shadows and speared forward at a speed faster than I'd ever traveled before. Even when flying with a griffin or with my own two wings, I'd never experienced speed like that.

The forest we'd been standing near breezed by in a blur, making it difficult to track where we were and where we were headed. I kept my gaze ahead, trying to keep track of some landmarks as we passed: a diamond shaped pond, a tree so wide you could carve a home into it, and a field covered in many wildflowers I'd never seen before—the most striking being a variation of one flower type that had black and red petals.

And the entire way, Byn's worries only seemed to build. Considering we were walking into the Ocrein Isles blindly—a place that had been closed off to the outside world for almost a decade and a half before the Battle of Shadows—I couldn't say I blamed him.

Eventually, after what felt like ages but also no time at all, we pushed through another copse of trees to reveal Castle Avyer.

Named after the first King of the Ocrein Isles, Castle Avyer was formed out of black earth and colorful crystals. Though, just having *heard* about the structure didn't do the palace any justice.

The foundations, pillars, and accents were all that black rock, but the majority of the castle was made up of crystals the color of a glowing sunset—colors that matched the sky. They must have found giant crystal clusters below and made them spread into shape. The castle wasn't quite as large as The Haven, but it was impressive nonetheless. The grounds around the castle were clean, comprised of organized gardens and shrubbery, with an occasional fountain or training ring. The closer we got, the more I admired the beauty of this hidden gem.

It seemed so... *peaceful*.

We stepped out of the darkness, the sun beginning to head beneath the horizon as we started toward the castle. Though before we could even step foot onto the castle grounds, another group of shadows flew our way, moving as quick as we just had been—if not a tad faster.

A burst of fire came to life in front of us, shattering that illusion of peacefulness I had been grasping at.

From out of the flames came a couple that I could only assume were King and Queen Rividian themselves.

Before we could utter a word, the queen spoke, her voice full of pure fury and disgust.

"We extend a helping hand during your time of need, King Thorntier, and *this* is how you repay us?" she seethed. "By bringing a *Northerner* to our doorstep?"

Chapter Twenty-Eight

If the shadows ever decided to take on the form of a fae, it would be the female who stood before me then.

Her ebony skin seemed to glow despite its rich, dark shade. Her black hair was done up in a hairstyle called locs—something my time observing the Southerners and Islanders back in Cairnyl had taught me. Almost every loc was adorned with a gold cuff or colorful jewel. And if the gold and jewels weren't enough, atop her head sat a crown made of a mixture of gold and that black metal I'd noticed before on the soldiers. A deep violet gown hugged her luscious curves, leaving little room for open interpretation. Confidence seemed to be etched into her very bones, but when I met her eyes—which were so dark they seemed to absorb light—all I could see was the outrage she was obviously feeling.

"*Well?*" she pushed, demanding answers.

Byn bowed his head. "Queen Rividian, it's great to finally meet you—"

"Save the pleasantries, King Thorntier. You forget that my last memory of you was when you were still a snotty nosed hooligan." She waved him off. "Now, answer my question, before I lose my patience," she said through clenched teeth.

An arm looped through hers, and for the first time, I noticed King Rividian.

The male, while handsome in his own rights, was eclipsed next to his wife's beauty. His soft brown skin had an olive tone to it, and his eyes were a warm, earthy color. He had a head of thick dark curls, and the shadow of a beard growing in along his jaw. He, too, wore violet, his silk shirt matching his wife's gown. His pants were black and his entire outfit was without a single wrinkle—something I couldn't relate to after our long journey.

At the contact of her husband, she seemed to calm ever so slightly as she took a deep breath and awaited our answer. I couldn't help but wonder if they, too, shared emotions somehow.

"King and Queen Rividian, it's my immense pleasure to introduce you to my wife and Queen of the South, Aviva Heartshire Thorntier," Byn announced, his voice strong and confident despite the whirling emotions I knew he was feeling.

Stepping forward, I dipped my chin slightly in an act of respect. "Aviva Heartshire *Ashford* Thorntier, Your Majesty," I corrected, my voice kind but unwavering. "Thank you for coming to our aid recently."

At that revelation, the royals before us lapsed into a stunned silence. I stood perfectly still as their eyes took me in, though what they were searching for, I didn't know.

Seeming to finally notice her own children at our sides, her gaze landed on Callum and Caelia.

"They speak truth?" she asked her son and daughter.

Callum stepped forward, that weight from before seeming to drag him down.

I wondered if his parents had ever noticed it.

"Yes, Mother. Aviva is Queen of the South—and an incredible one at that," he said. I had to hold back my grin at his words, though I hoped he knew I appreciated them.

The queen's head swiveled towards Caelia next, her eyes still holding the same question in them.

"My brother speaks nothing but truth," Caelia agreed, holding her head just a tad higher than before.

At that, the queen seemed conflicted at best as her eyes narrowed.

Though I supposed that was better than the fury she had harbored before.

Suddenly, her eyes began roving about our large group. It was obvious she was looking for somebody specific, though I wasn't sure who until she locked eyes with one of the fae behind me and repeated her question to them.

Then Rayven's deep voice rang out from the middle of our group. "Yes, Your Majesty. I apologize for using your lack of knowledge to my advantage when I came seeking your aid, but Queen Aviva is not the threat you seem to think she is."

I cringed internally as I realized what, exactly, it had taken to get the Ocrein Isles to come to our aid in the Battle of Shadows.

We'd only told them what they needed to know, it seemed.

Upon hearing those words, Queen Rividian seemed to deflate ever so slightly. "I see where your loyalties lie, spy," she said to Rayven.

The queen turned to look at her husband then, and an entire conversation seemed to pass between them within a handful of seconds.

Facing us again, the king said, "We will hear you all out, as we imagine you all wouldn't have traveled this far without good reason. Follow us, and we will ensure you all have accommodations in the castle." He turned to address his children. "And you two have some explaining to do."

Caelia and Callum shared a quick glance, but didn't object to their father's statement.

The tension in the air was still electrified as we headed toward Castle Avyer as one.

Making it past the grounds I'd found so calming before, we began filing into the main entrance of the castle. Upon entering, King Rividian instructed Lyra—the soldier who had been paired with Margo before—to lead us to one of the guest wings. Callum and Caelia, though, parted from our group as they fell in line behind their parents, heading deeper inward.

After stepping inside, I noted that the crystals making up the structure weren't *actually* the color of a sunset—it was simply reflecting the colors of the sky outside. Now, as night fell, the castle was shifting from hues of orange and pink to deep blue and silver, the light from the moon coming through and energizing the Northern zirilium running through my veins.

Once Lyra had led us to what felt like the farthest wing in the entire structure, we divided into pairs again, having been told most rooms would only fit two—some with one large bed, others with two smaller ones.

Quinn forced Byn and me into the room farthest down the dead end of the hall, just like our arrangement back in The Haven. I supposed it made her feel a bit more comfortable, knowing that if anybody ran into trouble, we'd likely be farthest from it. Though Byn tried to argue with her anyway, we all knew Quinn didn't take *no* for an answer.

"The king and queen will see you all in an hour for dinner," Lyra announced down the long corridor just before Byn and I shut ourselves into the room picked for us.

Byn leaned against the back of the door, resting against it as he took a deep breath.

"That could've gone worse," he said quietly, though I couldn't tell if he was attempting to reassure me, or himself.

The room itself was spacious—almost *too* spacious.

There was one large bed in the middle of the room, a small breakfast table with two chairs in the left corner, and two wardrobes. Besides that, the space was mostly empty. I supposed they didn't exactly get a lot of visitors, but the space itself felt cold—and not just because the walls, ceiling, and floor were crafted of earth and crystal.

Fortunately, the crystals were foggy enough in this area of the castle that we couldn't see through the walls into the next room, though I still spoke quietly, just in case there were listening ears.

"So," I began, "how long have you known about Rayven's abilities?"

"Years," Byn admitted as he rubbed the back of his neck. "But he made me vow that I'd never tell a soul. I didn't know Titan Wolves could be turned to shadow, either, until he returned from the Isles so quickly before the Battle of Shadows. He'd used a mixture of Willow and hastening the two of them to make it there and back in time to come to our aid."

"And I guess when Rayven came asking for aid, he didn't mention that you'd taken a Northern wife?" I inquired.

I wanted to be upset about it, but the more I thought about it, the more it made sense. The Rividian royals likely wouldn't have sent their aid if they'd known about me, and Byn had been under a vow.

"There wasn't another choice, Avi," Byn sighed, standing straight and peering down at me. "We both know we would've lost that battle without the Isles's help."

Though I didn't enjoy the sour taste of manipulation left in my mouth, I understood that sometimes sacrifices needed to be made.

Even if it was a part of ourselves we were sacrificing.

"I get it, I really do. But you could've warned me."

"I wanted to, truly. Callum and Caelia thought it'd be better to orchestrate an organic first interaction with their mother.

And since they know her better than any of us, I trusted them." Byn hung his head. "It won't happen again. And before you ask, yes, we're on the same page now."

I nodded, deciding to let this one go. At the very least, we needed to present as a united front—now more than ever.

"We should probably freshen up. Care to join me, my love?" Byn motioned toward the door off to the side, which I could only assume was the washroom. I could hear the teasing in his voice, and a small smile crept onto my lips as I realized how much more comfortable he was when it was just the two of us.

I quirked my mouth to the side, acting as though I was pondering, when a mischievous smirk overtook Byn's lips. Before I could take a step, he reached down and slung me over his shoulder in one quick move. Squealing, I wrapped my arms around his torso as my hair fell into my face, my circlet falling to the floor.

"*Thorntier!* Let me down!" I got out between laughs as he headed toward the washroom.

"If you insist, m'lady." Byn gently placed me back on my own two feet within the confines of the smaller room. Playfully, I shoved him away from me. His smirk only grew, and I couldn't ignore the fire growing in my core.

Logically, I knew now wasn't the time. But it'd been over a week and a half since I'd last been alone with my husband, and suddenly, he was all that mattered to me.

As my laughter died down, I realized his eyes hadn't left me.

He was drinking me in like I was the only thing he needed to sustain himself.

"I used to think I worshipped the Sun for my gifts, or even the Stars for guiding me," he said softly, raw emotion in his voice.

I cocked my head to the side, puzzled.

"But my worship of the Sun and Stars is nothing compared to the way I plan on worshipping you."

My entire face and ears flushed as he stepped forward, cupping my jaw with his hand, tilting my head up towards his. I could vaguely feel myself standing on the tips of my toes in an effort to draw closer.

His lips brushed mine as he said, "I'll praise you for as long as I breathe, Aviva."

Then our lips met in an all-consuming kiss, and if I had ever been more than that moment, I didn't want to remember.

***

"Teagan?" I knocked on the door across from Quinn and Ezra's, calling for my sister.

"Come in, I'm just finishing up with Margo."

Sliding into the room and shutting the door behind me, I noticed the space was set up pretty much the exact same as mine and Byn's room, except instead of one bed, there were two smaller ones. The crystals that made up Castle Avyer were now a mix of deep blues, whites, and silvers, as night had fallen swiftly over the Isles.

"Do you mind lighting a lantern and bringing it over?" Teagan requested from where she stood behind Margo, who was sitting at the breakfast table in the corner. Teagan seemed to be working on taming the young female's unruly short waves with countless bejeweled clips.

Upon realizing who had entered, Margo tilted her head my way and smiled. "Hi, Viva! Teagan is letting me wear my circlet tonight!"

"Margo, please sit *still*," her older sister sighed in a way I knew that wasn't the first time she'd asked Margo to stop moving.

Margo, realizing her error, looked straight forward again and sat up as straight and tall as she could. She was still fairly small for eight—almost nine now—but she'd grown a little taller over the past few months.

Grabbing an unlit lantern off the small table by the door, I called a small ball of blue fire to my palm and placed it inside. The blue flames cast a cool glow—so different from the warm light of the other small fires in the space.

Margo's eyes lit up as I put the lantern on the table before her, but to her credit, she didn't budge.

Teagan did a double take when I finally entered her line of sight.

I knew it wasn't my attire she was concerned with. I'd adorned myself in a deep indigo gown—one with a wide slit running along my leg, so that if I needed to, I could move freely. The sleeves were sheer and thin, and the entire gown was light. I'd gone with this one tonight to combat the warmth of the Isles, though it was also because I'd also picked out a pair of trousers for Byn to wear that matched the indigo color of my dress.

No, it wasn't my attire. It was my damp, limp, wavy hair that had her looking stunned.

"We've got to fix that," she said after a beat of silence.

With only ten minutes to spare before we needed to meet Lyra at the end of the hall, Teagan managed to finish Margo's hair and secure her small golden circlet to her head, as well as twist my hair up into a firm, elegant updo made of twists and braids. Some strands hung in short waves, and my silver circlet was placed atop the crown of my head.

Fortunately, Teagan had been ready to go before I'd stepped into the room. Her hair was in a simple but classy half-up style, with her own golden headpiece adorning her. For what might be the first time I'd ever seen, she had picked out a long green and gold dress. It fit her in all the right places, and it matched Margo's perfectly. Both green gowns had patterns of suns and flowers sewn into them with gold threading, though in slightly different patterns.

When all of us were ready, I grabbed hold of Margo's gloved hand and twirled her in a circle.

"You're going to be the prettiest princess at this dinner, Margo," I exclaimed.

Margo giggled, using my hand to spin herself again, then curtseyed dramatically.

As I watched her curtsey for a second time to an invisible crowd, I caught sight of Teagan looking our way. Before she caught my eye, I couldn't help but notice just how sad the eldest Princess of the South truly appeared. Her lips were tilted up in a soft smile, yes, but her eyes made it look as though she wasn't even in the room with us. She felt far away, like she was trying to outrun something nobody else could see.

Then our gazes clashed, and she looked like the same Teagan I'd always known.

Shaking my head in an effort to clear it, I said to them, "Let's go show them what fae from the mainland are *really* like."

Chapter Twenty-Nine

"Do you think the food is poisoned?" Matea whispered from my left.

I fixed a pointed look at my sister in warning, though I couldn't say I hadn't already considered that thought myself.

When our group had filed into the spacious dining room after following Lyra through Castle Avyer, we'd been surprised to find it empty—void of any of the Rividian royals. The room itself was constructed of the same earth-grown materials as the rest of the castle, including many of the room's components. The giant table in the center, the same one we all had taken a seat at, looked as though it had sprouted up from the floor. The people of the Ocre-in Isles seemed to be very in tune with their zirilium—at least here in the castle.

The rectangular black table had two crystal chairs on each end. Lyra had motioned for Byn and me to sit at one end, leaving the rest of the Valwain to sit closest to us—though my wings made sure I was the one left most uncomfortable.

Byn was to my right, with Teagan and Margo on the other side of him. Matea was on my left with Laurence next to her, then Rayven. Laurence had subtly tried to beat Matea to be closest to me—an act of protection I appreciated—but ended up between Matty and Rayven. Rayven, who had obviously been attempting to take a spot next to Matea, had gotten booted.

If Laurence realized the awkward predicament he'd found himself in, he didn't portray it. He was too focused on drinking in the surrounding details, keeping an eye on each entrance and exit.

The rest of the Valwain filled in almost the rest of the table. Four empty chairs remained on the other side. The two across from Byn and me, we assumed, remained empty for the king and queen—if they ever graced us with their presence. Next to that set of chairs, though, stood two extras for their heir and eldest princess—or so I was guessing.

"That wouldn't be a very intelligent move on their part," Ezra responded to Matty from the other side of the table. "We're the only thing standing between them and the North."

Quinn swiftly reached over and grabbed her husband's hand, squeezing. A warning, it seemed.

Byn leaned forward. "Ezra—"

"—is correct," Queen Rividian finished for him.

All heads at the table snapped toward the far corner of the room, where I assumed a hidden door was, though the way the light bounced around in the crystals made it difficult to tell.

Next to her stood her husband, who hadn't changed since we last saw him. The queen, though, had redressed into another gown—golden yellow to match the gold in her hair—that was even more revealing than the previous one, its neckline dangerously low.

Though the rulers before us had to be at least over twice my age, they had retained their youth and beauty impressively well.

Maybe it had something to do with having peace in their kingdom for over the past decade.

Byn rose to his feet. "I apologize for his bluntness—"

"Please, save the pleasantries. And stay seated. We're here to join you," the king said before they both crossed the space and took their seats at the opposite end of the table. Before anybody could utter a word, two shadows that I recognized as Callum and Caelia squeezed out from under one of the other, more noticeable doors, and speared toward the table. A moment later, the prince and princess were sitting next to their parents on their respective sides.

"Like my wife said, your friend Ezra here is correct—the only reason you've not been sent back home is because without you all, there's nothing stopping the North from coming after *us* next." King Rividian jerked his chin toward Ezra when mentioning his name.

"Though it seems you've already brought them here," the queen added smugly, throwing a blatant glare my way.

"I understand that our union may strike you as odd, but Aviva has more than proven herself. She is my wife and queen, and she deserves respect—despite your opinions," Byn stated matter-of-factly, not breaking eye contact with the queen across from us.

Something shifted slightly in her expression at the way he stood his ground, but it was gone as quickly as it had appeared.

"She might have earned your respect, but what has she done to earn ours?" King Rividian questioned. "Actually, let us start at the beginning. How did your union come to be?"

Before I could glance over at Byn to gauge his reaction and follow his lead, he placed a hand above my knee and squeezed softly. Encouragingly.

He was letting me handle this.

Callum and Caelia had been right. I would have to earn their respect my own way.

Taking a deep breath, I looked straight at the couple across from me, and started from the very beginning.

Leaving out the part about how, for most of my life, I'd been certain I'd killed my mother, I started with my father and the elixirs, claiming I began taking them after an *accident*. From there, it spiraled into how my father had proposed giving my hand in marriage to Byn in exchange for peace between the North and South. Byn chimed in briefly to mention that he'd have done nearly anything for peace after losing his parents, but that our union had been a blessing from the Stars after all. I started again with how my Southern zirilium began to emerge after I'd stopped taking the elixirs, then skipped forward to when Aurora had come to warn us of the impending battle—and how that warning had likely saved lives, especially civilians.

When vaguely mentioning that my father had met his doom during that battle, the king interrupted. "King Horace is no more?"

"Who rules the North now?" the queen added.

Internally cringing, I answered, "My father has met his end, yes. My twin brother, Dimitri, now sits on the Heartshire throne, and... he's decided to follow in our father's footsteps."

The rulers shared a brief glance, their shock evident.

"Carry on," Queen Rividian directed.

Taking a deep breath, I resumed with what we'd discovered since we'd won the war—with the help of the Isles. After that, I allowed some of the Valwain to chime in on our revelations. Laurence described how we'd noticed the records not making sense, and how Matea's suspicions had been enough of a push for us to pursue the matter. We recounted our time sneaking into the North—where I could feel the silent judgement radiating off the king and queen—and the encampment we'd unveiled while there, as well as how our zirilium had been temporarily snuffed out.

In the end, the reason why we'd come all the way to the Isles was glaringly obvious.

And yet, the rulers across from us still seemed to be questioning *me.*

"You mentioned you had Southern zirilium *and* your Northern ones. How is that?" King Rividian asked, looking my way.

"While in the South, I discovered that my mother hails from one of the South's noble families—the Ashfords. I'm not sure how our mother came to be with my father, but she ended up in the North—as the queen. Though, she wasn't seen often by the civilians—likely so her origins would remain secret."

"*Our* mother?" the queen pushed.

"Yes," I said, motioning towards Matea. "This is Matea Ashford, my half-sister. We share a mother, and as a matter of fact, her father was originally from these Isles."

The queen cocked an eyebrow as she took in Matea with a newfound interest, but she said nothing further.

"Entertain me—which zirilium are you able to wield?" the king said, eyes back on me.

Beginning to grow frustrated, I snapped, "*All* of them."

The king's eyes widened as his wife gasped, her hand flying to her mouth.

"*Et monlya,*" the queen whispered the Nolvym words—though it was so quiet, I wasn't sure I'd heard her correctly.

"*Et monlya?*" Byn questioned.

Adding in the same dead language so few new, I asked, "*What does that mean?*" Despite my studies of the ancient tongue, I didn't recognize the word.

The queen, seeming to regret having spoken, clenched her jaw shut.

The king, though, looked more than willing to fill in the blanks. He looked around at those sitting at the table, who all were trying to decode our conversation, before looking back at Byn in question.

"Whatever you have to say can be said before anybody we brought into this room," he reassured King Rividian.

Nodding, the king picked up the slack of his wife.

"*Et monlya* translates literally to *the one who commands earth and sky*. In the ancient texts of the ancestors, though, it was a title. A name for somebody to come. It's been so long, everybody simply assumed it was nothing more than a myth. And yet... here *you* are." He cast his gaze my way.

"It was a text written by *my* ancestor," the queen chimed in, clarifying. "Her name was Tarynama, and she was a fierce ruler. This war you are in started a few generations before her reign. It's noted that as a child, she'd been in an accident where they thought she'd died—but somehow, she'd just barely survived. Yet after the accident, it was said that she came back different. Wiser, but often more distant. She wrote that in her dreams, the Stars themselves would visit her. And that they would someday send *et monlya* to fix the mistake they had made."

"Mistake?" Teagan chimed in, pushing for more information.

The king and queen stalled, as if stunned by our lack of what seemed to be common knowledge to them.

"The star stones, of course," Caelia said, finally speaking up for the first time since making her entrance alongside her older brother.

The room went silent enough that I could *hear* Byn's breathing next to me—deep and deliberate, probably to combat the immense anxiety flooding between him *and* me.

When none of the Valwain said anything, Callum picked up where she'd left off.

"According to the records, the Stars told Tarynama that sending the star stones to your King Baron had been a mistake. That if they hadn't sent the stones, this war wouldn't have broken out. So they promised Tarynama a solution someday—a solution that may just be *you*, Aviva."

"*Me*?" My eyes widened, then I shook my head. "That's impossible. It's just a coincidence."

"My thoughts exactly. The Stars wouldn't make another horrible mistake—such as making *et monlya* a *Northerner*," Queen Ridivian hissed. "Who knows where her loyalties lie?"

I ground my teeth together as I listened to the queen doubt my motives and loyalties. Who was she to question me?

I could feel the air in the large room beginning to stir. The more my thoughts spiraled, the harsher the wind within the room became. Soon, our napkins were flying off the table, and our hair was flying in all directions as my emotions overcame me.

I was the physical embodiment of the wind of our realm.

And I was the very air they all breathed.

Finally fed up with always having to defend myself, I slammed my hands onto the table, rattling dishes as I stood. "You want to know where my loyalties lie? *I'm the one who slayed my very own father!*" I bit out aggressively, though I wasn't done there. "*I* am the one who has sacrificed my entire life for the good of my people—from *both* of my nations. *I* am the one who took down King Horace Heartshire of the North in the Battle of Shadows. And *I* am going to be the one who brings peace to *all* of Inphis—even if I *die* trying."

The hair on the back of my neck stood on end as the air in the room became further electrified with my zirilium—a storm lying in wait just beneath the surface of my skin. My breathing came quick and shallow as I stared down the table at the queen, refusing to look away from her intense gaze.

A few heartbeats of silence later, she began to clap ever so slowly.

"Now *that*, young queen, is how you gain my respect," she announced.

My brows drew together as I fought to keep my emotions—and my zirilium—in check. I was vaguely aware of Byn's hand on my lower back, guiding me back down to sit in my seat once again.

Just at Byn's touch, I was able to release the hold I'd had on my Northern zirilium.

They weren't necessary right now.

"My apologies, but he *did* have it coming," her husband said. "You did the right thing."

I loosened a breath, trying to steady myself as I responded quietly, "I know."

"Now that you know everything, you must know why we're here," Teagan said, her tone cautious.

"Hm?" Queen Rividian hummed, as if we had all the time on the continent to spare.

"We want you to open your borders long enough for you all to help us win this war—once and for all. And we want access to your navy to do it," Quinn spoke out, bold as ever.

The rulers looked shocked at her outspokenness, leaning back in their chairs as they glanced towards me and Byn.

"The general speaks with our voice when it comes to these things," my husband said, refusing to correct or reprimand Quinn.

"Truthfully, we imagined this was what you all had come for," the king responded, moving forward with the conversation after a breath of hesitation. "And my wife and I are in agreement. We'll do this for you all—lend our support, our soldiers, our navy. But we have a... *stipulation* of our own that we'd like you *Thorntiers* to consider."

"And once you agree, we can finally eat," the queen said, looking at the food before us that had gone untouched—and was likely cold by now. That was something Callum and Caelia had taught me during our journey—that in the Isles, nobody was permitted to eat in the presence of the king and queen until the royals themselves had begun to dig in.

"Alright, I'll bite," Byn said, breezing past the comment from Queen Rividian. "What do you want from us?"

At that, the two rulers shared a long look, a smirk growing on the queen's lips as they finally looked back toward us.

"Our stipulation is quite simple, really," she said airily.

And then King Rividian finally revealed what it was they wanted from us.

"As this conversation seems to have brought to light, the South *needs* the Ocrein Isles. And as it turns out, we need the South, too." He paused briefly, as if he wanted us to feel the full impact of what he was about to say. "As was done for centuries to strengthen royal and noble lines, we simply request that *your* princess marry *our* heir."

Chapter Thirty

The feeling of sweat rolling down the side of my face reminded me far too much of how blood felt on my skin. My body didn't seem to know if I should relish in it like I did with the prisoners back in Neokell, or panic as I did when I held my dying father in my arms.

"Focus, Dimitri," Mother chided, shifting her weight subtly from side to side, as though she was debating on when to strike.

Deciding to beat her to it, I then launched toward her as she shifted her weight forward instead of backward. Fireball in hand, I raised it over my head before slamming it down over her.

Realizing her error, her eyes widened slightly before she committed to the forward movement she'd already begun. She rolled under me as I was mid-air, avoiding the fire I had conjured to my palm. Her body seemed to remember whatever training she'd had many years ago.

Landing in a crouch as my fireball snuffed out, I panted heavily. She still fought like a Southerner.

The first few days after returning to Gatlyn Castle, I simply allowed Mother to rest and eat. I needed her to gain her strength, and now she was successfully back on the path to a healthy figure. After the first few days, though, she'd grown antsy—and honestly, so had I. We decided to begin our training that night, starting with earth. She'd claimed that rooting yourself in the earth was the easiest of my three zirilium, so I'd taken her word for it.

What neither of us seemed to know at that time, though, was what would happen once the alychite stopped touching her skin. The moment I'd unclasped the special metal cuff from her ankle, I'd been thrown back as Mother practically *erupted*.

The very ground beneath our feet shook as it cracked and fissured, crystals rising from deep within. Then the plants surrounded and climbed her, and the shadows circled, and I couldn't reach her despite how hard I tried.

Then she went up in a pillar of flames I thought would touch the clouds.

A few moments later, the fire went out, and she fell to the ground in a slump. The plants had burned off of her, the shadows dispersed, and the earth and crystals returned to how they had been—almost as though they'd never been disturbed at all.

She slept until the afternoon the day after that. Fortunately, we'd been so far outside the castle grounds that nobody had mentioned seeing anything to me—*yet.* Once she'd awakened, she and I reasoned that because it happened when the alychite stopped touching her, that the odd events from the night before had been a buildup of years of zirilium. That it had been lying beneath her skin until then, just waiting.

And we'd let it loose.

After that, we'd been much more cautious about taking the cuff off her ankle, though the eruption of power didn't happen again.

I'd decided the cuff would remain on for now. Just because she was my mother didn't automatically grant her my trust.

The night after, we officially began my training.

It'd taken the next four nights before I could move a rock larger than my palm around at will, even with us changing locations to try to connect to different types of rock and earth.

Though, once I'd done it the first time, it felt like a floodgate had been opened within me. My earth zirilium felt easier to access and tap into—a connection I hadn't possessed before then. And after conquering the basics of earth earlier that week, we'd moved onto fire.

My chest heaved as I stood from my crouch, turning on my heels to face my mother, prepared to try again.

Instead, she was already standing.

And the smile on her face could only be one of pride.

"You're beginning to use your zirilium based on your instincts, not your emotions," she praised.

"It just felt... *natural.*" I looked down at my hands in muted awe.

It had been just over a week and a half since we'd left the encampments outside of Neokell. The time since had mostly been consumed by meetings during the days as my advisors argued about our next moves, and training my zirilium with Mother during the evenings and late into the night.

The past few nights, she'd been forcing me to form different shapes out of my deep orange flames. Because I'd already associated my fire abilities heavily with my emotions, it had been much more difficult than I thought it would be to construct simple shapes and forms. We'd begun with a flame, then focused on how to control its size. Then we focused on the fire's heat level, then its form—my favorite being the shape of a longsword, which I'd accomplished just the night before.

In the beginning, when I first began with earth wielding, I was so tired I'd fall asleep the moment my head hit my pillow after training with Mother. Now that I'd been using my zirilium constantly for a couple of weeks, though, I could feel the difference. My mother had claimed that using your zirilium was similar to working a muscle—that it would gain strength over time with use.

Due to the sheer amount of time I was putting into these tasks and my training, my sleep schedule had become atrocious. I could see it in the dark circles appearing under my eyes, and in the way I could hardly focus on my daily meetings.

I was exhausted, but at least I was doing things.

I was still trying to push forward.

I would still win.

"That's how it's supposed to feel," she reassured me. "Your abilities are a part of you—they're not something foreign."

Still looking at my hands, I flexed them a couple times, relishing in the residual power I could feel in them.

"Let's go again," I said, sliding into a loose fighting stance.

Smiling softly—as she always had in my memories—she shook her head.

My heart felt as though it lurched out of my chest as she moved towards the door to the small training room we were in. Reaching out to stop her from leaving, I paused as she turned back around to face the center of the space.

She shot me an empathetic look once she noticed my hand still halfway extended toward her. She didn't comment on it, though; she simply lifted her arms towards the large, metal chandelier overhead and forced the flames to grow smaller and dimmer.

"Come," she said, moving to the middle of the training ring and sitting on the floor.

"What are we doing?" I questioned as I drew closer to her.

Mother remained silent, simply motioning for me to sit across from her instead.

Holding back a sigh, I lowered myself to the floor in front of her, positioning myself so we were face to face about an arm's length apart.

I watched as she closed her eyes and went so still, she could have passed as a statue.

Just as I opened my mouth to ask again what we were doing, she spoke.

"Do you feel them?" Her eyes stayed closed, her hands resting on her knees.

"Feel what? Who?" I looked toward the door in the corner of the room, thinking that maybe somebody had gotten past Val, who was guarding the door.

It wasn't until Mother responded that I understood what she'd meant.

"The shadows, of course."

That was why she'd dimmed the light in the room—to create more shadows.

"We're practicing shadow wielding?" I asked, looking at the darkest shadows in the corners of the room with a newfound interest.

"We're *feeling* them," she clarified. "Becoming aware of the shadows near you on a wielder's level is the first step to forming your initial connection with them."

Questions bubbled up within me, my curiosity beginning to get the better of me. I wanted to understand how it worked, and what she meant by a *connection*. What was it that made shadow wielding different from the other zirilium?

"I've felt other fae when they were in their shadow forms, but never just ordinary shadows," I said, eyeing a shadow nearby skeptically. "And I slipped into my own shadow form once—though only for a split second."

"That's good! You've already got a head start, then." I watched as Mother used her zirilium to rip a small chunk of the stone floor beneath us out of place—a piece no bigger than the size of her fist. When I raised an eyebrow at her methods, she reassured me she'd put it back after we were done.

Using her earth wielding, she suspended the stone in the air above us so that it cast a dark shadow on the ground between our forms.

"Shadows, much like crystals, have a unique energy to them," Mother said, her eyes peeling open to meet mine. "They're stubborn. You have to make them *want* to work with you by sending out your own energy to them and meeting them in the middle. Only then can you form a connection with shadows."

"None of that makes any sense!" I exclaimed, exasperated.

"It will, Dimitri. Now take a breath and focus on the shadow of the stone. Take in its shape, the different shades to it, the harsh and soft edges it possesses." Her eyes flicked down to the shadow between us.

Taking a deep breath to calm myself, I looked down at it and did as she'd said.

My gaze followed the outline of the shadow, taking in the sharp edges on one side and the fuzzy ones on the other. The entire shadow was dark, but I realized that the middle was a deeper color than the rest of it. Surrounding it was warm, dim light from the small chandelier overhead, making it appear even darker.

Oddly enough, it reminded me of Ziana's feathers and how they had such a depth to them.

Suddenly, I felt strangely compelled to reach toward the shadow—so I did.

I paused my movement halfway as the skin of my hand began to feel as though it was tingling.

"Keep going," Mother encouraged, her voice gentle, and I realized she must have been watching me.

Taking a deep breath, I slowly reached out further to the shadow. The closer I got, the more my skin buzzed with energy.

"Don't quite touch it. Get close, then send out your own energy toward it," she advised.

Stopping a breath away from the shadow, the tingling sensation growing stronger, I closed my eyes and took steadying breaths. Focusing intensely, I felt my zirilium flowing through my very bloodstream. I could feel it itching at my hands and fingertips, as though it, too, wanted to form that connection Mother spoke of.

So I allowed it.

Releasing the reins which I held my abilities by, that connection snapped into place so forcefully I *gasped*.

"That's the tether," Mother explained. "Move your fingers now, son. And open your eyes."

My gaze immediately drew to the shadow before me. It didn't *look* any different, but I could sense the energy flowing from it to me and back—as a full circle.

Doing as Mother instructed, I wiggled my fingers just a tad—that buzzing sensation lessened now that I'd accomplished my task. I watched, awestruck, as the shadow followed my movements perfectly.

"I did it!" I wiggled my fingers again, just in case Mother hadn't seen the first time.

I wanted her to be proud of me, I realized with a start. I wanted her approval.

And that single realization opened a gnawing pit in my gut.

Smiling, she responded, "Yes, you did. Now just—"

She was cut off as we both watched my connection to the shadow falter, then fail as it slunk back into its original shape.

"What happened?" I demanded, though my hands had begun to shake.

"Shadows are fickle things, Dimitri. They take years of practice to—"

"But I don't *have* years!" I reasoned, frustration bubbling inside me. And with those quickly emerging emotions—panic, anger, disappointment—a fraction of energy escaped me as the flames of the chandelier overhead grew and grew and *grew*.

She didn't understand. I *had* to master my abilities sooner rather than later, or we'd lose. *I* would lose, and I would fail at accomplishing the final task Father had given me. And if I couldn't succeed, *what was I besides a failure?*

"Dimitri, reel yourself back in!" Mother's hands clasped my shoulders, squeezing.

I centered myself on the feeling of her tight grip, gasping for air to counter the panic I felt.

Concentrating on the air entering my lungs, I clamped down on the loose energy I'd let run wild. The flames overhead immediately returned to their normal, small size, though the ceiling betrayed the evidence of my outburst with black scorch marks.

Panting, I pulled away from Mother. Then, I retrieved the alychite cuff and clamped it down over her ankle.

"You're dismissed," I breathed heavily. "Don't get caught heading back to your chambers."

She was only allowed to travel the castle through the hidden tunnels, though most of what she needed was brought to her chambers by either Val or Hugo.

"Dimitri, I—"

"*Now!*" I shouted, pointing in the direction of the hidden door in the corner of the room.

I watched as her face fell and her shoulders slumped. She looked defeated, almost. I knew I should've felt guilty, but I couldn't see past my own need to be alone.

I refused to be that vulnerable—that *weak*—before anybody else.

Including my mother.

As she departed without another word, I spiraled into a fit of disappointment and hatred—though I refused to admit to myself who I felt these emotions toward.

It'd only add to how inadequate I already felt.

And as the secret door shut behind Mother, my own spiraling mind engulfed me whole.

Chapter Thirty-One

The entire room broke out into chaos.

Each and every one of us, save for Teagan herself, was speaking all at once—either to each other, or toward the Rividian rulers across the table from us.

Surely we could make them see reason or offer them something else in return for their help. While my arranged marriage to Byn had somehow—against all odds—been a success, that generally wasn't the case, if history was to be trusted. More often than not, the two parties were stuck in a loveless, sad, lonely marriage—the two only together out of obligation.

If anybody deserved to grow old with somebody they loved, if anybody deserved to be happy, Teagan did. Even in just the months I'd been in the South, I could see how much she sacrificed not only for her people, but for her family and friends.

She deserved better than what was being proposed.

But what if there's no other way? a voice deep within me whispered fearfully.

Just as I was about to stand and demand they ask for something else, Teagan responded.

"*Enough!*" she yelled over all the loud chatter, slamming her fist against the table.

Breathing too deep to be natural, she looked around at her friends—her family—sat at the table beside her.

"This is nobody's choice to make but mine," she said. If I didn't know better, I'd have said I could already hear the defeat in her voice.

Looking toward King and Queen Rividian, she asked with a level voice, "There's nothing we can offer in place of my hand in marriage?"

Pressing his lips together in what *almost* looked like regret, the king shook his head. "Nothing."

Teagan nodded, releasing a breath slowly through her nose. I could see the thoughts swirling in her head rapidly, but there didn't seem to be another way out.

"Alright, but I have a stipulation of my own," she said.

"Teagan, absolutely *not—*" Byn halted when he saw the resigned look on his older sister's face.

"My baby brother," she said, soft enough that it wouldn't carry to the other end of the table as she placed a hand on his shoulder. "Let me do this for you. For us. For our *people.*"

Sorrow and helplessness washed over Byn's emotions. He would never deny his sisters or take away their ability to make their own choices.

He, as well as Teagan, Margo, and I, seemed to realize what this meant at the same moment.

Byn's eyes moistened, though no tears fell as he nodded slightly to Teagan. Upon seeing this, Margo reached a hand up and tugged on her sister.

"You *can't!* You can't leave, too!" the young female cried out.

She didn't want Teagan to leave her—as she must've felt their parents had.

"Margo," Teagan replied gently, sitting back down in her chair, though she was fully facing her little sister. "I will still see you all the time, alright? We'll work it out. I don't plan on abandoning you."

Before Margo could descend into a full-blown meltdown, Teagan looked up towards the other rulers. "My stipulation is that I will allow myself to be betrothed to your heir, but I will not marry until after we win this war. Do you have a problem with that?" she questioned.

"Father, don't I get—" Callum began, but was cut off when the king held up a hand to his son, effectively silencing him.

"No, Princess Teagan, we do not have any issues with that stipulation. This war will be over soon enough now," King Rividian replied, not giving his son a chance to speak.

"We'd like an official contract, and we'd like to read it once it's drafted up," Ezra said, speaking up when I least expected it. Though, it was a smart idea so nobody could go back on their word.

"Done," the queen said, then held her hand to her mouth and let out a sharp whistle.

A male that I could only imagine was one of the Rividian's advisors entered the room with a scroll.

He spread it out before the king and queen, where he quickly added in the stipulation of waiting until after the war was over for the marriage to become official.

After the advisor had read it over one final time, he handed it off to King Rividian.

"The kings and queens of each party will sign," he said, placing the scroll before him and his wife.

"*Father,*" Callum uttered that single word, his voice nearly breaking as he pleaded with all he had with those two small syllables.

"Sorry, my boy. This is for the best—whether or not you understand that just yet," his father responded, then signed his name without a second thought.

I watched as Callum seemed to deflate and shrink into himself—so unlike the strong, independent male I'd come to know—as he watched both of his parents sign away his future.

The scroll was rolled up and passed down the table, but when it got into Ezra's hands, Byn spoke out again.

"Stop," he said. "I want *my* advisor, Ezra, to read the contract now."

Sighing, the queen waved a dismissive hand in response.

A stunned Ezra, whose eyes had widened, quickly recovered after having been given a clear task. He took his time, reading each and every word, until he'd read the contract in its entirety—*twice*.

"It's as straightforward as can be, Robyn. If not a little vague," Ezra said, pointing toward a specific sentence on the scroll. "Like here, it simply says this union is between the *sole, living Ocrein Isles heir* and the *eldest living Princess of the South of Inphis*. The phrasing is strange, in my opinion, but we obviously know that it's referencing Callum and Teagan."

Byn nodded after hearing that, thanking Ezra for his efforts. A moment later, the scroll had made it to our end of the table, unrolled before Teagan, Byn, and me.

We allowed Teagan to read it before Byn asked her once again if she was sure about this. When she said yes, he only hesitated a moment longer before picking up the feathered pen and signing his name at the bottom, though the motion looked as though it pained him.

When Byn handed the pen to me next, I looked over at Teagan.

I was usually *so* good at reading people, but that skill seemed to evade me then. I didn't know if signing the contract was what was best for her—but I knew it was our best chance at beating my twin and the rest of the North.

After decades of the North winning the majority of the battles, I'd finally leveled the playing field for the South when I'd slayed my father. Now, we needed an advantage.

Repeating that in my mind—that we *needed* this—I signed away any possibility Teagan had of ever deciding her future for herself.

***

"What among the Stars were you *thinking?*"

Byn paced back and forth across Teagan and Margo's shared room.

After I'd signed the contract, the Rividian rulers had declared that it was time to eat—though hardly any of us were feeling hungry by that point. Margo, who had been so upset she couldn't stop her tears from dropping in to her plate, had left dinner early under the watchful eye of Lyra. She was somebody Caelia had given a nod of approval for, so Byn and Teagan had allowed their little sister to be led away.

Once we arrived back in our section of Castle Avyer, Byn had marched into Teagan's room after her. Wanting to make sure nobody else interrupted—and that my husband didn't get too out of hand—I'd been at his heels, closing the door behind the three of us.

"I was *thinking* that this sacrifice can help bring peace to our people," Teagan said, exasperated. "And you can't be upset at me now, when months ago you both did the same exact thing!"

Teagan looked between me and Byn as his pacing stopped before turning to face his sister.

"That was a decision you and I made *together*, Teagan," Byn responded, his voice raw with emotion. "You returned home as fast as Lychen would carry you, and we *talked* about it—along with the Valwain. Tonight, on the other hand, you cut me out of the equation—*all* of us out."

I could feel the despair coming from my husband, threatening to overtake my own emotions—though my feelings weren't too far off from his.

"Because I knew you would say no! And we don't have time to negotiate with them, brother. We need to end this *now*!" Teagan exclaimed.

"We could've found another way. We could've offered them resources, or coin, or even Titan Wolves, for Stars' sake! We could have given them *anything* else!"

"They've thrived without our resources and our coin for over a decade, Robyn. And you know Mother would've been disappointed if we'd given up any of our wolves—especially with so few left," Teagan reasoned.

"Mother would be disappointed that I've given up *you*!" Byn's voice broke.

The room went silent aside from the heavy breathing coming from the siblings before me. Just as I was about to open my mouth to add to the conversation, though, the door behind me creaked open.

Spinning on my heel, ready to slam the door in the face of whoever dared to interrupt, I froze in my tracks as my eyes lowered to see Margo's tear-stained face poking into the room.

"Come here, Margo," Teagan said softly, kneeling and opening her arms toward her sister. I watched, amazed yet stunned, at how quickly Teagan leveled out her breathing and plastered on a small smile.

I had a feeling Teagan had sacrificed a lot more than her future during her lifespan. Just in other ways than she had tonight.

Margo all but ran into the extended arms of her sister. I pushed the door shut after her, hoping to stall any other eavesdroppers.

"Did you enjoy your time with Lyra?" Byn asked her, lowering himself to the floor and sitting next to them.

"Lyra is kind." Margo nodded. "So is Calliope. But Cillian is *not*."

"Calliope, as in Callum and Caelia's teenage sister? And Cillian, the youngest?" Byn tilted his head.

"Yes! Lyra had taken me outside to the gardens, and we came across them in one of the smaller training rings. Calliope looked like she was trying to teach Cillian something, but they didn't have any weapons. When Lyra and I showed up, Cillian seemed like he was already frustrated, but Calliope made him shake my hand anyway while we were being introduced. But then he yanked my glove off and kept refusing to give it back! He thought I was scared of getting my hands dirty, I think."

Both Teagan's and Byn's eyes widened as they listened to Margo recall her time away from them.

"You have them back now, though. I hope you showed him who's boss," Byn said as he took both of her gloved hands in his and squeezed.

"Try not to worry. You shouldn't run into him again, as we're leaving in the morning. But if you see him again, steer clear, alright?" Teagan advised.

"Oh, I will. His colors were all wrong, anyway," Margo responded, sounding as though seeing the young prince again was the very last thing she'd ever want to do.

"Colors?" I finally spoke up after a wingbeat of silence.

At that one word, both of the older Thorntiers' eyes widened as their heads snapped my way. They looked as though they were quickly realizing they'd made some sort of mistake, though I wasn't sure what. I'd simply assumed it was Margo using her wild imagination, but at their reaction, I was beginning to have doubts. Even Margo looked regretful a moment later.

Byn sighed and hung his head, but before he could open his mouth to speak, Teagan warned him, "Don't."

"She was going to find out eventually, Teagan. We hide it well, but our parents hid it better. Plus, if Viva knows, then at least that's one more pair of eyes that can help us keep a more watchful eye on Margo," Byn explained.

At that, Teagan pursed her lips and looked back toward her sister. "It's alright," she reassured Margo. "Go see what colors Viva has."

The young female looked at each of her siblings, who nodded and encouraged her to head my way. Seeming to feel more confident, Margo bounded over to me. Taking my hand in her gloved one, she tugged me down to her level.

Kneeling, I watched as she unclasped her right glove at the wrist and slowly slid it off, letting it fall to the floor next to us.

She held her pale hand out toward the side of my face. I realized then that I couldn't recall a time where she had been without gloves on.

"May I?" she asked, her hand a short breath away from my cheek.

She'd been in a similar position with Ezra not too long ago.

Whatever this was, I could only assume the unofficial member of the Thorntier family also knew.

Nodding slightly, I placed my hand over hers as she brought it to my face. Our eyes locked as she ran her thumb over the skin of my cheek, but I remained still.

Waiting.

Within seconds, Margo's gaze wandered away from mine, slipping to the space around me. The very air I was existing in seemed to be extremely fascinating to her all of a sudden, though I didn't understand why.

"She's a soft lavender," Margo said after a moment, her eyes still searching the air around my figure. "With a mixture of all kinds of shades of blue. And a faint texture—like snow, or a fluffy cloud!"

"What... What is this?" I asked, tilting my head to look past her and toward Byn and Teagan.

"Margo sees the world differently than most fae," Byn started.

"When she touches things—or sometimes when things touch her, specifically her skin—she sees all sorts of things. Colors, shapes, textures. You name it, she sees it," Teagan carried on.

"But why hide it? If anything, it sounds like an awesome ability." I shifted my gaze back to Margo as she slid her hand from my face and into the ends of my hair.

Feeling another texture—something different than before—I realized.

"It's an unreliable ability that can affect her judgement on those around her—like how she did with the young prince, Cillian. She won't forget the colors she saw around him anytime soon, believe me," Teagan explained.

"Plus, we want her to live as much of a normal life as she can. If she didn't wear her gloves, our parents feared she'd become far too distracted by things that weren't really there. The leather of the gloves, she says, is a very faint color—one that's almost unnoticeable—so it's the best we can do for her," my husband said, running a hand through his hair and pushing it out of his eyes. "When she was younger, the trokavs said they'd never seen it before, but that it didn't seem to harm her. Still, it started to exhaust her—seeing things all the time. Hence why we limit it now."

I supposed that made sense. If Margo was constantly touching everyday objects, I imagined she'd become overwhelmed very quickly with different visuals only she could see.

She might even be deemed insane by some, if it became bad enough.

And that would *not* bode well for what was left of the Thorntier family.

No wonder they don't want this getting out, I thought.

As Margo reached forward to touch my dress next, I gently grabbed her hand out of the air and held it in my own. Drawing her attention to me, I smiled softly.

"You have a lovely gift, Margo. But I fear our world isn't ready to handle it," I said gently as I retrieved her glove from the floor.

"When will it?" she asked, her big brown eyes peering into my mismatched ones.

"You'll know when it's time. I promise."

Touching her skin as little as possible, I helped secure her glove over her hand once again. Not seeming to quite understand the gravity of her reality, she smiled up at me.

The gap in her toothy smile was slowly leveling out as a new tooth grew in.

Unable to help myself, I leaned over and placed a soft kiss on the top of her head, affection for the young female overflowing within me.

And as Margo turned back to face her siblings, I caught Teagan's and Byn's eyes as I made the motion of sealing my lips shut and tossing out the key.

Chapter Thirty-Two

A series of faint noises coaxed me from my fitful sleep. Even while asleep, I couldn't rest—especially after the extremely long day we'd had.

As the noises continued, I came to accept that it might be a long night, too.

Giving up on trying to ignore the sounds, I sat up in the too cold bed, my hand immediately reaching for Byn. My eyes flew open a second later, though, when my hand only met empty space.

Blinking twice as my vision adjusted to the darkness of the room, I swiveled my head toward the source of the noise at last.

Standing between the door and its frame, his bare back to me, stood Byn. He was rubbing one of his eyes, and his frame gave away just how exhausted he was, too. It seemed like whoever he was whispering with had dropped by unexpectedly, since Byn looked as though he'd just rolled out of bed and was wearing only a low-lying pair of sleep trousers.

Curiosity getting the best of me, I slipped silently out of bed—taking the blanket with me—and crept up behind him, wanting to know who stood on the other side of the door.

Standing on the tips of my toes, I looked over Byn's shoulder to peer right at Rayven.

"Hey, Rayven," I said with a small yawn. I moved back a step as Byn nearly jumped out of his skin, not having noticed I was up.

"Stars, Avi, you scared me." He clutched his chest, then turned back to his friend and lightly scolded him. "I told you not to wake her."

It was then that I noticed just how distraught the spy looked. His curly hair was unruly, as though he'd been tossing and turning in bed all night before visiting us. Desperation played on his face, and I couldn't help the way my brow furrowed when I realized he was fully dressed, too. I'd never seen Rayven so disheveled.

"My apologies, it's just—"

"What can we do?" I cut Rayven off, stepping forward with the blanket clutched around me.

Byn and Rayven shared a quick look before my husband said, "Rayven... his family lives on this Isle. He's considering going to visit before we leave, but he might be too late—we need to leave in a mere hour or two. The sun will be up soon."

"There's more to it than that, isn't there?" I tilted my head, peering up at Rayven.

He nodded.

The spy simply didn't want to face his troubles alone this time.

"It's just that..." Byn began speaking with Rayven again, but I turned back toward the room and quickly rushed to the bags we'd brought on our journey.

In a matter of almost no time at all, I'd dropped the blanket along with my sleep attire and donned an entirely new outfit. I threw on a more casual outfit, as I didn't know what I'd be walking into. The soft cotton top was a combination of different green shades, ranging from sage to deep forest green—like Byn's eyes. On top of the shirt was a brown under-bust corset with a pattern of suns on it. My trousers were a subtle brown color, and they were light enough to not make me immediately sweat. I laced up a pair of my boots, ran a gloved hand through my bangs and hair, and rushed back to the bedroom door.

Wearing the colors I most often saw Byn, Teagan, and Margo wearing, I headed for the bedroom entrance again. Throwing the door open, I almost caused Byn to fall over with the movement as I looked at Rayven and said, "Let's go."

Byn's lips parted slightly in surprise, though I could feel the respect and gratitude he was feeling at my offer. Each member of the Valwain was vowed to me, yes, but I was also vowed to each of them.

And I wanted to help in any way I could.

"You don't know what you're walking into, Aviva," Rayven warned, but didn't object. He was simply giving me one more chance to turn back around and return to bed—if I so pleased.

In response, I stepped out into the corridor and up to Rayven's side.

"The Rividian rulers are not going to be pleased if we're not both here to give our well wishes before we depart," Byn said, though we both knew I'd already made up my mind.

"Good thing they already signed the contract. They won't back out now," I reassured him, then stood up on my toes again as I planted a kiss on his cheek. In the blink of an eye, though, he cupped my jaw and tilted my face to align with his as he kissed me passionately—and quickly.

I forced down a gasp when he released me seconds after our lips met and had to force myself into turning away from him to face Rayven instead. Every fiber that made up my form could feel the distance growing between us as I began walking out of Castle Avyer with Rayven.

I may not have been the fae Rayven had been expecting to join him, but by the way his shoulders were a fraction more relaxed, I could tell he was grateful for my presence.

Once we passed through one door that led outside, Rayven reached out a hand toward me. "We don't have time to walk, run, or shadow wield. I'll hasten us there—if you're still up for coming."

I frowned at the uncertainty on his face, but gripping his gloved hand in mine, I quirked up one side of my mouth. "Let's get this bird in the sky."

Rayven nodded once, and then we were nothing and everything all at the same time.

Like it happened when we traveled to Castle Avyer, we moved faster than I ever had in all my years. The night surrounding us made us nearly undetectable with all the shadows about, and I was sure Rayven was grateful for it. He wasn't attempting to hop from shadow to shadow in an effort to be sneaky—he was simply relying on how fast we were going to be enough to keep us hidden.

That time, I didn't bother with trying to take in any details as we hastened. I trusted Rayven knew where we were going, and how to get back to where we needed to be. I just held tight to him and let myself enjoy the feeling of moving faster than even flight itself.

Time felt like it had paused as we traveled through the darkness, but I knew some moments had passed and we were drawing nearer when Rayven began to slow down.

Since slowing, I could take in more of our surroundings.

And what I saw took me by surprise.

It wasn't that I hadn't seen the dirty, poor sections of a kingdom or city before. It was just that the rest of the Isle was so beautiful, so charming, that I hadn't imagined a place that looked like where we were then.

Structures lined both sides of the uneven dirt path we'd ended up on. They were little more than shacks, if I was being honest. I imagined most of them only had one room in them. The roofs more often than not had tarps over them, as if to keep out any bad weather. And notably, there were no torches lit outside.

Even though I knew the Isles were home to many fae with Southern blood and zirilium, it seemed like the part of the Isle we stood in now didn't share those abilities—whether they weren't allowed or simply couldn't, I didn't know.

Rayven stopped at the end of the dirt road, releasing us from the shadows as his eyes locked on one shack in particular.

It didn't stand out from the others—it looked as though it was barely holding itself together, and seemed to be crafted of whatever could be found around, just like the rest of them in the area.

It was so, *so* different from the crystal castle we'd just come from, or even The Haven back in Cairnyl.

And yet, the shack before us was where Rayven had called home, once upon a time.

"What is this place?" I asked, my voice coming out quieter than I'd intended.

"The North isn't the only kingdom that shuns those without zirilium," Rayven answered, not removing his gaze from the structure down the path.

That explained why the shacks were made with scraps instead of chunks of earth, and why there were no torches lit anywhere.

None of these fae held those abilities.

In the North, they'd be considered *crids*.

"I haven't been here in twenty years," Rayven said, his voice an octave deeper than usual. "I was six when they sent me away."

Keeping my face calm and open, I stepped up to his side and peered at the shack with him, trying to imagine what he was seeing.

"My mother thought I'd have a better chance at a happy life if I went to go live with her brother, my uncle, on the continent. She... She wanted me to have everything she never had," Rayven spoke with regret in his voice. "She sent me away a couple months before the borders closed. I thought she and Beckett would join me someday, but the day after the borders were sealed, my uncle got the letter saying she'd passed."

"Rayven..."

"Beckett, my brother, is still here. We share the same father, though Beckett was always his favorite." Rayven pursed his lips, doing his best to push back his emotions. "And I was Mother's."

"I haven't heard about your uncle until now," I stated. Not a question, so he knew if he didn't want to explain, he didn't have to.

But he did.

"He reunited with Mother among the Stars."

We stood for a few moments, simply observing. No movement came from within the shack, though it was so early in the morning, that was to be expected.

"What do you want to do?" I asked gently. The situation and how it was handled was completely up to him—I was just there if he needed someone.

Rayven's eyes flickered to the door of the shack before turning to look at me. Within his gaze, I could see all the doubt, fear, and anxiety swirling within him. But between all of that, there was also a hint of something else.

A fraction of hope.

I placed my hand on his arm and squeezed. "You've got this."

That sentence, along with a deep breath, was all it took for him to slide up and knock on the shack door—the same knock the Valwain always did.

I slipped into my shadow form and moved closer to Rayven until I blended in with the shadow he cast under the moonlight. I knew he could sense me there, and I hoped he knew I would be there for him the same way he'd been there for me.

There came a shifting and stumbling sound from the other side of the door, and a moment later, it swung open to reveal who I could only imagine was Beckett.

We'd obviously roused him from sleep, as he was shirtless and his hair was an unruly mess of light brown curls that were a slightly looser pattern than Rayven's. Though, like his older brother, he had the same strong nose and olive brown skin. He couldn't have been but a year or two younger than Rayven. Beckett's skin was littered with small scars, though I couldn't tell what from—only that they'd come from all periods of life, as some looked fairly old while others appeared freshly healed. I watched as his eyes, the same light brown shade of his hair, widened when he realized who stood before him.

"Rayven?" Beckett asked, his voice ringing with disbelief. "Am I dreaming?"

"Not dreaming." The spy shook his head. "It's me, Beckett. I told you all those years ago that I'd see you again, and I meant it."

"How... How are you here? Where have you been? Are you staying?" Beckett began asking question after question, but as he opened his mouth to ask another, a different voice spoke out.

"It doesn't matter, because he's leaving. *Now.*"

Rayven's little brother's form stilled, as who I could only imagine was their father pushed his way in front of him.

Upon seeing the older male, who shared many characteristics with Beckett, Rayven dipped his chin.

"I'm not here to cause trouble, Father. I—"

"The name is Blaine, boy—I'm no father of yours," the old male spat. "And you're no brother of Beckett's. Now get lost again, before I *make* you."

At the threat, I crept forward and was ready to materialize when I noticed Rayven subtly motion for me to stand down.

All I could do was trust him.

"Please," Rayven said, his voice breaking slightly. "I only came to make peace."

"You came to cause trouble, just like you did when you entered the world. I'll say it one more time. *Get. Lost.*" Blaine took a half step forward and raised his hand into the air, causing Beckett behind him to flinch back.

I realized then where he'd likely gotten his scars.

Rayven, though, didn't shrink back or cower. He met his brother's gaze, looking past their father, and I could only imagine what Beckett could see in his eyes at that moment. The disappointment and the regret. And especially the longing to make peace and finally get to know his brother.

And yet, Rayven backed down. He broke eye contact with Beckett, quietly apologized for waking them, and turned away.

He paused just long enough to peer at a mid-sized rock along the dirt walkway, one that was weathered with time and had grass and moss growing around and on it. But if one looked close enough, two small handprints—one slightly larger than the other—could be seen next to each other on the top of the flat rock.

A craft two brothers made many, many years ago.

One that still remained.

Just like their bond, I realized. For just as we got down the dirt path and out of sight of the shack, but before I could return to my normal form, I could hear the sound of somebody running after us.

Peering back, it was none other than Beckett.

Realizing the same thing I had, Rayven turned back just in time to catch his brother as Beckett ran straight into his arms.

The two males held on in a tight embrace, and I thought I'd caught Rayven's chest heave in a held-back sob—though I couldn't tell for sure.

"I've missed you," Beckett expressed, his voice low—likely to avoid attracting any unwanted attention. Including their father's.

How he'd slipped out so soon after, I wasn't sure, but I was grateful to the Stars, anyway.

Rayven needed that moment. He'd needed to hold his little brother again.

I understood, though I almost wished I hadn't.

"Me too, Becks. There's not been a single day that's gone by that I haven't thought of you," Rayven replied, his husky voice raw with unchecked emotions.

Pulling back, Rayven cupped his brother's face in his hands. "Stars, how you've grown," he said, smiling, though his eyes were brimming with unshed tears.

"*Beckett!*" Blaine's voice could be heard from down the pathway.

Beckett looked up at Rayven, who was slightly taller, panic in his soft brown eyes.

"Take this," Rayven said, slipping a small, folded note to him, forcing Beckett's hand to curl around it tightly. "When you need me, you'll find me here. Follow the note, ask whoever you need to, for whatever you need to. Use the authority of the name written there to get you to me, no matter what, alright? You do what you have to, Beckett."

"Rayven," Beckett croaked, his voice giving out as his own eyes filled with tears. He looked *so* torn.

"I know." Rayven pulled him into another tight, but quick, embrace. "There will be a chance to leave soon with the navy—but only one shot. Do what you must and find me. This isn't goodbye."

Beckett's fingers dug into Rayven's back with how tightly he held on, before Rayven pulled back first. I could see the physical effort it took to leave his brother there. I knew, if he could force more than one fae into a shadow form at a time, that we would not be walking away from Beckett then. But Rayven knew as well as any of us that we needed to be on the ship back to the continent soon.

We'd already risked enough with this visit.

"Until the Stars align our paths once again." Rayven rested his hand on his brother's shoulder, squeezing once before letting go and taking a step back.

"Until then," Beckett said after clearing his throat. He held tightly to the note that had been tucked into his hand, as though it were a lifeline of sorts.

And in a way, it was.

When Blaine's voice could once again be heard calling for Beckett—this time slightly closer—Rayven took another step backwards, then another. Then, after one last look at his little brother, he turned and ran.

He ran and ran without looking back, wiping a sleeve over his eyes before any tears could fall. Once he was out of sight of his family, he shifted into the darkness of his shadow form. As the sky lightened a shade, he tethered himself to me, and then we were once again hastening across the Isle.

For the second time in just a couple months, Rayven and I shadow wielded ourselves away from the only remaining family we had left.

And as the night began to fade away to make room for daybreak, I wished to the Stars that we'd see Beckett again—*before* we joined them in the sky.

Chapter Thirty-Three

Sleep had eluded me for hours. It had gotten to a point where I was so antsy, I decided to visit the far western section of Gatlyn Castle, where Hugo's small chambers were. Though, when I hadn't found him there, I headed for the western tower—the place where the laboratory and infirmary were housed.

There, I'd finally found the royal trokav—who was still wide awake and working, to my surprise.

"What was it you said you were putting together?" I asked him, rounding the large stone table he was standing behind as he mixed together ingredients I couldn't—and didn't care to—name.

"I'm creating another batch of Lady Elore's strengthening elixirs. It'll help her continue to build up the muscle and weight she lost while... away," the older male answered.

Besides Val, Hugo was the only other fae I'd brought to light about the situation with Mother. With the shape she'd been in when I'd first found her, Hugo's intervention had been necessary if she were ever to function normally again—and swiftly.

Fortunately, Hugo knew his craft extremely well and took his position very seriously. Though I was now King of the North, Mother had at one time been the North's queen. That alone would make her a Lady of the court—if I were to ever allow it, that was.

Despite Hugo's appreciation for his craft, he also knew Mother *before*. Hugo had been there when my parents had married and had helped Mother deliver me and my twin into the world. Because of this, they seemed to have a fondness toward each other. It seemed like they were almost... *friends*, once upon a time.

I wasn't sure how I felt about the situation just yet.

"Do you predict she'll have to take them for much longer? She's started gaining her endurance back through our training as well." I picked up a small vial of orange liquid, tilting it from side to side to watch small particles within it move about.

"I'm hopeful that after a few more weeks of these elixirs, she'll be well enough to carry on growing healthy without them through training, lots of hydration, and good food." His eyes widened as he spoke before gently removing the vial from my hand, placing it back down.

"And you're up making them in the dead of night because..." I left my question hanging in the air between us as the older male shot me a slightly puzzled look.

"There is much to do, my king. The workflow doesn't just stop when I need to rest."

Much like the endless demands made of me by my advisors, it seemed Hugo, also, rarely caught a moment to breathe freely.

"You know," the trokav began hesitantly, "if you feel you need something—something I can provide—I would be more than happy to make it for you."

My blood ran cold as I processed what he was tiptoeing around.

"Are you suggesting I return to the elixirs?" I asked through clenched teeth. "The same ones that hid such big parts of me from not only those around me, but myself?"

"My king, ever since you've discovered your abilities, you've been different. You've been—"

"Stronger?" I asked, finishing his statement for him. "Or maybe you were going to mention how much more powerful I've become?" I could feel my fury bubbling up under my skin at just the idea of being tamed once again.

Hugo must have seen the pure anger flash across my face as I watched him begin to cower.

"It was simply a suggestion meant to be helpful—but let me know if there is *anything* else I can do for you, Your Majesty." He dipped his head as he turned back to the task he'd been working on when I'd arrived.

Clenching my hands into balls, I brought a fist down against the table next to us, hard enough to rattle the bottles and such littering the surface. I snatched one vial that sat before Hugo and that had been marked for Mother with Hugo's stamp of approval on top of the stopper. Without thinking, I threw it as hard as I could against the far wall. As the glass fell and liquid exploded, I turned on my heels without another word and departed from the room.

Alone in the corridor leading back to the western wing, I wrapped my wings around myself in a rare attempt to soothe my frayed nerves.

I don't need the elixirs, I thought. *I am more powerful than ever before. My name is Dimitri Heartshire, and I will not fail. I will conquer—and I will prove them all wrong. Just as Father instructed.*

Repeating those words to myself a few times in a row, I was able to steel myself against the world once more.

If each day I wrapped my heart in another layer of rock and earth, maybe over time, the protection would finally hold its broken pieces together enough to stop the hurting.

Taking a deep breath as I pushed my hair back and out of my face, I folded my wings back in, rolled my shoulders, and began the walk back toward the other side of the castle. Night was almost at its peak by now, so I needed to hurry.

My trip to Hugo's hadn't been in vain, after all.

***

After a detour that took longer than I'd believed it would, I realized morning would be upon the surrounding snow-capped mountains sooner than I'd thought. It seemed time had slipped away from me, and I needed to hurry if I wanted to show Mother what I'd done with my time since I'd dismissed her much earlier in the evening.

Picking up the pace, I spread my wings and flew through the empty castle corridors until I landed softly outside of Mother's chambers. It was technically very early in the morning at that point, though I didn't expect her to be awake just yet. Still, I knocked and hoped for an answer.

"One moment, please!" her voice rang out from within, sounding wide awake.

What was it about tonight that had sleep avoiding us all?

I stood outside the room, the vial slowly warming in my hand because of the prolonged contact with my skin, for another minute before Mother finally opened the door.

Standing between the door and its frame, Mother was gripping a fluffy robe tightly around her body. She must have thrown it on before answering the door in her sleepwear—though that didn't explain why she was breathing so heavily. As though she'd just ran ten laps around the castle.

But I was here to make peace after how I'd behaved the evening before. In spirit of that peace, I decided to let it go.

"I apologize for disturbing you so late—or early—but I'd like for you to come with me now, if you're able," I said, doing my best to portray myself as patient and thoughtful through the words I picked and the tone of my voice.

"Oh, alright." She tilted her head at my attire—the same dark, malleable clothing I'd worn at training. "Have you gotten any rest, Dimitri?"

I raised my eyebrows, surprised that she seemed to have notes of genuine concern lacing her words.

"Rest is for the weak," I responded, my tone light.

I had meant for my words to be a joke of sorts, though by the sadness that shadowed my mother's face, I wasn't sure I'd accomplished my goal.

Clearing my throat, I motioned to her chambers. "May I come in and wait while you get dressed?"

"Of course," she said after a slight pause, then pushed the door open as she headed toward her wardrobe.

As she picked out a fresh gown crafted of a soft, teal material, I lowered myself into the plush chair before the fireplace. My wings fit perfectly into the back of the chair, and I felt as though I could finally rest if I stayed long enough. Unfortunately for me, I had other things to do.

To keep myself awake, I took the time to look around at Mother's chambers. The first thing that drew my eye was that the hidden door to the secret tunnels was ever so slightly ajar. Though considering she and Val had been strictly using those to get around the castle, I wasn't alarmed. I also couldn't ignore the charcoal and parchment she had on the table before the fireplace—random lines and such drawn across each of the sheets. What they represented, I wasn't sure.

Having collected all the pieces of attire she needed, Mother passed by me in a hurry, her gown and other items clutched to her chest as she also held her robe together.

My eyes narrowed just before she shut the washroom door, as I could have sworn I had seen her wearing boots beneath the robe.

What had she needed boots for if she had only been in her chambers?

A few moments later, when she emerged wearing the gown and a pair of small-heeled shoes—no boots in sight—I let out a breath that had been trapped within me.

Shaking my head, I did my best to let the anxiety roll off me. It was still dark out, and there were only so many torches and candles lit inside the room. It was an easy mistake to have made.

"I'm ready now. Though you haven't said where we're headed," Mother pointed out as she shut the door to the washroom behind her and headed my way.

"It's a bit of a surprise." I stood, stretching like a griffin, before we exited the chambers and started down the corridor.

On another occasion, I'd have us take the tunnels, but it was still dark out. There shouldn't be anybody milling about the castle just yet.

"If it's only a bit of a surprise, can I at least know where we are going?" she asked, her steps light beside me.

"The greenhouse."

Mother's gait faltered as she paused, a soft gasp falling from her mouth.

"That was always my favorite place in the entire castle," she said softly, our gazes locking when I turned back to face her. She was searching for something there, but what she was looking for, I didn't know.

"I remember." I nodded, motioning for her to continue walking with me.

As a young child, I didn't recognize that Mother wasn't Northern. I understood she didn't have wings, but you saw that every once in a while from those that had gone to war. They often came back with pieces missing or bad scars—if they came back at all. I simply knew that she was my mother. I didn't need to know more than that back then.

Because of the simple workings of the young mind, I also didn't notice just how much time she'd spend in the greenhouse. Hours each day, if she could manage it.

Nowadays, I understood it better.

It made her feel closer to her origins.

And while she would never step foot into the land of the South again, I could at least provide her with a crumb of comfort.

I was still clinging to the hope that if I behaved, those I held dear wouldn't abandon me.

Like Father had.

Like my twin had.

Like I'd thought Mother had.

No, the word bounced around in my mind, cutting off my spiraling thoughts. *Not again.*

Taking a stabilizing breath, I realized we'd already arrived before the greenhouse doors. And with the concern etched onto Mother's face, I assumed she'd been trying to get my attention for a moment or two.

"Pardon?" I asked, slowly sinking back into my reality.

"I asked if you were alright, dear," she responded, tilting her head. "We can turn back and find Hugo if you need."

"No," I said, though it came off sharper than I'd intended. Before she could try to intervene again, I cleared my throat and motioned to the tall, foggy glass doors in front of us. "We've already come all this way. Let's go inside."

Mother shot me a skeptical look, but when I held the door open for her, she proceeded through without another word.

Upon stepping into the greenhouse, the substantially warmer air immediately engulfed us—so unlike the frigid temperatures almost year-round inside the rest of the castle and outside.

The entirety of the greenhouse was constructed of giant panes of glass in the shape of a dome overhead. The main doors connected directly to the castle, and another door on the opposite side of the dome lead straight into the forest behind Gatlyn Castle. The top of the dome had a perpetual layer of ice and snow on it, though with the slightly warmer weather this summer, one could see out from all the other windows. At the very center of the greenhouse floor lay a giant mosaic of the Heartshire family crest—an extended wing overlapping a crescent moon.

The same one that I could see inked onto the inside of Mother's left arm as she lifted her arms into the air, taking in the warmth the greenhouse offered.

That crest marked her as the North's. She'd had it since she and Father married—though I couldn't recall Father ever having a crest marked on *his* arm.

"Come this way," I said to Mother, motioning for her to follow me.

Making our way around the largest of the overgrown flowerbeds—something my twin and Aurora used to tend to by hand just often enough to keep the plants alive—I stopped in front of one of the smaller, raised plots. This one had its dirt freshly turned, and the soil was dark with recently applied water. On the surface, it simply looked like an empty flowerbed.

But not to me.

No, I knew what lay beneath.

Waiting.

"If I take your cuff off," I said, turning to Mother, "would you use your zirilium to make whatever is under this dirt grow?"

"It'd be an easy task," she answered, peering at the dirt with a newfound interest.

Crouching, I slipped the key I kept on me at all times out of my pocket and unlocked her alychite cuff, then placed it on the edge of the flowerbed.

"If you would," I requested of her, waving an arm toward the bed of dirt before us.

Mother eyed me curiously, but obliged as she moved closer to the dirt and sunk her hand into the wet earth. She closed her eyes momentarily, and I could tell she was simply reaching out with her zirilium—like she'd taught me to do over the past couple of weeks. And with her reach, I was certain she'd feel the dozens of seeds I'd planted there just a few hours before.

Within another moment, her eyes flew open as green stalks began to sprout rapidly, shoving the dirt out of the way so they could make their appearance for the first time. The stalks quickly started to resemble a real plant as they grew bright green leaves up their stems and gray bulbs on top.

And in mere seconds, they bloomed nearly all at once, causing Mother's mouth to fall agape at what was then before her.

Moon lilies.

Her—and my twin's—favorite.

The white and gray petals of each flower appeared nearly silver as the moon shone onto them through the glass overhead. The centers, though, were a bright purple color—unlike any other plant I'd seen before. It was native to the North and only grew there, as they weren't a flower that was easily accessible to ordinary fae. It was rare to find in the wild, and it was said that if they were, that whoever found them had the Stars on their side. Yet, most of all, the flowers served as a symbol of wealth and prosperity for my people.

Father used to keep them growing in the royal gardens and greenhouse, simply because he could. That was... he kept them *before* Mother had supposedly died. I had always assumed he couldn't bear to look at them after her passing. Now, I wasn't sure what to think. Maybe he simply didn't want any reminders of her in the castle.

The seeds planted in the bed before me were ones I had slipped out of Hugo's stash earlier that night. He kept some of them in his workspace—*always*. I was certain they had some sort of healing property, though I couldn't list exactly what it did. And with how poorly he'd hidden them—next to the orange vial I'd distracted him with—I couldn't imagine they were all that important.

"Where did you find these?" Mother asked, slickness wetting her eyes.

"I have my ways," I said as I watched her lean down and cup one blossom in her hands. Delicately, she took in the soft scent of its purple center.

The flowers seemed like they almost bent *toward* her as she gingerly wove a hand through them. Maybe they did it wasn't like I knew much about plant zirilium outside of what they could do in battle. I wasn't sure what to expect in a softer, kinder setting. But I did know that the scene before me forced a small fissure in the rock I'd formed around my heart. If I had to name it, I'd say it very nearly made me feel... *joy*.

"And... you're welcome to visit them anytime. Or we can find a small pot around here, so you can take a few to your chambers." I rubbed the back of my neck, a shade embarrassed. "Whatever you'd like, Mother."

She took a seat on the ledge of the flowerbed, then grinned up at me. "Thank you," she offered sincerely, then waved for me to come closer, which I obliged to. "Try now, Dimitri," she encouraged as she reached a hand *under* one of the nearest blossoms. I watched with a partial view as the shadow of that flower wrapped around her fingers in an instant, reminding me of the way an ivy plant would wrap around tree limbs in the forest.

When I hesitated, she patiently waited until I, too, reached out a hand toward the multitude of shadows coming from the moon lilies.

I closed my eyes and focused on my breathing. The tingling came quicker this time, though it spread slowly up my arm. I focused on the energy of the shadows that I felt through my zirilium, as well as conjuring the image of the specific flower and its shadow I knew was closest to my hand. I went over in my mind the different swells and divots in the flower's shadow, searing it into my mind's eye until the image was so clear I could nearly feel it.

And then, I *did* feel it.

The connection snapped into place, and I felt myself melt into the shadow. Or maybe the shadow melted into me—I couldn't tell anymore. I was bound to it, and it to me, and we were one as I began to move about.

Looking around, everything looked the same except for me. When I tried to look down at myself, I simply glimpsed a form constructed of black, wispy shadow. I grounded myself in that feeling—it was like being even lighter than when I was flying. As though all the weight of the continent had been lifted from me, even temporarily.

After memorizing that feeling the best I could, I released the binding connection I had with the shadow, appearing once again as myself next to Mother. The shadow sprung back into place without the outside influence of any zirilium.

"I knew you could do it!" Mother clasped her hands together. "You did it—you tethered yourself to a shadow!"

Tethered. I took note of the word, realizing that it fit much better than the binding way I'd been thinking about it.

"I did it," I said, looking down at my usual pale hands, then up at my mother excitedly. "I did it!"

Bubbling with pride and feeling positively overwhelmed, I went in to hug Mother for the first time.

But I quickly stopped in my tracks, freezing, when in a split second her demeanor changed as she flinched back from the almost-contact.

"I'm-I'm sorry," I said, retreating a few steps.

"Not your fault," she reassured me as she looked back toward the flowers, wrapping her arms around herself in what I assumed was an act of self-soothing.

Something I imagined she was far too accustomed to.

What had happened to her in her time away that caused her to react like that?

"Keep practicing," she advised as she ran a finger down a flower petal. "The more you practice, the easier it'll become."

I nodded, doing my best to take in her counsel, though my mind was elsewhere by that point.

I'd begun the evening with training and ended the session by letting my emotions get out of hand. I'd gone to visit Hugo, and ended the conversation by, once again, letting my emotions get the best of me. And now, even when I was trying to behave and to be good—to be who I *thought* everybody wanted me to be—my emotions still got the best of me, and I *still* did damage.

Maybe Father had been right all along.

Emotions *did* make one weak.

And I would die before I let the world see me become that.

Chapter Thirty-Four

The sun had just kissed the horizon when Rayven and I paused our hastening just outside of Castle Avyer's grounds. Slipping back into our physical forms, I tried to read the spy, to understand how he was feeling, but he'd slipped his brooding mask back into place.

It nearly looked like the past hour or two hadn't even happened.

Nearly.

"Do you need a moment?" I asked him, though I knew we both saw the Valwain and Rividian family exiting the castle as I spoke.

There wasn't any more time. But if Rayven needed it, especially after what he'd just experienced, I'd *make* time.

"We don't have time." Rayven shook his head, then held out his hand.

Withholding a sigh, I placed my hand in his, and in the blink of an eye we were hastened, appearing a wingbeat later behind our group.

Our family.

"About time you made an appearance," Queen Rividian said, announcing our presence and forcing all heads to swivel our way.

"Apologies for my tardiness, though I believe my husband is more than capable of bidding you farewell for the both of us," I said as I weaved through the members of the Valwain—all of whom were present and packed, ready to go home—to stand next to Byn. Rayven, I could feel, was hot on my heels.

"It's my fault we're late," Rayven said, dipping his head toward the queen, then to her husband next to her.

Queen Rividian gave Rayven a long, hard look that was almost a glare before turning back to face me.

"King Thorntier filled me in a bit more. If King Horace's son now has zinilium, I'm not sure even the star stones could help you win now. But I wish to the Stars that they'll be with you as you try. It's honorable, your efforts."

Much more honorable than closing our borders and hiding, I thought to myself.

"You know of the star stones? Are they not simply a legend of old?" I questioned after realizing what she'd just let slip.

The Queen looked annoyed at my questions, rolling her eyes, but she answered anyway. "Every legend and myth has a beginning, a seed of truth to it. Don't forget it, *et monlya*."

A chill ran down my spine at the title.

"Do you know more about them? Like where they can be found—if at all?" I pressed.

"I do not. If anybody were to know, it'd be the humans on the Levast Isles. But nobody has heard from them in centuries. We aren't even sure they're still alive." The queen sighed. "Now, be on your way, before you miss your ship back to the continent."

"Our fae will hasten you back to Regis," King Rividian said, waving toward the castle doors. Having been a signal of sorts, a group of guards exited the castle and began pairing up again with members of the Valwain.

"Callum will be meeting with our navy and prepping them to set sail first thing tomorrow, while Caelia will stay with you all.

The navy should arrive in Kyrish shortly after you all make it back to Cairnyl. The seas and winds have been kind to us as of late," the queen told us, motioning to Callum at her husband's side when mentioned.

Glancing at Callum, I couldn't help but notice—not for the first time—how different he seemed when he was around his parents.

Hopefully leading the navy would keep his mind occupied.

As we said our final goodbyes and expressed our gratitude, I couldn't help but catch Callum peering over at Teagan. She hadn't spared him a glance as she fussed over Margo, but Callum appeared extremely conflicted.

I wondered if they'd gotten to talk about their new arrangement, though I doubted they'd had the chance—or privacy.

As we turned away from the Rividian rulers and toward our group, I smiled at Byn as he expressed his excitement at being reunited with Atlas again. Then, I placed my hand in a female guard's and held on tightly as we crossed the Isle in a matter of moments.

Though even the beauty of the Isle couldn't dislodge the pit of nerves beginning to form in my gut at the thought of going to battle again so soon.

Unfortunately, though, there wasn't another option.

We wouldn't rest until the entire continent and beyond knew what peace tasted like.

***

It had taken a little over eight days to get back to Cairnyl after leaving Fallaine. The fae there had wanted us to stay, but we'd had to turn them down in favor of returning home. We let them down gently, saying we'd be back to celebrate once the war was over.

They seemed skeptical, but I couldn't blame them. The war seemed endless, as though it didn't follow the rules of time.

To them, the war would never end.

Our sense of urgency had motivated us to ride faster than before. Now, we had not only our own army at our fingertips, but the Ocrein Isle navy, too.

We couldn't mess up now.

We *would* free the fae trapped outside of Neokell.

Even if it was the last thing we did.

We'd arrived back to The Haven the night before last, promptly fell asleep, and were up at dawn with Giles at our door, requesting our presence for a day of back-to-back meetings. We'd explained, with Teagan's help, the agreement we'd come to with the Ocrein Isles.

Our advisors had not taken it well, to say the least.

But what we'd done had been done. All we could do now was move forward and make the most of what we had.

I hadn't seen Aurora since we'd returned, though, and I planned to change that today.

Knocking on her chamber door, I steeled myself for the sting of rejection I was almost certain she'd cast upon me.

Yet when the door swung open, her body almost slumped in relief. "Viva! You had me worried sick. It's been *weeks!*" she exclaimed as she looked over my form, as if making sure I was all in one piece still.

Stunned, I was silent for a moment before explaining. "I'm sorry, I should've told you we were leaving for a little while. We had some... business to attend to in the Ocrein Isles."

My friend's eyebrows furrowed. "Aren't their borders closed? How did you..." she trailed off, obviously confused.

"We took our chances, and it paid off. That's all," I shrugged. Not wanting to burden her with too much unnecessary information, I carried on to why I was there. "But I wanted to see if you'd like to spend some time with me today. I've asked for some small dishes to be brought to one of the lounge rooms for us—if you'd join me."

Aurora's lips pursed as though she was going to say no, so I was surprised when she nodded instead. "I'd like that."

I grinned at her response, then motioned for her to join me out in the corridor. But as we neared one of the lounge rooms, Byn, Rayven, and Quinn all exited from it, joining us in the hallway.

"Avi," Byn said affectionately once he caught sight of me. Stepping forward, he cupped the back of my neck, tilting my head up as he planted a soft kiss against my lips. I smiled against him, my gaze full of heat when he finally pulled back.

Once he stepped to the side, I peered at Rayven, then Quinn, who was shutting the door behind them. "Is that the lounge where the snacks are that I asked for? I hope you three didn't eat them all."

"No, definitely not. There's a lot of other..." Quinn's eyes flicked toward Aurora, and I realized she was censoring herself in front of the winged female, "*stuff* in there, though, that we can go over with you later."

I frowned slightly, but after what had happened with Ezra, I couldn't exactly blame the general for being overly cautious.

"That'd be great, thank you." I nodded. "We'll check out the other lounge, then. Come on, Aurora."

I grabbed Byn's hand and squeezed briefly before heading down the corridor to the second lounge room in the Valwain's wing of the castle.

I could smell the sweet, buttery scent of baked goods upon entering the room, letting me know we were in the right place that time.

Aurora and I let the door fall shut behind us as we made our way over to the small table by the orange stained-glass window. It had a lovely depiction of a tree making up the pattern of the glass, and I found myself feeling a spark of joy when looking at it.

As we sat before the handful of plates, I smiled at the dishes we'd been served, full of different pastries, breads, cheeses, and fruit.

Safe foods that the Southerners I was closest to had learned I liked. And therefore, Aurora should, too. Maybe Byn had overheard me requesting the snacks and had recommended these foods specifically. I wouldn't have been surprised.

"You're grinning like you've gone mad," Aurora said as she placed a flaky bread on her plate.

"Sorry," I said, clearing my throat. "I was just thinking. Please, help yourself."

Aurora observed me in a way that let me know she had thoughts of her own to share. Though, I didn't push. If she wanted to talk about whatever it was, she'd say something.

She groaned in satisfaction as the flaky bread—that she'd topped with a cream-colored cheese—hit her tongue. I lifted the side of my mouth up in a sly smile, happy that she was enjoying something of the South's at long last.

After a moment of us devouring some of the treats in front of us, Aurora paused and simply watched me again in a thoughtful manner.

I quirked an eyebrow at her, letting her know I'd listen if she wanted to speak. Taking that as an opening, she placed down the piece of fruit she'd been holding and had a curious look on her face as she asked, "You truly love him, don't you?"

Realizing she must have been watching me and Byn in the hallway moments ago, I smiled softly. "With everything that I was, that I am, and that I will become."

I watched as my oldest friend's eyes softened a fraction at my response. It was like I was finally getting through to her—the *real* her—not the shell of herself she'd been for the past couple of months.

"I'm glad you found your place, Viva," Aurora said gently before taking another bite of the fruit she'd set down.

"Your place could be here too, you know. If you'd let it be," I spoke tentatively, keeping my expression open and my gaze soft. I wanted her to know I really meant it. That she was welcome there.

Sighing, Aurora took a moment to contemplate.

"I'm not so sure. I uprooted my own life when I decided to leave the North to find you. I left it all behind, and now I wouldn't even know where to begin starting over, or if I even could."

"You could." I reached across the small table, placing my hand on top of hers. "You *can*."

Aurora remained hesitant, but she didn't seem as close-minded as before.

That moment was my chance to help change things for her.

And I wouldn't let the opportunity go to waste.

I stood abruptly, my wings flaring slightly in excitement as I reached out a hand toward her.

"Come with me. Let me show you something."

She looked up at me, our eyes meeting, as if she expected my offer to be some sort of trick, or something I'd revoke.

I wondered then if she knew how much she meant to me. How much she would *always* mean to me.

I grinned as she slowly placed her hand in mine and stood from her seat.

"Let's see what you've got," she said, her voice sounding a lot like a challenge.

I lead her through The Haven, offering soft greetings to those we passed by—who no longer stared or shied away from the presence of winged fae in the South. They smiled openly and greeted us in return—their queen and her friend.

I guided us toward the front of the castle, where the amount of civilians present was higher. The location I was leading us to was conveniently placed to be the most accessible to the public.

After what felt like ages with nerves eating away at me, wondering how she'd react, we arrived at our destination.

The Haven's infirmary.

I held one of the heavy wooden doors open for Aurora and filed in behind her, but almost ran straight into her when she paused just a few steps inside.

She was taking in the beauty, I realized, as I watched her gaze drink in the space.

The infirmary *was* jaw-dropping. It had a tall, peaked roof overhead, with hundreds of vines and plants hanging from it—some clinging to the stone of the ceiling itself, and others in small pots stuck to the sides of the roof. Each plant was different, though, and was something Chess's mentor had begun with just a handful of different vines. Since Chess took over as Byn's royal trokav, though, he'd added dozens and dozens more. He or one of his fellow trokavs tended to them daily, ensuring they were healthy. The plants weren't only to make the space more lively, though. Each one had a purpose, whether it be something the trokavs could've used to help heal somebody, or just a type that they could put next to patients' beds.

Aside from the masterfully crafted garden above, the infirmary had enough space for well over one hundred patients—if they squeezed a bit. There were rows and rows to our right of small cots, all of which were mostly empty aside from the folded bedding on each. Deeper inside, there were more spaces for patients that offered more privacy, if they needed it. Such as when loved ones had to say goodbye.

Fortunately, the team of trokavs Chess had left in charge while we were journeying to and from the Ocrein Isles had managed to clear out almost all of the remaining patients still present after the

Battle of Shadows. They had been the ones that had been hurt the worst, and needed the most time and hands-on care.

I explained all of this to Aurora as we stood just deep enough in the space to see each section as I pointed them out. Just as I was about to dive into the tall windows that allowed sunlight into the giant room and helped brighten patients' days, Chess caught sight of us. He stood to the left, opposite the rows of cots, where his main workstation was. It looked like he was grinding an ointment together as he headed over to us with the mortar and pestle still in hand, mixing nonstop.

"Hello! I wasn't expecting you today, Viva. Aurora." Chess dipped his head toward both of us respectfully. "To whom do I owe the pleasure?"

"Aurora here was training to be the Heartshire's royal trokav back in the North. I thought it'd be beneficial for her to see how things are done here in the South, and where the miracles happen." I wiggled my fingers at Chess as I spoke the word *miracles.*

"Oh, wonderful! It's a fantastic specialty to have, isn't it?" Chess asked, his voice light and welcoming toward Aurora.

"The best," Aurora agreed with a nod.

"Let me show you around!" Chess exclaimed as he threw all formalities out of the window, looping arms with Aurora and tugging her deeper into his infirmary.

Aurora looked back at me helplessly, but allowed herself to be led away. I chuckled, tagging along behind the duo.

I watched as Chess flitted around from one part of the infirmary to the next, explaining to Aurora not only what it was for, but also relating a brief memory of his to each space. My personal favorite had been when he recalled an encounter he'd had with his mentor. Chess had been much younger and had wanted to get out of an elixir test at the time. In order to do so, he used his zirilium to force a specific plant on the ceiling to grow faster than it should have—a plant that just so happened to drip its nectar into the elixir base for the test. It combusted right as his mentor picked it up, as the movement had caused the base and nectar to mix. Chess knew that this specific plant's nectar was only used for extreme ointments, and in small doses, but wouldn't cause *too* much harm. Apparently, his mentor had been so taken aback that he'd postponed the test in favor of figuring out why his elixir base was acting up.

I couldn't help but smile broadly as Chess recounted the memory, his eyes lighting up as he spoke and his breathing coming out short as he laughed. He was my age, and though I knew he'd experienced grief and hardship, he didn't let it define him. He still did his best to not only strive in his trade, but to be *happy*.

I could only wish that Aurora had caught sight of that, too.

That joy was within her grasp.

As the three of us wrapped up our round of the infirmary, we found ourselves near Chess's workstation once again.

"This was a fun visit. You're welcome here anytime—*both* of you." Chess's gaze bounced between Aurora and me as he spoke.

"Thank you," Aurora responded softly.

Perhaps she was finally warming up to the idea of the South.

"I have to go make my patient rounds now, but it was great showing you around!" The royal trokav waved as he walked backwards a few steps, then turned and retreated deeper into the infirmary, toward the direction of the private beds.

After bidding him farewell, I glanced toward Aurora. I smiled a bit when I realized she was looking around in wonder at the different sections of the infirmary that we'd been shown.

"You could be a part of all this, you know," I said, still observing her.

"Pardon?" Aurora asked, shifting her focus back toward me.

"You could make yourself useful here," I expanded. "You could find purpose again."

At those words alone, her expression shifted from awe to resignation. She appeared almost pained at the thought of what I'd mentioned, but I truly didn't understand why.

"Aurora, *please.* Just tell me what you're thinking. Let me *in*," I begged, taking a step toward her.

I watched as she hung her head, that emotionless mask back in place that she'd often had on before today.

I couldn't grasp it. She'd risked everything to come to Cairnyl—to warn *me*. She'd been with us for months now. What else was there to do besides begin to find her place there? To start over, to build a life?

I was missing something; I was sure of it. I just couldn't figure out exactly what.

"I don't know what I did, but whatever it was, Aurora, I'm sorry." I clasped my hands together, anxiously picking at the skin around my nails.

She took a deep breath before lifting her head again and peering at me. Ever observant, she placed a hand on mine, making me pause my movements.

"Can we go for a fly? Like old times—except just us this time," Aurora asked, briefly looking sad at the mention of it being just the two of us. Maybe what I hadn't considered was how she missed Dimitri—but if that were the case, why wouldn't she express that? Surely that was something we could relate to together.

I nodded, forcing the thought of my twin out of my mind before he was all I could think of.

"Of course. We can even visit Eden, if you'd like," I offered, moving toward the tall doors.

"Yes, I would like that," Aurora responded, though there wasn't a hint of any true emotion in her voice.

"We can have dinner together later, too, if you'd like. I promised Ezra I would help him with Margo's studies this afternoon, but I'd love to meet with you again later," I said as we exited the infirmary, keeping my voice light. I didn't want her to know that my nerves were eating me alive trying to figure out what I was missing and why she appeared so unhappy.

I could've sworn I saw Aurora's bottom lip quiver as I spoke, but when I glanced her way, her lips were tightly pressed together. And when she responded, her voice was clear.

"I'll consider it. You've given me a lot to think about today, Viva."

I frowned slightly at the lack of a solid answer, but nodded as we walked until we stepped outside into the sunlight. The sky above was a soft, midday blue and speckled with white, puffy clouds. There were guards milling about, though when they caught sight of me, they quickly found themselves occupied.

It was almost enough to bring a smile to my face.

Almost.

"Ready to get up there?" I asked, still peering up at the sky.

"Beat you to it," Aurora said, and when I turned back to face her, her feet were already off the ground as she hovered about twice my height in the air, her wings pumping steadily.

"Even with a headstart, I can still beat you to the den," I pronounced, mentioning our destination—where my griffin was.

"Let's see if you're right or not," she challenged, a small smile playing on her lips—though it had a sad undertone to the expression.

Deciding to let it go for right then, I leapt into the sky and flew after Aurora—who had, indeed, gotten a headstart.

***

After spending hours helping Ezra teach Margo about the different zirilium in an alcove of The Haven's library, I was exhausted. It hadn't occurred to me before then why Ezra had requested my presence specifically until the topic of study came up. Then, I spent the next few hours giving demonstrations of different zirilium—and explaining the ones that weren't safe to do while indoors, surrounded by flammable items and other fae. Margo had been disappointed when she realized she wouldn't get to see my lightning up close, but she'd understood well enough—after making me promise to show her another time.

Night had fallen over Cairnyl over an hour ago. I'd told Ezra and Margo earlier in our studies that I had dinner plans, but time had slipped through our fingers faster than we could try to catch it. Once we realized how late it was, I had to excuse myself as I apologized profusely.

Only as I turned the corner into the royal wing of The Haven did I allow myself to slow my pace from a near-run to a brisk walk. Aurora's chambers were at the other end of the corridor, but I took the opportunity to smooth my hair down and tame my bangs as I walked.

The wing was quieter than I'd expected, but considering it was nighttime, maybe I shouldn't have been surprised. Perhaps everybody else was feeling the exhaustion, too.

As I passed by the lounge room that Quinn, Byn, and Rayven had exited earlier in the day, I noticed the door was slightly ajar. I knew Quinn had shut it firmly behind her, but it was always possible that Byn or Rayven had visited again, and hadn't been quite as careful. Taking the liberty to protect whatever Quinn didn't want to reveal inside, I reached over and slid the door shut before carrying on down the corridor.

Stopping in front of Aurora's door, I knocked the familiar pattern of the Valwain.

"Aurora, it's me. Are you ready for dinner?" I called out when she didn't immediately answer the door.

When the moment stretched on, with silence the only thing greeting me from the other side of the door, I grew nervous that she'd decided against dinner. Focusing a thread of my energy toward one of the sun stones on my gloved hand, I channeled that into the stone of the floor beneath me. I reached out through that earthy material, feeling throughout the chambers on the other side of the door.

And came up empty.

"Aurora, I'm coming in," I announced as I reached for the handle—only for it to be locked. I bit my lip in a moment of contemplation before I funneled more energy into a moon stone. Holding out a hand to the lock, I froze it and the surrounding area, then backed up. I was suddenly grateful I'd decided on trousers today as in one swift motion I kicked the door in, the lock and ice shattering as one.

What I saw on the other side of the door made my stomach drop to the floor.

The room was empty.

Aurora wasn't there, nor were any of her belongings. The one bag she'd arrived with was gone, along with its contents. The dresses and other items I'd given her in her time with us, though, were folded and organized neatly on the perfectly made bed. Stepping closer, my anxiety spiked when I saw a folded paper atop one yellow dress.

And it had my name scrawled on the outside in Aurora's handwriting.

Aviva,

If you're reading this, you've already found that I've left.

I don't have a better reason than the fact that he needs me, Viva. You're gone, your father is gone, and I'm all he has left. If I stay gone, too, what then?

Please don't hate me when you discover all I've done.

But in the end, you have everything you ever wanted. It's his turn to get what he wants.

The Stars know he deserves it.

I'm so sorry.

Aurora

I read it once, twice, three times, trying to wrap my head around what had happened. It took me until after the second read-through for me to realize the *he* mentioned in the note was speaking of Dimitri—he was the only one that made sense in that context.

My breath was ragged, as if I'd just returned from a long run. I wasn't sure how long I stood there, stunned, reeling, reading it over and over. I glanced at the made bed, the bare room, the spaces where my friend had existed, where she no longer was—and a part of me mourned.

Then Byn's hands were cupping my face, turning me toward him. He must have been talking, asking me things, but all I could do was meagerly hand the note to him.

He read it once, then wrapped me up in a tight embrace. I could feel him pushing a wave of relaxation toward me through our intertwined souls, and I drank it in—just enough to slow my breathing.

And once there was enough air in my lungs again, it clicked.

I pulled from Byn's embrace, my eyes on the door and the corridor beyond.

"What is it, Avi?" he asked, following my gaze.

"Byn, what was in the room that you, Quinn, and Rayven were in earlier today?" I questioned, my mind begging the Stars for my gut not to be right.

"Our war plans, mostly. Maps, soldier and trokav counts, strategies—things of that nature. Why—"

Before he could finish his thought, I was slipping out of the room and breezing down the hallway until I was flinging open the lounge door—the same one I'd slid shut not long ago.

Only to find the main table in the center of the room bare.

The same place where I could only assume the plans had been earlier that day.

Byn rushed in behind me, then paused. Taking it in for a moment, he swore when he realized what had happened that day.

Aurora had betrayed us.

She'd betrayed *me*.

Chapter Thirty-Five

"You seem like you still have some energy left," Val noted, leaning against the hidden door she'd just slid closed behind her.

"Possibly." I readjusted the three new gold rings on my hands—each one holding a sun stone.

A day or two after I'd showed Mother the moon lilies, I'd taken a quick, discreet trip back to the Neokell encampments. I'd gone alone to save time, despite receiving a lengthy scolding from Val upon my return. But it had been necessary.

A necessary disappointment, Father's voice echoed in my mind.

I'd snuck in, not wanting my presence to be common knowledge, and made my way to where all the prisoner's confiscated items were kept. From there, I'd had almost too much fun picking out sun stones for myself. It had come down to a bracelet or the rings I wore now, but Mother had told me if I ever got ahold of sun stones, to cast out my energy and see which stones responded.

And these rings had practically sung in my presence.

Disgraceful, the voice announced.

It'd been weeks since then, though, and the sun stones had become like a second skin to me. They were comfortable and helped tremendously in focusing my zirilium—so much so that I had begun to best Mother in our training sessions, one after the other.

Except for when she played dirty, like she had tonight when she grew and used vines to trip me before I could advance.

It had been frustrating, making my blood boil, but she'd pointed out that Southerners would do much worse in battle. And at that, I couldn't argue.

"Lady Elore is in her chambers for the night," Val said, confirming that her latest task of escorting Mother through the hidden tunnels was complete.

I nodded once, not sparing her a single glance as I prepared to focus my energy on one of the many boulders we'd brought into the training room. I planned on staying there, tearing apart boulders one by one until the voices ringing out in my head quieted.

Or I passed out from exhaustion.

I was alright with either one, so long as the voice that haunted me was silenced.

As my advisors slowly moved things into place for our next battle, Father's deep voice replayed in my mind more often than not. Somehow, he continued to influence me, always criticizing, even in his absence.

It'd been so long since he'd gotten to me like he was presently, that I wasn't sure how to handle it.

I was relieved, though, that it was only Father's voice that time.

"Would you like to go another round?" Val's voice nearly made me jump. I'd been so locked inside my own head all day that I wasn't paying much attention to anything real.

Finally realizing that she wasn't leaving immediately like I'd thought she would, I peered over at her.

Only for my mouth to fall agape.

Val had changed out of her usual flexible, casual clothing and donned a pure silk floor-length gown. The black fabric hugged her upper body perfectly, while the bottom half flowed down her the rest of her form, a slit on each side exposing her long, pale legs every time she moved. On her hip and side were two large, blood-red flowers sewn into the dress, each one big enough to wrap around her front and back sides, visible at any angle. She had on black heels that made her just a hand or two shorter than I was, and she'd left her short brown hair down to rest just past her shoulders.

She was stunning, and I wasn't sure how I hadn't noticed it before.

"Griffin got your tongue?" Val asked, a cheeky smile playing on her plush pink lips.

"You look..." I trailed off as I took her appearance in once again, then cleared my throat to continue, "very nice."

"Thank you, Dimitri." Her smile grew a fraction as she dipped her head.

"Where are you headed?" I asked, finding myself drawn to her.

I wanted to be closer.

If only to clear my mind.

Or distract it.

"I was hoping you'd allow me an evening off. I was planning on hitting the town, maybe even stopping by my favorite tavern on the outskirts. Just to blow off some steam," she said, motioning toward the open windows and the city down below.

"That sounds like a lovely time," I replied. "The evening is yours to do whatever you please."

"*Whatever* I please?" Her cheeky smile returned, full force. "So if I asked you to join me tonight, would you?"

I paused, taken aback by her request. On one hand, it would be a nice way to keep my mind busy, since it'd been badgering me all day. On the other, I worried about what she meant on a deeper level. What did she get out of going to town with me? Why did she want to in the first place? Was it all some sort of ploy?

"Get out of your head for once, Dimitri," she said, crossing the room to stand before me.

"Take a night off and join me. You've been training non-stop—you deserve a break." She extended her hand toward me. "We both do."

When I hesitated, she added, "Plus, I can't go out looking like this all by *myself*."

At that, I broke into a small smile.

Then I reached forward and took her hand.

"Yes!" she exclaimed. "Now let's go find you something else to wear. Oh! Can I decide on your outfit? I promise I'll pick something almost as nice as mine!"

With our hands clasped together, she tugged me toward the hidden door she'd come from, which we both knew was the quickest way to my chambers.

I smiled at her excitement—a small, genuine smile. The action felt nearly foreign, but I welcomed the change with open arms.

Maybe the day could be salvaged after all.

***

The sign overhead read a single word: *Red's*.

If one didn't know what type of place it was, it would likely be overlooked and passed by. Fortunately for me, Val had guided us there, so I could only assume this was the tavern she'd mentioned. To my surprise, it was positioned at the top of one of the many towers Hollis was often known for. The entire city had a countless amount of these structures, all with large bridges connecting them, intertwining together like the web of a spider. The towers made life easier when majority of the population was always in the sky, anyway.

This particular tower was one of the few that extended farther beyond the main heart of the city. It stood tall and proud, right in between the clutter of the city and the space of the outskirts.

There were no windows displayed on the front side of the building—at least not that I could see from our spot on the sky bridge, standing in line to the side, waiting for our turn to enter.

It felt oddly... *normal*, to be forced to wait in a line with civilians for a change.

"The line usually moves faster than this," Val noted, peering forward to the front of the short line.

When one male before us turned his head back to look at Val, I couldn't help but note how his eyes lingered on her for *far* too long. In response, I loosely wrapped a wing around her form. When he finally peeled his eyes from her and looked my way, I bared my teeth in a threatening grin.

He quickly turned back around after that.

"We've got all night," I reassured her as the line began to move again. They must have sorted out whatever the issue was.

A few moments later, we arrived at the front, standing before a tavern guard.

"No weapons allowed," the male said, barely looking up from where he was examining a cut on his hand. I was confident he hadn't looked farther than the daggers on my waist.

A mistake on his part, truly.

"I believe you'll find yourself willing to make an exception this time," I said, taking a half step forward, which caused him to finally look up.

His expression of annoyance slipped as he came face to face with his king.

Not to mention that Val did, indeed, have a good sense of style. Though I found it a bit cheesy, she had picked out attire that matched hers. I wore straight black trousers without a single wrinkle on them, and a blood-red, long-sleeved shirt that had ruffles framing the V-shaped cut running halfway down my chest. I wore two Heartshire crest brooches on each side of the ruffles, with a chain connecting them that hung against my bare skin. It was more than I usually showed, but Val had insisted, and I found I couldn't turn her down. Not then, anyway.

"My king," the tavern guard said, dipping his head to look pointedly at my black shoes. "Of course. Please, go right on in."

I could hear those in line behind us begin to murmur at what the guard had just realized.

That their ruler walked among them.

Though instead of reacting, I tightened my wing around Val and lead her inside the door that the guard then held open for us.

Walking inside was equivalent to stepping into another realm. The floor was a black stone polished to perfection, reflecting the red lights back to us. The chandelier and torches weren't free flames like normal—they were all trapped within spheres of red glass, giving the entire space a specific glow to it. The walls were painted a deep maroon, one wall being covered in different pieces of abstract art.

But what surprised me most was the ceiling.

In the center of it was a giant stained-glass mural, much like the one in Gatlyn Castle's greenhouse. This one, though, was made up of different shades of red, black, and gray glass, laid out in a geometrical pattern above. That made it so even with the moon overhead shining its light over us, the glow it provided was skewed into whatever color of glass it passed through.

The entire space was unlike anything I'd ever seen before.

"Well, don't just gawk all night. Come on!" Val said excitedly as she stepped out of the safety of my wing and deeper into the tavern.

There was music coming from deeper within, the sound of stringed instruments and drums flowing through the air and becoming louder as I followed Val to the bar to the left.

When I finally caught up to her and slid into a seat next to hers at the bar, she motioned toward the barmaid before us.

"Dimitri, *this* is Red. This is her tavern, but her favorite role to play is the best barmaid I've ever met. She serves up a mean mixed drink," Val said, speaking loud enough to be heard over the music as she introduced me to Red, the tavern being her namesake.

To nobody's surprise, the female behind the counter had an unnatural shade of red hair, as though she'd found some way to dye it—though maybe the lights in there were messing with my vision a little too much. Her skin was pale enough that I imagined she didn't leave the tavern much, and her wings were a deep brown. She was pretty enough, though my eyes didn't linger on *her*.

"Nice to see you again, Valenia. It's been a while." Red smiled at Val as she leaned on the other side of the bar from us, then cast her gaze my way with a wink. "Though I see why you might've been busy."

I shook my head at the implication, but Val swept in before I could respond.

"Actually, I serve our king here now as his Right Hand. Tonight is the first night since he's taken me on as such that I could get him to loosen up and live a little," Val explained, nudging me gently.

Yet she didn't move away after like I thought she would, and I could feel the heat of her skin through the fabric of my clothing.

Red whistled as her eyebrows raised, looking at the two of us in a new light.

"Well, good for you! And you," Red fixed me with a pointed stare, "are fortunate to have her."

"I am," I confirmed, nodding my agreement.

Val looked at me with a hint of surprise masked on her beautiful features, but I carried on.

"Could you get us two of whatever Val's regular is?" I requested, placing a few silver coins on the bar and sliding them Red's way—more than enough to cover whatever we wanted.

"Be back in a moment," the barmaid said, snatching up the coins before the generous offer was retracted.

"So?" Val asked once Red had walked to the back of the bar. "Isn't it awesome in here?"

"It's definitely much more different from what I'm accustomed to," I said, glancing around again. The space was mostly full of packed tables, but over on the opposite side of the tower I could make out couples dancing to the music that seemed to be originating from over there.

"Hopefully a drink will help you loosen up." Val shook her head. I had to adjust my seat to be closer to hers in order to hear her, just a breath of space between our forms at that point.

As if on cue, Red returned with two short glasses of a honey-colored liquid.

"Let me know when it's time for the next round!" she called out, then turned to tend to other customers.

Val clinked her glass against the one I held, then smiled up at me before she took the first sip.

"Perfection, as always," she confirmed. "Try it!"

Following her lead, I took in a mouthful of the liquid and was pleasantly surprised. It had just enough fruit juice and syrup in it to take the edge off the aged alcohol, tasting much more satisfying than the alcohol I used to steal from Father's private stash.

"That's delicious," I admitted, taking another full sip.

"I hope you have a good tolerance built up if you're going to down it quickly," Val warned. "Red is known for the strength of her drinks, even if it doesn't taste like it."

"I promise I do," I reassured her.

I'd just downed my second cup when Val had finally finished her first. I'd learned that she didn't have nearly the kind of tolerance for alcohol like I'd imagined for somebody that frequented a tavern like Red's.

Once she placed her empty cup on the bar, I hopped to my feet. I was careful where I stood so as not to stumble. My mind felt a little foggy, but I much preferred that over the restless voices I'd heard on repeat for most of the day.

"Come dance with me," I requested, holding out a hand toward Val.

If she was surprised, she didn't show it as she placed her hand in mine and said, "I thought you'd never ask."

Feeling freer than I had in ages, I smiled mischievously at her before turning and leading us through the crowd toward the small dancefloor.

As we stepped onto the middle of the dancefloor, the song—which I'd heard before in passing—was reaching its climax. Just as the first verse was through and the chorus began with a beat drop, I shifted my feet swiftly in order to trip Val—then I caught her all in one swift motion, my arm wrapping around her lower back. The position we ended up in looked as though I'd dipped her, but her soft squeal of shock gave us both away. At her reaction, I laughed, and it felt like something that belonged to a version of myself from another life—but laugh I did.

Val, whose arms had quickly wrapped around my neck as I'd caught her, looked up at me in awe as I smiled down at her.

Standing us up straight as the song continued, I held her close as we danced, though she still looked star struck.

"What is it?" I asked her, moving my head closer to hers so we could hear each other.

"You're even more devastating when you smile," she answered, still peering up at me, though I couldn't seem to read the look twinkling in her eyes.

I flashed her a teasing grin just for the fun of it as one song bled into the next, the melody shifting to a faster pace.

We danced for what might've been hours, as I lost track of the number of songs that flowed between and around us. I simply let them take me and direct me in my movements, guiding Val through every motion and step. We glided together on the dance-floor the same way our forms moved in unison—silky smooth and without a flaw.

Together, the two of us laughed and smiled and danced freely, the alcohol allowing us just enough relief to leave the weight of our responsibilities behind for the night. There in that tavern, there was no war, no anxiety, no crowns or titles; it was just me and Val—two fae dancing until the end of time.

As the night went on, the crowd thinned out and the music slowed down. Once the moon could no longer be found through the thick, colorful glass overhead, the music faded out, signaling it was time to go.

As the last few notes played, I spun Val around so her back was pressed flush against my front. Leaning my head down so my lips lightly touched the shell of her ears as I spoke, I said genuinely, "Thank you."

"For what?" I couldn't ignore the chill bumps that erupted across her skin as my lips grazed her ear every time I talked.

"For pushing me to come tonight. I didn't realize how much I needed this."

"You're getting soft on me," Val teased. As the final song ended, she stepped out of my grasp, a small smile still playing on her lips, leaving her cheeks and ears a bright pink. "Let's get you home, Dimitri."

I imagined I could bribe the musicians and Red to let us stay longer, but Val was already taking my hand in hers and guiding me toward the exit.

After a rough and slow flight back to the castle, and a loud, laughter-filled walk toward the royal wing—where I'd also allowed Val a room down the hall—we finally came to a pause before the doors to my chambers.

A beat of silence followed our last bout of laughter as we caught our breath. Val was looking toward the doors of my chambers, but I only seemed to have eyes for her tonight.

It struck me as odd how quickly things could change. I'd once thought I would spend my life with a different female, and that I had found the love everybody seemed to spend their lives searching for. But if I thought I'd felt love before, then what was I feeling tonight?

I reached toward Val, wrapping a strand of her short, chestnut hair around my finger.

She turned her face back toward me, looking up as our eyes met. Whatever she saw there made her breath come faster, and I couldn't help the way my eyes left hers momentarily to peer down at her perfect lips.

"Dimitri..." she said, and if it sounded like a warning, I wasn't heeding it.

Not tonight.

I let go of the strand I'd been holding in favor of sliding my hand fully into her hair at the base of her head, cradling her. I gently tilted her head back as my other hand found her hip, pulling her even closer. I could smell her sweet scent all around me, hear her heavy breathing, and as both of our eyes slid shut, I leaned down, ready to taste and devour and conquer.

But when my lips were a mere breath away from Val's, a clattering sound rung out from the opposite end of the corridor, as if multiple objects had fallen.

Pulling my head back, I peered toward the source of the noise. Then, in an instant, I was backing away from Val as if touching her burned me.

"*Dimitri,*" Aurora gasped, her voice full of disbelief that I could hear despite the distance.

"Aurora, I..." I trailed off, looking between the two females before me.

Aurora, who I'd thought I'd been in love with for years. The female I'd been holding out for, in the hopes that she'd come around to the idea of an *us*. And she had almost done so—right before I sent her to the South to warn Aviva months ago. Though, when things hadn't gone according to plan, I wasn't sure if she'd be coming back at all.

As it turned out, it looked like she'd hatched a plan of her own.

And she was back.

She'd returned, and yet when I looked at her, none of that desire I'd felt for years was there anymore. What I'd felt for Aurora paled in comparison to what I'd felt tonight with Val.

But Aurora had scrolls, journals, and maps at her feet—the items she'd dropped. She looked like she'd flown straight there with all of it in hand.

And if Aurora's heart was what I needed to keep intact to win the war, then I could live with breaking Val's.

At least, I wished to the Stars that I could.

Glancing at Val, she was staring at Aurora, her gaze cold—absent of any and all heat I'd seen just seconds ago.

It seemed Aurora had returned with something in hand, after all. I'd hoped months ago that she'd return with my twin, but what lay at her feet might be even better suited for me now.

Although her timing could've been better.

Clearing my throat, I slid on the kingly mask I'd worn for so many years now—numb, disconnected, empty.

Like Father.

"Valenia, you're dismissed," I said, my voice as cold as the look she had trained on Aurora.

"What?" Val's gaze snapped to meet mine. Where she'd appeared cold and callused to Aurora, when she looked at me, an ember of that heat remained.

"Shall I repeat myself?" I questioned, placing my hands behind my back to keep myself from reaching for her.

She was who I wanted.

Who I *needed*.

And yet, there I was, pushing her away in favor of winning the war.

Conquer them all, Father's voice demanded. It echoed in my mind as I watched Val stiffly dip her head and mechanically walk away, passing Aurora without a glance. Val's posture was rigid, even as she rounded the corner and walked out of sight, heading deeper into the castle without another word.

And for the first time in a while, my heart ached as she left my sight.

Taking a deep breath, I focused on what I had to do next.

"Come," I said to Aurora, opening the door to my private chambers and motioning for her to follow.

A moment later she filed in behind me, using her foot to shut the door behind her. She crossed the space to the large table I stood beside, dumping the contents in her arms carelessly onto the table.

She was upset—I could see it in the tension in her shoulders—but I didn't have time for that right then.

"Where are they heading?" I asked her, glancing at the many items atop the table.

"It seems random," she shook her head. "They're aiming for some spot just outside of Neokell, but—"

"Neokell?" I asked, needing to be confident. "You're sure?"

I'd never shared all that I'd discovered with Aurora. I had wanted to spare her the horror of our reality.

And the horror of the real me.

The same one Val had seen, and had not backed away from.

"Yes," Aurora snapped as she unrolled one of the maps and pointed to where a sloppy circle had been drawn around where the old mines were.

And where the encampments were now.

Somehow, my twin had figured out exactly what I—and Father—had tried so desperately to keep hidden.

"They're coming *soon*," she warned, rolling the map back up.

"We have to act," I stated, my heart pounding as my mind reeled with the newfound information before me.

"Better do it sooner rather than later," Aurora said as she headed for the door.

She was upset, and likely needed space—I wasn't going to force her to stay if she wanted to leave.

But she didn't.

I watched as she slid the lock on my chamber doors into place, then turned back to face me, her voice slightly quieter.

"And Dimi?" she inquired, slipping another folded sheet of parchment out of her dress pocket.

"Hmm?" I hummed, tilting my head at her.

"There's *more.*"

Chapter Thirty-Six

Passing through Kyrish so swiftly had reminded me of the way we'd breezed through Fallaine to get to the Ocrein Isles.

Kyrish was a coastal town, one that was closest to the Levast Isles—where the humans remained in complete and utter silence. In peace, I imagined.

So unlike what we were facing here on the continent.

"Callum and the navy are passing around the Levast Isles as we speak. They should be here in time—he hopes," Caelia said, holding a small piece of parchment as she barged into the large tent.

A piece of parchment that had, obviously, come from the vial of a messenger corvid. The very thing we'd been waiting on all day.

It had been six days since Aurora had left and betrayed us all in one fell swoop.

Since then, the Valwain and the rest of the South had jumped into action, accomplishing much despite the tighter timeline. Even though Aurora had taken many of our plans, maps, and strategies, we still had the element of surprise on our side.

The North didn't know *when* we would strike, only *where.*

Plus, at the time of Aurora's betrayal, we hadn't yet factored the navy into our plans.

The North only knew a *fraction* of the might that was about to rain down on them.

This time, we were not afraid.

"He *hopes?*" Quinn questioned, cocking her scarred eyebrow at the princess.

"I know my brother," Caelia stared back at the general on the other side of the war table. "He'll be there, and he'll be right on time."

Quinn nodded firmly, then turned her attention back to the table before her, which displayed a raised, textured map of the entire continent.

Our entire realm, laid out at our fingertips.

The entire Valwain was present, along with Matea, Caelia, and a couple of Quinn's army captains. We'd set up camp in Glaytred Forest earlier that day, after sailing from Kyrish to the sparse edges of the forest. We'd borrowed nearly every boat in the coastal town, promising to bring them back as soon as we could.

The plans Aurora had taken showed our route to be by foot on land, but after she'd left, we decided to stay undetected as we set foot in Northern territory for as long as we could. Now instead of approaching Neokell from the south and sticking to the base of the mountains, we were approaching from the forest to the east.

Nearly everything was planned and plotted—there was only one loose end left.

A loose end I needed to tie up.

Allowing the rest of the Valwain to double check our army movements, I slipped out of the main tent and headed deeper into camp. We'd spread apart our set up that time, allowing for more space in between tents and such so that we'd be less likely to be seen if any Northerners flew overhead.

My boots crushed dry leaves underfoot as I walked through the darkness of night in the direction of Chess's tent. Yet before I could make it there on my own, a frazzled Ezra came running straight toward me out of the dim night.

"Aviva!" He came to a stop before me and rested his hands on my shoulders. "Chess and I did it. *We did it!* Come on!"

"Lead the way," I instructed, then we both broke out into a run.

A few moments later, we were dipping into Chess's tent, where I finally paused long enough to gather my bearings.

I'd handed over the small piece of alychite to Chess shortly after returning from our scouting missions in the North, asking him to find me an antidote of some sort. I didn't care how weak or strong—anything helped. He'd quickly recruited Ezra to the task, realizing that the knowledgeable fae could be a big help.

And he turned out to be right.

Inside the tent were half a dozen large tables, each scattered with different vials, beakers, small, controlled flames, and countless ingredients. It was, in all honesty, a mess—but Chess always seemed to know exactly where everything was amongst his space.

Upon noticing my presence, Chess held up a small bottle of elixir that appeared a murky, light gray color.

"We finished just in time, Viva!" he exclaimed. "We'd finalized the main ingredients earlier this week, but I wanted to make it a little more potent. It turns out that burdock root was just the thing we were looking for!"

"Chess, Ezra, you two are incredible," I praised them.

The two males shared a proud look as I ducked deeper inside. Once I got near enough, Chess handed over the vial.

"We only had enough time and resources to make this one dose. If your predictions are right, then once we're in and deep enough to be away from the wall, the rest of us shouldn't need a dose, anyway," Ezra explained.

And there it was.

A new weight settling onto my shoulders.

My duty was to somehow find a way to open up the wall for our people to get through. I was the one with the largest arsenal of zirilium at their fingertips—not to mention that with my wings, I was essentially the only fae who could blend in effectively.

The entirety of the battle relied on my ability to be quick on my feet, use my zirilium wisely, and not get caught.

"Thank you," I said, looking up from the elixir vial. "Thank you both. I'm sure it'll work great."

Chess beamed at that, but quickly seemed to remember something else.

"I almost forgot to give this to you," he said, fishing a second vial out of his pocket—that one with a darker liquid in it—and handing it to me.

Though when he handed it to me, I realized he was handing me more than just the ink-like substance I'd used in the North before.

He'd also slipped the now slightly dirty cloth out of his pocket, holding it against the vial as he placed both items in my palm. The same cloth that held the small piece of alychite—the material fitting in the palm of my hand as he gave it back to me.

"Just in case." He nodded.

To anybody else—even Ezra—it looked like he'd just been handing me a second vial.

But what I held in my hand now was much more than that.

"Just in case," I repeated, tucking both of the vials and the shard away into one of my own pockets. The dark gray leathers I wore were form fitting, though I'd also managed to snag one of Caelia's black chain-mail tops, which I'd slipped on over my leather tunic. All of my sun and moon stones had been charged, the gloves adorning my hands. Even my hair was braided tightly down my back, courtesy of Teagan.

I was, more or less, ready for what was to come.

Or at least, I was as ready as I could be.

As I wished Ezra and Chess the best before slipping out of the tent, I tucked the vial into a small pocket against my ribs. Ezra had insisted on playing a part in the battle that time around, so Chess had offered him a spot with his trokavs. Ezra didn't possess zirilium, but he could still be an extra pair of hands and eyes wherever needed—not to mention his vast knowledge. The male had gladly accepted the task, though if you looked at him long enough, you could see the anxiety etched into his features.

Margo had gone to stay with Nan and Pops—they'd been the only fae left that Byn, Teagan, and I felt comfortable enough around to leave the young female with. Byn and Teagan knew the Ashfords from years of them serving as nobles, but to me, they were family.

They'd been more than happy to help us, and once Nan answered the door with residual paint on her trousers and baked goods in hand, she had quickly won Margo over.

Now, I walked through the forest aimlessly. We'd already eaten dinner, and though I knew I should be doing my best to rest before the battle looming over us, I couldn't find it in me to sit still.

Who would I face on the battlefield this time?

And what would this cost us?

Questions such as these bounced around in my mind as I started walking faster and faster until I broke into an all-out run. I couldn't fly for risk of exposing our position.

So I ran.

I ran until my lungs burned, until my muscles cramped, until the effort it took to keep moving outweighed the voices trying to rule my every thought.

I was so focused on putting my own foot in front of the other that I didn't hear the sound of paws running toward me until Atlas nearly knocked me over.

Having to force myself to an abrupt stop in order to not run directly into him, I yelled out a strong, "*Hey!*"

"Don't blame him, my love, I asked him to," Byn called out as the duo came to a stop before me, then he slid down from his Titan Wolf's back.

"How long have you been following me?" I asked, placing my hands on my hips and trying to act like I wasn't gulping air down.

"Long enough," he replied, stepping forward and gently taking hold of my chin, tilting my face up towards his.

"Why?" My voice grew quieter as the weight on my shoulders began to feel suffocating once again now that I was stagnant.

"Well, you might've blown our cover if you ran any farther," Byn said, nodding toward where up ahead the forest became much thinner—something I hadn't even noticed.

It might've been over before it'd even begun, and it all would've been my fault.

My lungs tightened at the thought.

"Plus, I can feel it too, you know," Byn said, meeting my eyes. "The pressure you're feeling. The anxiety, the fear, the terror. It feels like the sky is pressing down on you, right? That's how I felt before the Battle of Shadows. And you know who grounded me then?"

I peered up at him, worried that if I tried to speak, my voice would break.

"You did," Byn answered for me, then leaned forward and rested his forehead against mine. "You did, because you're the strongest, most capable fae I've ever met. You're intelligent, and quick-thinking, and you trust your instincts—which never seem to steer you wrong. And if anybody can kick this battle off positively and in our favor, it's you, Avi."

I bit my lip to keep it from quivering as I listened to him speak.

"And if at any time you need to push some of that fear my way, I'll happily take it from you. But come early morning, do not let your emotions rule you any longer. It'll only mess with the control you have over your zirilium. Let it all out now, so that you're ready by the morning," Byn reasoned.

Then he paused, allowing me space to express myself if I so pleased.

But I didn't want to talk.

I wanted him to *feel*.

So instead, I reached up on the tips of my toes and kissed him deeply.

The action wasn't only a melding of our lips and bodies as we melted into each other, but it was also me opening the doorway between the very fibers that made up who we were. Usually, that doorway was cracked just enough for us to reach through, or for emotions to slip between us.

But this time, I reached inward and threw it wide open.

And with that connection solidified between us, I let him in completely.

And he engulfed every bit of me.

The greens of him bled into the blues and purples of me, creating multiple different shades and patterns in response. I let him feel all of me—the stress, the fear, the longing, the regret. Everything I'd been holding onto for months—it was his to feel, too.

The stress of failing and, therefore, disappointing those I held dear.

The fear of making the wrong call and risking everything we'd worked for.

The longing for a brother and friend I wasn't sure I could save anymore.

The regret at taking a life—even though I knew Father had acted horrendously, I still couldn't help but wonder what I could have done differently.

All of these and more, I let Byn in the same way he swept into my mouth, tasting each part of me the same way he reached through that open doorway and touched every part of my very soul.

And as he did, I could feel his emotions, too, as they mixed with mine where our cores met. He was proud of me and was confident in my abilities. Yes, he was anxious—he didn't want to lose anybody else—but it didn't seem to be eating him alive like it had just mere months ago. The negative feelings within him had their space, yes, but they were outshined by the positive ones. The joy at being with me, the comfort of having a solid plan in place, the peace of believing the Stars were on our side. All of this and more seemed to radiate from him to me, until I finally felt all of that, too.

We were going to be alright.

I was going to be alright.

And as we slowly broke apart, retreating into ourselves as that doorway went from being wide open to cracked, like it had always been, I decided on something.

My fear would not conquer me any longer.

***

Byn and I rode back together on Atlas, who seemed to need no guidance in where we were headed, despite the sky still being dark above us. I'd ran much farther than I thought, directly toward the edges of the forest—in the opposite direction from where Neokell awaited us.

As we approached the middle of camp, we came upon a large crowd of soldiers surrounding Quinn and Caelia. It seemed the general was wrapping up a speech she was giving to them.

"—and *that* is why we're here today. It isn't just about your duty and serving the crown—it's about doing what's right for our people. And I mean *all* of our people!" Quinn yelled out, raising her sword into the air with the last sentence. "Now, everybody get to their positions!"

As the soldiers began to disperse, Byn slid down from Atlas's back and shook hands with each one he could reach. He offered soft words of encouragement, praise, or thanks, greeting nearly every one of them by name. At least, the names of the Southern soldiers. He didn't seem to know many of the names of the Ocrein Isle soldiers, though he still made an effort. They'd never gotten to go home since the Battle of Shadows, and I wished to the Stars they knew how much we appreciated them.

As they passed me next, I placed my fist over my heart, making eye contact with whom I could and nodding my appreciation and well wishes.

The energy in the air felt charged—the same way it did before a lightning strike hit. Everybody seemed nervous, but also a tad excited.

Because after today, we'd be one step closer to having peace across our realm.

I was sure of it.

The soldiers trickled out of the center of camp, heading west toward Neokell—and the encampments—to take their places hidden in the forest.

After most of them had dispersed, I caught Matea approaching Atlas—who sniffed the top of her head once and huffed before letting her get closer.

"You ready to do this?" she asked, now standing at Atlas's side and peering up at me, her arms crossed over her chest.

"I am," I responded, my voice coming out firm.

Matea just barely raised an eyebrow, letting me know she noticed the shift within me, but she must have decided not to mention it.

"Don't forget who you are while you're out there, alright?" she said. "And remember that we'll be right on the other side of the wall, ready to pounce. You might feel alone, but you've got an entire army behind you, Viva."

She dipped her head, though there was no sarcasm behind the act—just respect and... *love.* I could see it in her eyes as she met my gaze again.

I smiled at the realization, but before I could comment on it, a voice rung out.

"Dawn is quickly approaching!" Caelia called out, looking up toward the sky, which had lightened just a shade.

If we started running late, it would put our entire plan at risk.

At that single sentence, I realized there wouldn't be a big goodbye like last time. Chess and Ezra seemed to have already departed to set up small infirmary stations out at the thinner parts of the forest, and Teagan had been assigned to keep an eye on the outside of the main gate. Matea was already slinking away in her shadow form, having said all she needed to say a moment ago. Quinn and Caelia had followed their soldiers out of camp—leaving only Rayven, Laurence, Byn, and me in the middle of the camp.

Rayven was sticking close to Byn as they both strapped on a few extra daggers. Though I knew I wasn't seeing things when Rayven's worried eyes caught on Matea as her shadow slipped into the forest, in the direction of the army. Laurence, though, approached Atlas's side as Matea had, Eden's reigns in his hand.

At the sight of the duo, I slipped down from the giant wolf's side and threw my arms around Eden's neck.

"I miss you," I told her, to which she let out a soft chirp sound in return. We'd been so busy as of late that Laurence had spent more time with my griffin than I had.

Turning to Laurence next, I smiled at the older male. "You got everything you need?" I asked him.

"Do *you?*" he questioned—ever worried about me instead of himself.

"I've got all I need." I nodded, patting the pocket on my ribs where two vials and the cloth were being held.

He nodded firmly, then hesitated. He was looking at me not only with concern etched into his features, but also pride.

Before he could get emotional on me, I pulled him into a tight embrace—one he returned strongly.

"You be safe out there, alright?" His voice was lower than usual, heavy with the emotion he was holding back.

"You too, Laurence," I said, patting him on the back twice before releasing him.

I knew I should be as anxiety-filled and nervous as everybody else seemed to be, but I couldn't find those emotions in me anymore. If they were still in there somewhere, they'd quieted down in favor of a different feeling.

Hope.

"I'll see you on the other side of this," I said to the older male, patting him on the shoulder before he dipped his head once and departed, likely heading to his position.

I reached a hand out to Atlas, gently resting it along his side and grounding myself in the moment.

I needed to be entirely present.

"Are you ready for this, Avi?" I heard Byn ask from above.

Looking up to where my husband awaited me on Atlas's back, I realized he and I were the only two fae left there.

His hand was extended to me, and I noticed he was wearing an extra ring today—one with his family's crest engraved on it. As though he wanted to carry a piece of them with him.

The time had come.

Taking a deep breath, I nodded.

"I'm ready," I confirmed as I slipped my hand into his.

Chapter Thirty-Seven

The closer I got to the towering wall surrounding the encampment, the more difficult it became to hold on to my shadow form. I had the wall up ahead to thank for that.

Once I was close enough to make out the largest of the odd alychite spikes poking out from the structure, my zirilium gave out completely. I could feel the moment it became blocked—like a flame flickering, then being smothered. I came to a stumbling stop as I was thrown back into my physical body, barely catching myself before I face planted, as I had been barreling forward at full speed.

Walking for some of the way, I followed the flow of the wall from the edges of the forest, heading toward the largest of the watchtowers up ahead.

The same one from before that Matea and I had discovered was much easier to wield our zirilium around.

With the sun nearing the horizon and soon to rise, I broke into an all-out run.

I knew patrols and guards were hidden within the forest, though I also knew I didn't need to worry about them.

The Valwain and army had that covered.

I was grateful I'd already had Byn help me ink my wings so that they blended in with my dark outfit, the dim sky overhead helping me to blend into the darkness of the forest still. I'd also tucked my blinding white hair into a charcoal-colored cap with a cloth concealing the lower half of my face—both being similar to the kinds I'd often seen some guards and soldiers of the North wearing. They'd don attire like this mostly during winter, but we were willing to risk it. I should still blend in enough to get by.

Plus, the face covering helped to negate the smell threatening to overpower my senses.

A few moments later, I was approaching the watchtower.

I'd passed multiple other, smaller watchtowers on the way, but the one up ahead of me then was different.

Last time we were here, we'd figured out the specific structure up ahead had significantly less of the alychite shards poking out of the wall in favor of having large structural supports. With the supports in the way, there hadn't been room for hardly any of the metal in that area.

Which gave me the perfect opening.

As I got within range of the wide stretch of stone that made up the watchtower—no alychite in the area—I could feel my ziril-ium spark back to life within me, the stones on my gloves buzzing with energy once again. I could tell it wasn't at full power simply because of my proximity to the insane amount of alychite there at the encampment, but it would have to be enough.

With access to my abilities again, I slipped into my shadow state, using the shadows of the watchtower to tether myself to. It flowed easily, as if even the shadows knew I was there to help. As if they, too, couldn't stand the horrors going on behind these walls.

I slid up the shadow cast by one of the structural supports until I reached an open side window. I knew if I were in my physical form, my heart would be pounding—but there in the darkness, I was confident I was safe.

That feeling of security faded swiftly, though, as the sun finally peeked over the horizon.

Then, as I curled myself into a dark corner of the tower and the sun shone through the open window, the wingbeats began. There was a countless amount of them—all I knew was that the noise blocked out all other sounds.

They were heading into the forest beyond the wall to relieve the night shift.

The night shift that, if all had gone to plan, had already been incapacitated by the Southerners hiding out in the top of the trees.

Our scouts had noted that more Northerners scattered the forest than the first time we had visited, letting us know they were expecting us. Fortunately for us, they still weren't aware of exactly what they were facing.

And as the wingbeats quieted down, having flown out to wherever their assigned position was, I wound myself down the staircase, checking each floor and finding them all empty. It seemed that by sending out so many to monitor the forest, they hadn't planned on keeping an eye on what they held within.

Their mistake, I thought as I made it to the bottom floor.

After ensuring there was nobody else around, I stepped out of the shadows I'd wielded to get me that far. I quickly double checked everything was in place—my wings were a solid, dark gray, my hair was hidden in my cap, and even my boots had large enough soles to add to my height. Only males were to serve as guards and soldiers in the North, so the extra height would help me blend in, too. Elaera—my sword that Dimitri had gifted me as young teenagers—was strapped to my back, the silvery hilt blending in with those common in the North.

Though, I felt I was missing something.

Looking around, I caught sight of a black jacket hanging by the door. I rushed to grab and don it, finding that it fit surprisingly well. The male it belonged to must have also been small in stature.

There was a family name embroidered over my heart—*Brewick*.

Deciding that would have to be enough, I headed for the door, stepping out into the early morning sunlight—and into the encampment.

Keeping my head down, I set off at a leisurely pace around the inside perimeter of the wall. I clinched my teeth as I left the safety of the giant watchtower and its lack of alychite. My zirilium quickly faded from my senses as I made it past the edges of the watchtower. There seemed to be even more of the spikes on the inside of the wall than there had been outside, forcing my zirilium somewhere so far into myself that I couldn't access it.

My goal now was to find the weakest point on the east side of the wall that I could.

And bring it down.

The watchtower I'd entered through was on the south side, so as I slowly shifted directions while following the edges of the wall, I kept my eyes peeled. I checked out the support and structure—and the gaps in between—of the wall as I walked, noting every detail, but still not finding exactly what I was seeking.

Just as I was about to pick up my pace, the door of the small watchtower I'd just passed swung open.

"*Hey!* Where do you think you're off to, soldier?"

I froze in place, taking deep, calm breaths as I turned on my heels to face the male. Peering up at him from under my cap, he appeared older, his hair graying at his temples and wrinkles setting in on his face. His wings were a deep brown, and he wore the usual dark attire of the Northern army—except that he wore a broach with the Heartshire family crest on it. Being the symbol of the North as a whole, those who wore the crest were only those who had earned it.

That meant the male before me was likely an army captain—a lieutenant, at the least.

"Did you not hear me clearly? Why aren't you with the others?" The male took a threatening step forward, the door he'd come through still wide open behind him.

I had options, ones that I ran through as quickly as I could. I could try to answer him, but my voice alone would give me away as a female, and my cover would be blown. If I tried to rush him and attack now, with the distance between us, he'd have enough time to fly away or call for help.

So, it looked like it was time for a little acting.

I took a loud breath, as though I was going to answer, then forced myself into a coughing fit. I doubled over, hiding my face further and my eyes that could give me away. I knew the type of males my father would appoint as higher ups in his army—those that were ruthless and cold-hearted—and I doubted my twin had gone back on any of our father's decisions.

And I could use that knowledge to my advantage.

I stumbled forward, still coughing and taking heaving gulps of air into my lungs.

"Something wrong with you, fledgling?" the male asked, using the term *fledgling* in a demeaning way—a way to display my younger age and his superiority.

As I gasped for breath, I leaned against the wall of the watchtower next to us. Fortunately, I'd stumbled forward just far enough to accomplish what I had in mind.

"Alright, enough of this," he said, advancing on what appeared to him as my compromised form. When his boots came into my line of sight, I knew he was close enough.

In an instant, I shot upright and used his own momentum to push him toward the open door, throwing all of my weight and might into the move. The male, being caught so off guard, stumbled further, allowing me to shove him again—even harder than the first time—straight inside of the watchtower.

I swiftly shut the door behind us, wishing to the Stars above that nobody had seen or heard us.

"What is happening here?" he demanded, finally righting himself.

I lifted my head to meet his gaze as I answered, "*Justice.*"

With that word alone, his eyes widened and his mouth parted in an effort to call out. For who, I wasn't sure, because before he could utter a word, I was on him.

I pounced, forcefully kneeing him between the legs with as much strength as I could muster. A squeaking sound was the only noise that left his mouth as he fell to his knees. With his upper body now lower and therefore easier for me to reach, I quickly grabbed toward the front and back of his head, shifting to bring his temple down onto my knee with all of my might in the same movement.

The male fell to the ground, out cold from the sudden knock to his head. Forcing air into my lungs so I could remain concentrated, I did a fast sweep of the floor of the watchtower we were on, searching.

"Perfect," I said under my breath as I found a rope in a large chest of other tools and weapons.

Returning to the male, who was still crumpled on the ground, I made quick work of moving him to one of the wooden posts that held up the ceiling and tying him firmly in place. After securing him, I ripped off a large strip of his own shirt and tied it tightly around his head so it covered his mouth.

He wouldn't be going anywhere for a *while*.

Wiping my hands on my trousers, I slipped back out of the watchtower and carried on walking along the wall, though much faster than before.

It only took another few minutes before I finally saw the perfect spot for what I'd been looking for.

There were still structural supports at that point of the wall, but they looked as though maybe they'd been placed first, as they had obviously been weathered down over the years. They were full of cracks, and one of them already looked slightly off center. All I needed to do was help speed up the route they were already on.

Slyly observing my surroundings, I pulled the small vial of light gray liquid out of my pocket.

The alychite-combatant.

This better work, I thought as I popped the cork off and brought the elixir to my mouth. I downed it in one big gulp, cringing at the awful, spoiled taste now coating my tongue.

Tucking the empty vial away, I paused for a moment, waiting for something to hit me.

A minute passed, then another, and I could feel the panic scratching at the edges of my mind.

And then it hit all at once.

It felt like coming up for air the way my zirilium slammed back into my body. It was as though a switch had been flipped within me, the usual hum of my abilities flowing through my veins once more.

Flexing my hands in front of me, I smiled.

Chess and Ezra's hard work had paid off, after all.

Checking once more to ensure nobody was in sight, I got to work.

Using my earth zirilium, I tore down the weathered supports that were holding up the section of wall that stood before me. I'd never been more grateful for my multiple abilities until that moment.

Though, once all the supports sat in piles of rubble, the wall still hadn't shifted.

The wall itself was much too large for me to tear down on my own. Earth wielding was an ability I had yet to strengthen and build up as much as I should have, and I was regretting that now.

I'd have to find another way to open up the wall.

And I had to do so quickly—before the Northern higher ups of this place realized their males weren't coming back.

Just as I was debating tearing the wall down with my bare hands, I heard the heavy footsteps of somebody running in my direction.

Spinning on my heels, my back to the wall, my eyes immediately caught on a male sprinting toward me. He appeared to be Southern, and when the morning sun glinted off the alychite cuff on his ankle, I realized quickly that he was a prisoner here.

And so were all the other males that came into view behind him.

They were practically a small army themselves, though I knew they weren't the army I should be worried about.

The first male kicked up dirt behind him with how quickly he got to me, a rusted pickaxe as his weapon of choice. The other males, still far off, were yelling battle cries as the first one descended upon me.

He was tall, and though he looked underfed, he still had muscle to him—likely from the amount of labor he was forced into. He swung his pickaxe toward my shoulder, to which I ducked away from with seconds to spare.

"Friend or foe?" he ground out between clenched teeth as he circled me.

"Pardon?" I asked, debating on reaching for one of my daggers. I didn't want to hurt the male—we were here to help, after all. Though if he got in my way and didn't allow me to finish my task, I might not have much of a choice.

"Friend. Or. Foe?" he ground out again, slower this time.

"*Friend!*" I answered, dodging another swing of his pickaxe. "We're here to help. We're not leaving until each and every one of you are safe and free."

"We?" he asked, his voice straining as we made rounds around each other.

Before I could respond, though, I realized the other males were advancing—and I wouldn't be able to take them all.

The male swung, though each time he did, it was toward a non-vital point of my body. I noted that as I sidestepped him, causing him to stumble toward the wall behind me. And as he was righting himself, I took a few steps forward and called for my zirilium through a sun stone.

With the energy I needed boiling beneath my skin, I inhaled deeply, then released a long, deep breath, spitting fire straight from my core. I turned my head as I did so there was a half-circle of thick blue flames surrounding me and the first male, the wall at my back protecting us where the fire couldn't.

The males on the other side of the flames yelled out, holding different tools in the air as though they were proper weapons. Yet, the ones who got close enough to feel my flames quickly found out just how hot they burned.

Turning back to the male behind me, I realized he seemed slightly less hostile with us now being obscured from view.

And yet, he still advanced again.

"Do you want out of this place or not?" I asked, backing up a step.

"*Of course* I do. Now take this from me." He motioned to the pickaxe as he charged forward. Not knowing what else to do besides listen to him, I gripped above and below where his hands lay on the handle of the pickaxe and yanked it from him harshly.

"Now what?" I asked as he retreated a few steps, as though he was reassessing the fight now that he was weaponless.

"Aim for the cuff," he instructed, beginning to circle, his fists raised as though he was going to attack again.

"Why are you doing this?" I questioned, not sure if he could be trusted or not.

"They took the females and children—threatened to slaughter them all if we didn't kill you and anybody else that tried to enter.

The males on the other side of these flames might not stop—not while the cuffs are on. But that's because they don't know what happens when they come off." Then he threw a punch toward my jaw that would've knocked me out if I hadn't ducked.

"The cuffs... they're alychite. Your zirilium should return once they're off, right?" For the sake of the performance we seemed to be putting on, I swung the pickaxe toward his side, to which he swiftly rolled out the way of.

"Let your aim be true and you'll find out exactly what happens," he said, a sort of finality to his voice when he kicked his leg high, as though to knock me down.

Hoping I was reading the situation correctly, I adjusted my aim as I brought the rusty pickaxe down on the thick cuff—right where the seam of the metal was.

Exactly where I imagined it was weakest.

The material dented and cracked, but didn't fall off the way I thought it would. With no time to spare, I threw the pickaxe to the ground and conjured fire to my hand—enough that it coated me like another glove—though it didn't burn me.

Needing no instruction this time, when the male kicked again, I grabbed his leg midair with both hands, making sure my flame-covered hand landed on the cuff attached to him.

Then I pushed all of that fire into the alychite until it melted from the male's skin, ensuring that none of the fire burned him.

And as the last drop of alychite dripped off his flesh, I was thrown back and to the ground as the male seemed to *burst*.

The amount of energy leaking from him as he stumbled backwards, closer to the wall, was beyond extreme.

Then the earth crumpled beneath him.

It looked as though the earth was something soft as it gathered close to him. Then, almost as though he was giving himself over to the forbidden act of the reckoning, he fell to his knees and let his zirilium take him.

The male—who was obviously a powerful earth wielder—screamed as his power went out of him in waves of earth. I quickly spread my wings and leaped into the air before the first wave of rippled earth could smack into me. The moving earth dowsed the fire that had surrounded us, putting it out, though the males beyond that point were quickly knocked to the ground before they could advance further.

I watched as the first wave of rippling earth reached the wall, causing it to sway dangerously.

With the second wave, it began to crumble.

And with the third, it fell.

"*Get out of there!*" I called out to the male as large chunks of the wall began to rain down around him. Though I knew if I got any closer, I'd likely be struck myself.

"This was my purpose, friend," he called back over the sound of rocks falling. "Now I'll get to be with her again—among the Stars."

With those final words, the last—and most powerful—wave of his power went out of him. The other males who had just got to their feet fell once again as the final wave knocked them down—just like the last of the wall fell.

Landing directly on top of the male.

"*No!*" I cried out, though I knew there was no saving him as his zirilium immediately gave out after the last of the wall landed. The earth he'd been involuntarily wielding settled back down into place as the power lost its source.

Chest heaving, I sent a silent wish to the Stars that they welcomed the fallen male with open arms.

Then, I flew through the long stretch of fallen wall and paused on the outskirts of the forest.

"My people!" I called out, ripping the cap and jacket from my body and letting them fall to the ground below. "Spare anybody you can that has a metal cuff on them—melt the cuffs off if you can!"

With those words to guide the army I knew was waiting for my signal in the forest, I turned back toward the encampment and shouted, "*For all of Inphis!*"

Countless shadows came spearing out of the forest, crossing through the fallen wall and into the encampment. When the shadows took on their physical form, I noted that each had been carrying another soldier with them. With the hundreds upon hundreds of shadow wielders and their counterparts inside, they began to face off with the other males that had charged me earlier.

Though, as I heard Quinn instruct the next wave to make their way inside, the sound that I often heard in my nightmares drowned her voice out.

Thousands of wingbeats arriving from the west.

I watched as the host of the North approached, having come from the Salic mountains beyond the encampment.

They'd been waiting for us to show our hand.

And they'd used prisoners to soften the battlefield.

The battle that had yet to truly begin.

Though what shocked me more than their horrific strategies was what I saw at the front of the winged host heading for us.

An almost pitch-black griffin—Ziana—lead the army.

And on her back sat my brother.

Dimitri was coming.

Chapter Thirty-Eight

Dimitri was coming for *me*.

Father had nearly always stayed behind the safety of his armies, letting them take the fall for him. Even when he did get his hands dirty, he was never on the front lines leading his soldiers into battle himself.

Yet, there was my twin heading toward me, doing exactly that.

For him, this was personal.

And because I knew he'd strike down anybody who stood between him and me, I realized I'd have to beat our soldiers to him.

Steeling myself for what was to come, I began flapping my wings in large strokes—heading straight for Dimi.

Flying as quickly as I could, I pulled Elaera from her sheath, which lay against my back. I wanted to be prepared, since I knew Dimitri wouldn't be leaving without a fight. Then I focused on recalling our previous confrontation.

He'd been primarily fond of using his fire zirilium, though I knew he also had the ability to wield shadows after he slipped in and out of his shadow form, even if it had been brief. It had obviously surprised him, too, though there was no telling if he'd been able to strengthen his abilities since then—or if he had any others.

As I neared, I could make out my brother's bone white hair—the same shade as mine—pushed back out of his face. He was dressed in a deep red color that made up his trousers, top, and overcoat. His outfit, to my surprise, was detailed with the gold fit for a king. He also had on gold rings, I realized, though the morning sun reflected off them oddly.

Gold had always been abundant in the South, while in the North, the same could be said of silver. Father always wore silver—I'd never even seen him *touch* gold.

I imagined if Dimi still had Father's advisors in place, that they'd protested about this small act of defiance, though it seemed like my brother lacked any concern over the matter.

When I came within shouting distance of him, meeting at what I imagined was the middle of the encampment, I paused, holding myself in the sky.

"Brother," I said, calling out loud enough so he could hear my greeting.

He guided his griffin a few wingbeats closer before pausing.

"*Sister,*" he responded, though his tone rang with sarcasm.

"We don't have to do this." My heart skipped a beat as his army caught up to him, thinking they'd come for me first. Instead, they gave me and Dimitri a wide berth, continuing toward the Southern army I'd help bring here today.

"I fear we do, though, don't we?" he said, lifting himself from Ziana's back and flying on his own. It wasn't until then that I realized another figure—somebody smaller—rode behind him. But before I could glance under the hood of their cloak, Ziana dipped down toward the battlefield below, taking the mystery rider out of sight with her.

"We could call a truce. Right here, right now," I offered, though I could tell by the set of his shoulders that it was no use.

"We both know you wouldn't leave here without these prisoners," he responded. "And I'm not giving them up without a fight."

I watched as he drew Tarrious—our father's black, onyx crested sword—from its sheath at his side as he spoke, signaling just how serious he was being.

"There are other ways than this, Dimi," I called out, desperation breaching the tone of my voice as I motioned to the beginnings of what would be a bloody battlefield below us.

"If there are, I don't know them," he claimed. "And even if I did, I would still choose this, Viva. Father gave me a final task, and I will *not* fail in this."

With that, he surged forward so quickly, I barely had time to lift Elaera over my head in time to block a bone-shaking blow. Metal sounded against metal as Dimi retreated a breath, then swung again.

Again and again he swung, aiming for critical points on my body. He had the upper hand here—he'd caught me off guard, and now I couldn't seem to catch up enough to carry out any hits or swings of my own. I was left defending myself over and over again as we flew around each other in circles, far above the battlefield.

"You know—" Dimitri began, but as he began to speak, he left his side exposed—something *he* had taught me to never do. Surging forward at the opportunity, his sentence was cut short as Elaera drew first blood when I sliced open his side. The cut wasn't deep enough to kill him, but as my twin sucked his teeth, I knew it'd been deep enough to hurt.

"*You* taught me that," I noted, gaining on him as I brought my sword down toward his sword-wielding shoulder. "Aren't you proud, brother?"

Grinding his teeth, he blocked my blow with Tarrious, though by his contorted expression I knew I'd hit a sensitive spot in his ego by drawing blood before he could.

"*Proud* isn't the word I would use to describe what I'm feeling," he ground out as he arced wide. I did my best to spin out of range, but the sudden bloom of pain and warm blood on my upper arm quickly let me know I'd hadn't been fast enough.

"This bores me," Dimi stated—his demeanor much too calm for my liking—before he conjured fire to his other hand. Touching the fire to Tarrious, the flames leaped to the blade, coating it completely. "Now *that* is more like it."

Flying backwards a few beats, I moved just in time to miss the first swing of the fiery sword.

"You seem like you have more control over your newfound zirilium," I noted, trying to distract him for even a moment. "Found a teacher? Maybe right here in this encampment?"

The smirk that grew over my brother's face looked so much like our father's that my chest ached at the sight.

"Yes, actually," he replied, taking a moment to dramatically swing Tarrious in an arc in front of him. "*Mother.*"

With no further explanation, he began to advance on me. Though before he could, a loud crack of thunder rattled my teeth with how high in the sky we were.

Snapping my head to look above, I realized the weather wielders were crafting one of the largest wielder-made storms I'd ever seen. A good storm was all the North needed to sway any battle in their favor. And if what I'd seen of the battlefield below was still accurate, the navy had yet to arrive.

Somebody had to stop the storm.

Or at least slow it down.

I gasped as I felt Tarrious and its flames bounce off the black chain-mail armor I had covering my torso. If I didn't have it on, that may have been a critical strike.

And yet Dimitri had taken the opportunity with no hesitation.

Meeting his eyes, I searched deep in his gaze for the brother I once knew better than I knew myself. He had to be in there somewhere, and yet right then, he remained lost to me.

I felt a fissure tear in my heart as I realized I'd have to eventually give up on him.

I hoped the dip in my emotions didn't stumble Byn, who I could feel was drawing closer. But as the clouds began to thicken overhead, I knew I had more to worry about than both my twin *and* my husband.

This was about *all* of Inphis.

Lifting my chin in an effort to not look as troubled as I felt, I called out to Dimitri, "Catch me if you can."

Then I tucked my wings in close to my body and nosedived.

A controlled fall took more skill than it might have appeared. And to get to my destination, I had to fight every urge in my body to spread my wings and simply fly the rest of the way there. But I knew falling was faster, and right then, every second mattered.

Before I could get too close to the ground, I angled myself just right, then spread my wings wide. Gliding along a perfectly timed air current, it carried me closer to the western towers. The weather wielders seemed to be somewhere in between the middle of the encampment and the western towers, and since my twin was in the middle, I chose the towers instead.

I considered going directly for the weather wielders, but they were generally very heavily guarded, and I wasn't sure of their exact location. Plus, since the storm overhead wasn't slowing down, I knew they were still safe enough to be wielding the sky—and I doubted I could take them all on my own.

I touched down on the flat roof of one of the towers, rolling to a stop and quickly jumping to my feet. I'd always been a faster flier than my twin, and I knew the drop I'd pulled had bought me extra time, too—though it still wouldn't be much.

I could feel Byn drawing closer again—as though he was following the soul-tie between us to me—but I blocked out that feeling in favor of focusing every piece of myself on the task before me.

I clenched my eyes shut tight as I funneled all of my power into the moon stone on the third finger of my left hand—the one I used to weather wield. Throwing as much energy into it as I could muster, I flung my open hands in the air and connected with the sky.

With small storms, it was easy to form a fist and put an end to it in one motion. But with how much energy was behind this storm, I could barely bend my fingers against the raw zirilium I could feel fighting against my attempt to slow down the storm formation.

Digging deeper into myself, I realized there were so many more levels to my zirilium than I'd ever known. Funneling more and more of myself into this one act, my fingers slowly began to bend, forcing the storm to slow ever so slightly.

But it wouldn't be enough.

My mouth fell open in a scream as I burrowed even *deeper* into the core of my power. I fell to my knees as my entire body shook with the effort to close my fists and pause the forming storm overhead—even if only for an extra moment.

A moment on the battlefield could mean life or death.

And not only were my soldiers, my people, on *both* sides of this war—but so were my friends. My *family*.

And for them, I could do anything.

It felt as though my very flesh and muscles were ripping themselves from my bones with the physical strain this was putting on my body. And yet, I pushed harder. My voice gave out as I dug a tad deeper, funneling every fiber of my power and energy as a wielder into the act at hand. I could vaguely feel my body violently shaking, but I was so far down inside of my own zirilium that it felt like a distant thought—not even a concern.

Then, with that final push, I closed my fists—the energy of an entire storm now being held in my hands.

I gasped, once again able to recognize the sudden agony I felt as the pain in my body from using so much energy. Back in my own body, I quickly folded in on myself, bringing my closed fists to my chest and holding them there. I still shook violently, the power of the energy I was holding back buzzing within every inch of me, fighting for a way out. Still kneeling on the tower's roof, I looked up and was reassured to find that the storm that had been circling overhead had paused its formation. It hadn't dissipated, but it looked as though it had frozen in time, and I knew that so long as I kept this energy trapped within me, I could spare the Southern army a few more moments.

Then I felt the edge of a sword being pressed against my throat.

I hadn't been enough.

"You know, twin," Dimi started, leaning over my kneeled form to keep Tarrious pressed firmly against my neck. "Aurora said you'd grown soft. *Weak*, even."

He let out a menacing chuckle before adding, "But I guess she didn't see this side of you in all her time spent among the *filth* of the South."

Knowing that if I tried to speak, I would likely shift the sword, I stayed silent. I was still shaking so hard that I felt the sword against my neck begin to slice through my skin anyway—without Dimitri even needing to press further.

"All that power was wasted on you, though," he sighed. "We could have been the most powerful of the entire realm—*together*."

Suddenly, Dimitri gripped my braided hair and pulled my head backwards, better exposing my throat.

"I... didn't want it to come to this, you know," he said, his voice a breath softer before it hardened again. "But nothing can stand in my way. Even you, Viva."

There.

The twin I knew was still in there, buried deep under layers of hurt.

And if I died today at his hand, at least I knew I'd gotten to hear a glimpse of him one last time.

I stared up at the still frozen clouds overhead, my body screaming at me to let go—though I still refused.

I'd meet the Stars with my fists still clenched if I had to.

I would give my people my final moments.

It was all I had left to offer.

And as I felt Dimitri shift his weight slightly, likely readying himself to spill my lifeblood, I decided I was alright with that.

Then, my brother's form went rigid behind me as a voice, one dripping with hatred and fury, spoke slowly from behind him.

"Drop the sword, Dimitri."

The voice belonged to somebody I would always recognize.

Byn.

Chapter Thirty-Nine

The tip of a sword pressed into the space between my wings. Shifting either way would likely cause damage to them, and pushing backwards wasn't an option. The only way out was forward, but with the hold I had on my twin, it wouldn't be simple—at least not if I didn't want to lose the leverage I had over her.

In that split second of hesitation, though, I made a miscalculation.

I had assumed that with Viva holding back the efforts of over a hundred weather wielders, she'd be too exhausted to fight back. Instead, though, it seemed hearing her husband's voice sparked life back into her once again as the back of her head connected with my nose in a nasty *crunch.*

Before the blood could even flow from my broken nose, I flung a tether out toward a shadow near the edge of the tower roof we stood on, trying to avoid falling into the sword at my back. I solidified a connection in a near instant, my body dissipating into shadows as I speared toward the edge. I was intrigued that my nose didn't ache while within the shadows, but tucked that observation away for another time.

Returning to my physical form, I could feel the blood now gushing from my nose. It fell down my face and clothes, but I didn't bother trying to stop it before reaching my hands up and swiftly setting it back into place. I didn't flinch, didn't wince—I simply stared at those who were on the other side of the roof from me.

King Thorntier—*Robyn*—had thrown himself before my twin, cupping her face in his hands with a gentleness I wasn't sure I'd ever seen before. He was speaking low enough that I couldn't hear him, but I saw her shaking her head in response to whatever he'd said.

Seeing such softness at another male's hands caused me to look down at my own bloodied ones.

Had I truly been ready to take the life of my sister just a mere moment ago?

The same female who I had cared about more than anybody else—and possibly still did. Would I have been able to do it?

And if so, who—or *what*—did that make me?

"Call off your army, Dimitri," Robyn said, now standing between my twin and me.

He was protecting her.

When had that stopped being *my* task?

Hatred bubbled up within me, stirring my zirilium, though I couldn't tell who I hated more—Robyn or myself.

That hatred added another layer of hardness around my heart, sealing away the guilt I was beginning to feel.

I hadn't been made to feel such things.

I had been made to *rule*.

To *conquer*.

And that was all I had left.

Sinking back into the numbness of my everyday life, I met Robyn's eyes and smirked.

"I don't think I will. I appear to be winning, after all." I motioned toward the battlefield that remained of the encampment below and around us.

The male prisoners I'd sent after Aviva had softened the battlefield a fraction. They'd fought, yes, but once the alychite cuffs started coming off, their zirilium had also begun to erupt, the same way Mother's had. They'd been a decent distraction while the actual army swept in and took over. Now, even without the storm I'd been planning because of Aviva still holding it back—shaking so badly I thought her body might split in two—we would likely win here today. The North often had the upper hand as we could attack from above, and it could become extremely difficult to watch all around you *and* above you as a soldier. Not to mention that two of their strongest wielders just so happened to be at the top of a tower with *me*, instead of fighting with their people.

Before Robyn could respond, though, my head snapped sideways, my eyes searching out something I couldn't see just yet.

Something I could only *feel* approaching from the shadows.

"What are you looking at?" Robyn's gaze followed mine.

"We have company," I responded.

But if I was about to be outnumbered, I was at least going to get a few good hits in first.

I was, after all, the embodiment of the embers of the fire I held within.

Summoning flames to coat my hands, I balled them into fists and began advancing on the Southern King. To his credit, he stood his ground, refusing to leave my twin unprotected. He conjured his own flames, and with the way he was planting his feet, I knew he had tapped into the stone of the tower, too.

My first punch had been blocked by his own hand—as planned. But as my second swing was about to make contact with Robyn's jaw, a movement to my right caused my attention to sway.

Then, the shadow I felt approaching before was on me, moving faster than I'd imagined somebody's shadow form could move.

I stumbled back a step, then two, as the dark form circled around my body like a snake. They moved so quickly that even when I tried to knock them away from me, they'd already moved to another spot.

After disorienting me, I saw a brief glint of a blade before the cuts began. I winced and flinched, covering my face with my hands as I was bombarded. It was as though they were mostly shadow, but a small part of them, like their hand, was physical every few seconds—just long enough to run a dagger across my skin.

"Rayven, stop!" Robyn called out, but the shadow figure didn't slow down.

Blood ran from every wound, my clothes ruined and tattered, but whoever they were, they carried on. Finally, after trying so many times to knock their form off me, a manic laugh escaped my lips before I slid into the darkness, too.

My wounds ceased hurting and bleeding immediately, though they didn't stop. Now, they were circling me, coming closer and closer, forcing me to shrink in on myself to avoid them.

I didn't know much about the capabilities of fighting while in shadow form, but at least they couldn't cut me anymore.

"*Rayven!*" Robyn said, his voice so strong and demanding that even I hesitated briefly. The other shadow did, too, and stared at me as though making a decision.

"Rayven, please, take Viva away from here. She refuses to stop until they're here, and it isn't safe for her up here," Robyn explained, nearly begging.

How pathetic, I thought.

The other shadow, seeming to have been moved by what the Southern King said, slowly backed away from me and toward my sister.

It wasn't until they materialized that I understood.

It wasn't Rayven, as Robyn had thought.

Instead, *Matea* stepped out of the shadows, kneeling next to Viva.

My... *sisters.*

Robyn looked upon her, shock written across his features, though there was an underlying level of understanding mixed in, too.

I slipped back into my physical form, forcing my arms to stay by my side instead of trying to stop any of the bleeding.

"I've got you," Matea said gently, wrapping her arms around Viva's vibrating shoulders. But before they departed, she locked eyes with me.

"Where is my mother?" she asked—no, *demanded.*

"Not here, *sister,*" I sneered, blood dripping into my eye from a gash in my eyebrow.

"*Don't call me that,*" she seethed. "As a matter of fact, don't call *either* of us that. You're nothing to us, Dimitri. *You are nothing.*"

With those final words, she dissipated into shadows, taking Viva with her.

Though as their dark forms slid away, another smudge of black marred the sky above—and was coming closer.

Ziana. And on her back sat Val.

Robyn followed my gaze, though he didn't shrink away from the fight approaching him.

That was something I could appreciate.

Yet before Val could make it to us, the most powerful surge of shadow zirilium I'd ever experienced washed over me. Not my own—no. Whatever it was, it was approaching from the gaping hole Viva had managed to tear into the wall.

And it was approaching *fast.*

"What did you bring?" I asked Robyn, an edge of horror in my voice.

"What are you—" He was cut off by the sound of my soldiers screaming coming from the battlefield.

It was hundreds—no, definitely *thousands*—of shadows that began pouring onto the battlefield from the hole in the wall. Their presence was so numerous and overwhelming that I could feel the weight of their power pressing against my bones. I barely even registered Ziana and Val landing on the opposite side of the roof from all the energy electrifying the air.

"I'll say it again, Dimitri," Robyn ground out, taking a step forward as he motioned to his army—and my falling soldiers. "Call off your army."

As I opened my mouth to refuse, though, a callused hand landed on my arm.

And the relief I felt at that single touch struck me to my core.

Turning my head to look at Val, she nodded slightly, then dipped her head toward the battle below.

She wanted me to look.

Slowly, I did as she pleased.

It was a bloodbath, I noticed.

And it was Northern blood being shed.

If I ever wanted to win, I had to plan my next moves wisely. And remaining here, I realized, would only weaken us. Weaken *me*.

And that wasn't something I was willing to allow.

Turning back to Val, I met her eyes and did my best to convey that I understood.

Pointing a finger at Robyn, I stated, "This is just the beginning, Thorntier." Grabbing hold of my Right Hand, I added, "Let's fly, Val."

Tethering myself to a shadow nearby, I wielded us onto Ziana's back before the Southern King could try to interfere. Materializing again, Val sitting before me in Ziana's saddle, we took flight toward the battlefield.

Though as we headed forward to retreat, I couldn't ignore the way Val stared backwards—right where Robyn stood—and where my twin had kneeled.

Chapter Forty

I was nothing, and it was bliss.

I had a vague recollection of Matea wielding us away—away from Byn, and away from Dimitri.

I could still feel the strain on my zirilium—the shocking amount of power I was utilizing, of which I didn't even know I had possessed. Though after the darkness embraced me, my body didn't feel as though the very fibers of my being were ripping apart. It was a small, quick reprieve—before Matea let go of the shadows that had been holding us so gently.

And the agonizing pain returned, flooding each of my senses.

I fell to my knees instantly, unable to hold myself upright as I kept my fists clenched tight.

"Viva, let go!" Matea said, kneeling before me.

I managed to just barely shake my head in response.

"Dimitri is about to retreat, I promise. Let *go,*" she tried again.

But for all I knew, that was what Dimi wanted us to think.

So instead, I held on.

I heard Matea curse before she wrapped her arms around my shaking body, holding me.

It was all she could offer, and I couldn't have been more appreciative.

Moments passed before the word *retreat* spread across the battlefield like a wildfire.

And then, one by one, I could feel the weather wielders I'd been grappling with slowly let go of their hold on their zirilium. The storm overhead, which had been frozen in time, slowly dissipated as each wielder turned from their task in order to retreat. With each wielder that stopped fighting my efforts, a small wave of relief was reintroduced to my body. With each wave, I became more and more aware of my body once again.

Now, I could feel the sweat coating my skin, the pressure and ache of my muscles, and the way I was shaking.

And as the last of the weather wielders let go, the hold I'd been keeping on my zirilium went out like a doused torch. I collapsed into Matea's embrace, breathing heavier than ever before. My hands felt numb from the strain of holding back so much power, and the reserve I'd dug my zirilium out of felt like a dried-up well in my core.

I was so focused on what I felt lacking, though, that I barely felt Byn approaching.

"*Avi,*" I heard. Then he was all I could focus on as his pride, his awe, his amazement washed over me—*through* me.

And he was feeling all of that about *me*, I realized with a start.

In the beat of a wing, I was passed from Matea's arms to Byn's as he murmured sweet encouragements to me.

I may have been across the border from Cairnyl and no longer welcome in Hollis, but in that moment—there in his arms—I knew I was home.

"Talk to me, my love. Are you alright?" Byn said, drawing back and cupping my face in his hands.

Peeling my eyes open, I was met with the forest green of his—and the immense concern and anxiety there.

Simply to ease his mind, I nodded, though when his brow quirked, I could tell he didn't believe me.

"Find Chess," Byn instructed Matea, only taking his gaze off mine for a few seconds.

Without arguing or objecting, I felt more than saw Matea dissipate into shadow and depart toward the forest.

Once we were alone, Byn brought his forehead to mine, his expression still etched in worry.

"What were you thinking?" he asked.

"I couldn't let them gain the upper hand—especially not before the navy arrived," I said slowly, my breathing still heavy.

"You're going to be the death of me," he murmured, pressing a gentle kiss to my forehead as I felt Matea quickly approaching with another energy.

Matea and Chess slipped out of the darkness, the trokav not at all affected as Laurence had been by traveling through the shadows. Byn shifted to be at my side as Chess did a quick examination of me, checking things like my heartbeat, my eyes, my breathing, and my limbs for any major causes of concern. When he didn't find anything immediately wrong, but still saw my weakened state, he started piecing things together.

"This isn't physical. She used up a *ton* of her zirilium, didn't she?" Chess began sifting through his different pouches attached to his belt and on a strap across his chest, obviously looking for something.

"To put it simply, yes," Byn answered for me.

"To put it *not* so simply, she's the reason the storm ceased during the battle," Matea added. "The Battle of No Rain."

"That was *Viva?*" Chess asked, obviously shocked.

"I'm right here, you know," I said, trying to put a sarcastic tone to it, though it seemed to fall short.

After another moment of Chess double checking his pouches, he finally yanked a tiny vial out of one on his hip. "Found it!" he exclaimed, then popped off the top and held it out toward

Byn and me. "Here, have her take this. It'll restore most of the energy she used to hold back the storm."

As my husband brought the open vial to my lips, I nearly cringed away from the smell—then fully cringed at the taste as the liquid coated my tongue. It tasted like somebody had tried to make mud pies into a real thing—in liquid form.

Nonetheless, I'd taken worse elixirs in my lifetime, so I forced myself to swallow every last drop.

I could feel the liquid settling in my stomach, almost instantly getting to work. The elixir quickly began to fill in that spot deep within myself where I'd clawed out the energy I needed to hold on to the storm and bend it to my will. But not only did it seem to re-energize my zirilium, it seemed to soothe my aching body to a degree, too. My muscles didn't feel as though they'd been shredded any longer.

Inhaling deeply, I felt like I had finally caught my breath.

I looked at Chess in awe, placing a hand on his arm. "Thank you."

"Happy to help." Chess smiled and dipped his head.

With Byn's attentive assistance, I carefully got to my own two feet again. I stretched my limbs, then my wings, grounding myself in the feeling of my body. As I was pulling my wings back in, I felt through the earth below a large creature sprinting toward us from the direction of the battlefield.

Within seconds, Lychen came bounding out from the edges of the ruined wall, passing by countless Southerners and navy members celebrating our victory. Though it had felt to me like the battle lasted for some agonizing days, to my surprise, it was only late in the morning.

When Lychen grew near, Teagan slid off the wolf's back, followed by Quinn. And out of Lychen's shadow appeared Rayven and Laurence.

Almost the entire Valwain was present—all except for Ezra.

I could see the panic creeping onto Quinn's features, though Chess seemed to notice first.

"He's helping my trokavs wrap and bind any wounds that are still bleeding," he explained, motioning toward the forest behind us where the trokavs had been set up.

Relief washed over her expression, and she nodded once in thanks before getting down to business.

"We have minimal casualties—due to how short the battle was, and due to them not having the storm on their side," Quinn reported. "I'd imagine the same sort of news on the North's side. It was more so the *prisoners* that took the brunt of it all. Though, once the North retreated, they finally got brave enough to tell us why—the lives of the females and children were on the line. The prisoners that died did so with honor."

"Did they find—" Byn began asking, only for Quinn to finish his sentence.

"The females and children? Yes, they had been taken up into the mountain where they, along with the males, have been forced to mine for alychite and other minerals each day, dawn to dusk."

Byn nodded, though his expression shifted from reassured to concerned within a few seconds. "This doesn't end here, Valwain." He looked around at each of us. "Dimitri will only become more determined, more dangerous. If we ever want to truly end this war, we'll have to get two steps ahead of him. We need to think wisely about our next moves."

"I… I might have an idea, but it's quite a stretch," I warned.

"Let's hear it," Teagan pitched in, and I noticed as she motioned for me to continue, there was a long slice down her forearm, still bleeding. Chess must have not noticed yet, or he'd have already patched the princess up.

"I think we should—" I quickly cut myself off as a blur of black feathers caught my eye from afar.

I gasped, realizing that despite everything else we were juggling, I'd made a promise to a stranger—to Valenia.

"We'll be right back," I said to the Valwain, taking hold of Byn's hand and shadow wielding us in the direction of the black feathers. My wielding felt a bit sluggish, causing us to move slower than I'd have liked. I nearly lost sight of the blur of black, but I moved just fast enough to keep him in my sights.

He crossed through the hole of the wall, where the navy—which seemed to be full of kind-hearted fae despite their profession—was guiding the prisoners out of the encampment. Some fell to their knees when they made it past the wall, as they'd never been beyond the confines of this place until that moment.

Breezing passed one of those kneeling fae, I shed the shadows that were carrying us as we finally caught up to the one I'd been after.

"*Kaison!*" I called out toward the young male, who was a few strides ahead of Byn and me.

He came to a stop, turning around slowly. His frame was much too small for a fledgling of his age—ten, if I remembered correctly. His dark hair was limp and his clothes were barely more than rags hanging onto his pale, too-thin form. He'd most definitely lost weight since whenever the portrait of him had been painted, though it was still *him* standing before me.

"How do you know my name?" he asked hesitantly, his gaze shifting from me then to Byn, and then back to me. Even his voice sounded weaker than I imagined it should have.

I slowly dropped into a crouch as I pulled the portrait Valenia had given me out of my pocket. It had become slightly crumpled at the edges, but it remained whole as I unfolded it and held it out towards him.

"Your aunt sent me," I said gently as he drew near and took the picture from my grasp. "Her name is Valenia, right?"

His head snapped up at the mention of her name, as though beyond surprised. Then he nodded.

"She... she really sent you? Is she here?" Kai began to look around.

"It's just us, sweetheart," I said softly. "My name is Aviva, and this is my husband, Robyn. Your aunt asked us to keep an eye on you for her—just until she can come for you."

"Aviva as in the Princess of the North? I heard you were taken by the South, and yet..." His gaze slid to Byn, who had crouched down next to me.

"I promise, there's much more to the story than what you've heard," Byn reassured him.

Kai nodded, though he had a curious glint in his eyes.

"Would you do me a favor, Kai?" I asked him, drawing his attention back to me.

"Of course," he responded.

"Would you be willing to come with us so I can uphold the promise I made to your aunt to keep you safe? And I promise—you *will* be safe." I held out my hand toward him, palm up.

The fledgling paused for a moment, contemplating. I watched as he looked down at the portrait in his hand, his younger self staring up at him.

"Auntie Val always said names were important. That you can't give somebody your full name unless you trust them," Kai said, shifting his gaze toward me. "But she gave you her name. And if she trusts you, then I trust you, too. So... yes, I'll go with you."

I smiled as he placed his hand into mine and handed the portrait back. I slipped it back into my pocket as I lightly gripped the young male's hand.

"You won't regret this, I promise," I assured him.

"I know," Kai said matter-of-factly.

I felt Byn's warmth in my own chest as I reached for his hand with my spare one. Walking back in the direction of the Valwain, Byn finally asked what I knew he'd been wondering.

"What was it you were going to say to the group?"

I bit my lip at the question, wondering how stupid of an idea it was. But at least if it was truly that bad, Byn could tell me and save me the embarrassment of presenting the idea to the rest of the Valwain.

I sighed, leaning toward him so Kai couldn't hear me as I finally said what I'd been considering.

"I think we should visit the humans on the Levast Isles."

Chapter Forty-One

We'd taken one of the mid-sized ships we still needed to return to Kyrish, sailing slightly farther east than the rest of the navy.

After the Battle of No Rain—Matea had called it that enough for it to stick—it had taken what felt like ages to get all the prisoners out of the encampment. We welcomed the Southerners and Islanders that had been imprisoned with open arms, though the Northerners were a different story. I knew how fae of the North were loyal to a fault, their ego often getting in the way of rational thoughts. So as each Northerner crossed through the torn-down wall, they were given two options: remain there outside Neokell and find their own way, or come with us and help take down the regime that placed them there—for the small price of a vow to the Thorntier line.

So Teagan, Byn, and I all stood just outside the wall, Northerners approaching one by one to kneel and vow their loyalty to a Thorntier.

And we left behind not a single Northerner.

After crossing through Glaytred Forest with the entire army, navy, and encampment of fae, we loaded everybody up onto any ships we could. It turned out to be more crowded than anticipated, but it worked, and we only needed to make it to Kyrish, where the navy would remain temporarily.

Well, *they* only needed to make it to Kyrish.

Ezra, Matea, Laurence, Rayven, Byn, and I all loaded up onto the mid-sized ship and set sail for the Levast Isles. Teagan had needed to get back to Margo, *and* she could call the shots in mine and Byn's absence. Caelia and Callum decided to stay with their navy the same way Quinn had decided to stay with her army—despite the longing I could see in her eyes when she watched her husband walk onto the ship with the rest of us.

Now we were sailing closer to the human lands than any fae had in centuries.

As the Levast Isles came into clearer view, I wondered why nobody had tried harder to contact the humans before now. Surely, despite the fact that they weren't fae, they could still help turn the tides of this war. But as two ships came into view speeding toward us—the wind on their side—I wondered if maybe those before us had been wise to leave the humans be.

"Do you think they're friendly?" Laurence said, our small portion of the Valwain all standing at the nose of our ship, watching the two vessels approaching.

"There's a reason the humans have closed off their borders for so long, and I don't think the reason is friendliness," Rayven answered with a sigh.

"Regardless, we're only here to talk with them. If they refuse to help us, we'll figure something else out," Byn said, attempting to reassure us all. Though I felt anything *but* reassured—and I knew my husband was on edge, too, despite the brave expression he'd donned.

The two other ships approached quickly, and once they were near enough, I flinched as they shot arrows into our ship's foremast, a rope attached to each arrow. Then, as swiftly as the ships arrived, the humans did. They used some sort of leather and cloth straps to hold firmly onto as they zipped from their ships and onto ours using the ropes they'd put in place. With our three ships connected by the ropes, it seemed easy enough for them to board.

"What are you *fae* doing this close to our Isles?" the first one who landed hissed, a long dagger already in his hand. "You know well that your *kind* isn't welcome here."

"We're coming here in peace. We don't wish you any harm or wish to drag your people into anything." Byn held up his hands in a mock surrender as a dozen more humans from each ship arrived—men and women alike.

The first man's gaze flickered to Byn's golden circlet before meeting his eyes again.

"Then why come here at all?"

"Because of me," I said as I stepped up to my husband's side. "I come seeking knowledge, and I've heard this is the place to find it."

When the man's eyes shifted to me, a faint flash of recognition crossed his features, although I wasn't entirely sure why. I knew for a fact that I'd never met him—or any other human—before in my lifetime.

"Please," Byn added when the man didn't answer. "Take us to whoever is in charge, if you must. We can plead our case if necessary, but we came all this way. Please give us just one chance."

"Oh, you'll be meeting the queen alright. And you *will* plead your case." The man brought his hand to his mouth and whistled a series of six loud notes. A few moments later, the other two ships had lined up on either side of us and laid planks down between the edges of each vessel.

As the other two dozen humans used the planks to return to their respective ships, they hung their heads in disappointment when they realized they wouldn't get to fight anybody, the first man stayed put on our deck.

"So, what's your name?" Laurence asked the man.

"Dexter. But you won't be here long enough to need to use it," Dexter stated. "Tell your ship's captain to keep up. We're taking you to Queen Calista *right now*."

***

As we walked toward the middle of the largest Isle, I realized hidden tunnels weren't something that only the North utilized.

When we'd finally set foot on the main Isle, Dexter pointed out a small tunnel in the rock-face of the beach. Having no choice but to follow him, we stepped into the dimly lit tunnel and began the trek that Dexter claimed lead to the stone fortress, which Queen Calista resided in and ruled from.

After multiple forks in the tunnel and following Dexter blindly for what felt like days, we finally got to the other end.

And walked directly into what I could only imagine was Queen Calista's throne room.

It was much more modest than I'd have imagined for royalty, but considering she called her castle a *fortress*, I wasn't too surprised. The queen didn't seem to need to flash her wealth or status in such ways to let her subjects—and others—know that she was in charge.

I could tell simply by her eyes that she was the one they idolized.

Queen Calista's gaze raked over our group with a piqued interest, though her near-black eyes spoke of wisdom that must have been far beyond her years. She had tawny tanned skin similar to Rayven's, and deep brown, sword-straight hair flowing down to her waist. She looked young, as though she couldn't have been much older than Byn—likely Teagan and Rayven's age. And yet even the way she held herself spoke of having had time to perfect her every movement. She sat perfectly still upon her throne, not a single hair out of place or any shifting of muscles or limbs. Only her eyes moved as her gaze followed us, Dexter leading us to the center of the small throne room to stand before his queen.

"Kneel before Queen Calista!" Dexter commanded.

My muscles tensed as I forced myself to keep looking forward and not toward Byn for comfort and reassurance.

We might have been farther out of our element here than I'd originally thought.

"My sincere apologies, but my wife and I have vowed to never kneel to another." Byn motioned toward me, then our posse behind us. "My friends here, also, will only kneel to us. I hope you can understand that this does not affect the respect we have for you, Queen Calista."

The woman before us was silent a moment, simply observing us as though she had all the time in the world at her disposal.

"I see," she finally said. "I was curious about who was invading my lands, but a Thorntier king and a Heartshire queen wasn't what I'd imagined."

"You know who we are?" Byn asked, surprise radiating from him.

"Of course I do. Just because us humans don't partake in the outside world doesn't mean we're clueless."

Byn dipped his head slightly. "Right, of course. My apologies."

"We come seeking your help, Queen Calista," I added, trying to begin pleading our case. "We're here to find information about the star stones."

"Oh, I know why you've come, child. But the Levast Isles have stayed out of the war for this long, and I don't plan on that changing anytime soon, I fear," the queen answered, looking down her straight nose at us.

As she spoke, though, I felt a shadow shift ever so slightly near the dais of her throne.

A shadow with one unfamiliar energy, and another that I knew *extremely* well.

Two unexpected visitors.

"You know, usually I would accept that answer," I said, taking a step forward. "But not today. Because despite what you claim, you're already involved in the war, aren't you? In fact, you've already chosen a side."

As swiftly as I could manage, I drew the small alychite crystal from my pocket and threw it directly at the shadow that I knew for a fact differed from the rest that were in the room.

And the second the crystal connected with the shadow, it sucked the zirilium from them, forcing the fae hiding within the darkness back into their physical forms in an instant.

Then, standing where the shadows had been, was Dimitri, along with a smaller, hooded figure behind him. The cloaked figure must have been the unfamiliar energy I'd felt, though there was something about the second fae I thought I recognized.

"Hello, twin," Dimitri smirked, his gaze locked on mine.

I could feel the frustration and anger flowing from Byn, but it was also originating from within *me*.

Forcing myself to keep my hands open at my sides instead of in fists, I tried once more with the queen.

"Queen Calista, *please* reconsider your stance on this matter. Dimitri is the main reason that the war has yet to come to its end. This could all be over today if you'd only—"

"See what I mean, Queen Calista?" Dimitri said to the woman on the throne, stepping closer to the dais. "They're only here to try to use your people and your knowledge. The South hasn't changed, but the North has. And as I mentioned before, *we* aren't looking for a one-sided partnership."

When my eyebrows furrowed, and Byn's expression shifted to confusion, Dimi began to explain. "The Queen received your letter," he said, motioning toward who sat on the throne. "Thanks to me, of course. You really should train your birds better if you're going to be sending them this far."

Before any of us could speak or question what was being said, the queen held up a sheet of paper, small enough to fit in a corvid's vial, but what stood out was the seal at the bottom.

It was the Thorntier family official seal, one that matched perfectly with the ring on Byn's...

Looking down at my husband's hand, I realized the ring that had been there before the Battle of No Rain had gone missing.

Byn must have realized what I had a second later, but the queen spoke before we could.

"I don't appreciate threats to me, *or* to my people. I also don't appreciate you all invading our waters in an effort to force a landing on *my* islands," Queen Calista said, rising to her feet.

"When the South's corvid got lost on its way here, running into me instead, I figured I would help it deliver the message myself. Though, I hadn't been expecting such a threatening message to have been sent—especially when the humans have minded their own for so long in this war," Dimitri explained further.

This has to be a sick, twisted joke, I thought.

Dimitri had woven together the perfect scheme to paint the South as the villains in the war.

And the human queen seemed to have already made up her mind.

"Queen Calista, please, you don't understand—" I started, though was quickly cut off.

"I understand better than you'd imagine, *child*, and I've heard enough. Besides, I have made my decision," she declared. "If I must choose a side in this war for it to finally end, then I'd rather be on the side that *doesn't* threaten the lives of humans before we've even met."

We all watched as the queen and Dimitri turned to face each other, and I couldn't help but notice the menacing, crazed glint in my brother's eyes.

"I accept your offer, King Dimitri Heartshire of the North," Queen Calista announced.

Dimitri lifted his chin slightly. "I'd like to also receive whatever information my sister was seeking, if that's alright."

The human queen nodded. "Done."

"Then it's settled," Dimitri said, holding out his hand toward her.

I surged forward as I watched Queen Calista reach out toward my twin's hand, trying to stop her from making such a grave mistake. But before I could take two steps, the human guards closed in, blocking us off from the dais and those on it.

"I vow to uphold my end of our deal," Queen Calista said, taking hold of Dimitri's hand.

"And I vow to uphold mine," Dimitri echoed, then shook her hand.

That act alone now made the humans our rivals.

We were officially in enemy territory.

"Fetch the ancient scroll about the star stones for our new ally," Queen Calista ordered, and a guard slipped out of formation to do so.

Grinding my teeth, I fought back the zirilium begging to be released.

If I couldn't get what we'd come for, there was no longer any reason to remain in the Levast Isles.

"Well then, I suppose we can see ourselves out," I said, falling back to my spot at Byn's side.

Then Queen Calista chuckled. "Child, you and your people still tried to force a landing on my Isles, *and* threatened our lives." She took a step down the dais, nearer to us. "You won't be leaving here alive."

At those words, more guards funneled into the room, surrounding our small group and closing in on us. Slipping in with the guards, though, was a small woman I imagined was a scribe or librarian of sorts. She held a thick scroll, the one I imagined Dimitri had asked for.

The one we had come all this way for.

And the one I wouldn't be leaving without.

As the guards closed in, pushing us in toward each other, I kept my eyes on the scribe nearing the dais—though when her gaze met mine, she gave pause.

"Opal," the human queen called to the scribe. "Bring me the scroll."

But the scribe didn't move as the guards attempted to seize us, Opal's eyes locked on mine.

It was in that moment that I realized not *all* the humans present seemed to agree with their queen.

Wanting to keep my family safe above all else, I gave my zirilium an outlet as I began to force vines up through the stone of the floor. Forever in tune with me, I felt Byn pitching in, turning his back to me to guard the other side of our posse. Together, we forced enough plants up to wrap around each of the guard's feet and up their legs, forcing them to remain in place.

Looking back toward Opal, I realized she was still hesitating.

"*Now*, Opal," Queen Calista ground out between clenched teeth, holding her hand out toward the scribe. "And guards, *hurry up*. I tire of this."

The human queen didn't seem stressed in the slightest about the fact that we had put her guards on pause. She mostly seemed concerned with the scroll that had yet to reach her.

Which meant I still had a chance.

I met Opal's eyes and wished to the Stars she could see just how much was at stake.

Please, I mouthed to her, my last attempt.

Opal's eyes flickered to the floor as she slowly made her way closer to the dais—and closer to me.

Before she turned to go up the dais, she paused again.

Then, she ran straight for me, betraying her queen.

The same queen she seemed to no longer support.

"*Opal!*" Queen Calista yelled as she watched her own scribe defect.

I kept my eyes on the scribe, tome clutched to her chest, even as Dimitri surged forward to try to stop her. But before he could go far, the second cloaked figure behind him reached for the shard of alychite I'd thrown at them earlier, and with a gloved hand, held it to the side of his bare neck.

Dimitri went rigid and motionless, though his hands balled into fists at his sides.

"What is the meaning of this?" Queen Calista called out, standing as Opal nimbly made it through the hoard of guards surrounding us. Ushering her to the middle of our group, I turned to face the dais once again.

But before anybody could respond, the very foundations of the stone fortress began to *shake.*

Then I watched as the cloaked figure finally revealed themselves.

As they pushed their hood back, I realized why their energy felt familiar earlier.

"*RUN!*" Mother screamed as the ceiling above started to cave in on us.

My heart dropped to the cracking floor below us as I looked at her. Older than I remembered, but still just as stunning.

"Mother?" I questioned.

"*Mother!*" Matea cried.

Though as we both surged forward to get to her, strong hands pulled us backwards.

Byn and Rayven had their grips on us, holding on tight as they forced us backwards toward the tunnel we'd arrived through.

"We have to leave! We have what we came for!" Byn said over the sound of chunks of falling stone hitting the floor around us. I barely registered that some of the human guards had already fallen to them.

"No! *Please!*" Matea begged, tears slipping down her face. "I've never been so close!"

I gulped back my own cries as I struggled against Byn, but we continued moving backwards until all of us, including the scribe, were entering the mouth of the tunnel.

The last thing I could make out through the moisture in my eyes was the ceiling caving in over the dais—and it landing directly on top of the three figures that stood upon it.

Chapter Forty-Two

"Queen Calista!" I called out.

Mother betrayed me and disappeared once we'd been knocked to the ground by the rocks *she* had caused to fall.

I'd deal with her another time. But right then, all that mattered was keeping this alliance.

Using my earth zirilium, I wielded stones out of the way, clearing a path toward where the throne had sat. I heard a faint groan once I got close enough, and started attempting to wield one of the larger chunks of stone away.

Under it, I found Queen Calista—thankfully, in one piece and *not* squished.

"Help me up, you fool," she ordered.

Grinding my teeth, I did as she asked, wielding the rock from her throne and helping her to sit upon it.

Standing before her then, I finally noticed why she'd needed the assistance.

She had a long chunk of stone impaled all the way through her thigh. And it was bleeding heavily.

"Wait—" I said, but before I could stop her, she surged forward and simply ripped it out of her leg.

Then I watched in absolute amazement as her flesh deep within the wound began to rapidly knit itself back together, bit by bit.

Something that mortal humans *didn't* do.

I kept my eyes on the wound, eyes glued to it as her leg righted itself. Finally, after another moment, her skin wove itself back together and didn't leave behind a single trace—not even a scar.

Now that I was paying more attention, I realized she didn't have any cuts or bruises marring her skin either.

As if she *hadn't* just been knocked to the ground and trapped by the collapse of her own throne room.

There was only one explanation—but I feared if I was right, it would rewrite history as the fae knew it.

"You're..." I trailed off, unable to say it aloud.

"Yes, child. We all are." She motioned toward the ruined throne room below her, and as if on queue, her guards began to shift rocks and emerge from the rubble—all of them alive, all of them without a scratch.

It turned out that the humans weren't just going to be the perfect allies for their knowledge.

They were also the very thing that had been wiped from the fae's history.

The humans were *immortal.*

Epilogue

The tears that had fallen were still wet against my skin by the time we'd made it back to our ship.

Ezra had led the way through the tunnel, Laurence bringing up the rear, with Rayven and Robyn forcing me and Viva—my little sister—farther and farther away from our mother.

The female I'd been searching for my entire life.

She'd slipped through my fingers like fine sand, and I wasn't sure I'd ever fully recover.

It felt as though I'd left part of my heart back in that fallen fortress.

Now, we were forcing our way through the other ships that had blocked us in on both sides, and though Viva had been trusted enough to be released, her logic winning her over, I had not.

I turned in Rayven's arms to face him, pounding on his chest.

"Let me *go*! I have to go *back*!" I pleaded, the tears beginning to well in my eyes once again.

"Matea, please," the spy said softly, his voice husky as ever.

Everything about him pissed me off, but deep down, I knew he was right. It would be stupid to return after we'd just barely escaped with our lives.

"I can't just leave her there," I said, my voice cracking pathetically.

"We'll get her back." Rayven gently rested a hand against the back of my head, cradling me against his chest.

I took a moment to allow myself to find comfort in his act of kindness. It was a privilege I rarely allowed myself.

"Maybe sooner than you realize," he added, his grip on me loosening as he lifted an arm, pointing toward the shoreline we'd just left.

And running full speed out of the tunnel we'd exited moments before was the same female I'd just been crying over.

She'd made it out.

I watched, stunned, as Viva helped water wield the ocean below to allow for her to make it to the ship.

As she boarded the ship, I fell to my knees.

After decades, my mother had finally, at long last, returned to me.

About the Author

Photo by Alaina Hope

Alaina Hope was born in Houston, Texas and was raised just north of the sprawling metropolis. She has two younger siblings who mean the world to her, and a cat she's had since she was seven, who *still* serves as her writing companion.

When she isn't writing or reading, she's hanging out with those dear to her, or traveling across the country to see some of her closest friends.

Most of all, she can't wait to provide you with the *final* installment of Aviva's and Dimitri's story!

Made in the USA
Coppell, TX
08 June 2026

78630443R00249